HIGH MAGIC

ABOUT THE AUTHOR

Born in Heliopolis, Egypt, Frater U.·. D.·. has been working within the magical tradition for decades. He lived in Africa and Asia and trained with yoga and tantra masters, as well as studying languages and literature at the universities of Bonn and Lisbon. He is recognized as the founder of Pragmatic Magic, and has written articles for many magazines, including *Unicorn, Thelema: Magazine for Magic and Tantra, Anubis* (Germany), *The Lamp of Thoth,* and *Chaos International* (Great Britain). His published works include *Practical Sigil Magic.* Among his translations are the books of Peter Carroll and Ramsey Dukes and Aleister Crowley's *Book of Lies.* At present, he lives near Bonn, Germany, working as a freelance writer, translator, and workshop speaker.

TO WRITE TO THE AUTHOR

If you wish to contact the author or would like more information about this book, please write to the author in care of Llewellyn Worldwide and we will forward your request. Both the author and publisher appreciate hearing from you and learning of your enjoyment of this book and how it has helped you. Llewellyn Worldwide cannot guarantee that every letter written to the author can be answered, but all will be forwarded. Please write to:

Frater U.·. D.·.
℅ Llewellyn Worldwide
2143 Wooddale Drive
Woodbury, MN 55125-2989

Please enclose a self-addressed stamped envelope for reply, or $1.00 to cover costs. If outside U.S.A., enclose international postal reply coupon.

Many of Llewellyn's authors have websites with additional information and resources. For more information, please visit our website at http://www.llewellyn.com.

Frater U.:. D.:.

Llewellyn Publications
Woodbury, Minnesota U.S.A.

First Edition
Fifth Printing, 2010

Cover background © 2004 by PhotoDisk
Cover design by Lisa Novak
Editing by Tom Bilstad
Translated by Melinda Kumbalek, from the German edition:
Schule der Hohen Magie © 2001 by Frater U:. D:.
Published in Germany by Ansata Verlag.

Library of Congress Cataloging-in-Publication Data

U.D., Frater, 1952–
High magic : theory & practice / Frater U.D. — 1st ed.
p. cm.
ISBN: 978-0-7387-0471-5
1. Magic. I. Title.

BF1611.U3 2005
113.4'3—dc22 2004060751

Llewellyn Publications
A Division of Llewellyn Worldwide Ltd.
2143 Wooddale Drive
Woodbury, MN 55125-2989, U.S.A.
www.llewellyn.com
Llewellyn is a registered trademark of Llewellyn Worldwide Ltd.

Printed in the United States of America

OTHER BOOKS BY FRATER U.·. D.·.

Secrets of Western Sex Magic
(Llewellyn Publications)

Practical Sigil Magic
(Llewellyn Publications)

High Magic II
(Llewellyn Publications)

Where Do Demons Live?
(Llewellyn Publications)

CONTENTS

FOREWORD

TABULA SMARAGDINA HERMETIS

1. Verum, sine mendacio, certum et verissimum.
2. Quod est inferius, est sicut quod est superius, et quod est superius, est sicut quod est inferius, ad perpetranda miracula rei unius.
3. Et sicut omnes res fuerunt ab uno, meditatione unius: sic omnes res natae fuerunt ab hac una re, adaptatione.
4. Pater eius est Sol, mater eius est Luna; portavit illud ventus in ventre suo; nutrix eius terra est.
5. Pater omnis thelesmi totius mundi est hic.
6. Vis eius integra est, si versa fuerit in terram.
7. Separabis terram ab igno, subtile a spisso, suaviter cum magno ingenio.
8. Ascendit in coelum, iterumque descendit in terram, et recipit vim superiorum et inferiorum. Sic habebis gloriam totius mundi. Ideo fugiat a te omnis obscuritas.
9. Hic est totius fortitudinis fortitudo fortis; quia vincet omnem rem subtilem, omnemque solidam penetrabit.
10. Sic mundus creatus est.

11. Hinc adaptationes erunt mirabiles, quarum modus est hic.
12. Itaque vocates sum HERMES TRISMEGISTUS, habens tres partes Philosophiae totius mundi.
13. Completum est quod dixi de operatione Solis.

THE EMERALD PLATE OF HERMES TRISMEGISTOS

1. True, without error, certain and most true.
2. That which is above is as that which is below, and that which is below is as that which is above, to perform the miracles of the One Thing.
3. And as all things are from One, by the meditation of One, so all things arise from this One Thing by adaptation.
4. The sun is its father, the moon its mother, the wind carries it in its belly, its nurse is the earth.
5. This is the father of all creation.
6. Undivided and absolute is its power if it is turned to earth.
7. Separate the earth from fire, the fine from the coarse, gently, with great ingenuity.
8. It ascends from the earth to the heavens and descends again to the earth, and receives the power of the superiors and of the inferiors. Thus thou hast the glory of the whole world. And all obscurity will flee before thee.
9. This is the force of all forces, overcoming every subtle and penetrating every solid thing.
10. Thus the world was created.
11. Hence are all the adaptations of which this is the manner.
12. Therefore I am called Thrice-Great Hermes, having the three parts of the philosophy of the whole world.
13. That which I have to tell is completed, concerning the operations of the sun.

(English translation based on Frater U.·. D.·.'s German translation of the original Latin)

An Introduction, or "Welcome to the Club!"

Magic, a word that's been shrouded in mystery for thousands of years. How many minds have already pondered this subject? Magic is probably one of the most difficult, most diversified, and most fascinating of all the occult sciences—either as a supporter or opponent, as an initiate or as an unknowing person! Magicians were (and still are) often considered to be loathsome creatures with no desire whatsoever to conform to an external temporal power. They were viewed as people willing to commit the crime of not accepting the concepts of "reality" and "the healthy limits of morals and decency" as forced upon them by religion and society, priests and world leaders; as people who refuse to serve any gods or goddesses apart from their own, no matter whether they call them Hermes or Hekate, Baal or Baphomet, Lilith or Lucifer, idealism or materialism, rationalism or irrationalism, I or myself—the list goes on.

The magician, whether male or female, was always a psychonaut, a soul searcher, someone who wanted to peek behind the "Veil of Isis"; a person who could never rest until he or she discovered (or at least had a good idea about) "what holds the world together deep down inside." Zoroaster was considered a magician, as were Moses, Salomo, Milarepa, and even Jesus Christ. Raimundus Lullus belonged to this crowd of different thinkers and, more importantly, different doers. Jacques de Molay, Agrippa von Nettesheim, Theophrastus Bombastus Paracelsus, Doctor Faustus, Athanasius Kircher,

Cagliostro, the Comte de Saint Germain . . . the list could go on forever, packed full with truly historic figures, and an infinite number of mythical ones as well. Despite all the persecution by the church and government, this list never ends, not even in modern times, this so-called "Age of Enlightenment," this time of rationalism and materialism. Witnesses along the way included Robert Fludd (also called Robertus de Fluctibus), Dr. John Dee, Edward Kelley, Frances Barrett, Alan Bennett, Eliphas Levi, Papus, Stanislas de Guaïta, Sâr Merodack Joséphin Péladan, Samuel Liddell McGregor Mathers, Arthur Waite, Karl Kellner, Theodor Reuss, Aleister Crowley, Austin Osman Spare, Ludwig Staudenmaier, Musallam, Rah-Omir Quintscher, Herbert Fritsche, Franz Bardon, and Gregor A. Gregorius.

For the time being, we prefer to not mention those who are still alive (and this list keeps growing and growing) for reasons of modesty and the lack of historical distance required. Besides, it's simply impossible to mention them all, and we'll encounter many of these people frequently enough throughout the course of this book anyway.

So you see, if you decide to pursue the path of magic, you'll find yourself among quite colorful company. Like in any large family, these include geniuses and skilled experts that stand out among the rest, but also simpler souls, and even a few quacks (who are actually quite necessary in fact!). Magicians are all individualists who prefer not to be categorized or labeled in simple terms that do nothing to promote understanding, but who actually distort the picture instead. The apparent contradictions in the writings of magic authors can be explained by this fact, as well as by magic's extreme subjectivity that we will encounter again and again.

This book is intended to give you a comprehensive and well-rounded introduction to practical magic. This includes thorough background information about the Black Arts, which all magicians draw on, whether consciously or subconsciously. Studying the older authors has many advantages, but some disadvantages as well. But when done in a sensible fashion and accompanied by a keen awareness of history, it saves us the trouble of having to "discover the wheel" all over again. Plus, there is much to gain through the rich experience and vast knowledge of our forefathers.

Of course, in order to properly judge their work, sound knowledge of the historical background and context of these ideas is required. For example, the role played by Christian phrases in medieval spell books[1] can only be understood if one also is familiar with the intellectual history of the period in which the magician lived, such as the supremacy of the church and the dangers of witch-hunts. Therefore it's absolutely necessary to treat our forefathers with the utmost respect.

But this respect must also be critical. Just because it's old doesn't automatically mean it's good! Lots of things have found their way into traditional magic that we can (and should, if we really want to progress) rely on comfortably. This includes the secretiveness of early times as well as the static recitation of individual formulas without explaining the basic laws and structures of magic, which can be used by any halfway intelligent beginner to create such formulas him- or herself in just a short period of time. For this reason, our training manual will not be short of criticism where it seems appropriate. Of course, you don't need to agree with everything we say; even our statements reflect merely a subjective approach to magic, which is the only way it could possibly be, because magic can't be anything else!

The statements that you're now expecting mainly concern the practice of magic. Since each person has a different idea of what "practice" actually means, we're going to clear up the matter right away, so that everyone knows exactly how we define it: Magical practice means the application of magical laws, teachings, and techniques and observing the results.

Magic that only takes place on paper is a ridicule of magical knowledge and magical wisdom. With magic, one desires to influence every aspect of one's fate that seems beyond control by using just ordinary measures—and the magician can succeed! We'll be exploring and investigating microcosmic and macrocosmic laws, techniques that lead to material success and those used for mystical reflection and spiritual growth.

Modern magic is primarily a path to self-discovery or spiritual wholeness. Unlike religion and mysticism (not to be confused with mystics), magic fundamentally denies that spirit and matter exist as opposites. Instead, it considers them to be one—a unity, a whole. The spirit is in no way "better" than matter, and matter isn't "unholier" than the spirit. Both complement one another, learn from one another, and are interwoven into a fine tissue that we call "reality" (which in turn is responsible for posing our greatest thinkers with seemingly unsolvable problems, and enticing our simpler thinkers into coming up with fast, superficial answers and shallow systems for solving these problems!).

Please always keep a critical distance. Don't accept anything without examining it first until you can confirm it through your own practice. Always be a researcher, a psychonaut who travels to new regions and those that have already been visited throughout the centuries, and discover your own impressions of the climate there, the condition of the soil, the riches and the dangers, and . . . yes, even the residents there.

Anything that you haven't experienced yourself is meaningless: a paper dream, a hollow promise of unspeakable adventure and treasures in the deepest depths of your soul, with limits beyond imagination that you could barely just begin to explore. Only your personal experience can bring this world and this universe (or these universes) to life and make magic more than just a fantasy of wayward, delirious spirits such as some biased pseudo-skeptics seem to believe.

Magic can only be as vivacious as the magician his- or herself. Without magic, the magician is meaningless, and don't be surprised if one day you discover that without the magician, magic is just as meaningless!

And one more thing: If you choose this path, you need to understand right from the start that it never ends; once you begin with magic, it will always be a part of you. Only a few have allowed themselves to be swayed from this path once they've overcome the first obstacles and taken their first breaths of magical freedom.

Magic can give a person everything, but it can take everything as well if one doesn't understand that he or she is obligated to serve. Not some senile or crazy old god imposed upon him by others, but rather serving that which makes one a human being: one's purpose and goals in life, one's "Holy Guardian Angel" as it was called in medieval magic, one's "Will" or "Thelema" as expressed by one of the greatest magicians of the twentieth century, and one's Self or the discovery and integration hereof as defined by modern-day psychoanalysis; in short, everything that makes the seeker a magician, an aspirant, a pilgrim, a humble student, and a dignified master.

Modern magic aims to satisfy and make use of both sides of your personality, the rational as well as the intuitional. Modern brain research refers to two halves of the brain. In simple terms, the left half is connected to the right half of the body and it's responsible for the rational, such as thought, calculation, planning, and so on. The right half of the brain controls the left side of the body and, along with it, the intuitional, such as feeling and sensation, trance and vision, and so on. We'll encounter this principle shortly in the first definition of magic in the next section where magic is described as being an "art" and "science."

And now we'd like to say, "Welcome to the club of magicians!" May your magical path be rich and colorful, delightful and frightening, challenging and easy, humorous and individual, through and through, just like it was for all our magical ancestors and for those who contributed their vast experience to this book, with all the riches and shortcomings, strengths and weaknesses, wisdom and foolishness for you to examine, imitate, supplement, expand on, and adapt to your own needs and realizations.

My own personal magical motto is: "VBIQVE DÆMON . . . VBIQVE DEVS . . ." In English this means: "THE DEMON IS IN EVERYTHING, THE GOD IS IN EVERYTHING." This is a challenge for us to always see and respect both sides. Maybe you've heard of the colloquial German proverb *Was dem einen seine Eule, ist dem anderen seine Nachtigall* ("One man's owl is another man's nightingale"). In English there is a similar saying that's a bit clearer and more drastic: "One man's meat is another's poison." If you take this basic principle to heart, you'll not only learn to be tolerant of different thinkers, but you'll also develop a certain resistance against the oh-so-sweet but often insidious traps from "the great authorities" who usually did nothing other than any good magician would do: They created one's own universe and environment from one's own reality. That always was a good thing, and it still is, but a person should only breathe in an atmosphere that's suitable for him or her. And that's why we'd like to adopt the following motto, used by the old gentlemen from the magic mountain of Drachenfels, for this book as well. Use it as "instructions" to help you make use of everything that we're offering you here:

"LOOK & LEAP"

—Fra U.·. D.·.
VBIQVE DÆMON Æ VBIQVE DEVS Æ

1. So-called "grimoires."

WHAT IS MAGIC?

Before we start discussing the actual practice of magic, we first need to know what it's all about. Throughout the years, an endless number of definitions of the word "magic" have popped up, and we'll have to deal with many of these in order to understand the concept of magical practice.

Probably the most famous definition came from one of the most significant magicians of the twentieth century, Aleister Crowley (1875–1947):

Magic is the Science and Art of Causing Changes to Occur in Conformity with Will.

Although this definition actually describes the core of magical practice quite well, it's a bit too general and generic for the layperson and beginner to understand. Usually something quite different or special is expected of the term "magic," namely a discipline that's more concerned with "subtle" influences, such as the shaping of one's destiny and "coincidences." Plus, the above definition offers no clue whatsoever as to the techniques and methods used in magic.

Some authors such as Israel Regardie and Francis King have taken this into account and have attempted to expand on Crowley's definition:

Magic is the science and art of using states of altered consciousness for causing changes to occur in conformity with will.

This solution isn't exactly the best either, but it's good enough for the start. Let's take a closer look at it since this definition already contains one important practical formula.

First of all, the terms "art" and "science" are important here. Often the term "occult science" is used, but the occultist (or occult scientist) generally defines "science" quite differently than the "exact" or "natural scientist" does. In the attempt to earn the recognition of orthodox schoolbook science, many occultists (and even magicians) have tried to use the word "scientific" to describe their discipline. This is only true as long as magic uses scientific methods. In technical jargon, it's "empirical" or "empirically scientific," which applies to everyday practical magic at least. This means that magic first aims at what is visibly successful.

On the other hand, the term "art" refers to the more intuitive area of magic that includes "fine instincts" and feelings in general, as well as the sensitivity for subtle energies (such as those involved in the various types of clairvoyance). Dreams and visions also fall under the "art" aspect of magic, but thought and the knowledge of correlations, on the other hand, belong to the "science" aspect.

In summary, magic makes use of both the so-called "rational" and "irrational" components of the human personality. Since the word "irrational" has a negative connotation in this age of rationalism ("irrational" is often equated with "foolish," "mad," "crazy," "ill-considered"), we prefer to call it "the intuitive side" of the magician.

We see that magic actually aims at achieving the spiritual totality and unity of a person. This has purely practical reasons, because only when both sides work together harmoniously can magical results be achieve, results that often appear as though they would disprove all (scientific) laws of nature, which of course isn't true, as we'll see throughout this book.

But magic, however, is even more than the art and science of achieving unity of the soul. Let's begin with everyday practical magic, also called "lower magic," which is a term that's certainly not meant to be derogatory, but rather serves the purpose of distinguishing from the more mystical-religious "high magic" in terms of the techniques and contents involved. In practice, a person needs to use both aspects (the rational and the intuitive) to effectively perform a successful act of magic. This happens through two of the three most important basic components of the magical act, namely the combination of will and imagination. (We'll discuss the third factor shortly, namely "states of altered consciousness.")

We've illustrated this in Chart 1. Look at the diagram closely for a few minutes and try to add more features to each appropriate column. Try to think of other things that would belong to the area of "art," and some that would fit into the "science" column as well. You'll also notice that we've created a relationship between "art" and "imagination," as well as one between "science" and "will."

Art	Science
* right side of brain	* left side of brain
* left side of body	* right side of body
* intuition	* logic
* vision	* thought
* sensation	* consideration
* premonition	* calculation
* synthetic	* analytical
* cyclical	* linear
* mythical	* factual
* federalist	* centralist
* creative chaos	* maintains order
* symbol-logical	* formally logical
* irrational	* rational
Imagination	Will
Magic	

Chart 1: Diagram of the basic structure of magic

"Art" corresponds to "imagination" by means of its intuitive nature, while "science" corresponds to "will" through its reflectivity and its clear and precise objectives. Thus we already have a preliminary equation: WILL + IMAGINATION = MAGIC.

Actually, this was considered to be the ultimate basic formula of magic for many years. Some disciplines such as positive thinking, in which certain events and situations are intentionally ("will") visualized ("imagination") as realistically as possible, work almost exclusively according to this principle, and are quite successful in doing so at that. But if we look at our definition once again, we'll notice that there's something still missing in this equation: the "states of altered consciousness." These states of altered consciousness that are used in magic are referred to as magical trance or gnosis. It's important to remember that the magical trance usually has nothing to do with the hypnotic full trance in which the will of the hypnotized person is largely shut off or controlled by someone else. This would also violate the statement "in conformity with will," because here we mean a clear and conscious will.[1]

But if we're already using our imagination and will, why do we still need magical trance? In order to understand this, we need to understand the structure of our psyche and how it works, because we like to assume that magical power and the ability to perform magic is an inner-spiritual occurrence.

Conscious Mind
Censor
Subconscious Mind

Chart 2: The basic structure of the psyche

In Chart 2, we present a simplified form of the common model of the human psyche as provided by modern psychoanalysis. First we see the conscious mind, also known as the daytime or waking consciousness. In the lower portion of the chart we can see the subconscious mind, which is also called the unconscious. This includes everything that usually escapes our conscious mind. Although it's constantly active, we usually only notice it when we dream. The so-called censor is located between the conscious and subconscious minds. It represents a sort of "two-way filter." On the one hand, it ensures the selective perception of the stimuli of the outside world. On the other hand, it protects the conscious mind from the uncontrolled flooding of information from the subconscious mind, which includes repressions and complexes. The censor is assigned a vital function, namely the maintenance of what we generally call "spiritual health." It's of great importance to realize this to prevent us from thinking of the censor as an "evil enemy" that's just trying to spoil us magicians from having fun in life! But unfortunately, this happens quite frequently.

Admittedly, the censor has a considerable disadvantage as well, namely that it's extremely conservative. Only reluctantly does it allow the conscious mind to make direct and immediate contact with the subconscious mind, thereby escaping its control. You could compare it to a slightly distrustful "palace guard," a loyal, brave servant to his master, but sometimes too worried about his own safety to allow and admit new situations without careful examination.

Actually one of the most important "tricks" in magic is temporarily turning off the censor in order to directly tap the source of power (the subconscious mind) and assign it specific tasks. This happens through magical or gnostic trance. This state often resembles the hazy period just before falling asleep in which the conscious mind is still active but quite subdued. In this state, it can exchange information directly with the subconscious mind, e.g., in the form of images. During magical trance, the censor is in a way "put to sleep." Ideally, it would "sleep" very lightly and only awake in an emergency. By the way, this corresponds to the role of the sword in magic, as we'll see later on when we discuss the ritual weapons.

Thus, we now have the complete structure of magic that corresponds to our extended definition as depicted in Chart 3 below.

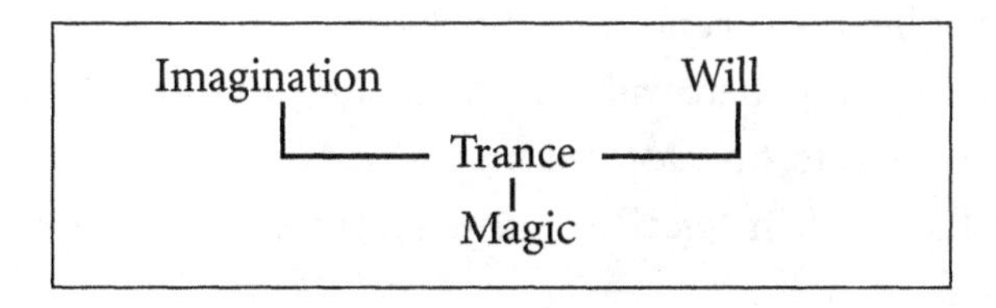

Chart 3: The basic structure of magic (II)

In comparison, Chart 4 (next page) reflects the same concept in the form of a "mathemagical equation." It would be best for you to study these charts carefully and even memorize them since we'll be running into similar formulas throughout the course of this book. This isn't just a game! On the contrary, formulas are mnemonic abbreviations to help us memorize rules and laws from which practical derivatives can be gained. One goal of this book is to point out the basic structures of magic and to clarify them. In this respect, this is an entirely new concept since most of the magical literature available today is written like a "recipe book." Instead of explaining the basic laws that govern magic, most authors—even the older ones—usually just provide individual "recipes." Rituals for protection from an enemy, magical glyphs for happiness and prosperity, amulets to prevent the plague and cholera, mantras (magic words) for "attracting a prince" or conjuring spirits, recipes for getting rid of warts, magic potions for "winning the love of a man/woman," and so on. Even (and especially!) the traditional magical "practice literature" of most recent times follows this principle. Unfortunately, what's often misunderstood here is the fact that such recipes are not effective "automatically" by themselves! This is a mistake that many people, especially beginners, continue to make again and again. They constantly search for the "real, true, 100 percent effective ritual" or the "ultimate magical formula." Even today there are more than enough quacks around who'd be eager to hold out a hand and sell you a recipe without explaining the conditions necessary to make it work.

Now I'm not saying that all such recipes are completely useless. But if we're not able to understand the basic formula of magic first before we use them, they're not even worth the paper that they're written on. And even if they do work sometimes, it can be easily seen that will, imagination, and gnosis played an important role as well.

However, once you're familiar with the basic laws and formulas of magic, you can create your own "recipes" on the basis of these, in the same way that every magician basically writes his or her own grimoire or "book of magic."

A large part of our work here will deal with doing just this. But as with any other discipline, the basics need to be mastered first, otherwise "1 + 1" will never be learned! These basics are the "mathemagical," structural formulas that we'll continually confront you with in various versions.

$M = w + i + g$
<u>Legend</u> M = magical act w = will i = imagination g = gnosis (mag. trance)

Chart 4: The first basic formula of magic

As seen in the above statements, we can see that the focus of a magical education must be on the training of WILL, IMAGINATION, and TRANCE in order to enable efficient work within this paradigm or model of explanation. There are a number of magic books that are dedicated to this. For example, the books by Franz Bardon (especially *Initiation into Hermetics*) contain a number of basic exercises that focus on self-discipline and mental training, such as visualization and imagination. Bardon's exercises are excellently structured and you can make a great deal of progress in magic by using them. Admittedly, progress is slow as a snail if the prescribed time schedule is strictly adhered to. For example, you must be able to visualize an object for ten minutes without the slightest loss of concentration, and be able to achieve a state of empty mind for this length of time as well. Without a doubt, this can be very useful to magic. However, practice has revealed that such maximum requirements tend to scare off people unnecessarily, especially beginners, and that they can even distract from the actual principal of magic. The fear of not doing the exercise "properly" or not being able to master it is often an obstacle that can be avoided. In other words, it can be done much easier and faster, which sigil magic proves, and that's what we'll be dealing with in the next section.

But that doesn't mean that the magician-in-training can avoid hard, diligent work—on the contrary, even a "master" with decades of successful experience needs to repeat certain basics once in awhile to avoid "getting rusty." Especially since one of the things that makes this discipline so interesting is that you can never stop learning; there's always something new, something undiscovered and unknown, and, above all, something that's unmastered. The challenges are countless and a person that always keeps his or her eyes open will never get bored with magic. That's why we're presenting this basic maxim right at the start of this book:

Diligent practice on a regular basis is the key to acquiring magical skills!

You should know that it's entirely up to you how fast or how slow magic "works" for you. Although there's no denying that some people have a certain "talent" for magic in various degrees, the importance of this talent is usually drastically overestimated. Never make the common beginner's mistake of envying the "naturals" who seem to be able to accomplish many things in magic straight off (without painstaking work and previous training). In fact, you should actually feel quite sorry for them. Since they've been "given" so much and many things fall right into their laps, they usually lack the self-discipline and severity of those with less talent who have to earn every little thing with sweat and tears. In magical terms, this self-discipline and severity represent the important aspect of grounding since they're the best protection against two of the most common and most dangerous illnesses of magicians: overestimating oneself, and the persecution complex. A good magician is humble in the same way a good warrior is humble: One knows his or her own limits way too well to be deceived by wishful thinking. A warrior never makes the mistake of underestimating a problem, the enemy, or a challenge. He or she thinks and acts economically with a minimum of effort and maximum efficiency. The warrior is of sound character because he or she learned to master willpower throughout training and knows how to distinguish between judgments based on emotion and those based on facts. Ideally, the magician is a technician without being a technocrat, someone who's mastered one's discipline to a tee, and who knows its legitimacy as well as its weaknesses, and he or she respects and admires one's trade and all those who have learned it and are still learning. All of these qualities are rarely just handed to a person; they have to be acquired through hard work. Natural talents often tend to oversee these requirements and usually learn them the hard way by running into walls or through the painful process of mistakes and failure.

But life is way too short anyway for any single person to completely cover the entire field of magic and the occult. Time is running short, regardless of whether you're eighteen or eighty! This causes a demand for didactic and pedagogical economy. We've taken this into account by only recommending exercises and procedures that are as versatile and comprehensive as possible from an educational point of view. Put in more colloquial terms, our exercises aim at killing as many birds as possible with only one stone. At the same time, they're designed to train the will, develop the imagination, and provide access to controlled trance. For this reason, we'll avoid strictly dividing our training manual into the three sections (willpower, imagination, and trance) as might seem appropriate for our model. In the next section we'll discuss this topic in depth. But for now we should be content with getting acquainted with the basic elements of magic listed here and thinking about them for awhile.

Instead of holding you up (such as some magic authors like to do) for months, weeks, and years with exercises that seem to have no direct relationship to the practice of magic (which is often just a misjudgment by the beginner!), we'd like to introduce you to magical practice right away with no major preparations. This means, however, that the exercises at the end of this section might seem to demand things from you that seem sheer impossible at first. But don't worry, everyone's in the same boat! Just do your best and always remember that many things can only be accomplished through practice itself.

TO KNOW, TO WILL, TO DARE, TO BE SILENT

Before we go on to the practical part of this first section, we'd like to give you another maxim to think about that surfaces repeatedly in esoteric literature and is (rightly so) highly esteemed. "To know, to will, to dare, to be silent" is the challenge that's posed to occultists. We only want to mention it briefly here, but it should serve for further meditation.

To Know

Without the knowledge of what we as magicians are doing, we're not only aimless but we also run the risk of not recognizing the basic laws of our magical work, causing us to occasionally make some disastrous mistakes. However, there were times when this "knowledge" was misunderstood or strongly overestimated. This doesn't just mean pure intellectual knowledge, which is naturally also a part of it, and we'll be providing you with comprehensive information throughout this course as well. But mainly it means intuition or that gut feeling from deep down inside that can only be achieved through personal experience. The most any teacher can do is show the student how to gain this kind of intuitive knowledge, but the student needs to go through the actual learning process him- or herself.

To Will

In the long run, a magician who doesn't know what he or she wants is hopelessly destined to fail. Only an unyielding will (and an uncompromising desire, which is not the same!) can lead a magician safely to his or her goal. Actually, many modern-day magicians regard the ultimate goal of high magic to be the recognition of one's own true will, or Thelema. If the will begins to sway, the whole magical operation automatically strays off track as well. That's why mental training, or training of the will, always includes cognitive training and disciplining because every person is naturally inclined to act according to the pleasure principle whenever he or she has the opportunity. Although there's principally nothing wrong with this, it often leads to negligence and convenience. This kind of person is quite successful in avoiding the conscious pursuit of one's own will.

To Dare

This is probably the basic principal that has been violated most frequently throughout the history of magic. Countless pages written by authors of magic are filled with the utter fear of practice, as though they're afraid that magic could actually work! And it actually does, although a magician can only be truly efficient if he or she has the courage to stand up for what one will feel is necessary and worthwhile, in action as well as in thought. Please note that we've not yet said one word about the dangers of magic. It's not as though there aren't any. But magic is actually no more dangerous than driving a car. Thorough training and diligent practice are the best prerequisites for successful, risk-free magical work. If a student driver is continuously filled with images of fear about how dangerous driving is, the only thing that's accomplished is that he or she has been made into an intimidated, and therefore poorer, driver who even seems to attract accidents and bad driving habits. The same holds true for magicians. Watch out for the warnings of "well-meaning" nonpractitioners who can already imagine you rotting in hell or an insane asylum just for reading about theoretical magic! Instead, you should listen to the more experienced "journeyers to the East" and psychonauts who know exactly what dangers are actually real and which ones are just imagined (and that's most of them!). Think about the statement made by Martin Luther: "A despairing ass will never produce a happy fart." Actually, the fear of magic itself is one of the greatest dangers a person will encounter on his or her magical path! For exactly these reasons, the importance of confronting one's own fears is not to be underestimated.

To Be Silent

Lots of nonsense has been written in the past about the obligation to secrecy. Often this commandment was confused with the tendency to hide one's own uncertainty behind secretive insinuations ("I have to be silent about that," "True initiates will know what I mean," etc.). Sometimes occult knowledge was jealously guarded and intentionally withheld from the "profane masses." But at the most, this is the behavior of a fossilized priesthood that's worried about maintaining its predominance founded merely on the ignorance of the people they rule. At worst, the main intention here is to lead the ignorant astray so that they're easier to exploit. In reality, the mysteries protect themselves exceptionally well and it's impossible to "unveil" them, because their actual "secret" is contained in the experience that the initiate makes with them. These realms of experience can never be taken away from the magician and can never be tarnished by an outsider or an ignorant person. Nevertheless, it's advisable to not be all too open about your own occult interests as the prejudices that a magician encounters even in these modern times of "enlightenment" and "tolerance" are still great, as is the energy wasted on defending oneself against such opposition. This defense ties up a lot of your power and should therefore be avoided whenever possible. Besides, if I allow myself to use another idiom, being silent also means "putting a lid on the pot," meaning that by stoppering a bubbling cauldron, one creates the necessary amount of pressure to cook. This pressure is the magical power that we call *magis*.

And now let's move on to practice.

---

1. An exception to the rule of nonfull trance is made by the so-called "possession religions" that we can mainly observe in some cultures: Voodoo, Macumba, etc.

STRAIGHT TO PRACTICE

THE LESSER BANISHING RITUAL OF THE PENTAGRAM

INTRODUCTION TO THE LESSER BANISHING RITUAL OF THE PENTAGRAM

The Lesser Banishing Ritual of the Pentagram is sort of like the smallest common denominator among all magicians from Western, Hermetic-oriented traditions. It's practiced from Europe to America, from Asia to Australia, everywhere that men and women, magicians of all types, work with these traditions. The number of variations is large, but the number of significant differences between them is relatively small. Without exaggerating, it can be said that the Lesser Banishing Ritual of the Pentagram is one of the most important pieces of basic equipment that the Western magician uses. It serves various purposes: general protection, a part of a larger ceremony (usually as an introduction and conclusion), casting the protective circle, and an exercise to train the imagination as well as visualization, concentration, and trance skills.

In short, the pentagram is an ancient symbol used in Western tradition to represent the five elements—Earth, Water, Fire, Air, and Spirit (Ether). When a person stands up straight with legs spread apart and arms stretched out to the side, he or she naturally forms a pentagram. The pentagram (also called the Druid's Foot and five-pointed star) was viewed as a representation of the microcosm, in contrast to the hexagram (Star of David or six-pointed star), which is assigned to the planetary powers (therefore representing the macrocosm). The traditional classification of the elements can be seen in Illustration 1. First we'll explain the technical procedure of performing the ritual, and then later discuss the details and finer points.

In addition to the Lesser Banishing Ritual of the Pentagram, there's also the Greater Ritual of the Pentagram that we'll deal with later on in the book.

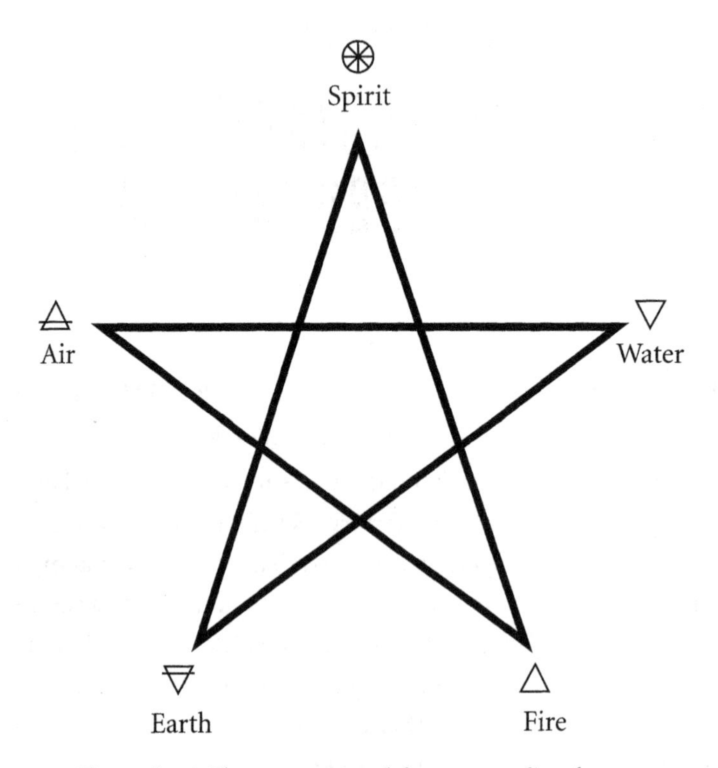

Illustration 1: The pentagram and the corresponding elements

The allocation of the elements also corresponds to certain ways of drawing the pentagram for various purposes. Technically speaking, the Lesser Banishing Ritual of the Pentagram uses the banishing Earth pentagram, meaning that it banishes starting from the earth. In other words, the magician stands with "both feet on the ground" in this ritual, which aids his or her stability and concentration while in gnostic trance. This is why we recommend the beginner to practice this Lesser Banishing Ritual of the Pentagram as presented here one to two times daily for several months until it becomes second nature to perform. This exercise can substitute certain other imagination and visualization exercises and is a tremendous aid in developing ritual magic skills.

First, we'll present the complete Lesser Banishing Ritual of the Pentagram. Second, we'll comment on it in more detail later, which will make looking it up at a later date for reference much easier. Once you've thoroughly studied the explanations, you might need to look up the technical details on occasion to make sure you're doing it right.

PRACTICE OF THE LESSER BANISHING RITUAL OF THE PENTAGRAM

The Lesser Banishing Ritual of the Pentagram is divided into four parts (five when used at the end of a larger ritual):

1. Kabbalistic Cross
2. Drawing the pentagrams and the circle
3. Invocation of the archangels/visualization of additional symbols
4. Kabbalistic Cross
5. License to depart (only at the end of a larger ritual)

The ritual is performed while standing facing the east; the gestures can be made with either the right or left hand since the direction the lines are drawn remains the same in either case. You can either use your magical dagger or your extended index and middle fingers, with your thumb resting lightly under them.

1. Kabbalistic Cross

Using your fingers or dagger, draw down energy from above and touch your forehead, vibrating powerfully:

ATEH (= Thine is)

Touch your breast and vibrate powerfully:

MALKUTH (= the kingdom)

Touch your right shoulder and vibrate powerfully:

VE-GEBURAH (= and the power)

Touch your left shoulder and vibrate powerfully:

VE-GEDULAH (= and the glory)

Fold your arms across your chest and vibrate powerfully:

LE-OLAM (= forever and ever)

Fold your hands in front of your forehead, slowly pull them down to your chest and vibrate powerfully:

AMEN (= so be it)

2. Drawing the Pentagrams and the Circle

Draw the first pentagram facing the east. Inhale while pulling your hand back to your chest, then sharply stab your fingers or dagger into the middle of the pentagram while powerfully vibrating the god-name:

JHVH (Yeh-ho-vah or Yod-heh-vau-heh)

Keep your arm outstretched and turn ninety degrees to the south, draw another pentagram, and stab it in the center, vibrating powerfully:

ADNI (Ah-doh-nai)

Keep your arm outstretched and turn ninety degrees to the west, draw another pentagram and stab it in the center, vibrating powerfully:

EHIH (Eh-he-yeh)

Keep your arm outstretched and turn ninety degrees to the north, draw another pentagram, and stab it in the center, vibrating powerfully:

AGLA (Ah-geh-lah)

Keep your arm outstretched and turn ninety degrees back to the east, completing the circle that connects the centers of each pentagram.

Illustration 2: How to draw the lines in the Lesser Ritual of the Pentagram

3. Invocation of the Archangels/Visualization of Additional Symbols

Still facing the east, stretch out your arms to the side and visualize yourself as an oversized black cross with a large red rose blooming at the front intersecting point. When you're satisfied with this visualization, vibrate the god-names while visualizing the archangels in gigantic human form.

Speak and vibrate the names powerfully:

Before me RAPHAEL;
Behind me GABRIEL;
On my right hand MICHAEL;
On my left hand AURIEL;
For about me flames the pentagram,
And above me shines the six-rayed star.

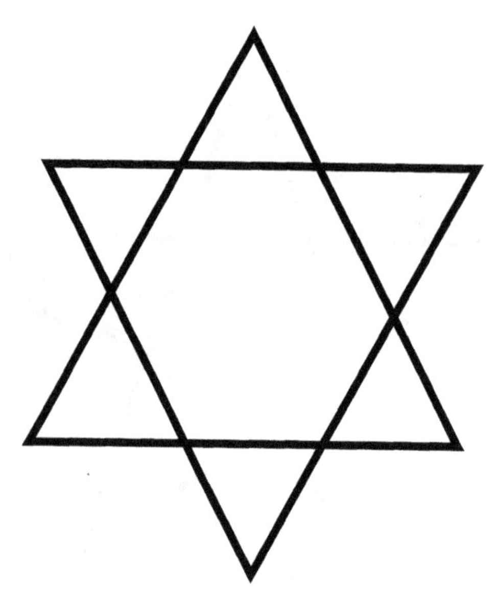

Illustration 3: The hexagram

4. Kabbalistic Cross

Repeat step 1 above (Kabbalistic Cross).

5. License to Depart *(only at the end of a larger ritual)*

Refer to the text below for explanations on this.

COMMENTS ON THE LESSER BANISHING RITUAL OF THE PENTAGRAM

1. Visualization while performing the Kabbalistic Cross

The hand you use draws down a beam of white light from above, through the crown of your head and into your body, through your solar plexus and down to your feet, then from your right to left shoulders until your body is illuminated by a cross of light.

2. Drawing the pentagrams and the circle

The pentagrams are drawn in front of your body in the direction of the arrows (see Illustration 2) and should be about three feet tall. I would recommend synchronizing your breathing to drawing the lines of the pentagram (ascending lines—inhale; descending lines—exhale; horizontal line—hold breath).

Visualization while drawing the pentagrams and the circle:

The hand used for drawing projects, like a laser, colored energy (bluish white, silver, or red), causing the pentagrams and circle to continuously radiate inside the room.

The god-names should be vibrated as powerful as possible until "the walls of the temple tremble," as stated in old texts. This isn't a question of volume. The temple is your body and the god-names should "echo to the end of the universe" in each direction, penetrating everything in its path.

3. Invocation of the archangels/visualization of additional symbols

As with the god-names, the names of the archangels should also be vibrated long and slow, making "the walls of the temple tremble."

Imagination/visualization while invoking the archangels:

Raphael in the east rules the element of Air. He wears a yellow gown and carries a staff, and sometimes an anointing pot. During the invocation, a light breeze from the east brushes your face.

Gabriel in the west rules the element of Water. He wears a blue gown and carries a chalice while standing under a clear, flowing waterfall. You can hear the water splashing behind you in the west and can feel the moisture.

Michael (or Mikael) in the south rules the element of Fire. He wears a bright red gown and carries a sword of fire. You can feel the heat to your right in the south.

Auriel (or Uriel) in the north rules the element of Earth. He wears an earth-colored gown that's brown and olive green, and carries an ear of corn while standing in the middle of a wheat field, perhaps on top of a pentacle. You can feel the firmness of the Earth to your left in the north.

Imagine the hexagram above you in gold.

Don't forget: You visualize the pentagrams and the circle, hear the vibrated god-names, imagine yourself as a big black cross with a rose, and see/feel the archangels and elemental powers . . . all at the same time! Don't be disappointed if it takes you several months before you can do all of this properly. Practice makes perfect, and there's no way of avoiding this unless you're a natural. But even a beginner's imperfect Lesser Banishing Ritual of the Pentagram is highly effective as long as it's performed with a great deal of concentration and effort.

4. Kabbalistic Cross

Now repeat the Kabbalistic Cross according to step 1.

5. License to Depart

For larger operations of ceremonial magic, the Lesser Banishing Ritual of the Pentagram is used as an introductory ritual for protection and casting the magic circle. It's repeated at the end of the operation to conclude the whole ritual.

In this case, the second Lesser Banishing Ritual of the Pentagram is followed by a license to depart. This dismisses any beings (or disperses any distracting thoughts, associations, and feelings) that might have been attracted by the ceremony. There's no standard license to depart, but it could be worded as follows:

I now dismiss all spirits and energies that have been attracted to this ritual. Go in freedom—may peace be with you and me!

In the following part of these explanations, we want to discuss the individual parts of the Lesser Banishing Ritual of the Pentagram, the various aspects of its use, the logic behind the direction the lines are drawn, and more. Let's begin the same way the ritual does, with the Kabbalistic Cross.

1. The Kabbalistic Cross

Regardless of any religious and cultural associations, the Kabbalistic Cross serves mainly two purposes:

a) It gives the magician a feeling of inner harmony and centralization, and causes the balanced activation of his or her body's subtle energies. In this sense, it's similar to exercises we're already familiar with from letter magic (Kerning, Kolb, Sebottendorf), but from other cultures as well (such as the "small circulation" of energy from chi kung or tao yoga). The importance of this function cannot be overemphasized! Sometimes just performing the Kabbalistic Cross on a regular basis is enough to promote healing, inner peace, and, above all, magical protection. This can also be achieved through the second factor that will be discussed in the next paragraph, and the experience of countless Western magicians has proven its extreme effectiveness.

b) The statement it makes ("Thine is the kingdom and the power and the glory forever and ever, amen!") strengthens the self-confidence and self-assurance of the magician, eliminating any fears[1] of magic that he or she might have while, on a metaphorical level, producing the certainty that can remove any destructive doubt about his or her own will. After all, "thine" refers to the magician directly, according to the ancient motto "Deus est Homo, Homo est Deus" ("God is Man, Man is God").

Nonetheless, it's not necessary to deliberately reflect on the meaning of these individual Hebrew mantras while vibrating the words (the same applies to the god-names). They work much stronger through sound, which is why it's so important to vibrate them out loud. Later with enough practice they'll even work when you say them silently to yourself (for example, in look-alike magic).

Drawing down the white light connects heaven and earth (kabbalistically speaking) inside the magician's body, making him or her a living symbol of the union of traditional opposites, such as "spirit/matter," "light/shadow," "good/evil," "solve/coagula" ("disintegrate/unite"), or, in Eastern terms, "yin/yang." Thus, the magician becomes the embodiment of the Hermetic law "As above, so below." This abbreviated law is taken from the Emerald Plate of Hermes Trismegistos, which reads: "That which is above is as that which is below, and that which is below is as that which is above, to perform the miracles of the One Thing."

We realize that the Kabbalistic Cross alone offers enough material for contemplation to occupy the magician philosophically for a long period of time, which proves the value of well-considered, traditional symbolic acts. Nonetheless, from a metaphysical-mystical perspective, the practice itself should never be neglected, as it unfortunately has been for way too long with magic in the past and still is sometimes today. Such lack of symbol-logic can cause unconscious conflicts within the magician that question his or her magical success in the material world (the concrete) as well as the philosophical (the mystical). If you want to join that which is above and that which is below, thought and actions must cooperate harmoniously. Empty speculation must also be avoided, as well as blind action without spiritual basis.

2. The Pentagrams, the Protective Circle, and the God-Names

Thoughts on the deeper symbolism of the pentagram alone could fill many pages. In the first part, we've already given you the essential information so that just a short summary is necessary here. The pentagram symbolizes, among other things, the five elements: Earth, Water, Fire, Air, and Spirit.

With this, it represents the material, earthly world, which our ancestors also called the "sublunar" world (meaning "located below the moon"). In the early days, the moon (and everything feminine) was considered to be the epitome of deception, seduction, and illusion (at least by the more patriarchal-influenced Western occultists). This led to the claim that there was such a thing as "lower" and "higher" magic. Nowadays, there are at least some open-minded magicians who won't accept all the old nonsense without constructive criticism and view the situation a bit differently, thanks in part to modern psychoanalysis. They've realized that there's little use in overemphasizing one pole (e.g., the "cosmic," "divine," "spiritual," or whatever you want to call it) at the cost of the other one. After all, magic is also art: on the one hand, the art of creating a certain balance; on the other hand, the art of removing it and replacing it with a new one.[2]

Knowing this, we're confronted with the pentagram. Just by drawing it, the pentagram symbolically enables us to direct the energy of the elements for our use. This will become clearer in the third section of this book when we explain the direction the lines are drawn in connection with the Greater Ritual of the Pentagram. Just a word here in advance: Drawing the lines of the pentagram joins the elements with one another. On the tarot card I ("The Magician"), the magician is usually portrayed standing at a table (or altar) while juggling the four elements represented by the wand (Fire), the chalice (Water), the sword (Air), and the pentacle (Earth). He can only manage this due to his inherent spirit, which is often represented (such as in the Golden Dawn tarot deck) by the lemniscate (a figure eight lying on its side, the symbol of infinity) that's marked on his hat or floating above his head.

In the end, performing magic simply means saying "yes" to the sublunar world of the elements. That's why the pentagram is the ultimate symbol of magic. By placing the four pentagrams in the four cardinal directions (also called "corners," a symbol that we'll discuss later in this book) during a ritual, we acknowledge ourselves to be "below" while at the same time putting the knowledge and (hopefully!) wisdom (e.g., True Will or

Thelema, gnosis) from "above" into action. This is our home; as already mentioned in the first section, we ourselves embody the pentagram when we stand with our arms and legs spread (think about Leonardo's famous painting of the Vitruvian man!), and, when we mark our circle with pentagrams, protecting the circle with their harmony. Drawing the pentagrams is the practical application of the "choreography of energy movements," which is a phrase sometimes used to define magic.

The protective circle also plays a significant role in the practice of magic, which we just want to touch on here.

The circle is the symbol of infinity since it has no beginning and no end. Inside the circle, the magician literally stands in his or her own center, in the middle of the circle, and in the middle of his or her own infinity.(At least the magician should be, in the ideal situation; in any case, he or she should strive for it.) Sometimes the circle is even drawn or visualized as a ball. The circle protects against unwanted external influences, but this doesn't just happen automatically; it occurs when the magician counters it with his or her own centeredness. The circle, therefore, is a symbol of concentration—the temporary switching off of everything that's unnecessary and distracting. The magician draws his or her concentric circles from one's own center and projects them into the world; the circle is one's symbolic microcosm, and the universe that the magician controls as its master and creator. But every universe is only as good as its creator! In this sense, the circle is the magician's incentive to pursue perfection, or at least the improvement of skills, knowledge, and wisdom.

In practice, it's not enough to just visualize or sense the circle, it should also be felt physically and it should be as noticeable as a brick wall. The magician should never leave one's magic circle during a ritual, because that means he or she would be leaving one's own center, which could cause horrible consequences, such as illness, confusion, or even insanity and physical death, depending on the type of energies that one is working with at the time. Compare leaving the circle to tinkering with a live power line: If you remove the protective isolation, you're in deadly danger. Of course, the circle also protects against your own energies, especially those of your subconscious mind. In this sense, it works like a kind of projected censor and filter, so to speak. The circle is also permeable, but only for the powers intended and invoked.

The god-names vibrated in each of the four cardinal directions have meanings of their own, but this is by far secondary to the mantric, vibratory significance. Nonetheless, for better understanding, these meanings should at least be mentioned here briefly.

JHVH (Jehovah or Yahweh) is generally translated as "I AM WHO I AM"—the self-definition of the creator god from the book of Genesis. A god is a god, and man should view this fact as a challenge to be what he is as well. This can be compared to the recognition and pursuit of one's True Will (Thelema), the establishment of contact and dialog with one's Holy Guardian Angel, the realization of one's own destiny, and so on. Papus presented a comprehensive list of kabbalistic speculations about the relationship of the four elements to each of the Hebrew letters of this "unspeakable" name of God, but this isn't the right place to go into detail on that. Another important fact to know is that JHVH is often referred to as the Tetragrammaton, which literally means "four-word" or as the "four-letter name of God."

ADNI (often written ADONAI) literally means "Lord" or "my Lord." Generally it's also the name that an orthodox Jew reads aloud at the place in the holy scriptures when the Tetragrammaton is mentioned, because one's never allowed to say JHVH.

EHIH (often written EHIEH) is translated as "I will be." In the pentagram ritual, this represents the magician's will.

AGLA is not a word in itself, but rather an abbreviation formed from the first letters of a whole sentence (a technique that's described in the Kabbalah as notaricon): "Athath gibor leolam Adonai," which means "Thou art powerful and eternal, O Lord!" Once again, there are a number of mystical speculations related to this, most of which, of course, are based on Jewish occultism.

The exact reason for this specific allocation of the god-names to the four cardinal directions or elements is unclear, especially since there are some discrepancies when compared to the Greater Ritual of the Pentagram, as we'll see later on in the section dealing with this.

Above all, powerful vibration of the names is important since it enables quick access to their subtle energies, even for a magician who's not familiar with the Judeo-Christian tradition.

3. The Invocation of the Archangels and the Visualization of Additional Symbols

The cross that the magician visualizes (which is actually isosceles) is, among other things, an ancient symbol for the union of the spiritual (vertical axis) and the material (horizontal axis), with the human being at its intersection. Here's also where the rose of insight and wisdom blooms. But it's also the rose of silence, meaning the challenge to keep silent about one's royal art.[3] Keeping silent is, as we've already seen, a very significant energy technique that serves to increase magical power, just like putting the lid on a pot of boiling water will create pressure and explode. By incorporating the "cross of the world," the (silent) wisdom of perfection grows inside the initiate.

One element of the Lesser Banishing Ritual of the Pentagram usually causes problems for non-Christian magicians: the invocation of the archangels. Now and then, the visualizations might seem like devotional kitsch to you, and some of you magicians who were raised as Catholics might think back in horror on those little pictures of guardian angels from your childhood. This is just one reason why attempts are often made at replacing these figures. This would be easy to do since they mainly represent the elemental powers, as already mentioned. If you like, you can replace them with other formulas, such as "I Call Upon Thee, O Powers of the East, O Powers of Air" or "O Powers of the South, Powers of Fire." But this is, of course, an "unorthodox" version of the Lesser Banishing Ritual of the Pentagram and, when working in a group with other magicians, you should first clear up the exact procedure you want to use.

There's much to be said for personifying the elemental powers and making them appear as figures, even if you can't really appreciate the colorfulness that resembles A. E. Waite's tarot deck (which came much later, of course). After all, a large majority of ceremonial magicians work with such images. Through the contrast that the magician consciously creates internally and externally (e.g., by projecting one's own images from deep inside), the subconscious mind can deal with such projected energies more skillfully.

Surely a magician should always confront and analyze such ideological (symbolical) systems that are foreign to one's self, or those that he or she doesn't understand or even abhors. That's one of the best ways to learn, and it releases magical energy as well.

The names of the archangels have certain meanings or associations as well, which don't always correspond to the archangels' functions in the Lesser Banishing Ritual of the Pentagram. In order of their invocation:

RAPHAEL—"The Healer of God," which is why he's sometimes associated astrologically and astromagically with Mercury.

GABRIEL—"The Mighty One of God"; in the gnostic speculations he's often associated with the spirit as the bringer of life, or the logos.

MICHAEL—"Who is like God?"; guardian angel of the Jewish people, also called the "Sword of God" (or of the Demiurge); Michael was also the figure who expelled Adam and Eve from paradise after eating from the Tree of Knowledge.

AURIEL—"The Fire of God"; also one of the important angels.

Consider the fact that the formula EL (or AL) has always played an important role in magical literature. This is a Hebrew term for "God," and as an ending it means "divine" or "of God." The well-known formula ELOHIM that we'll run into later is the plural form. Strictly speaking, it means "gods"—a fact that's quite significant in Jewish and gnostic traditions to the never-ending debate about monotheism. Is there only one "God" or many? It's also significant in our magical dealings with god-forms, especially in planetary magic.

Lastly, we still need to mention that the radiant pentagrams are strengthened through visualization, and (this is new) that the hexagram is also visualized or imagined above the magician's head. While the pentagram represents the five elements, and therefore the "sublunar" world mentioned earlier, the hexagram portrays, among other things, the "astral" world. This is understood to be the sphere of stars (Latin *astrum*, plural *astra*), which is why each of the six points also corresponds to one of the seven planets of classical astrology. (The sun, being the central planet, is located in the middle of the hexagram.) The hexagram is also a symbol for the fusion of the cosmic polarities "male" (upward-pointing triangle) and "female" (downward-pointing triangle); in this respect, it can be seen as a counterpart to the oriental yin-yang symbol (also called "monad"). As the "Key (or Seal) of Solomon," the hexagram is a traditional symbol of magic just like the pentagram. Through its visualization, the magician is aware that he or she is not only working in the transient world of the elements (which are "merely" a product of primeval duality), but, more importantly, that one's using the cosmic primary powers as well. Plus, it reminds the magician that one doesn't have to "carry the cross" alone according to the laws of the material world. The hexagram could also be seen as a sort of "magical beacon" pointing the way toward higher insight and wisdom that the magician uses to illuminate the path that one follows.

We can see from this analysis (which is still quite short, even though we seem to have covered many details) that the Lesser Banishing Ritual of the Pentagram is actually a little *summa summarum*, or "summary," of Western ritual symbolism—a sort of "Encyclopedia of Symbols in Action." After all, we should never forget this aspect, regardless of all the fun we're having speculating and theorizing about the symbolism; the golden rule of Western magic is to recognize the symbol, be able to experience it, and use it in a practical sense—all at the same time! Only then can your head and hand work together to attain spiritual and physical totality and healing (from "heal" or "to be whole"), which is the highest goal for nearly all magicians of the Western tradition (even if other words are often used to describe this goal . . .).

PRACTICAL EXERCISES

The Importance of the Magical Diary

The results of magical operations should always be monitored. This prevents self-deception and delusion while at the same time assuring the precise and accurate estimate of one's own strengths and weaknesses.

The means for this monitoring is your magical diary. If you don't have one yet, get yourself a thick, stable notebook to use only for your magical work. You should make daily entries, even if you happen to neglect your training program on occasion! Then you would write why you were "lazy." By the way, in your magical diary you should even record your thoughts relating to magic, e.g., about the magical literature that you may have read, or questions that you can't follow up on until later.

Leave plenty of room for adding entries and comments at a later date.

Never underestimate the importance of your magical diary. Otherwise, you'll soon learn the hard way through practice. Consider your magical diary to be a "reality anchor" that prevents you from losing control and drifting away. In addition, it's also a "logbook" of your psychonautic journey and after a few months and years it will become a rich source of information about your development as a magician.

Also, make sure that your magical diary never gets into unauthorized hands!

EXERCISE 1

CONFRONTING YOUR FEARS AND DETERMINING THEIR CAUSE

Sit in a firm, comfortable position and relax; then take a few minutes to think about everything that you're afraid of. Think about your fears neutrally without forming an opinion. Just accept them like you would while practicing the state of empty mind technique, such as in Buddhist satipatthana meditation or zazen.

After awhile, ask yourself, "Who is it that's afraid?" Repeat this question again and again until it's almost like a mantra, but without consciously forcing an answer!

Write down any answers, insights, or personal impressions that you might have.

Duration of the exercise: about fifteen minutes.

Frequency of the exercise: at least three times a week, preferably right after waking up or just before going to bed.

Practice this exercise on a regular basis for at least one month and then write a summary of the results. Later you'll occasionally repeat this exercise.

EXERCISE 2

KABBALISTIC CROSS

Practice the Kabbalistic Cross three times a day for a week. Preferably you should do this right after getting up in the morning, or right after taking a bath or shower, while your body's still wet. During the exercise, make sure your face is directed toward a light source (natural or artificial); this will help you feel the light's energy stronger and absorb it easier. However, you don't need to actually concentrate on the light. While practicing, pay attention to how your body feels.

If you can't work without being disturbed, you can even do the exercise in the bathroom at work during your lunch break; just vibrate the mantras softly, but powerfully.

The Kabbalistic Cross can be repeated as often as you want whenever needed. It can also be used to store energy when you're feeling weak, sick, nervous, or afraid and is an exceptionally effective form of magical protection.

EXERCISE 3

PRACTICE OF THE LESSER BANISHING RITUAL OF THE PENTAGRAM

After practicing Exercise 2 for one week, start practicing the Lesser Banishing Ritual of the Pentagram. Optimally, you should do this twice a day, but once a day is acceptable too. Of course you should make sure that you're not disturbed while practicing.

For now, you don't need any special clothing or other accessories, or even a special practice room or temple. You should just practice on a regular basis at the same time and place whenever possible.

Keep practicing Exercise 2 three times a day on a daily basis, counting the number of times you perform it during the Lesser Banishing Ritual of the Pentagram as well. So if you perform the Lesser Banishing Ritual of the Pentagram twice a day, you only need to do Exercise 2 one more time, and if you only do the pentagram ritual once, you need to do Exercise 2 twice more.

The Lesser Banishing Ritual of the Pentagram can also be repeated as often as you want whenever needed. It's also used for storing energy when you're feeling weak, sick, nervous, or afraid, and is a very effective form of magical protection.

Don't despair if you have problems visualizing/imagining all of the details with the desired clarity and focus, or can't seem to do it at all. This will happen with time. Avoid putting yourself under lots of pressure to succeed; just work as best as you can, and as thoroughly as your ability allows.

The Lesser Banishing Ritual of the Pentagram will probably accompany you throughout your entire life as a magician; as a minimum, you should do Exercise 2 on a daily basis during the entire time of your training. At first that may sound like it's very time-consuming, but later you'll really only need no more than five minutes for this, especially when we get into the astral and mental techniques of working. Until then, you should only work physically (not mentally or astrally!) as described here in order to create a solid foundation for mental and astral magic, which is much more difficult (and risky).

---

1. Some of the worst fears in this sense are paranoia and megalomania, which is quite typical of many beginners but is actually nothing more than a new kind of "fear turned upside down" and, psychologically speaking, is just a compensation for an inferiority complex. Both complexes can result in fatal misjudgment or loss of touch with reality.
2. Because in no way is there such a thing as just one correct balance, as many falsely seem to think. Here's an example. Balance and equilibrium within a group of gangsters means the smooth and "harmonious" performance of their work; for those being robbed, on the other hand, and for the general public that's threatened by the gangsters, this means "danger on the streets and in parks," "lack of protection of life and property," or the imbalance and disadvantage of those who are weaker. If a "strong leader with an iron hand" (e.g., a draconic leader or politician) reestablishes "law and order," this usually results in an imbalance for different thinkers. Political persecution is the consequence, and corruption, unrest, and finally rebellion can result, which may even lead to overthrow and a new regime.
3. *Sub rosae,* or "under the rose," is still used sometimes today to describe information and agreements that are confidential or even secret.

PRACTICAL SIGIL MAGIC (I)

INTRODUCTION TO SIGIL MAGIC

The following introduction to sigil magic can be applied to magic in general. Even if you're already familiar with sigil magic, I recommend that you study the following information closely and integrate it into your magical practice. This will help prevent you from getting on the wrong track, which can rob quite a bit of your time.

In the last section, we mentioned one of the basic formulas of magic: WILL, IMAGINATION, and TRANCE. This formal structure enables us to understand our magical work better, and allows us to derive and apply many of the laws of magic from our own understanding.

Now let's take a practical approach. You already know that the censor, the authority that all-too-often makes life as a magician difficult for us with its pseudo-rational doubts and objections, is located between the conscious and subconscious minds. This censor can be averted entirely (or at least in part) through the means of trance. Magical power lies in the subconscious mind. If we can succeed in "smuggling" commands or statements of intent past the conscious mind to the subconscious mind, our experience has shown that this enables the desired result to manifest within the scope of one's powers (which are actually quite tremendous).

The desire to achieve a specific thing automatically generates the opposite effect, namely failure, according to the law of *actio et reactio.* The fact that we're usually unaware of this countereffect doesn't change the situation. Our psyche has learned to cleverly disguise it in many ways: doubts, fear, moral or religious concerns, uncertainty, and yes, even the plain old fear of success itself, which is rarely admitted. These are the manifestations of this anti-energy. "All suffering stems from desire," said Buddha. This definitely applies to the magical level as well until we've learned to make the distinction between desire and will. But this isn't always as simple as it sounds, so we'll start by using the more straightforward method of directing our desires straight to their destination by means of magical technology.

People who are not strong enough to face their opponent openly in battle need to use cunning and camouflage. Consequently, we disguise our desires and statements of intent, enabling them to march right by the "palace guard"—namely our censor—unhindered, straight to the armory of our inner soul. The best way to do this is to give them a "harmless" disguise that hides their true intentions, such as through the use of abstract images and glyphs (symbols) that we call "sigils."

Now you might object and think that all the effort isn't really necessary if you just use the technique of suggestion. In fact, such techniques (e.g. Couéism, positive thinking, self-hypnosis) often do work quite well. These techniques are no strangers to magic and are often applied as helpful tools, but they shouldn't be confused with magic itself! Anyway, if you take a closer look, you'll see that these systems are really not as "simple" as they may seem at first, and that their rate of success rarely even comes close to that achieved though sigil magic.

Let's look at a concrete example. You'd like to make a good impression on an important person, such as during a job interview. Now by using autosuggestion, positive thinking, or similar systems, you'd prepare yourself for the interview by suggesting to yourself several times a day that you'll make the desired good impression and get the job. Depending on the situation and your talent, this would require at least five to ten minutes of work a day for several days in a row—maybe even for weeks or months. On the other hand, with sigil magic, you can achieve the same goal (provided that you have some experience) with a minimum amount of effort applied just once for about fifteen minutes—and with a much higher success rate, as proven. Afterward you never have to think about it again; in fact, you're even required to forget!

But the minimum of time and effort involved isn't the only advantage of sigil magic. This is truly an organic method through and through, and we really mean that literally: Austin Osman Spare, the founder of sigil magic, once said, "Sigils will flesh." They become an integral part of the human organism, which, in turn, applies all of the strength and power available in every one of its cells to convert them into action. Later on we'll discuss what this actually means and apply in practice as well by using the example of atavistic magic.

Everything that we enter into our subconscious mind is processed there: Facts, experiences, and associations are stored; uncomfortable thoughts are repressed and, as a result, can even become a tremendous explosive force (such as a complex, neurosis, or even psychosis). In magic, the function of the conscious mind is to define the predetermined goal, acting as a sort of "pilot." It's cultivated through spiritual training and exercises in concentration, discipline, and will.

The subconscious mind, on the other hand, has the responsibility of converting the commands and goals as promisingly as possible, acting as the "engineer." It's trained through ritual and association/analogies (more on this later), through trance training as well as through the use of symbols.

The censor is assigned the function of protecting the entire process, keeping everything "running" and eradicating any undesired internal or external factors. It's the "duty officer." Since at first it will more likely cause difficulties rather than stimulate our magical ambitions due to its ultraconservative and overcautious attitude that's additionally strengthened through a magic-hostile environment and upbringing, it will be evaded and "re-educated" by working with the gnostic or magical trance. Experience has shown that it will eventually come to terms with our magic, becoming a valuable ally that takes over a large part of our work on the robotic or automatic level while also providing effective magical protection. Once the magician is able to merge it with his or her True Will (Thelema) through constant practice, it will become its embodiment, therefore fulfilling the function of what is referred to as the "Holy Guardian Angel" in the Magic of Abramelin, or the "clan totem" in African magic (as well as in other so-called "primitive" systems of native peoples).

In this respect, evading the censor is actually an important part of our further development. It's trained by experiencing the effectiveness and success of your magical work. Chart 5 summarizes this.

Psychological Authority	Developed by
Conscious Mind	discipline training will training mental training
Censor	avoidance trance experience magical success
Subconscious Mind	ritual trance training symbols

Chart 5: Magical training—the development of psychological authorities

Now we have enough information to understand the basics of how sigil magic works so that we can get started. In practice, using the example from above, you would first formulate your statement of intent, then convert it into a glyph or sigil by means of graphical manipulation, and then charge this sigil, implanting it into your subconscious mind through gnostic trance. Here's a detailed description of how that works.

THE PRACTICE OF SIGIL MAGIC (I)—THE WORD METHOD

Before we get to the actual practice of sigil magic, we first need to state our intention. At first, we'll only be dealing with the so-called "word method" of sigil magic, but later we'll be dealing with other techniques as well.

The Statement of Intent and its Formulation

The word method of sigil magic is based on a distinctly formulated "statement of intent." This should be worded as clearly and precisely as possible because the subconscious mind has the fatal tendency to interpret some commands way too literally. Let me tell you about a real situation that happened to one of our seminar participants once since his example illustrates this principle quite well—here's his report:

> *A colleague from work is a passionate horseman who often participates in tournaments and competitions. Well, there was one riding competition that he was particularly interested in, and it was his dream to win it at least once in his lifetime. Since he was familiar with the technique of positive thinking, he used an affirmation that was worded as follows: "I will win the tournament. I will win the tournament." He repeated this several times a day.*
>
> *Finally the big day arrived and he participated in the tournament just as planned. Although he tried his best, he only crossed the finish line fourth. Now, imagine how baffled he was when he received his consolation prize—an aftershave called "Tournament"! You could almost hear the universe laughing out loud . . .*

Now be honest, did you ever think this situation would turn out the way it did? Probably not! After all, this example can teach us a lesson in more ways than one. Firstly, it shows how careful we need to be when formulating our magical statements of intent in order to avoid misunderstandings. Secondly, we realize how literal the subconscious mind understands some commands—and how it may cause "coincidences" to occur in order to obey these (misunderstood) commands. Thirdly, it illustrates the principle of "success on another level" in which we often just barely "miss the point," being not even able to count it as a true failure since the instructions were officially carried out. All experienced magicians are familiar with this phenomena and, after all, this is what often makes magic so colorful and surprising. The reason we often just hit scattered targets instead of the desired "direct shots" will be discussed more closely in the next section when we deal with the "symbol-logical fuzzy relation."

On the other hand, the statement of intent shouldn't be overly precise. A statement like "I want to win exactly $7527.24 on March 14 in the lottery" is loaded with too many specific commands to have any hopes of success. Although such formulations just may actually work sometimes, it only happens in spite of the formulation and certainly not because of it!

It's similar to divination with tarot cards, which generally have pictures on them. If you want to use the cards to make predictions about the future successfully, you need to ask the proper questions that the pictures can answer—a principle that's violated much too frequently. So pack your statement of intent into such a form that's not too vague in order to prevent the possibility of misinterpretation insofar as possible (which, of course, can never be done 100 percent of the time), but also allows enough room for the imagery of the subconscious mind to effectively take action. Of course there are no set rules or patterns to follow—you'll just have to rely on your instinct and ever-growing experience.

However, as a rule of thumb, you can note that your statement of intent should be clear and precise. "Clear" means that you should eliminate any ambiguities.

If you say "I want to get rich," this includes the possibility of winning the lottery, but also the possibility of your favorite aunt passing away and you inheriting her house—or you getting "rich in experience," for example, by falling for a trickster who talks you into buying "dead certain" stock in an Australian gold mine that turns out to be not even worth the paper it's printed on . . .

On the other hand, the requirement of "preciseness" is easier to fulfill. It simply means that the statement of intent should be aimed at a specific goal and that it shouldn't be formulated too vaguely. If you use a statement of intent such as "I want to do well," this spell may or may not bear fruit—in any case, it's questionable as to whether or not you'd even notice the effect. So try to be as precise as possible without overdoing it.

We recommend always starting your statement of intent with the same phrasing, such as "I will . . ." or "It is my will to . . ." This conditions your subconscious mind the more you practice and trains it to automatically activate every time a new sigil is charged.

Avoid the following when formulating your statement of intent:

a) *Negative formulations*—these are usually ignored by the subconscious mind and therefore turned into just the opposite. "I will not get sick" turns into a fatal "I will get sick." Try to formulate them in a positive sense, as in the example "I will stay healthy."

b) *Abstractions, foreign words, and all too complicated formulations*, unless they're already imprinted "in your flesh and blood" (and I mean that literally!) through your job or another activity. The subconscious mind of an average person would have no idea what to make of words like "diphenylamine" or "gnoseology," but they'd pose no problem for the subconscious mind of a chemist or philosopher. Nevertheless, even such specialists should always stick to clear, precise formulation. By the way, you can even formulate your statement of intent in your colloquial dialect if that's how you normally talk and if you find it difficult to use proper standard language.

c) *Outrageous goals* that clearly surpass your own sphere of influence. Although magic is much more powerful than you might think, it's not omnipotent. Charging sigils for "world peace" or "wiping out international terrorism" is a sheer overestimation of your abilities. Of course you can always do things like this to satisfy (or pacify) your own conscience, but this has nothing to do with targeted, success-oriented, and, therefore, pragmatic magic.

Always remember that with every act of magic you perform, you owe it to your subconscious mind to aim for realistic goals that lie within its sphere of influence—anything else is a dangerous delusion! A person who concentrates on magical goals that one will never be able to reach is automatically programming his or her entire magical personality for inevitable failure, thereby blocking all opportunity to expand one's magical skills. That's why you should stick to "little things," especially when you're just starting out. Also take the following rule to heart:

Even Use Magic for Things That Are Already Very Promising!

With this little trick, you're programming your subconscious mind for success, thereby giving it the chance to develop further until you've reached the point where you're really able to "move mountains" and accomplish exceptional things.

Now if you get the impression that you need to master sigil magic like an expert before you can even start, don't worry—just the opposite is true. Because only practice can show which of these rules is more important for you and which ones you can ignore. After all, it's a mistake to think that one person's subconscious mind functions exactly the same as another's. Each person is different from the next; we can only provide a sort of "statistical average" here that has led to astonishing success in nearly every case.

The question as to whether a statement of intent is correct or not can only be monitored through the success of the operation itself. In cases of doubt, however, you should rely mainly on your feelings and intuition. Through constant practice, you'll surely develop the necessary "fine touch."

Making a Sigil with the Word Method

Generally, making sigils is one of the easiest and most uncomplicated aspects of sigil magic. After you've followed our directions to make your first sigil, take the time to read through our instructions once again before you start charging it.

Let's take an example from everyday or practical magic: "I will make eight hundred dollars tomorrow." (Make sure you set a time span—this will make it easier for you to monitor the results later.)

First, write your statement of intent in block letters on a piece of paper:

I WILL MAKE EIGHT HUNDRED DOLLARS TOMORROW[1]

Now cross out all of the letters that are repeated each time a repetition occurs. Each letter is only used once.

I WxxL MAKE xxGHT xUNDRxx xOxxxxS xxxxxxxx

The letters that remain are:

I, W, L, M, A, K, E, G, H, T, U, N, D, R, O, S,

Now we make a sigil using these letters:

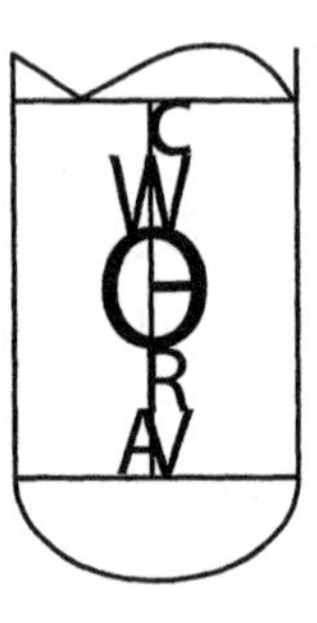

Illustration 4: The first sigil

You see that we've made a little picture by lining up the letters on top of each other. Now although a sigil shouldn't be too complicated to prevent overchallenging the subconscious mind, it shouldn't be too simple either since this makes forgetting the sigil more difficult (see below: "Banishing"). A simple square or circle is way too easy to forget. Plus, if you take a close look at the sigil you should be able to recognize all of the letters you used—at least theoretically.[2]

When simplifying the sigil, you should also make the letters more abstract. This could look like the example in Illustration 5.

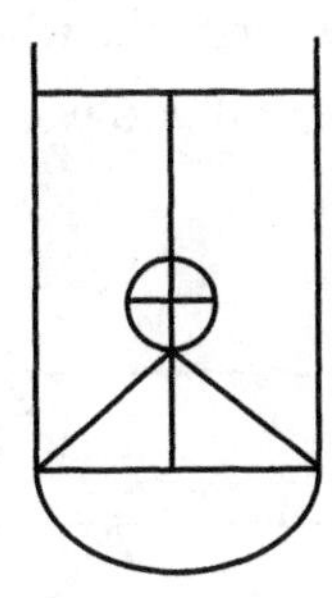

Illustration 5: The simplified, abstract sigil

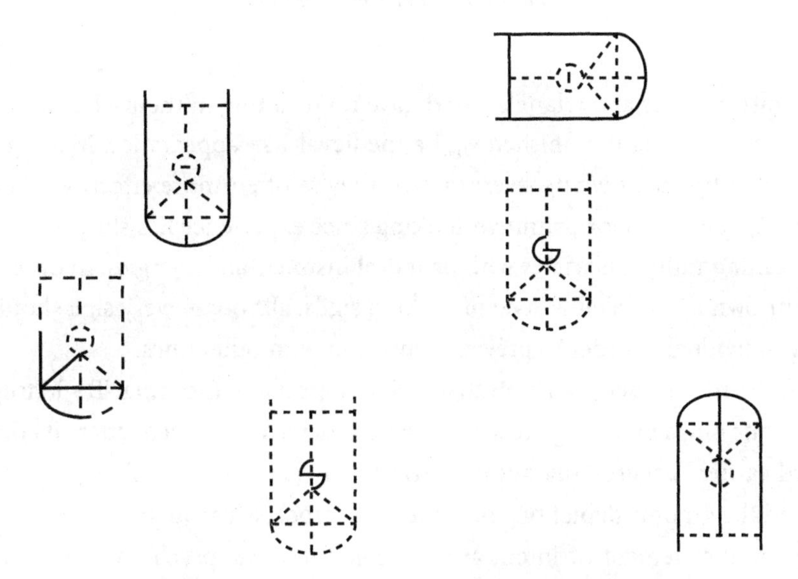

Illustration 6: Some of the letters contained in the completed sigil

You'll notice that we've left out quite a bit from the first sigil, but that we've added some things as well. Nonetheless, it still contains all of the letters from the list above, even if we've used a little trick. One line can be part of several letters at the same time, and the letters count even when they're upside down. That way, the arch can be used for the *U* and the *D* at the same time, as shown in Illustration 4; in the same way, the remaining letters can easily be found in the finished sigil as well. In Illustration 6, we've also shown the letters *K, G, S,* and *M* in order to clarify the whole process better.

You can even decorate the sigil a bit if you want to give it a more "magical" appearance, as in Illustration 7 below.

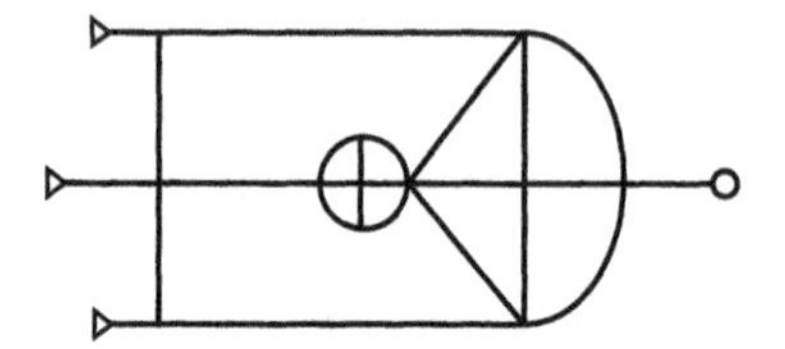

Illustration 7: The decorated sigil

The decorative circles and triangles used have no meaning in themselves and serve the sole purpose of giving the finished sigil a medieval-like appearance. Making sigils requires no artistic talent whatsoever; in fact, they're often more effective when they're "homemade," awkward, or primitive-looking since experience has shown that the subconscious mind rather associates with primeval instincts and energies. In time you'll develop your own unmistakable style of making sigils, although every sigil should still be uniquely individual in order to prevent confusion with other ones.

The finished product is a glyph that has no detectable meaning. Try letting friends examine your finished test sigil to see if they can determine which letters it contains. As explained earlier, just crossing out the extra letters is a way of coding the statement of intent, and the graphic depiction continues this process. Through coding, the contents of the magical statement of intent are smuggled past the psychological censor undetected so that it cannot erect any barriers or blockades and the subconscious mind can tackle the job unhindered.

In summary, the word method of creating sigils proceeds according to the following scheme:

Write down the statement of intent in block letters.
Cross out the letters that appear more than once.
Create a graphic sigil using the remaining letters.
Simplify and decorate the sigil, making it more abstract.

Chart 6: Making a sigil (word method)

That's all you need to know for now about this method of making sigils. This is plenty of information to get you started. Experience has shown that this method will lead to excellent results as long as you heed our advice contained in this section.

Charging the Sigil

Charging a sigil that was made using the word method is done in a spasmodic (convulsive or jerky) way. It involves exertion and there are many methods for storing the energy required for this.

Austin Osman Spare recommended the so-called "death posture" to charge a sigil, although he failed to describe this in detail. Nowadays, most practitioners have agreed that the goal of the death posture is to achieve a complete state of empty mind. Once this is achieved, the sigil can be charged and implanted into the subconscious mind.

Please note that the word "charge" in relation to sigil magic means something entirely different than the energizing of talismans and amulets. In the latter, magical energy is directed into an object (sometimes spasmodic as well), which turns it into a storage medium for this polarized power. The charging of a sigil, on the other hand, can be compared to a computer program that's loaded or stored into the memory of the computer. In other words:

A sigil is charged by implanting it into the subconscious mind.

Metaphorically, you could compare it to a cartridge that's loaded into the chamber of a revolver. It's important to keep this difference in mind, otherwise it may lead to future misunderstandings. This is why we'll be using the phrase "to activate" from now on.

Principally it doesn't matter which form of the death posture you choose for activating your sigils. The important thing is that you can adequately achieve a state of empty mind. The term "death posture" refers to the "death" of all thoughts; for the same reason, an orgasm is sometimes called "little death." This death of all mind activity is accompanied by a temporary dissolving of self-awareness (ego).

The phrase "state of empty mind" has caused quite a sensation in esoteric literature in the past, and it's considered the ultimate goal of all yoga techniques and other Eastern forms of mediation. But it would throw us way too far off course to delve into such questions now, e.g., whether samadhi yoga or satori in Zen Buddhism are possibly nothing more than the temporary shutting-off of the thought process and self-awareness—something which their followers strictly deny. For now it's fine if you can just imagine the state of empty mind being comparable to a moment of extreme anger or joy—a state in which the entire outside world is either concentrated into one single thing or disappears entirely, and no thoughts about one's own identity can exist. The best way to achieve this state of mind is through physical stress, which is emphasized by the first of the following two techniques for activating sigils.

The Death Posture (I)[3]

The magician can either stand or sit. The sigil is either hung on the wall or placed on the table in front of one's self, clearly visible. The magician takes a deep breath and closes one's mouth, eyes, ears, and nostrils using the fingers of both hands. Then he or she holds one's breath until it's nearly unbearable. But one doesn't let go yet—he or she keeps holding one's breath. While doing so, he or she should think neither about the sigil nor its purpose. Then—just before fainting—one opens the eyes as wide as possible and stares at the sigil while exhaling and refilling one's lungs with fresh air. Then the magician abruptly closes the eyes again and banishes the sigil (see section "Banishing the Sigil" further below).

Another option is to stare at the sigil while standing on your tiptoes, holding your arms in an unnatural, uncomfortable position twisted and turned behind your back, and leaning back so far that you can just barely keep your balance.[4]

The Death Posture (II)

This version of the death posture is much milder than the first, but works just as well when done with the proper intensity. However, it requires a bit more practice. It should be performed while sitting and is well suited for people with heart or breathing problems.

The sigil is placed on a table in front of the magician, who sits up straight and places one's hands on the tabletop around the sigil. The thumbs form a ninety-degree angle, the hands lie flat on the table with the tips of the thumbs touching, and the sigil lies in the open square formed by the hands (see Illustration 8). Stare at the sigil with your eyes wide open; don't blink or close your eyes, even when they start running.

Now the magician starts twitching muscles one by one, starting with a lower leg, then the next, then both at the same time. This twitching should be firm and relaxed; it should only take a split second, but needs to be very intense. Then the magician continues by twitching the upper legs in the same way, then the buttocks, hands, arms, and finally even the scalp. After practicing a few times, twitching the whole body should only take about a half a second.

At the climax of twitching, the magician rips open the eyes even further while still staring at the sigil; then, he or she abruptly closes the eyes and banishes the sigil (see "Banishing the Sigil").

Banishing the Sigil

After activating the sigil, it needs to be banished—this is the first step in forgetting the entire operation. The easiest way of banishing is to let out a loud, hearty laugh. At first your laugh will probably seem a bit fake, but that doesn't matter. Actually, laughing is one of the most uncomplicated ways of achieving a state of empty mind, as mentioned above.[5]

In addition, the magician should distract oneself from the magical operation by concentrating on something profane. The less it has to do with magic, the better. Activities like watching TV, playing computer games, or exercising are all good methods of distraction.

The "channel" leading to the subconscious mind that was opened through trance needs to be closed again completely after charging the sigil. It would be entirely wrong to meditate after charging a sigil, like some of my students did at first. In colloquial terms, it can be compared to the principal of "putting the lid on the pot." Only when the lid is firmly put on the pot can enough heat be generated to cook the meal properly. Therefore, when we open ourselves up through trance in order to implant our sigil into our subconscious mind, we need to close this opening as soon as we're finished so that no energy can escape. For the same reason, the sigil also needs to be forgotten. If the magician is constantly reminded of its shape and contents, the rational mind will interfere with the process and endanger the operation with doubt, curiosity, or impatience. To make another metaphorical comparison, imagine how you would plant a seed. You would dig a hole in the ground, put the seed in the hole, and cover it up again with soil. No gardener on earth would ever dream of digging up the seed once an hour to see if it has already sprouted and is doing well. That would ruin the whole thing. We'd be doing a similar disservice to our subconscious mind by constantly checking up on it to see if it were working properly (even if it were to happen unconsciously and instinctively). This is another aspect that you might not have suspected of the challenge "To keep silent" from the phrase "To know, to will, to dare, to keep silent" that we mentioned in the first section. After all, it's often necessary to keep silent and still with your own subconscious mind so that it can work without being hindered.

Ideally, the magician should forget not only the external appearance of the sigil, but also its intention. This is extremely difficult to do in practice since the magician usually only does a magical operation for something that's very important to him or her. That's why we recommend preparing a whole bunch of sigils for various long-term goals and keeping them all in the same place until you can no longer remember which sigil is for which purpose. Not until then should you activate the sigils.

If one of the sigils suddenly escapes the subconscious mind unwillingly, it should be activated once again and banished. Usually it's enough to just divert your attention away from the sigil until it disappears again, and the best way to do this is through laughter.

Now let's summarize the main points of sigil magic once again in the chart on the next page:

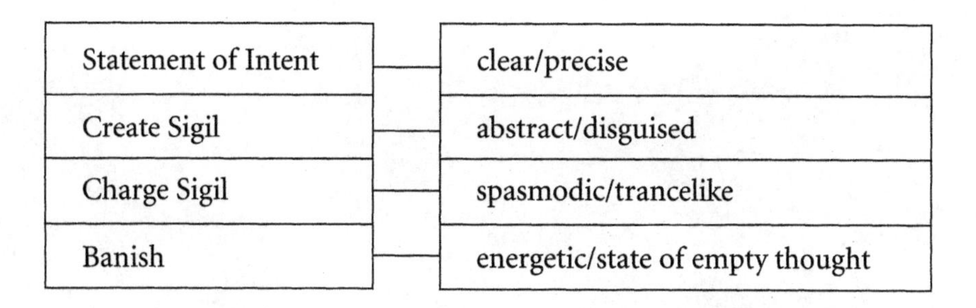

Chart 7: The four steps of sigil magic

---

1. By the way, always write out numbers, such as "thirty four" instead of "34" and so on. Punctuation marks such as hypens, commas, periods, exclamation marks, etc. are not used either.
2. However, this examination is only done before charging the sigil; afterward, it's not recommended for obvious reasons.
3. *Warning:* Avoid this technique if you suffer from heart palpitations or are at high risk of a heart attack and/or you suffer from any kind of lung problems, high blood pressure, or vascular problems. In this case, only use the second method that's described in the next section called the Death Posture (II).
4. If a milder version of this technique is used, e.g., by not holding one's breath for quite so long, it can even be used by people with the above-mentioned physical ailments.
5. Whoever doesn't believe this should just try laughing real hard while trying to concentrate on a math problem!

Introduction to Ritual Magic (1)

MAGIC IS A SYMBOLIC ACT

Rituals are often described as "dramaturgical myths" and this description can surely be applied to a large number of the ceremonies performed in traditional magic. Ritual participants can witness and actively participate in mythological themes—such as the life, death, and reincarnation of the sun god Osiris, or the union of Simon and Helena—by "staging" them symbolically or allegorically in a temple or sanctuary (be it with or without an audience) within a more or less fixed ritual structure. However, the difference from an ordinary drama is that rituals are not designed for entertainment or amusement, and not much importance is placed on aesthetics and philosophical contemplation; rather, they're aimed at fulfilling a specific and concrete purpose, whether mystical or with intentions of magical success.

This realization also has many important consequences for both ritual and nonritual magic. You've heard of magic being called the "art of illusion." Well, this includes much more than just stage entertainment where virgins are apparently sawed into pieces and then brought back to life and rabbits are pulled out of apparently empty top hats. A magician is a master of illusion. He or she sees through things, learns the laws of nature, uses them to one's advantage, and forces reality to comply with them. Of course that doesn't mean that a magician's results are merely "imagined," or based on optical or other perceptional illusions. Actually, the effects of magic are no less real and concrete than our reality as a whole, even though they may be more difficult to grasp and detect. You could compare it to working with microbes. The unaided (in magic, "untrained") eye is unable to see microorganisms (in magic, "magical energies and effects") and cannot even confirm their existence; but with the help of microscopes and the proper training (in magic, "the training of perception and intuition"), we're able to do this. Therefore, our view of reality is dependent on the way we perceive things.

Please note that we're talking about the way we perceive things and not the precision with which we perceive things. Only materialistic scientists would do the latter because they represent the ideology that in the end everything in the universe is measurable and therefore perceptible with our five normal senses, if science would just make sufficient progress. Even the supposedly accurate and unerring measuring instruments that scientists use are nothing more than extended human sensory organs. Actually this is nothing but a change in our current form of perception. One of the goals of a magical education should therefore be the training of one's magical perception.

In this sense, we can apply the above-mentioned concept that (ritual) magic is also "sacred theater," or a "mystery game." The proof can be found in the basic structure of the subconscious mind that if "pretending" is practiced frequently enough, it will cause the desired real effect on a material or conscious level. We're all familiar with a negative example of this. If you keep telling yourself that no one likes you or that you're a ridiculous loser and have nothing but bad luck in dealing with other people (such as with the opposite sex, but also with colleagues, superiors, and so on), you'll indeed become the kind of person that you insist you already are: You'll become a person that no one likes with absolutely no attractive charisma. The same holds true if you keep insisting on failure ("I won't get the job," "I'll never pass that test!", "No woman/man could ever put up with me"). Psychology calls this a "self-fulfilling prophecy."

Techniques of autosuggestion, such as positive thinking and working with affirmations or self-hypnosis, prove that this method works in a positive way as well, meaning that a constructive opposite can also be achieved.

This is usually not clear enough to beginning students of magic. When practicing the Lesser Banishing Ritual of the Pentagram, if you feel that the complicated visualizations of this basic ritual just don't seem to work despite all your efforts, remember the following basic principle:

Anything that you cannot actually perceive during the visualization must either be imagined or accepted as reality until you are able to do so!

This means moving away from older magic authors such as Bardon, Crowley, or Gregorius who usually place great importance on perfect visualization before actually performing a magical operation. However, modern practice has shown that this is nothing but an extremely time-consuming misunderstanding. In reality it's fine (at least for the start) to just accept a visualization as being real (even if you can't "really" perceive it) in order to achieve the desired effect. In other words, your Lesser Banishing Ritual of the Pentagram will protect you even if you're not able to see the archangels with all of their colorful details as long as you practice it frequently enough and, in this way, program your "magical database" or "the subconscious" to associate this ritual with protection as well as inner and outer centering.[1]

Often, the beginner will stand in the circle, perform the ritual correctly (meaning according to the instructions), and merely hope that the pentagrams are actually flaming around him, the god-names are "echoing to the end of the universe," and that all of the archangels as guardians of the elements are present.

Only after practicing for awhile—which can take days or years, depending on how talented you are—will the actual effect take place. You'll be able to perceive the visualized symbols, figures, mantras, and so on with the same reality that you perceive things in the everyday world. Then the magician will instinctively feel a physical touch if one accidentally brushes with the boundaries of the "imaginary" circle—a sure indication that his or her subtle perception has developed well. This is the largest obstacle that needs to be overcome, and then it's just one more small step until you can perceive the magical energy of other people. From now on we're going to call this "magical energy perception", or simply "energy perception."

At first, energy perception is developed by means of a trick, namely by declaring its reality without actually being able to perceive it. We can derive a theory from this that can be applied to all aspects of magical practice that you should definitely remember:

The art of magical illusion is achieved by forcefully and repeatedly declaring illusions to be reality until they have actually become reality.

Notice that the concepts of force and repetition are stressed here. Fact is, the subconscious mind is a creature of habit that mainly learns through repetition. First the length of practice is of importance, followed of course by the respective energy input required. Such a process can be understood as the creative formation of one's own universe.

After all, rituals also serve the purpose of creating this magical illusion by setting "reality markers" through movement, analogies, and even the initial process stages of imitation and acting out, regardless of whether we prefer to establish these in the magician's psyche or on the astral plane. It's often said that rituals work like "astral beacons," attracting nonincarnate entities (beings) like moths to a light. This is one important reason for saying the license to depart after every ritual (not only after the Lesser Banishing Ritual of the Pentagram).

Even if you don't happen to believe in the hypothesis (and it's really no more than such) of nonincarnate entities (although most magicians do, with some exceptions), there's good reason to assume that every ritual leaves behind tracks in the deepest layers of the psyche. The more psychologically minded magician might argue that subconscious, often repressed soul material is activated by the ritual and therefore needs to be banished afterwards to prevent it from getting out of control and taking possession of the magician.

"VISUALIZATION" AND MAGICAL SENSORY PERCEPTION

The term "visualization" as commonly used in magical literature has often led to misunderstandings. Maybe the following sentence will shatter all your well-loved prejudices (or misjudgments), and your own practice will surely convince you that it's correct:

Magical sensory and energy perception does not occur
through any of the known sensory organs.

The theories about the "third eye" or other postulated subtle organs that are often used to explain magical perception still do not change this fact. In no way do we want to deny the existence of the third eye—but it's useless to start off by identifying it with the thymus gland, only to later switch it to the mysterious pineal gland, and finally to switch it to some other center, which is exactly what the history of magic has done. And it's nonsense to believe that such models could actually help the training of magical perception.

The concept of the third eye has led to the fact that magic has been reduced to optical perception only throughout the centuries, when in reality it's quasi-optical at the most and, in addition, represents only one of many methods of magical perception. After all, clairvoyance doesn't just involve seeing, but also smelling, hearing, tasting, and feeling. But all of these terms are merely just vague approximations for a form of perception that really resembles more of a "sensing" than seeing, hearing or feeling. Only a small minority of magicians and other sensitive people are able to perceive things equally well with all of these senses, even if this is desired in the interest of higher accuracy and therefore trained as such. In reality, although subtle perception is articulated in a way that may seem to resemble other forms of sensory perception, it's not identical to these and they should in no way be confused.

Although magical perception usually takes place on a quasi-optical level for most people—meaning that they seem to actually "see" the subtle energies—there are countless exceptions. In fact, many magicians are extremely nonvisual types and cannot really visualize anything at all. But that doesn't mean that they're poor representatives of their trade; it only means that they're skilled in other things and may be able to smell, taste, or feel the subtle energies instead. But if you insist on focusing your training on optical perception for experiencing subtle energies like most magical literature does, those of you that could reach the same results with other forms of perception will have unnecessary difficulties.

In other words, if you have the feeling that you can't really "visualize" properly, just try using another form of perception instead. Don't force yourself to "see" the magical circle or the pentagrams at all costs; try to "feel" them with your hands instead, or to "smell," "taste," and even "hear" them. For example, a visually oriented person will find it hard to imagine how one could differentiate between a red triangle or yellow square by simply "smelling" it, but for a "nose" or olfactory person this wouldn't be any problem at all. An auditory person, on the other hand, can "hear" the difference between various colors and symbols, and the haptic person can "feel" it.

So if you should happen to run across the word "visualization" in other books on magic, just replace it with the word "magical imagination" and concentrate on the "sensory organ" that works best for you at first. Later, of course, you should train the other forms of perception as well since this would expand your entire range of perception, allowing more information to be taken in and processed, which would result in greater flexibility in decision-making and a larger variety of possible outcomes. But such maximum demands are usually more of a stumbling block for the beginning students that tend to frustrate them and rob them of all motivation.

PRACTICAL EXERCISES

EXERCISE 4

PRACTICAL SIGIL MAGIC (I)

Perform at least one operation of sigil magic per week for three months according to the instructions in this section using the word method. Enter the operation into your magical diary, but cover up the sigil after activating it by taping a sheet of paper to the sides so that you won't accidentally see and deactivate it when paging through the diary. Don't forget to write a date on this cover-up sheet that tells you when to monitor the success or failure of the operation. Here it's extremely important to leave room in your magical diary for later entries, which should be dated as well.

EXERCISE 5

TRAINING OF MAGICAL PERCEPTION (I)

This exercise is practiced alongside the Lesser Banishing Ritual of the Pentagram. During the first month of practice, you should perform the entire exercise at least twice a week. On each of the other five days you can do one of the five steps of the exercise (letters a, b, c, d, or e) after performing the pentagram ritual. In doing so, during the first month you should pay close attention that you really do practice each individual step equally without putting more emphasis on a certain one.

During the second month, it's enough to just do the entire exercise at least twice per week. After the third month, just do the exercise whenever (and as often as) you feel necessary. If you notice that your magical perception is improving from this exercise (and that will most likely be the case), try intensifying things for awhile by extending the length and duration of the exercise. Don't stop performing this exercise until you're completely satisfied with your magical perception. But even then, we recommend you repeat it once every quarter year so that you don't get "rusty."

a) After performing and vibrating the Kabbalistic Cross for the second time following the Lesser Banishing Ritual of the Pentagram, keep your eyes closed, stretch out your arms, and walk around the circle, trying to "feel" it. Try not to visualize or imagine the circle in any way when doing so—this won't be necessary at all, even if you don't have much success at first. Usually you'll sense the subtle energies as a soft tingling feeling, or a feeling of warmth or cold, or maybe you'll even feel a slight electrical shock. Carefully note all of your perceptions in your magical diary.

b) Proceed as in step a) except that you'll work with the sense of hearing this time. While walking around the circle, first try hearing each of the god-names that you vibrated in the corresponding directions. (Keep silent while doing this; don't try to help your perception by vibrating the names again.) Then stand in the middle of the circle and try to hear all of the god-names at the same time, each one echoing from its corresponding direction. Carefully note all of your perceptions in your magical diary.

c) Proceed as in step a) except that you'll work with the sense of smell this time. While walking around the circle, first try to sense the general smell of the room you're in. Try to determine if the ritual has made a difference in the smell. (Next time you can consciously compare the smell of the room before and after the pentagram ritual.) Carefully note all of your perceptions in your magical diary.

d) Proceed as in a) except that you'll work with the sense of taste this time. While walking around the circle, first try to sense the general taste of the room you're in. Pay attention to your sense of taste before and after the ritual. Carefully note all of your perceptions in your magical diary.

e) Proceed as in step a) except that you'll work with the sense of sight this time. While walking around the circle, open your eyes real wide and try to see it without purposely focusing your eyes. At first you'll probably only see a vague shimmer, like a fog or mist in the air, as though it were subject to a high degree of heat. This is a good sign. After awhile the contours of the circle will become more distinct. Do the same with the symbols, and finally with the images of the archangels as well. Carefully note all of your perceptions in your magical diary.

Don't be discouraged if you can only record minimal success or none at all in your magical diary. After all, this exercise is meant to thoroughly train your magical perception! First, in combination with the following Exercise 6, you'll get a good idea of where your strengths lie concerning subtle energy perception. These are not necessarily identical to your strengths in your everyday perception. That way, a generally auditory, or even musical, person might "smell" or "see" magical energy better than he or she can hear it, while an extraordinarily haptic person, on the other hand, might find out that he or she can "hear" or "taste" better when it comes to magic.

EXERCISE 6

TRAINING OF MAGICAL PERCEPTION (II)

After practicing the previous exercise at least four times in its complete form and the short version just as frequently, answer the following question in your magical diary directly after completing the full version of the exercise:

1. Which form of magical perception is easiest for me? Is it easier for me to "see," "feel," "taste," "smell," or "hear," or is there some other form of perception that works best for me that I'm not (yet) able to put into words?
2. After answering the question in 1 above, try to use your "best" form of perception more in the future. So when you run into the phrase

"magical imagination" later on in this book, interpret it as meaning your own personal best form of perception, unless you're specifically asked to use another method. (For example, if we say "Imagine a silver crescent," you can also "hear" it, "feel" it, etc., and don't need to visualize it if this form of perception is more difficult for you than another. But if the instructions say "Visualize a ball of energy above the circle," this clearly means that you need to use your quasi-optical sense of perception.

EXERCISE 7

PRACTICAL DREAM WORK (1)

Working with your dreams is a particularly effective way of training and expanding your magical perception because the specific attention you pay to your subconscious mind flatters it, making it more willing to help you with your magical efforts. In addition, working with dreams helps improve your trance control, divination skills, astral travel, and several other magical practices, in particular those of a shamanistic nature.

Let's start very basic and concentrate on simply remembering our dreams. If you've never worked with your dreams before, you might think that this would be extremely difficult, but that's definitely not the case. All you need is a little patience and something to write with next to your bed—and then you're ready to go! Before falling asleep, tell yourself that you'll remember your dreams in the morning. (You can support this work by making an appropriate sigil.) At first you should keep this thought firmly in mind while falling asleep, allowing it to sink into your subconscious mind.

When you wake up, don't move for a few minutes until you can recall your dreams as well as possible. Then write down your impressions using short keywords. You can also use drawings and sketches to record certain impressions; sometimes this will give you a much more precise impression of the energy and intensity of the dream than a description in words could ever achieve, no matter how detailed it may be.

If you wake up suddenly in the middle of the night after having a dream, write it down immediately. You can even make notes in the dark if you don't want to wake up completely, as long as you write legibly.

Instead of writing down your dream right away, you can speak it onto a tape recorder that you keep next to your bed. This has the great advantage that you can record more details in a shorter period of time, and much more realistically than by writing. Of course, the disadvantage is that it's fairly time-consuming to listen to the tape later on and write everything down (which is absolutely necessary for later review and comparison).

Keep a separate diary for recording your dreams; don't record them in your magical diary. As you get better you'll notice that you'll be writing more and more, and your magical diary will literally be overflowing with dream work. (There will come a time when you'll consciously try *not* to remember your dreams, but we'll get to that later.) Only if your dreams are directly related to a magical operation should you additionally write parts of your dream in your magical diary. Often it's enough to just make a cross-reference to the corresponding page in your dream diary.

It's possible that you may not have any luck at all in recalling your dreams during the first few days or even weeks. This problem can only be solved with persistence. Keep trying every single night and you're sure to succeed someday!

You might even discover that your magical activities will cause you to dream much more vividly. That's a good sign since it reflects the growing willingness of your subconscious mind to cooperate.

FURTHER READING

Let's keep the cross-references to other useful books to the bare minimum. After all, even the most ambitious and well-meaning magician just doesn't have the time to weed through hundreds of other books parallel to working through this one. Besides, it's not our intention to divide up magical knowledge into many different pieces such as most books do—on the contrary, this book is designed to save you the trouble of having to consult various sources.

Nonetheless, there are so many excellent standard reference books available, such as on astrology or herbal lore, that we feel it unnecessary to delve deeper into subjects such as the signs of the zodiac or various herbs and their blossom time.

Frater U.·. D.·., *Practical Sigil Magic*

This monograph delves even deeper into sigil magic. It covers the atavistic magic of Austin Osman Spare, explains the Alphabet of Desire, and provides an overview of the classical planet sigils and magic squares as compiled by Agrippa von Nettesheim.

Thorwald Dethlefsen, *Challenge of Fate*

A brilliant introduction to esotericism and magical thought. Dethlefsen's book describes the basics of astrology and the use of analogies and correspondences in a very clear way.

---

1. *Warning:* Don't make the mistake of neglecting your practice on the basis of this comforting fact! This mechanism only works as long as you're in the process of learning with the intention of developing optimal visualization, imagination, and similar skills. Otherwise, your subconscious mind will become dulled and interpret your careless practice with the actual goal. This will result in the programming of long-term errors in perception that can be devastating and may even take an entire human lifetime to eradicate. So, it's really not as easy as it sounds.

INTRODUCTION TO RITUAL MAGIC (II)

PSYCHOLOGY OR SPIRITUALISM?

The question as to whether magical phenomena are actually projections of our own internal abilities and powers, or might be caused by the influence of nonhuman beings (spirits, demons, astral beings, or the like) has interested parascience for decades. The principle that supports a more psychological explanation and believes that everything magical arises from deep inside the magician's soul itself is called animism (from the Latin word *anima,* "soul"); the other principle that's based on the existence of real nonhuman living beings (and those made up of subtle energies) is called spiritualism (from the Latin word *spiritus,* "spirit"). It's important to remember this difference since it appears in literature over and over again.

But in reality, these two models of explanation are not all as different as their supporters like to think. We can illustrate this by using the example of the wave-particle dualism of light, which has puzzled physics for quite some time. Light sometimes behaves like a wave and sometimes like a particle—regardless of the conditions of the experiment! It would therefore be wrong to unilaterally refer to light waves while simply ignoring the physical reality of the light particles, and reverse. In the end, the physicists themselves decide which way the light should behave in their experiment or in their concept of the world.

The same holds true for the magician. The concept that our reality is always the reality of the description should be confronted at an early stage; our reality merely reflects that which we are able to express and perceive in one way or another.[1]

You'll be running into this important principle of modern magic again and again throughout the course of this book.

In practice, we need to choose the approach that's most likely work, and whatever that might be depends on a number of various factors, such as one's own spiritual composition and ideological preferences, but also on practical aspects as well. As antirationalistic as it may seem, experience has shown that it's wise to not worry about the apparent contradiction between animistic and spiritualistic models of explanation; the easiest way to do this is by simply "ignoring" the temptation to ponder their degree of truth.

During a ritual, it's the experience or perception of energy that counts. Intellectual or even academic concepts such as animism or spiritualism have no business here. If you prefer the spiritualistic approach and want to believe that you're dealing with real spiritual beings, that's just fine. If, on the other hand, you prefer the psychological approach and view your ritual work as the external ("projecting") confrontation with your own soul, you'll get good results as well.

This book doesn't intend to sway you toward one way or another, because the principals that govern a magical ritual are exactly the same in both cases. However, this usually only becomes clear through lots of experience. That's why this section already begins training the flexible application of the various philosophies and ideologies.

THE BASIC STRUCTURE OF A MAGICAL RITUAL

Now let's talk about the basic structure of a magical ritual. If we take a look at the history of Western ceremonial magic, we'll notice that two main currents developed parallel to one another; they never joined, and they never stimulated one another in any mentionable way. We're talking about the cyclical or circular ritual form, and the angular or square ritual form.

For now we're going to focus on the circular form since this is easier for the beginner to learn than the angular form and can be performed effortlessly alone.

The angular structure, on the other hand, requires a great deal of basic knowledge about symbols and is more suited for working in groups of at least three people. Of course there are plenty of exceptions to the rule, but this statement can definitely be applied to get the general picture. Moreover, the angular structure is predominately found in dogmatic and purely mystical systems.

To avoid any misunderstandings, we need to point out that the term "circular" doesn't just mean that a magical circle is used, but also refers to the structure of the ritual itself. This is the point we'd like to focus on here. The following description of the ritual structure can be found in nearly all of these types of rituals, even though the practitioners and authors of these rituals are rarely aware of this. However, it would be quite helpful for you to understand this basic structure in order to avoid symbol-logical errors or contradictions when developing your own rituals.

A typical ritual of the circular tradition is structured as follows:

1. Preparation of the ritual
2. Opening banishing/purification
3. Main part
4. Closing banishing/purification and license to depart
5. Follow-up work after the ritual

Chart 8: Basic structure of a ritual

Below is a detailed description of the individual points of this chart.

1. Preparation of the Ritual

Preparation includes determining the goal, selecting the proper utensils, choosing the right time for the operation, establishing the structure of the ritual, dividing up the roles (for group rituals), and, of course, inwardly preparing for the ritual and concentrating on its purpose. Often a ritual is proceeded by a period of fasting or not sleeping, ecstatic dancing, or other practices that promote ritual gnosis, as well as by ritual washing and certain forms of cleansing. Putting on ritual clothing, lighting incense, and performing other activities necessary for the ritual are important parts of the preparation as well.

Often just planning the ritual has a similar effect on a subtle level as actually performing it. Once you actually begin, you realize that the work has already been done! Nonetheless, you should still perform the ritual even if it's just symbolic "topping on the cake" and to say a word of thanks. After all, this phenomenon also shows that thorough preparation is half the work.

2. Opening Banishing/Purification

We've already discussed this in connection with the Lesser Banishing Ritual of the Pentagram.

3. Main Part

The main part of the ritual is reserved for special magical operations. This includes, for example, calling upon energies to polarize, direct, and "utilize" them, but also to simply experience them. Invocations, the charging of talismans and amulets, mystical experiences, evocations, the influence of others—the list of possibilities is endless, and we don't want to go into this in more detail until later.

Generally, meditation belongs to the main part of a ritual as well, and sometimes a more casual part is included too—for example in festive group rituals such as to honor Pan, the moon goddess, or other energies where sacraments can be consumed, or where you can even laugh or talk.

4. Closing Banishing/Purification and License to Depart

The closing banishing/purification and license to depart symbolically signify, among other things, the return to everyday consciousness. We've already discussed this part of the ritual in connection with the Lesser Banishing Ritual of the Pentagram as well.

5. Follow-Up Work After the Ritual

Careful follow-up work is just as important as the ritual itself. This not only includes writing in your magical diary, but also monitoring the results of the operation and evaluating the ritual itself (including constructive criticism!). Later on in this book we'll be discussing the art of noticing and interpreting the effects of magic in more detail, especially in everyday practical magic.

Circular rituals usually proceed more or less in a symmetrical way. If the ritual is opened with the Lesser Banishing Ritual of the Pentagram for banishing and purification, the ritual is closed with this as well; if the "veil of mysteries" is opened with a symbolic gesture, then it needs to be closed at the end of the ritual, too, and so on.

Cyclical symmetry is one of the most important aspects of this ritual form and should always be upheld. If this symmetry is unintentionally neglected, it often impedes the success of the entire operation since this would be comparable to attempting to force a square peg into a round hole—and situations like these are rarely taken well by the magical subconscious. At best, nothing will happen at all (or at least nothing perceptible), and at worst it could magically backfire with the activated energies turning against the magician. By the way, this simple but plausible law is most frequently violated in connection with magic for healing, money, and love, as well as in magical warfare.

But that's enough for now about ritual magic. However, we recommend that you think over the information in this section thoroughly since it will surely help clear up many things that a complete beginner might have trouble understanding at first.

APPLIED PARADIGM SHIFTING

A paradigm is a set of basic ideological or technological assumptions or beliefs—and therefore a model of explanation. Since magic is always a "reality dance," it would be logical to experiment with various paradigms.

The magician should become familiar with various philosophies of life not only in theory, but more importantly in practice as well. Only then can one control every aspect of his or her own reality production (and magic is nothing more than that!) to fit one's individual needs, regardless of whether these concern everyday practical magic or are of a more mystical nature. After all, there's a little bit of truth in every philosophy of life in the sense of "probability," just like there's a good deal of falsehood in the sense of "improbability." Nothing is absolute; at best, it just may seem that it is.

This relativistic principle is in no way as modern and iconoclastic as it may seem at first. Traditional churches, theologians, and cultural historians have often accused occultism of being a "pseudo-religion" with syncretic influence, and therefore dubious, fabricated, and inconsequential. The dictionary defines "syncretism" as "a fusion of different religions, denominations or philosophical doctrines, generally without any form of inner unity." Surely occultism and magic in general can rightfully be described as such a mixture if you disregard the fact that this much-abused "bastard philosophy" was born out of the attempt to recognize at least a minimum amount of inner unity in all religious, mystical, and magical systems and institutions (which in turn fed this philosophy with energy and convincingness), and that occultism is now widely tolerated due to its respect of all other paradigms (a fact which some of the more homogenous systems of thought and belief could learn a lesson from). In any case, regardless of all this, the great strength of occultism and magic lies in their variety and diversity.

After all, every pantheon (or system of gods) is just a reproduction of a certain psychology—either personal or collective—that's disguised in mythical pictures. On the one hand, however, despite the many similarities there are surely just as many different psychologies as there were and are people. And on the other hand, each and every person has countless faces and personalities that often cannot be covered by just one pantheon.[2] For this reason, the everyday psychology of polytheism is generally much more refined and practice-oriented than monotheistic systems. This can be seen in the fact that the latter, following an initial period of blossoming, almost always develops into a sort of quasi-polytheism that often just thrives in the dark. This is how the trinity and sainthood developed in Christianity; in Buddhism, one Buddha was turned into thousands, especially in Tibetan tantra but also throughout the entire mahayana system; in Islam—similar to Christianity—the Shiites flourished with their many saints and near-prophets; yes, even Judaism, which is particularly strict, developed polytheistic elements alongside the Kabbalah with its teachings of angels and demons as well as the sephiroths, which are often embodied individually as well.

We can illustrate this with an example that was, in turn, borrowed from Hermetic occultism. We're familiar with the Roman god and astrological planet Mercury that represents the principle of the intellect; however, it's also equated with the Greek god Hermes and ancient Egyptian god Thot (also called Tahuti, pronounced "Djahuti" or "Dahaut"). One quick look at Crowley's list of correspondences and analogies in *Liber 777* shows that these three gods also share similarities on a practical level—for example, the number 8, the color orange, and the metal mercury. But analogy is not the same as equality: Mercury is not Hermes or Thot, even if all three aspects are one and the same basic principle. The magical novice may not recognize the often subtle differences between these three embodiments right away, and all too often an experienced magician will mention them in the same breath as though they were interchangeable. But later during magical rituals and in everyday practical magic it will become obvious that this is definitely not the case: Mercury is far more playful than Thot, and even though he cannot deny his relationship to Hermes considering their shared cultural history, he's nevertheless quite different from him in many ways.[3]

Ibis-headed Thot, on the other hand, is much stricter than both other deities and he was originally a moon god who was considered the master of time—a function that was assigned to Chronos or Saturn in the Hellenic and Roman pantheon.

Such reflections are in no way meant to ruin the painstakingly acquired "unit of the smallest common denominator" that's characteristic for the equation of the three gods. This unit is present without a doubt and is often not revealed to the initiate until after deep meditation. Rather, our intention is to point out the differentiation that our "mixture of gods" enables. During a magical ritual, such a mixed pantheon gives us the choice between highly subtle different hues—for example, the experienced magician would prefer to use the energy of Thot for an operation concerning the strict interpretation of a law. For a case involving fraud in which one may even be working on the side of the defendant, Mercury would be more appropriate. Forensic medical reports, on the other hand, would fall under the scope of Hermes, and so on.

All of these examples are just approximations that are subject to change depending on subjective assessment and experience. But they at least reflect the value of this magical skill of being able to comfortably work with several systems at the same time, or, to put it in more modern, colloquial terms, changing paradigms like the shirt on your back. This results in the following mnemonic phrase that should definitely not just remain theoretical, but should also be applied in daily practice as well:

The magician chooses one's beliefs like the surgeon chooses his or her instruments.

Let's give this piece of information the finishing touch by adding another guiding principle that stems from modern-day Chaos Magic, making it particularly effective through its fairly clear-cut wording:

Belief is just a technique.

Even if you don't fully agree with this sentence, we recommend meditating on it over a longer period of time and at least adopting it as a valid working hypothesis (even if just for reasons of later discussion). Because when we start discussing the magic of Austin Osman Spare, this sentence will play a central role—in our practice as well.

The contemporary practice of brainwashing has shown that it's relatively simple to turn an atheist into a Christian, a Hindu into a Maoist, a Christian into a Buddhist, or a fascist into a communist—at least temporarily. The prerequisite for this is merely the specific and skillful application or removal of certain stimuli. Certainly political brainwashing is a form of torture; but instead of playing helpless and complaining about a world that allows such atrocities to happen, we should focus on the positive aspects that can help us as magicians if we adapt such techniques to optimize our magic. On the one hand, the systematic and intentional shifting of paradigms can destroy the illusion that we're dependent on our beliefs and can only define ourselves according to such. A person who doesn't strive for the absolute in the external world will never again be subject to the illusions that the external world may present as absolute reality. ("Nothing is true, everything is permitted" was supposedly said by the old man in the mountains.)This person's also immune to the temptations of religious, political, and social indoctrination and has mastered (in the sense of Mao Tse-Tung) the philosophical guerilla attack.

On the other hand, rigid systems are always subject to limitation. Through frequent, conscious system shifting the magician creates a much larger area for maneuvering; he or she not only becomes more versatile, but even has more potential because he or she has become aware of the illusionary character of limits and no longer needs to accept them helplessly as before.

However, it can also be useful as well to stick with one system of beliefs or thoughts for a longer period of time as long as your flexibility doesn't suffer from doing so. This can help avoid that certain superficiality that's an inherent danger of the other practice.

Now rigid belief systems are not completely useless, otherwise they surely wouldn't have had such a strong grip on our everyday reality for thousands of years. They give people something to hold on to, even if for just a fragile moment and even if they have to pay a very high price for this wobbly security (such as the loss of freedom and intellectual independence); after all, they'd much rather have it this way than feel utterly helpless at life's mercy. In particular, people who are unstable and insecure have trouble coping with the delicate balancing act between the various realities.

Magic has always been similar to walking on a tightrope without a net, and it's surely not wrong to say that a magician usually has one foot in the grave and the other in the nuthouse. The trick is keeping your balance without landing in one or the other, thereby enjoying the complete freedom of someone who walks the line. But in order to do so, thorough grounding is an absolute must.

THE IMPORTANCE OF GROUNDING

The true shamans of primitive tribes seldom concentrate on just being shamans. In addition to their jobs as a medicine man or woman, healer or sorcerer, they carry out their usual tribal responsibilities as well, such as hunting, gathering, fishing, or farming. In fact, the best method of grounding is having a normal, everyday job. The reasons for this might not be clear to everyone right off, which is why we'd like to go into it a bit further.

If we think about the above statements a bit more, we'll discover that magicians often have to function in quite extreme states of consciousness that differ considerably from everyday reality. Although they'll be integrating their magic (and therefore their applied gnosis as well) into their everyday life more and more with practice, this doesn't mean that the borderlines between the two become blurred—they merely become more permeable. These are two entirely different things, and shamanistic cultures in particular show us again and again how serious the problem of spiritual stability is dealt with by these "magical experts." For example, every member of such a tribe accepts the fact that there are spirits and that one can perceive them and communicate with them, but this is definitely not true in our rationalistic civilization. Such a person who sees spirits and talks to them regularly will probably end up in a padded cell, which is how our culture deals with such deviations from the norm.

But if a member of a native tribe constantly sees spirits that haunt one wildly, and if one even neglects his or her everyday obligations to the community for this reason, this person would certainly be declared insane and he or she'd be expelled from society.

We'll find a similar situation among the ancient kabbalists. In the old days, whoever wanted to study the Kabbalah with an initiated rabbi not only had to be of a certain age, but also had to prove that they had both feet on the ground in their job as well as in their everyday life.

During my own seminars I've noticed again and again that people who seem to be anchored in their jobs more than average actually make the quickest progress in magic.

Managers, for example, who already work seventy or eighty hours a week still seem to find three or four hours for their magic, and such people are usually able to apply it to everyday situations with lots of creativity and intelligence. On the other hand, people who have lots of free time on their hands seem to have more trouble progressing with their magic. Being subject to job-related or financial stress is surely favorable for maximum performance in all areas, but this phenomena has much deeper roots.

We need to remember that the extreme situations mentioned above that magic confronts us with are particularly tempting to the more psychologically unstable who are lacking material roots. But usually such people are not really looking for magic itself, but rather some sort of playground where they can let out their psychological problems without being disturbed; or they're searching for a substitute for the usual types of therapy. In extremely rare cases, magic can offer them both of these and even heal them (in the sense of "heal" = "to make whole"). But usually these types of people tend to feel attracted to the negative, destructive energies in magic since these appear to be of greater intensity in their eyes.

In a certain way, this is a vicious circle. For successfully practicing the magic arts, a certain degree of psychological tension is absolutely necessary, as we'll see later when discussing astromagic. (This is one reason why most magicians are generally quite boring people.) If you look at it this way, magic does indeed fulfill a therapeutic role for many practitioners because it allows them to specifically direct their psychological tensions and imbalances into something constructive, thereby gaining control of them as well. On the other hand, extreme magical experiences can sometimes unconsciously trigger psychological disturbances. But it's important to remember that it's not the magic that can drive a person insane. On the contrary, it does nothing more than tear open the veil covering our psychological sham existence in which an occasional swamp blossom can thrive among the shadows that silently poison the organism as a whole (which the psyche is naturally a part of). Confronting one's own fears—which every good magician does thoroughly—is a good example of this process.

Being embedded in a "normal" everyday job helps to stay grounded and gives magicians something to hold on to at times when they feel that the ground is being pulled out from under their feet; it protects them from the possession of complexes/demons by constantly confronting them with a different reality that is, for the most part, unmagical in which they also face challenges that need to be mastered. Of course, having a job that demands high performance is no cure-all for magical problems, but experience has shown that it usually can help to avoid such problems or get them under control.

But magic demands much more, of course, and this can be accomplished by regularly practicing the Lesser Banishing Ritual of the Pentagram and the Kabbalistic Cross. Other exercises for grounding and stabilization will come later, but the important thing for now is probably just a healthy degree of self-confidence, as long as it's not muddled by arrogance or the overestimation of your abilities. After all, only a person who knows and realizes one's limits is able to overcome them.

---

1. This is the deeper meaning of the shamanic saying "What you perceive is what is true."
2. There's a similar phrase in the Egyptian Book of the Dead: "In every part of your body lives a god."
3. Hermes, for example, wears distinct symbols of a god of death or souls, just like Thot does—psychpompos—while Mercury (at least in a later astrological sense) predominately represents the aspects of a god of trade and communication.

ELEMENTAL MAGIC

THE GREATER RITUAL OF THE PENTAGRAM

The Greater Ritual of the Pentagram has been a standard ceremony in Western ritual magic since it was developed in this form by the initiates of the Golden Dawn. At first we'll only be dealing with the invoking form, not the banishing form.

The goal of the ritual is to charge the magician with the power of all the elements in harmonious balance. In contrast to the Lesser Banishing Ritual of the Pentagram, this ritual is mainly used for invoking and seldom for banishing (exceptions will be discussed later), and the element of Ether or Spirit is included when drawing the symbols and vibrating the formulas. Another difference from the Lesser Pentagram Ritual is that no point is activated in the middle of the pentagram; instead the symbols of the elements are energized by means of a separate mantra in the same way as in hexagram rituals, which we'll discuss later.

Each element is drawn in a certain direction; to invoke, draw toward the element, and to banish, draw away from the element.[1]

The invoking pentagram of one basic element is, at the same time, the banishing pentagram of the opposite element, and reverse. This way, "invoking Air" also means "banishing Water," and so on.

In order to understand this concept better, it's helpful to know that the four basic elements are divided into two groups:

Those considered to be *active* elements: AIR and FIRE.

Those considered to be *passive* elements: WATER and EARTH.

Accordingly, a distinction is also made between an actively and passively balanced pentagram of ETHER or SPIRIT; occasionally this is referred to as an equilibrated pentagram.

Those considered to be *opposite* elements: AIR—EARTH and FIRE—WATER.

We'll be dealing with the elements in more detail later on, which is an intentional decision on our part because we feel that, in this case, sensory practice should come first before delving into the intellectual superstructure. That's why we're just using general keywords here to describe the elements in the order they occur in the ritual:

Air: the principle of intellect; communication and language; analytical (differential, separative) thought

Fire: the principle of instinct; will, sexuality, and aggression; spontaneous ("hot-headed") action

Water: the principle of feelings; emotion, intuition and dream/vision; synthetic (connecting, combining) sensation

Earth: the principle of structure; perseverance and concentration; deliberate maintenance and creation of order

Ether/Spirit/Quintessence: the principle of the superior; meaning and purpose; the ("fifth") essence of the other elements; shaping the supreme

The rest of the Greater Ritual of the Pentagram follows the same structure as the Lesser Banishing Ritual of the Pentagram (abbreviated as LBR).

THE PRACTICE OF THE GREATER RITUAL OF THE PENTAGRAM

1. Kabbalistic Cross
2. Drawing the pentagrams and the circle
3. Invocation of the archangels/visualization of additional symbols
4. Kabbalistic Cross

The ritual is performed while standing facing the east, the gestures can be made with either the right or left hand since the direction of the lines and the other details remains the same in either case. You can either use your magical dagger or your extended index and middle fingers with your thumb resting lightly under them.

1. Kabbalistic Cross

(See Section 1)

2. Drawing the Pentagrams and the Circle

Facing the east, draw the equilibrated active pentagram of Spirit. While drawing, powerfully vibrate the formula:

EXARP (Ex-ar-pay)

Illustration 8

In the center of the pentagram, draw the eight-spoke wheel of Spirit while powerfully vibrating the formula:

EHIH (Eh-he-yeh)

Now draw the invoking pentagram of Air. While drawing, powerfully vibrate the formula:

ORO IBAH AOZPI (O-ro-Ee-bah-Ah-oh-zohd-pih)

Illustration 9

In the center of the pentagram, draw the symbol of Aquarius while powerfully vibrating the formula:

JHVH (Yeh-ho-vah *or* Yod-heh-vau-heh)

Keep your arm outstretched and turn ninety degrees to the south. Facing the south, draw the equilibrated active pentagram of Spirit. While drawing, powerfully vibrate the formula:

BITOM (Bi-toh-meh)

Illustration 10

In the center of the pentagram, draw the eight-spoke wheel of Spirit while powerfully vibrating the formula:

EHIH (Eh-he-yeh)

Now draw the invoking pentagram of Fire. While drawing, powerfully vibrate the formula:

OIP TEAA PEDOKE (Oh-ee-peh-Teh-ah-ah-Peh-doh-keh)

Illustration 11

In the center of the pentagram, draw the symbol of Leo while powerfully vibrating the formula:

ELOHIM (Eh-loh-hee-mm)

Keep your arm outstretched and turn ninety degrees to the west. Facing the west, draw the equilibrated passive pentagram of Spirit. While drawing, powerfully vibrate the formula:

HKOMA (Heh-koh-mah)

Illustration 12

In the center of the pentagram, draw the eight-spoke wheel of Spirit while powerfully vibrating the formula:

AGLA (Ah-geh-lah)

Now draw the invoking pentagram of Water. While drawing, powerfully vibrate the formula:

EMPEH ARSEL GAIOL (Em-peh-heh-Ar-ess-el-Gah-ee-oh-leh)

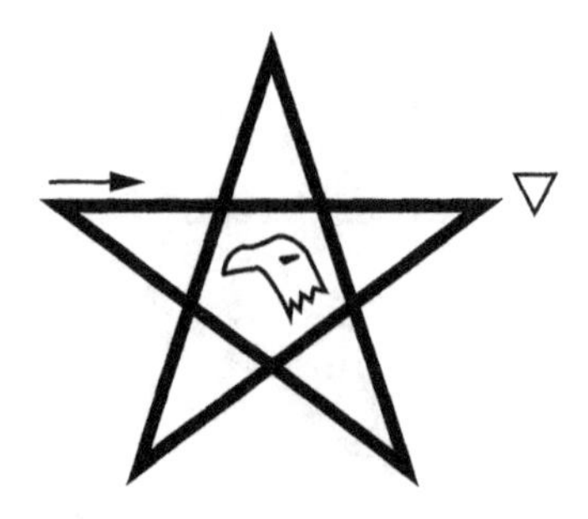

Illustration 13

In the center of the pentagram, draw the symbol of the Eagle while powerfully vibrating the formula:

AL (Ah-ll)

Keep your arm outstretched and turn ninety degrees to the north. Facing the north, draw the equilibrated passive pentagram of Spirit. While drawing, powerfully vibrate the formula:

NANTA (Nah-neh-tah)

Illustration 14

In the center of the pentagram, draw the eight-spoke wheel of Spirit while powerfully vibrating the formula:

AGLA (Ah-geh-lah)

Now draw the invoking pentagram of Earth. While drawing, powerfully vibrate the formula:

EMOR DIAL HEKTEGA (Eh-moh-ahr-Dee-ah-leh-Heh-keh-teh-gah)

Illustration 15

In the center of the pentagram, draw the symbol of Taurus while powerfully vibrating the formula:

ADNI (AH-DOH-NAI)

Complete the ritual facing the east by invoking the four archangels and performing the Kabbalistic Cross, just like in the Lesser Banishing Ritual of the Pentagram.

3. Invocation of the Archangels/Visualization of Additional Symbols

(See page 25)

4. Kabbalistic Cross

(See page 23)

Theoretically, the Greater Ritual of the Pentagram can also replace the Lesser Banishing Ritual of the Pentagram and be practiced alone. In this case, you'd have to add the usual license to depart at the end of the ritual.

However, the Greater Ritual of the Pentagram is usually proceeded by the Lesser Banishing Ritual of the Pentagram and the ceremony is concluded with the LBR as well. This may seem to be quite elaborate but if you think about the actual purpose of the Lesser Banishing Ritual of the Pentagram—namely the banishing of undesired powers and thoughts and the resulting cleansing of the temple inside (spiritually/physically) and out (spatially)—it's symbol-logically entirely correct. Plus, the Greater Ritual of the Pentagram as described here is used purely for invoking and doesn't have anything to do with banishing.[2]

Comments on the Greater Ritual of the Pentagram

Just like the Lesser Banishing Ritual of the Pentagram, the Greater Ritual of the Pentagram contains a number of symbolic references that can be interpreted in many ways. It would be impossible and inappropriate to discuss these here in detail. That's why I'd recommend that you first gain a few months of experience by practicing the Greater Ritual of the Pentagram and meditating on its internal symbol-logic and structure before attempting a more complicated interpretation. After all, the main purpose of this ritual is to experience the elements firsthand and to become familiar with their powers. That's why we're just going to mention a few details here.

THE MEANING OF THE FORMULAS/GOD-NAMES IN THE GREATER RITUAL OF THE PENTAGRAM

The Hebrew Formulas[3]

JHVH

(Jehovah or Yahweh) is generally translated as "I AM WHO I AM"—the self-definition of the creator god from the book of Genesis. One should view the fact that a god is what it is as a challenge to become like this god. This can be compared to the recognition and pursuit of one's True Will (Thelema), the establishment of contact and dialog with one's Holy Guardian Angel, and the realization of one's own destiny. JHVA is also referred to as the Tetragrammaton, which literally means "four-word" or the "four-letter name of God."

ELOHIM

(or ELHM) is the plural form of AL (see below), or more specifically of ELOAH, "goddess." That's why it is often translated as "gods" or even "goddesses." The fact that this god-name appears frequently in the Bible in a plural sense quite justly causes doubt as to the radically monotheistic nature of the early Jewish religion.

AL

(or EL) is generally translated as "God," but originally meant "magnificent, powerful" (also see ELOHIM).

ADNI

(often written ADONAI) literally means "Lord" or "my Lord." Generally it's also the name that an orthodox Jew reads aloud at the place in the holy scriptures where the Tetragrammaton is mentioned (because one's never allowed to say JHVH).

EHIH

(often written EHIEH) is translated as "I will be."

AGLA

Agla is not a word in itself, but rather an abbreviation of the first letters of an entire sentence, namely "Athath gibor leolam Adonai," translated as "Thou art powerful and eternal, O Lord!"

As with the Lesser Banishing Ritual of the Pentagram, it's not clear why the individual formulas are assigned to their corresponding cardinal directions.

The Enochian Formulas

Enochian is a ritual language developed by John Dee (1527–1608), an English magician, alchemist, scholar, and astrologer for Queen Elizabeth I, with the assistance of his medium Edward Kelley during a series of rituals. This is a completely autonomous language with grammar and pronunciation rules that continue to puzzle linguists today. It's part of an extremely complicated and highly effective system called Enochian Magic, which is too extensive to discuss in these pages. It's sufficient to briefly explain the meanings of the Enochian formulas that are used in the Greater Ritual of the Pentagram. However, we'd like to point out that the spelling of the Enochian words may vary slightly depending on the source, as may the pronunciation. Here we've used the versions that are most widespread today.

ORO IBAH AOZPI

This formula stems from the Enochian Quarter of Air and is generally interpreted as being a secret, holy god-name. It's translated as: "He who cries aloud in the place of desolation."

OIP TEAA PEDOKE

This formula stems from the Enochian Quarter of Fire and is generally interpreted as being a secret, holy god-name. It's translated as: "He whose name is unchanged from what it was."

EMPEH ARSEL GAIOL

This formula stems from the Enochian Quarter of Water and is generally interpreted as being a secret, holy god-name. It's translated as: "He who is the first true creator, the horned one."

EMOR DIAL HEKTEGA

This formula stems from the Enochian Quarter of Earth and is generally interpreted as being a secret, holy god-name. It's translated as: "He who burns up iniquity without equal."

The following four formulas are the Enochian rulers of the lower elements in groups of four (Air of Air, Fire of Air, Water of Air, and so on) who reign over the sixty-four serviant angels. These formulas are formed from the first letters of the first of these beings and therefore have no direct translation. The affixes *E, B, H,* and *N* (in parentheses below) refer to the Cherubic Tablet of Union, or the Black Cross of Enochiana, so that each name contains five Enochian letters.

(E)XARP: Reigning Serviant Angel of Air.

(B)ITOM: Reigning Serviant Angel of Fire.

(H)KOMA: Reigning Serviant Angel of Water.

(N)ANTA: Reigning Serviant Angel of Earth.

As with the Hebrew god-names, it's fine to use the Enochian formulas at first merely for their highly effective phonetics and not let yourself get distracted by their deeper meanings.

THE ELEMENT SYMBOLS INSIDE THE PENTAGRAMS

We're already familiar with the eight-spoke wheel as a symbol of Ether or Spirit from the allocation of the elements in the pentagram. It portrays the sun wheel and represents both the all-penetrable and omnipresent as well as the centeredness and the center around which everything revolves.

Instead of the usual triangular alchemistic symbols used to represent the elements, the Greater Ritual of the Pentagram uses the cherubic or astrological symbols. This may confuse some beginners at first, which is why we'd like to briefly explain this.

The Biblical cherubs (or kerubs, Hebrew *Cherubim*) are the angels and guardians of heaven that are understood by Western ceremonial magicians as guardians of the elements. Each cherub is composed of four parts with each part stemming from a different creature; namely an eagle, a lion, an ox, and a man.

This is the reason why the cherubs were considered to be the Israeli equivalents to the Egyptian sphinxes. Two of these symbols can be found in the Greater Ritual of the Pentagram in the pentagrams of Fire and Water, whereby in the case of Fire, the astrological symbol for Leo is used as well. This holds true as well for the symbol of Taurus in the pentagram of Earth.

A beginner with little knowledge of astrology may find it difficult to understand the symbol used in the pentagram of Air, which resembles water. One might expect the eagle's head here instead. In the writings of the Golden Dawn, this is substantiated by the fact that the air contains water in the form of rain and humidity. This may not seem very logical and convincing to some, but let's not forget that the astrological zodiac sign Aquarius is an Air sign, and this is also the symbol that we're dealing with here.

The eagle, on the other hand, which might remind the beginner of Air, is also the alchemistic symbol for distillation, which indicates a watery process. In addition, many early astrologers used to use it in place of the watery sign of Scorpio. This makes the eagle's relationship to the element of Water thoroughly understandable.

The element of Earth, on the other hand, is assigned the astrological symbol of Taurus, which indeed actually belongs to this element and is meant to represent diligence. Please note that in contrast to the customary astrological symbol for Taurus, the circle in the one used here contains a dot, similar to the astrological symbol for the sun. This also indicates the "horned sun," which is linked to the Persian-Roman Mithras cult with its death and fertility themes.

For a more profound understanding of the Greater Ritual of the Pentagram, it's important to keep in mind that the elements do not remain static inside the circle or the pentagram itself—they stand in direct interaction with one another, and the choreography of the movements of their energies is one of the cosmic prerequisites for both animistic and spiritualistic magic. *Panta rei*, "everything flows," is how Heraclitus described it, and our attempts at using structure to capture this flow must not lead us to the misleading assumption that we're dealing with undynamic constants. Within the ritual circle and inside the pentagram, we must consciously realize that the elements do not act as opposites with a direct line of connection. In this circle, Air does not stand opposite of Earth, and Fire opposite of Water as some naive authors with no knowledge of symbol-logic claim—but rather Air and Water, Fire and Earth.

In the pentagram as well, the contrasting pairs do not stand opposite one another, but rather one above the other—they're only connected indirectly.

Because AIR—EARTH or FIRE—WATER acting as opposites would balance each other out, causing a standstill—or in more modern terms, entropy. After all, no element is stronger, or for that matter "better," than the others. Only Ether stands above the polarity of the subordinate elements and is often considered to be the origin thereof.[4]

You might want to meditate on this symbolism for a while and absorb it until it becomes intuition. This will make your practical work with the element energies much easier later on. In order to make this easier for you, we've purposely not included an illustration of this concept. Instead you should fill in this diagram yourself with the proper energy links in the lower box since this will help you load this information into your subconscious mind.

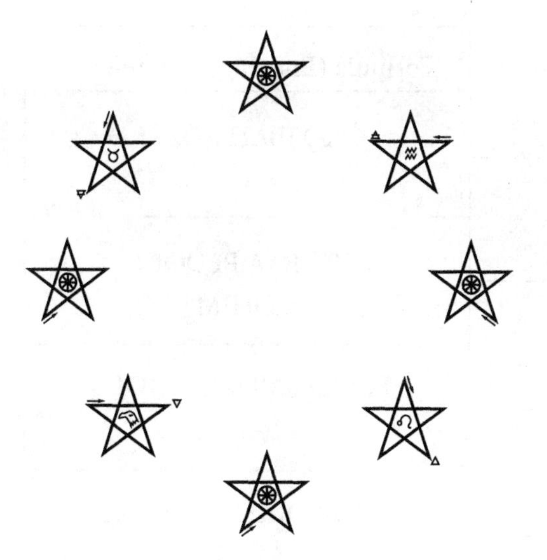

Illustration 16: The dynamic arrangement of the elements in the circle and pentagrams (fill in yourself)

For later reference, we'd like to summarize the directions of the pentagrams once again in the chart below, along with the formulas used and the correct order of the invocations. Later on as mentioned we'll be going into more detail about the directions of the pentagrams.

Element	Pentagram	Formula (Enochian/Hebrew)
Air		ORO IBAH AOZPI JHVH
Fire		OIP TEAA PEDOKE ELOHIM
Water		EMPEH ARSEL GAIOL AL
Earth		EMOR DIAL HEKTEGA ADNI
Spirit or Ether (active)		EXARPE (East) EHIH (East) BITOM (South) EHIH (South)
Spirit or Ether (passive)		HKOMA (West) AGLA (West) NANTA (North) AGLA (North)

Chart 9: The symbols and formulas used in the Greater Ritual of the Pentagram (all pentagrams are invoking)

It would be a good idea to repeat the order of the invocations in the Greater Ritual of the Pentagram in tabular form as well:

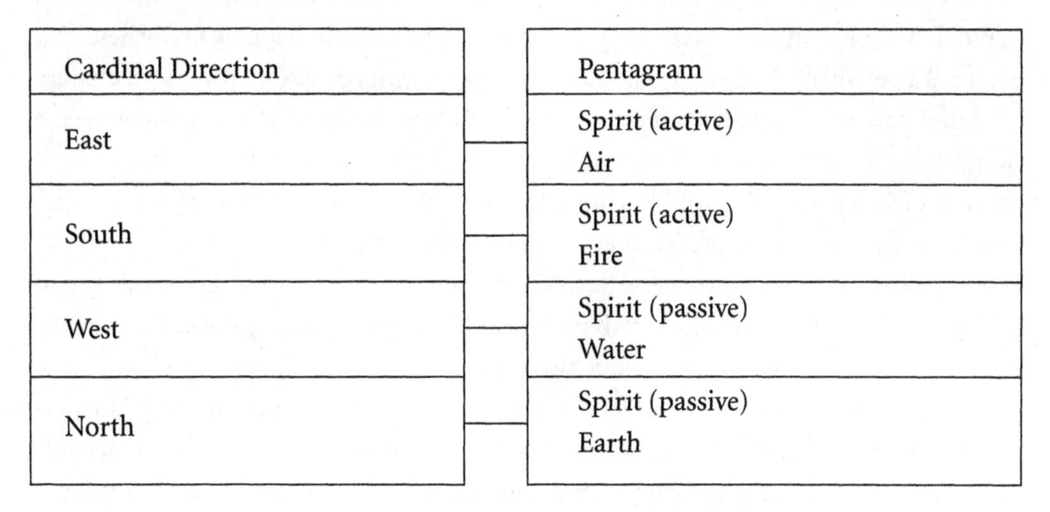

Cardinal Direction	Pentagram
East	Spirit (active) Air
South	Spirit (active) Fire
West	Spirit (passive) Water
North	Spirit (passive) Earth

Chart 10: The order of the invocations in the Greater Ritual of the Pentagram (all pentagrams are invoking)

THE SYMBOL-LOGICAL FUZZY RELATION AND MAGIC

The left side of our brain, which operates rationally and analytically, continuously strives for clarity, predictability, and precision. Our rationalistic civilization places a great deal of value on this since unpredictability, such as that of natural disasters, is considered to be something dangerous and life-threatening.

The intuitive and synthetically active right half of the brain, on the other hand, prefers imagery that's unpredictable and imprecise. The fact that this makes it susceptible for subtle cosmic and spiritual correlations is seldom understood today.

But precision has its limits, just as imprecision does. In both cases, too much is not desired, although this is seldom practiced willingly.

Let's have a look at this using an oracle as an example. In divination, the following rules are quickly learned:

The less precise the message of an oracle is, the more likely it is to be accurate.

The more precise the message of an oracle is, the less likely it is to be accurate.

If someone asks you to read his oracle and you predict "Next week many things in your life will change," the skeptic may just shake his head at such a "wishy-washy" statement. However, your rate of accuracy is most likely to be extraordinarily high—after all, you didn't say exactly what was going to happen, how it would happen, and when! You achieved a potentially higher rate of accuracy by limiting the precision of your prediction.

But if you were to predict "In exactly one week from today at 3:03 pm, you'll meet a blond man at the train station on track 6 who'll give you a check for $2044.84," your chances of being accurate would be next to nothing as compared to your first prediction. You achieved a more precise prediction by limiting the rate of accuracy.

Of course, both examples are extreme cases and shouldn't deny the possibility of achieving a high rate of accuracy with precise predictions—but daily divination usually operates in the gray area between these two extremes.

We only want to illustrate the fact that images and symbols generally escape the scientific definition of precision for the most part and should therefore be treated accordingly. Once we've comprehended this mechanism, we'll find it easier to work constructively with symbols such as the elements, tarot cards, or astrological aspects, just to mention a few examples.

According to definition, symbols are always ambiguous and can never be interpreted in just one fixed way. Besides, they're way too subjunctive as well. For example, just ask your friends what they associate with a circle or square as a symbol. Surely their answers will overlap in many areas, which only means that although symbols are ambivalent, they are in no way arbitrary. But the answers will differ in many areas as well—which, on the other hand, means that symbols can do more than just transport one single meaning.

A tarot deck consists of pictures and when we ask it a question we need to formulate it in such a way that the pictures can answer it. Questions about telephone numbers or lottery numbers will usually be futile for this method of divination, although sometimes it's difficult to realize this when we're frustrated by the caprioles of our subconscious mind and its magic. (Remember the example about the horse-riding competition and aftershave in the last section?)

The thing we like to call "the symbol-logical fuzzy relation" that we've illustrated here with a few humorous examples plays quite a concrete role in your magical practice.

For example, it's much easier to perform magic for "wealth" in general instead of trying to aim for a specific sum of money. In the same way, it's much easier to use magic to help us live out our own True Will instead of using it to influence the external world by making sexual partners, enemies, wealthy aunts, etc. submit to our will. This has often been used as an argument to support the idea of a basically moral and ethical functioning cosmos, but this reasoning is in no way compulsory. Once again we're talking about karma as a moral-free law of cause and effect. People who formulate their goals too precisely forge their own chains that will often prevent them from reaching this goal in the end. Later on we'll delve into this subject a bit deeper when talking about the "neither-neither" principle in the magic of Austin Osman Spare. Here's another example. You want to contact a certain person but don't have the address. It would be much more promising to charge a sigil for "making contact" with the person in general instead of specifying the means of contact by telephone or letter, for example.

Our main intention here is just to point out that there's no purpose in wanting to destroy symbols and pictures (which is exactly what we work with in magic) through rationalization. With this concept, we're not claiming that precise magical operations are not possible at all. If a magician wants a certain apartment or a certain job, or to win a specific lawsuit, magic can certainly be used to achieve this, but it's just much more difficult than aiming for more general goals. The challenge posed to a skilled magician in the rationalistic paradigm surely lies in the technical precision of one's magic; but the beginner should avoid becoming fixated on achieving precision accuracy. Even the most experienced magicians usually only hit stray shots, which is not a deficit as long as the general direction of these is correct. The secret of a successful master magician is the ability to define the goal as precisely as possible while leaving the path to its realization wide open, and only specifying the minimum in detail required to prevent unwanted results.

Plus, the symbol-logical fuzzy relation in magic has powerful advantages that no exact science can match. On the one hand, it comprises the magical power of the subconscious and the right side of the brain much easier when skillfully used since these react better to something that is blurred or unclear (which is not the same as "inaccurate"!). Pictures and symbols react. On the other hand, it gives us the ability to recognize relationships and opportunities where a rationalist may only see separation and limitation. Indeed, even the simple basic principle of sympathetic magic, that everything always stands in relation to everything else, is rooted in this fuzzy relation concept, which can even be expressed in a mathematical equation for better illustration:

$$M \propto 1/P_s$$

Legend
M = magical act
P_s = symbol precision

Chart 11: The first basic formula of magic

The degree of magical success is inversely proportional to the degree of (rationalistic) precision of the symbols used in the magical operation.

But that's enough information for now. It will surely take some time for this to "sink in." Later we'll talk about it in more detail.

PRACTICAL EXERCISES

Exercise 8

KABBALISTIC CROSS (II)

Practice the Kabbalistic Cross three times a day for eight weeks. Preferably you should do this right after getting up in the morning, or right after taking a bath or shower while your body's still wet. During the exercise, make sure your face is directed toward a light source (natural or artificial); this will help you feel the light's energy stronger and absorb it easier. However, you don't need to actually concentrate on the light. Proceed as you're used to from Exercise 2, but with one difference: Don't touch your body with your hand when drawing the lines! Keep your hand five to ten inches away from the corresponding point of your body. This will train your subtle perception and get you accustomed to working with your body's energies;

it will also aid your ability to see and feel auras and represents a preliminary stage in mental/astral training.

While practicing, pay attention to how your body feels. Determine if there are any differences when touching your body while practicing, and write these down in your magical diary.

Exercise 9

PRACTICE OF THE GREATER RITUAL OF THE PENTAGRAM

Perform the Greater Ritual of the Pentagram once every two weeks at a time of your choice for at least four months. Do this like you'd perform any normal ritual:

1. Banish with the Lesser Banishing Ritual of the Pentagram
2. Perform the Greater Ritual of the Pentagram
3. Meditate on the elements
4. Banish with the Lesser Banishing Ritual of the Pentagram and license to depart

Pay particular attention to how you perceive the elements. After doing this four times, you can combine this exercise with Exercise 5 in order to fine-tune your energy perception even more. To do so, you'll need to adapt Exercise 5 to fit the Greater Ritual of the Pentagram.

Exercise 10

APPLIED PARADIGM SHIFTING IN PRACTICE (I)

a) Go to a Catholic church one Sunday and observe the magical aspects of the Mass. How is the ritual structured?

b) Do the same with a Protestant church service and note the differences from the Catholic rite.

c) Do the same with church services and rituals of at least two other denominations of your choice (either Christian or non-Christian, such as Greek Orthodox, Adventistic, Mormon, Jewish, Islam, Buddhist, Hindu, etc.). The more you familiarize yourself with various religious rites by personally experiencing them, the better.

d) Later, try outlining the basic structure of each ritual including the sequence of events, the utensils used, the role distribution of those involved, the actual procedure, and so on.

The reason why we recommend Christian rituals at first is that they usually require no special effort to view them since there are churches nearly everywhere that hold services.

Even if you're not a religious person you can still learn from such personal experience. Last but not least, you'll also learn firsthand how much magic in these ancient religious cults has survived up to the present day—but also how little knowledge and understanding of this magic remains.

Try to be as inconspicuous as possible at these religious services and just experience the energies passively instead of trying to play an active role. Maybe you'll even be surprised to see that many rituals can develop quite a unique magical energy, even if the congregation and priests, or ritual leaders, may not be aware of this.

You should complete this exercise within a two-month period but feel free to repeat it later as often as desired.

Exercise 11

Training of Magical Perception (III)

The 180° Gaze

You've already become familiar with the idea behind this technique in Exercise 5e. This is definitely one of the best methods for training your magical perception (e.g., of auras). And now we'd like to intensify this exercise.

a) Place two tall glasses or bottles about thirty inches apart on an otherwise empty table. Sit directly in front of the objects so that they block your visual field on the left and right sides. Now defocus your eyes by allowing everything to become blurry as already practiced in Exercise 5, enter a state of empty mind ("nonattachment, non-lack of interest"), and observe the empty space between the two objects. Write down your perceptions (duration: about ten minutes).

b) Take a walk outdoors in a place that you're familiar with and practice the 180° gaze by blurring your vision (technically called "defocusing") and neutrally observe what you optically perceive, for example the space between the trees, or the area surrounding other walkers (duration: about ten minutes, relaxing your eyes afterward).

You can repeat this exercise as often as you like but you should do it at least fifty times within a period of six months. You can vary the exercise as well to make it less time consuming, for example by doing it at work for a few minutes, or while waiting for a traffic light, and in other similar situations.

Experience has shown that this exercise can help you learn to perceive auras fairly quickly and it will increase your sense for subtle energies as well.

Exercise 12

PRACTICAL DREAM WORK (II)

To follow up on Exercises 4 and 7, we're now ready to take the first step in learning dream control. This will not only help you make more direct contact to the astral realms of your subconscious, but it will also save you a lot of work when later learning trance techniques.

Make a sigil to have a certain dream. Don't make it too precise at first; for example, it's fine to work toward dreaming about a yellow cat, an African landscape, a skyscraper, or absurd everyday objects such as a shoehorn or a toothbrush. Try creating such a dream at least once a week by charging a sigil accordingly. Technically speaking, this work could be called dream incubation. Carefully note all success as well as failure in your magical diary.[5]

You've surely noticed that our training program is becoming increasingly demanding. At first this will be noticeable in the great deal of time it involves, which is quantitative. Later the amount of time involved will drop a bit, but the qualitative challenges will increase. This holds true no matter what you learn, not just in magic, and it would be a good idea if you keep in mind that learning always requires you to sacrifice time and energy. Of course, you could and should set your own pace. But since most of the exercises in this book continue to build on previous exercises, meaning that they're hierarchically structured, you should at least try to do them in the correct order even if you may not be able to stick to the time schedule. But keep in mind that it will be fairly difficult to make up any material you might skip; if you're interested in magical practice but tend to slack off in your work, you'll find it quite hard later on to comprehend the theoretical parts of this book due to a lack of experience since we'll keep referring to the practical experience you've made more and more throughout the course of this book.

BIBLIOGRAPHY

Horst E. Miers, *Lexikon des Geheimwissens*

Even if Miers' work is lacking in many aspects in reliability and objectivity, it's nonetheless considered one of the most comprehensive and exhaustive encyclopedias on the subject of the occult. Above all, it covers the various smaller groups and movements throughout the history of occultism up through the early 1960s (after this time, the information included is sparse and vague). Highly recommended as a book of reference when used with the appropriate discretion.

Hans Biedermann, *Handlexikon der magischen Künste*

This volume is one of the most scientifically respectable encyclopedic collections of the occult up to the start of the nineteenth century. An absolute classic that no magical library should be without; it contains a number of original quotations from old sources and a great deal of illustrations, and stands apart from the rest with its competent objectivity.

---

1. This is why the Lesser Banishing Ritual of the Pentagram is considered to be a banishing ritual, using only the banishing pentagram of the element of Earth, as already mentioned in the first section.
2. In the Golden Dawn tradition, various grade signs were performed after drawing the individual pentagrams for each element. Nowadays, this practice has basically become extinct. After all, this would be pretty meaningless for magicians who didn't "grow up" in this system and never went through its various grades. (The Golden Dawn no longer exists in its original form. Only a few self-appointed successors are still active in this tradition today.)
3. For better clarity, we'll repeat the meaning of the formulas/god-names from the Lesser Banishing Ritual of the Pentagram.
4. By the way, we usually prefer to say "Ether" instead of "Spirit" since we want to avoid the negative physical associations that often accompany this superelevation of the spirit as common to Western magic.
5. *Warning:* For this exercise, it's absolutely essential that you cast a protective circle around your bed, and the best way to do this is with the Lesser Banishing Ritual of the Pentagram. The place you sleep tends to attract astral energies and since this is not your intention with this exercise, you shouldn't neglect this form of protection until you're spiritually and physically steadfast enough to be able to do without such protective measures on occasion. If you leave the protective circle during the night (e.g., to go to the bathroom), you need to cast it again. You can do this mentally as well, provided that you've practiced Exercise 2 on a regular basis.

PLANETARY MAGIC (I)

INTRODUCTION TO THE HEXAGRAM RITUAL (I)

In Western ceremonial magic, the pentagram is a symbol that represents the microcosm of the elements, while the hexagram is a symbol of the macrocosm of the planetary spheres. In simpler terms, the pentagram represents the "earthly" aspect of creation while the hexagram portrays the "cosmic" aspect.

But this seems to be the only aspect of the hexagram ritual that all magicians can agree on: There are so many versions of this ritual, some grossly mutilated or completely twisted in meaning, and some authors (such as Miers in his *Lexikon des Geheimwissens*) even doubt that the hexagram ritual was genuinely passed down throughout magical tradition at all. Crowley distinguishes between the "Greater" and "Lesser Ritual of the Hexagram," while the Golden Dawn only referred to the "Hexagram Ritual" in general, or to the "Lesser Ritual of the Hexagram," that is if we're to believe Regardie. These are basically identical to Crowley's versions despite their different names, but you should always pay particular attention to such "minor details" in magic, especially when reading authors who come from a dogmatic and strictly literal tradition. For practical reasons and because the Golden Dawn tradition is not specifically focused on one certain magician like Crowley's is, we'd like to use the Golden Dawn system as a reference here, even if some of our details may differ.

Modern magic has taken excerpts from what the Golden Dawn calls the "Hexagram Ritual" (or Crowley's "Greater Ritual of the Hexagram") for use in practical planetary magic. This seems completely logical and justifiable, which we're about to see. But before we start thinking about that, we first need to take a look at the basic structure of the hexagram ritual according to the tradition of the Golden Dawn.

In order to do so, we need to take a look at the symbolism of the hexagram itself. In Illustration 17, you'll see the basic symbols that make up the hexagram. The upwards pointing triangle stands for the male principle (not just for the element of Fire), and the downwards pointing triangle stands for the female principle (not just for the element of Water). The hexagram is ancient in this form and interpretation and can be found in Eastern cultures as well, such in Hindu tantra in the meditation symbol "Sri Yantra" where it's understood as the union of *Shiva* (male principle) and *Shakti* (female principle). Its symbolic message also corresponds to the Chinese yin-yang symbol (the so-called tai chi).

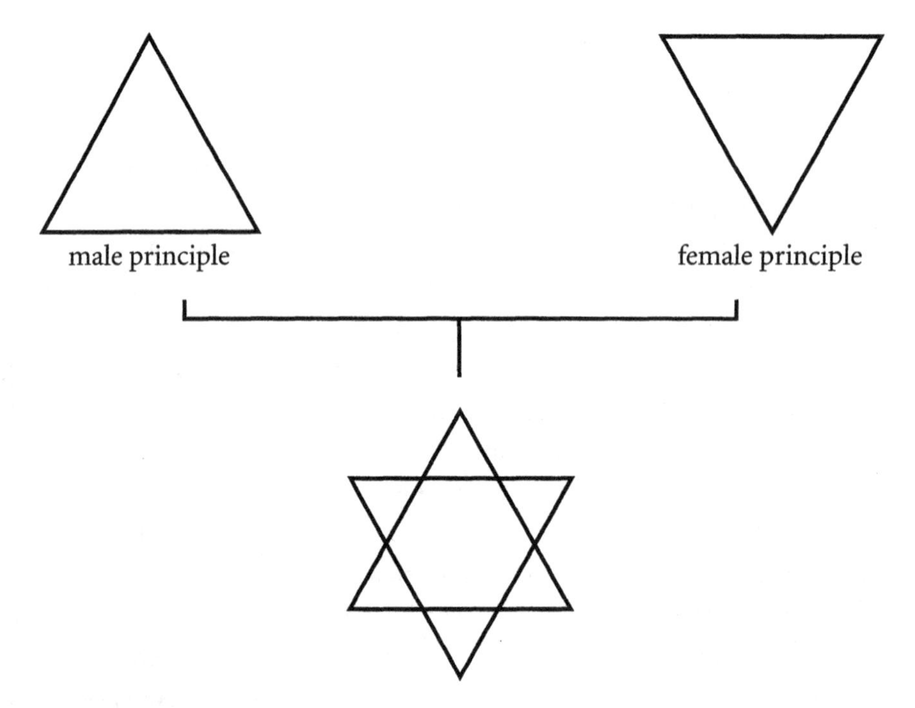

Illustration 17: The structure of the hexagram

In the Western tradition, the hexagram is also called the "Seal" or "Key of Solomon," and is even more popular under the name "Star of David."[1]

The relationship to the biblical King Solomon will be discussed in more detail later when we mention the influences of Judaism and the Christian tradition on Western magic. For now it's sufficient to mention that Solomon has been the archetype or epitome of the wise (and sometimes even blasphemous) magician since the early days of time.

So we can see that the hexagram represents the basic polarity of all existence. But its symbolism goes much deeper since it also stands for the (macrocosmic) spheres of the planets in the same way the pentagram symbolizes the (microcosmic) spheres of the elements. This is also why the hexagram was used to portray the mystical or theurgical path, while the pentagram was used to portray the magical or demonic path. But this in no way prevents the magician from working with the planetary powers in everyday magic and turning to the aid of the hexagram to do so. Such a distinction between "mystical" and "magical" is purely theoretical anyway, as we'll see later on.

The magician generally finds it easier to comprehend the model that works with the elements since these have a direct influence on his environment. In a way, one's "grounded" or anchored in concrete tangibility. Working with the planetary powers, however, involves contact with more subtle powers that are often regarded as supreme (keyword: "our fate is in the stars"), which could be interpreted as aspects of inner spiritual structures just as well.

Since the hexagram plays such an exceptional role in planetary magic (which in turn is extremely important to our work as magicians), we need to deal with each of the planetary principles in detail. Of course, our book isn't able to go into as much detail as literature on astrology can, which is why it's vital that we recommend further reading later on. However, only a handful of astrology books actually deal with the magical aspects of the planets. We'll be discussing the individual planetary principles in more detail later on as we progress with our training in planetary magic, so a rough summary will suffice for now. Those of you who are already well familiar with the planetary powers can just skim over the next section.

THE PLANETARY POWERS IN MAGIC

Magic usually recognizes seven "classical" planets, which need to be understood in an astrological sense. This means that the sun and moon (which, astrologically speaking, are not considered to be planets at all) are certainly viewed as such in magic. This represents the geocentric worldview that all celestial bodies revolve around the earth as its axis—an outlook that's still valid in magic today in symbolic form. To put this in magical terms, it means that the magician stands at the axis of one's own universe and everything rotates around him or her. At the same time, this concept also contains one of the greatest dangers of magic, namely megalomania, which can lead to a serious overestimation of one's own abilities and delusional self-importance. The only way to avoid this is by systematically monitoring your results—especially in everyday practical magic—and applying the appropriate objectivity and sobriety. We've already mentioned one of the basic principles of Western magic, and it wasn't just Aleister Crowley who supported this viewpoint in the twentieth century:

DEUS EST HOMO—HOMO EST DEUS

"God is Man—Man is God": indeed a daring claim that's nonetheless proven every day in magical practice, but only if we understand it correctly. If we view magic as a means of self-finding and self-realization, it will become clear that we first need to put ourselves in the center of everything. But the interesting question here is "What do we actually mean by 'ourselves'?"

There's one common misunderstanding that especially the beginner needs to avoid. The astrological or magical planets have very little in common with the celestial bodies we know from astronomy. Of course, horoscopy makes use of the tables of celestial bodies called ephemerides (which are, by the way, astronomically and not astrologically calculated) and the movement of the actual planets in the sky serves as a point of reference, but the interpretation of this movement is purely mantic, or omen-based. Despite astrology's claims to being scientific (as defined in the rationalistic-materialistic sense of the nineteenth century), this system is and remains intuitive art and not an exact science.

Symbol-logically it makes no difference at all to the magician what the planets Mercury or Mars really look like, or what gravity they have there and what the atmosphere is made up of. The symbolic planets have just as little (and as much) in common with the physical ones, just like a poem called "O Sweet Rosemary" would have with the botanical plant of the same name. The only way to find a correspondence in both components is by applying C. G. Jung's psychoanalysis and its principle of synchronicity (in which the relationship of equality is transcribed causally with nonrelated events) as well as its analogies, which we'll run into later in connection with the magical principles of symbolic correspondences. In other words, in magic we'd never assume that Mercury's power of attraction or the cosmic rays from Mars are influencing our earthly well-being, but rather we view the moving stars as living external symbols, which may indicate the occurrence of certain events and situations, but certainly not cause them.

Like every pantheon (as the planets have been since ancient Chaldea), the planetary powers offer us above all extremely sophisticated psychology and existential teachings with the help of which we as magicians can define our goals clearly and tackle their realization.

The three "nonclassical" planets (Uranus, Neptune, and Pluto) are designated as such because they were discovered quite late: Uranus (which is called "Herschel" in older literature after the person who discovered it) was first sighted in 1781 with the help of the telescope; Neptune's discovery followed in the year 1846 by Galle (after previous calculations made by Leverrier and Adams); Pluto wasn't sighted until 1930 by Tombaugh. Even today, there's still no standard astrological interpretation of these three planets, although the various astrological schools at least reflect some similarities in their renditions. After all, the symbolic powers of these planets—also called "trans-Saturnian planets" since they lie beyond the classical planetary sphere bordered by Saturn—are considered extremely difficult to handle magically, which is why we'll only be dealing with the classical planets here.

You should memorize these seven planets along with their symbols and most significant correspondences as soon as possible. For better illustration, we've listed them in Chart 12 along with their astrological/magical symbols, their corresponding kabbalistic numbers, and their Hebrew formulas in the hexagram ritual. Other correspondences (such as metal, color, sephira, and so on) will follow later in connection with magical correspondences and planetary rituals.

Therefore, just like the elements, the planets are symbol-logical principles of order and structure. In this sense, they fulfill a function similar to the sephiroths of the kabbalistic Tree of Life, the three aggregate states of alchemy (sulfur, mercury, salt), the three Indian gunas (sattva, rajas, and tamas), as well as other comparable symbol structures.

They divide up the magical world and make it manageable. No more, but also no less: It would be a fallacy to believe that these are "objective" correspondences such as, for example, a physicist would define them. Let's just view them as helpful analogies that make our practice of magic a bit easier.

Planet	Symbol	Number	Ritual Formula
Sun	☉	6	YOD-HE-VAU-HEH ELOA VA-DAATH ARARITA
Moon	☽	9	SHADDAI EL SHAI ARARITA
Mercury	☿	8	ELOHIM TZABAOTH ARARITA
Venus	♀	7	YOD-HE-VAU-HE TZABAOTH ARARITA
Mars	♂	5	ELOHIM GIBOR ARARITA
Jupiter	♃	4	EL ARARITA
Saturn	♄	3	YOD-HE-VAU-HEH ELOHIM ARARITA

Chart 12: The planets: astrological symbols, kabbalistic numbers, formulas in the hexagram ritual

THE SYMBOL-LOGIC OF THE PLANETARY POSITIONS IN THE HEXAGRAM

Each point of the hexagram corresponds to one of the seven classical planets with the exception of the sun, which is located in the middle. This is immediately clear if you view the sun as the "sum" or "essence" of all other planets, comparable to Ether or Spirit in the world of the elements. In addition, the allocation of the planets to specific points of the hexagram coincides with the corresponding kabbalistic sephiroths. Saturn (which corresponds directly to the sephira Binah) is at the very top and stands for the totality of the upper triad, made up of Kether, Chokmah, and Binah; the moon corresponds to the sephira Yesod, Jupiter corresponds to Chesed, Mars to Geburah, Venus to Netzach, and Mercury to Hod.[2]

In classical theory, the planets are divided into so-called "octaves," which doesn't need to concern us yet in detail. The only thing we need to point out is that the opposite planets (Saturn/moon, Jupiter/Mercury, and Mars/Venus) are "agreeable" to one another. The fact that they form counterpoles in the hexagram doesn't mean contradiction, but rather just the opposite.[3]

You'll find the positions of the planets depicted in Illustration 18.

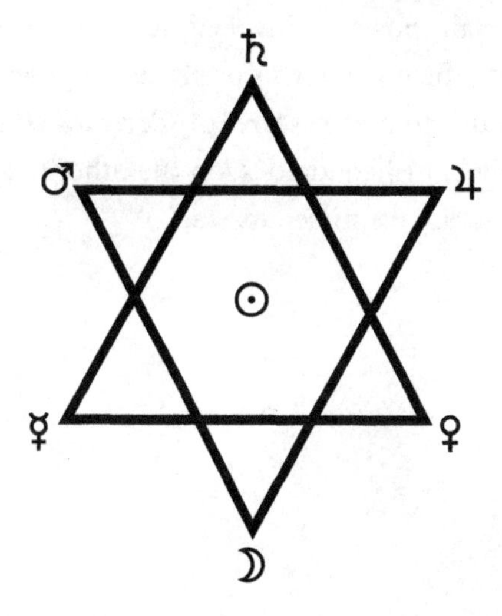

Illustration 18: The hexagram and the positions of the planets

Please memorize the position of the planets in the hexagram right from the start; you'll need this throughout your magical career again and again since the location also determines the direction the lines are drawn in each planetary hexagram. Unlike the pentagram, the hexagram in its classical form cannot be drawn in one single line without lifting the hand, therefore two separate but interlocking triangles are drawn. In doing so, the following rules apply, so please memorize these as well:

Invoking is always clockwise.

Banishing is always counterclockwise.

The first hexagram always begins on the point corresponding to the planet.

The second hexagram always begins on the point opposite the planet.

Charts 13a and 13b will show you how to draw each planetary hexagram. We need to describe the hexagram ritual in such a complicated way at first because its various forms and versions will not become clear until you've studied its basic principles.

On that note, here's one more comment on the principle of invoking and banishing. According to basic symbol-logic structure, a magical operation should always be designed as symmetrically as possible. If, for example, the "veil to the magical world is opened" at the beginning of a ritual, it needs to be symbolically closed at the end of the operation as well. If a certain power is invoked, it needs to be dismissed as well. The term "banishing" is a bit confusing in terms of planetary powers or deities since the beginner often understands this to mean "scare" or "drive away." Actually, only demons or elemental powers are truly banished; deities, on the other hand, are never driven away due to their superiority, but are dismissed instead.[4]

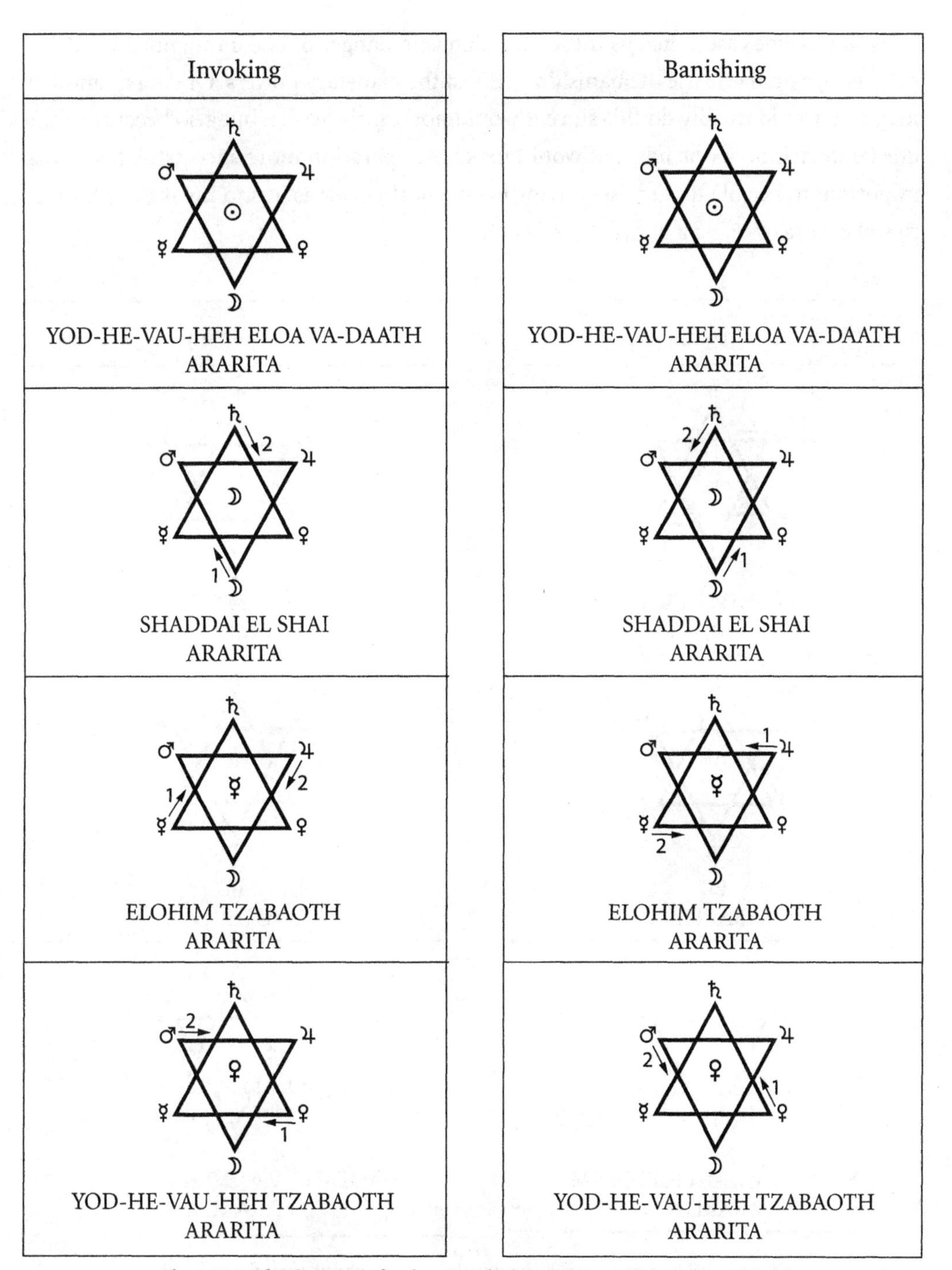

Chart 13a: The directions for drawing the hexagrams and their formulas (1)

Only in extreme cases, such as if the magician is in danger of becoming uncontrollably possessed, would one use the banishing against the planetary powers. Of course, another magician would usually do this since it would not only be easier, but also because of the greater detachment one has that would make the operation more successful. It's just as important to be able to dismiss or banish a magical power as it is to invoke it. This dismissal occurs by using a banishing symbol.

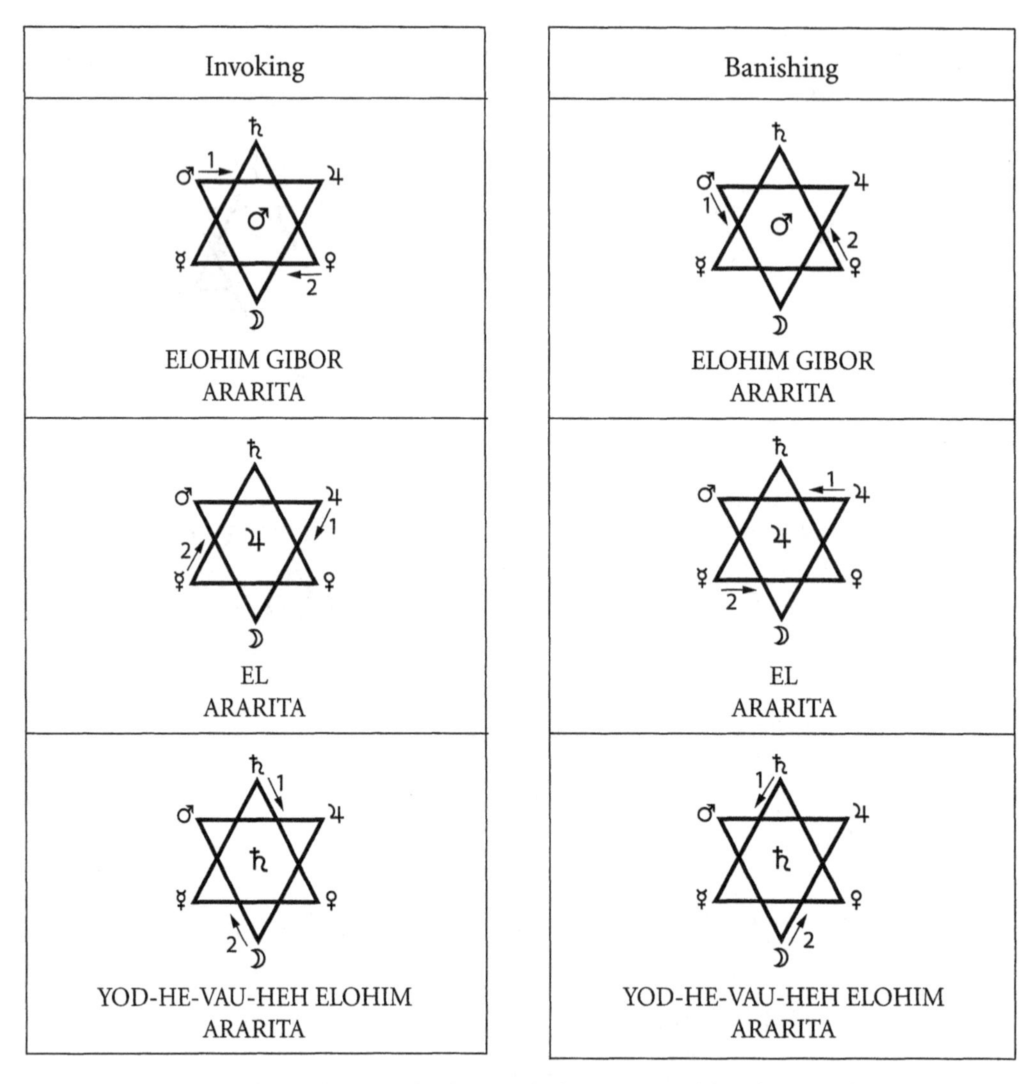

Chart 13b: The directions for drawing the hexagrams and their formulas (2)

The hexagram of the sun is made up of all other six planetary hexagrams together while drawing the sun symbol in the middle of each and vibrating the sun formula. This happens in the following traditional order: 1. Saturn; 2. Jupiter; 3. Mars; 4. Venus; 5. Mercury; 6. moon.

First draw the Saturn hexagram while vibrating the sun formula, then draw the sun symbol in the center (the circle with the dot in the middle) and vibrate Ararita, then do the same with the hexagrams for Jupiter, Mars, and so on.

AN OUTLINE OF THE PLANETARY PRINCIPLES

Here's a short summary of the planetary principles. In parentheses we've listed the Latin descriptions that are sometimes used in literature.

Sun (Sol)

Basic principles: vitality, reasoning, consciousness, center of being, centeredness, potency, giving, creating, linear knowledge, intellectual analysis, structuring.

Practical magical application: Improving the quality of life, magic for health and prosperity, gaining wisdom and centeredness, stabilizing one's magical identity, promoting general and specific plans in a business, health, or power/political sense.

Moon (Luna)

Basic principles: femininity, intuition, emotion, sensitivity, dream, fertility, receptiveness, producing and dissolving, change, inconsistency, rhythm, cyclic knowledge, emotional synthesis, sense of structure.

Practical magical application: divination, clairvoyance, anima work, dream work, sex magic, magic dealing with emotions, improvement of subtle perception, magic dealing with decomposition and uncertainty, improving the perception of cycles and rhythms.

Mercury (Mercurius)

Basic principles: the intellect, language and speech, communication, healing, cunning and shrewdness, thievery, business sense, recognition of structure.

Practical magical application: magic for healing, money magic, help with examinations, interviews, business negotiations, etc., and the support of intellectual activities.

Venus (Venus)

Basic principles: harmony, union, love, eroticism, beauty, art, romanticism, flair, harmonization of structure.

Practical magical application: creating harmony, finding lovers, magic for influencing emotions, money magic, supporting artistic and promotional projects.

Mars (Mars)

Basic principles: driving force (dynamics), self-authority, sexuality, passion, fighting, competition, aggression, courage, self-protection, the fight for structure.

Practical magical application: rituals for attack and protection, work dealing with authority, finding sexual partners, improving the quality of life, work with the gnosis of anger.

Jupiter (Iovis)

Basic principles: overview, luxury, wealth, abundance, religion, generosity, grandeur, ethics, expansion, growth, widening structures.

Practical magical application: magic for wealth and prosperity, magic for luck and happiness, the support of healing operations, gaining philosophical-ethical insight, rituals of self-assertion.

Saturn (Saturnus)

Basic principles: restriction, concentration, severity, initiation, concretization, grounding, perseverance, wisdom, trueness to detail, sickness, death, time (also known as Chronos in this function), compulsory structure.

Practical magical application: finding a job, real-estate matters, improving concentration, the concretization of material projects, magic dealing with death.

Of course, the great number of practical magical applications possible is in no way exhausted with this short list. Also, don't let it bother you that some aspects seem to overlap. For example, money magic can be performed using the sun, but also using Jupiter, Venus, or Mercury, although there are slight differences, which we'll get to later when we discuss the individual planetary rituals. For now, just familiarize yourself with the principles we've mentioned.

THE PRONUNCIATION OF HEBREW WORDS IN THE WESTERN MAGICAL TRADITION

The Hebrew Kabbalah is considered one of the basic pillars of Western magic. This mainly has historical reasons of a spiritual and religious nature: Christianity, as it developed from Mosaic or Jewish beliefs, gave rise to a strict orientation to the Bible that can even be fanatical at times.

The modern relationship between shamans or native tribes to average New Agers resembles that of medieval occultists to their Jews: a somewhat exotic people whose religious customs seemed so strange to noninitiates that it was often suspected that Judaism contained the knowledge that was sought in vain in one's own religion. Thus, one adopted the Jewish doctrine that Hebrew is not a normal language like all others, but rather the primeval language of creation itself. In this sense, these languages contained magical power, and exact knowledge of their esoteric legitimacy was considered a prerequisite for all serious magic. The same still holds true with Hinduism and the Sanskrit language, which has had such a major impact on mantramism that it led to the belief that some mantras are as "dangerous" to noninitiates as weapons are to children. By the way, that held true until well into the twentieth century and especially the classic authors of magic literature such as Levi, Papus, Guaïta, and even Mathers, Crowley, and Waite always attached great importance to kabbalistic and Hebrew (which are not necessarily identical) formulas.

You've already encountered a number of Hebrew formulas (god-names, names of archangels) in the Lesser Banishing Ritual of the Pentagram, the Greater Ritual of the Pentagram, and now in this section in the hexagram ritual. In the case of the pentagram rituals, we made suggestions as to how to pronounce these words using phonetic spelling for easier use. We'll do so in the future as well, for example in the next section where we'll explain the hexagram ritual in more detail. Even though we tell you what these formulas actually mean, we still need to point out that the acoustic or mantric effect they have is much more important. Later during your mantra training, you'll also be working with formulas from Sanskrit, Pali, Arabic, Japanese, and ancient Greek to familiarize you with the differences in the quality of energy of each language.

The pronunciation of ancient Hebrew has not been perfectly preserved. Like every other language, it underwent phonetic development that cannot easily be reconstructed. By the way, this holds true for all Semitic languages since their alphabets have no—or just some—vowels. For example, when a Hebrew or Arab writes the word "KTB," this could be read as "KATABA" or as "KITABU," but even "KATABU" could be possible as well. Of course, each of these words means something entirely different (e.g., in Arabic *kataba,* "to write"; *kitabu,* "book"; *katabu,* "they write"), which makes these languages quite difficult for an American to learn. However, some older texts contain "diacritical marks" for vocalization that make such literature much easier to read. (In Hebrew, these are various dots and lines such as the segol, the tzere, and the shew na', while in Arabic these special marks include the fatah, the kasra, and more.) But there are even various renditions of entire sentences as a result of the various possible ways to interpret the consonant structure. In the Semitic linguistic area, special genres of literature (especially in poetry) have even developed to play with this structure, creating aphorisms and poetry that can be read and understood in a countless number of ways.

In the nineteenth century, the study of Hebrew—along with Greek and Latin—was considered part of a humanistic general education, which certainly influenced magic and its authors as well. Of course, this doesn't change the fact that the pronunciation of Hebrew ritual formulas was never really standardly defined.

The magician should be aware of this when encountering kabbalistically influenced texts that may claim that there's only "one true" pronunciation of special Hebrew words, and may not even reveal what it is. Indeed, there's only "one true" way to pronounce every magical formula, namely, the most effective way! But this is always subjective and only the magician can decide what's effective for oneself. Our recommendations for pronunciation have been taken from practice and do not necessarily have anything to do with "proper Hebrew." If we use modern spoken Hebrew as a basis (so-called Ivrit) and take the example of the Kabbalistic Cross, we'd have to say "wa" instead of "ve,, whereby the "w" is spoken softly like the English word "wine" and the "a" would be short. The word "Malkuth" on the other hand, would be pronounced similar to "Mall-chút" with a short "a," a long "l," and a guttural "ch" similar to the German "ch" in the word "doch." The pronunciation of the formula "Ateh" in original Hebrew is extremely difficult to explain without going into a scientific exposition; an attempt would be "A'-tteh," dropping the voice after the "a" such as in the English word "baboon," a powerful "t," and a sharp, short "eh" in the second syllable, which is emphasized. The last example makes it clear that the acoustic effect would be entirely different if we used the relatively harsh, short, and guttural sounds of the modern Hebrew language. A long, sonorous mantra, on the other hand, has the advantage that it can actually make the walls of your "inner temple" quake, which is why we prefer it here. Most modern magicians, however, usually don't even realize that "their" Hebrew isn't necessarily that of Orthodox Jews or Torah scholars, and are unknowing of the actual reasons for this. But it would nevertheless be helpful if you'd learn just a few rules of Hebrew pronunciation, as least the ones that linguists have written down.

For now, it's fine to just familiarize yourself with the so-called "sun letters" and their principle of assimilation. We'll do without printing the Hebrew letters here and just print their transcription in Latin letters, using the English transcription that's most common in magical literature.

The Hebrew sun letters are the dental sounds and sibilants Samekh (s), Shin (sh), and Daleth (d), as well as the sounds Resh (r), Lamed (l), and Nun. These assimilate the end consonants of the previous word, for example the "l" of the previous article "Al" (or "El"). Although the word for "sun" is written AL SHAMASCH, it's pronounced "ASCH-SCHAMASCH" (the sun letters are called so because of this example word). Using the moon hexagram as an example, SHADDAI EL SHAI should correctly be spoken "SHADDAI ASCH-SCHAI." We've already taken this into account in our description of the rituals, but won't explain it again.

---

1. Some competent authors (particularly journalists) have confused the hexagram with the pentagram in the past, and the other way around as well. This is probably due to the fact that the hexagram is sometimes referred to as a "pentacle," which may cause confusion among beginners.

2. If you're not yet familiar with the kabbalistic Tree of Life, just skip this information for now since we'll be dealing with it in more detail at a more appropriate time. This kabbalistic information is meant to serve as a reminder to those readers who have already memorized the symbolism of the Tree of Life so that they can now actually apply what they've learned.

3. Of course, there are certain limits to this statement as any experienced astrologer will know. We're merely stating the doctrine of the Golden Dawn here in short form.

4. The word "deity" in modern magical terms describes a personified principle that rules over a certain aspect of being; for example, Mercury is the "lord of speech," Saturn the "lord of initiation," and so on. In this sense, the deity is always superior to or higher than the magician since it rules over the aspect that it embodies. Mercury not only rules over speech in general, but also over the communication skills of the magician him- or herself, such as one's skill in winning arguments.

INTRODUCTION TO RITUAL MAGIC (III)

THE MAGICIAN'S TOOLS

Since rituals are symbols in action (as we've already seen) in an entirely physical sense as well, we'd like to take a look at the tools that a ceremonial magician works with.

This equipment is often called "magical paraphernalia." You should keep this technical term in mind when reading other magical literature, if you choose to do so. Our discussion of the magical tools will stretch over the entire book. The focus hereby will be on the following items:

1. The Temple
2. The Robe
3. The Belt
4. The Headband
5. The Sandals
6. The Dagger
7. The Cup
8. The Wand
9. The Sword
10. The Pentacle
11. The Altar
12. The Crown
13. The Hat
14. The Bell
15. The Incense Burner
16. The Lamp
17. The Lamen
18. The Phial
19. The Oil
20. The Chain
21. The Scourge
22. The Ring
23. The Mask
24. The Mirror
25. The Book

These are just a few of the most important tools—other objects such as talismans, amulets, general and specific fetishes, stones, incense mixtures, aroma oils, tulpas, shields, element tablets, combat daggers, or chaos spheres all belong to special areas of magic that will be discussed later on in the appropriate context.

Now don't let this scare you into thinking you'll have to turn your apartment into a magical house of horrors. Our list is just meant to serve as a complete reference, like many other things in this book, and in no way does it mean that every Western magician has all of these things, especially right from the start since obtaining or making these things usually takes years, if not decades. Plus, you usually can't just order magical instruments through a catalog, and even if you actually do sometimes, these instruments still need to be charged and subtly calibrated, which involves a considerable amount of effort. And after all, everyone knows that the true initiate has mastered the techniques of the empty hand. But in order to truly master these, experience has shown that about 90 percent of all beginning magicians need to learn how to work with physical tools first, which is what we'll be discussing here.

Always keep in mind that magical tools are merely symbolic aids that are meant to bring the magician's spirit into a certain gnosis. By structuring one's universe externally as well as internally with symbols, one's creating "anchors" for various states of consciousness. One consciously projects part of one's self and then retrieves this part by working with it practically or epistemologically. Although this process can be understood as rationally and intellectually as just described, the act itself happens in an entirely different way. A person who looks at his or her dagger and consciously thinks "You are the projection of my will and nothing more than a tool that I can just as easily do without" won't have much success when working with the dagger. After all, there's a reason why magic is sometimes called "controlled schizophrenia," although "controlled projection" would probably be more fitting. This externalization (projection) must be absolute in order for it to develop its own momentum and become effective in the desired sense. On the other hand, this shouldn't be carried too far so that magicians are completely helpless when they don't have their own tools at hand or if they might even be lost. But paradoxically we can usually only gain this independence from our magical tools by working with them for so long that we've either internalized them or that they really exist on a psychological level (astrally). Only a very few highly talented naturals are able to master the techniques of the empty hand right from the start, and often this mastery is proceeded by yearlong training in other disciplines, such as yoga, meditation, autogenic training, alchemy, oriental martial arts, or others. Even such natural talents should still work thoroughly with physical tools in their magical practice, even if it's for the mere purpose of sufficiently grounding their own work and developing a feeling for the various energy qualities.

But why are material tools so effective? The psychological explanation says because they make an impression on the subconscious in a direct and subtle manner. The subconscious is commonly known to be a bit "childish" at times, at least in the opinion of our supposedly "adult" intellect. Like a child, it loves bright colors, powerful stimuli, and clear statements. It's no secret that many people have trouble with ritual work, especially at the beginning of their magical career. And certainly the significance of the ritual in magical work shouldn't be underestimated. Of course, there are other ritual-free forms and subdisciplines in magic that are just as effective and far less elaborate as we've already seen in the second section on sigil magic. But ritual offers us the opportunity to perceive the choreography of magical energies in a controlled situation as well as to capture these and use them for our work. Moreover, only the ritual is able to calibrate the magician's psyche with a lasting effect toward magical work, magical perception, and—probably most importantly—magical success.

The importance of rituals and ritual objects can be seen in everyday life. No matter what kind of ritual we observe—rituals of greeting, job promotions, anniversaries, award ceremonies, marriages, baptisms and funerals, political elections, military taps, or even the ritual structure of sporting events—people are always busy performing symbolic acts with the intention of structuring their cosmos and making it comprehensible by creating points of reference and orientation, which in turn create opportunities for acting and maneuvering. In this sense, magical rituals are the logical and consequential continuation of a proven living technique that already governs our entire existence anyway. Of course, with the difference that we as magicians design our rituals ourselves for the most part, making them ideally more accurate and without letting them become reduced to nothing but hollow, meaningless shells.

In doing so, magical tools function both as an unconscious reminder and as an energy storage medium for subtle powers. (Psychologically speaking, this is basically the same.) However, the fact that these objects often develop a strange life of their own cannot be explained entirely in psychological terms. But we'll get to that later.

For now, let's have a look at the first item on our list—the temple.

THE MAGICAL TEMPLE

The magical temple is a place where only magic is practiced. This is usually an isolated room or corner of the room that's dedicated to magical work. Many magicians don't decide to have their own temple until after many years of practice; until then, they may temporarily transform their living room or bedroom into one for magical work. As the need arises, you'll have to decide for yourself how you want to solve the problem of a magical workplace; you've probably already found a solution if you've been doing the exercises given here. The reason why we've chosen to top our list with the most elaborate item is that creating a suitable temple is really no problem at all if you've understood the concept behind it. Let's talk about what the ideal temple looks like so that you know what's important and what you can easily do without when planning your special spot.

The ideal temple is a room that's only used for magic and otherwise remains closed. Only the magician is allowed to enter, or colleagues or clients whom he or she performs magical operations with. Curious outsiders have no business snooping in the temple—remember the esoteric oath to keep silent! The magician keeps one's temple in proper order, allowing no outsiders to clean there or possibly even pick up things. The temple should be well ventilated since the incense mixtures used during rituals can cause quite thick clouds of smoke. On the other hand, the temple doesn't necessarily need to have a window since you usually work in the dark anyway (with few exceptions) since this aids concentration.

The temple can be painted or designed in white or black or any other color that the magician feels appropriate. According to our experience, a neutral black or white is best since the level of distraction is much less. Plus, these are so-called "noncolors" (technically speaking, "uncolored") that causes a certain energetic neutrality. Don't let those New Agers scare you into thinking that the color black can have "negative effects." Maybe you could counter such a statement by saying that, optically speaking, every object is actually lacking the color that we associate with it.

In other words, a rose "is" not red—red is much more the only color that it's not, since the rose emits this color. In some traditions, black is also the color of protection and concentration—and magic. White, on the other hand, is the color of purity and permeability as well as mysticism. But when in doubt, you should put more trust in your intuition than in spoon-fed color theories. However, if possible, avoid flowered wallpaper or loud patterns that could distract your eyes or have an irritating effect on the ritual gnosis.

The temple holds all of the equipment that the magician needs for one's work, including the ritual instruments as mentioned above, but also candles, candleholders, incense mixtures, charcoal tablets, parchment (for talismans and amulets), string (for knot magic), crystal balls, and meditation pillows as well as the usual shelves, cabinets, or cupboards for storing these objects. The floor of the temple should be made of highly inflammable material since the incense often causes sparks. Any windows should either be covered or not transparent from the outside.

That's all for the basic requirements, but this list can be expanded in any way you like. Most magicians prefer candlelight rituals, but some also like to work with electronic lighting effects, which require the proper equipment, of course. A person who prefers the romantic tradition completely without electricity won't even need a power socket.

The size of the temple depends on the individual needs of the magician as well, depending on whether one mainly works alone or together with other magicians. In any case, the temple should at least be large enough for the altar (when available) and the magician to cast the circle around it.

For classical demon evocations, additional space is needed outside the circle for a triangle. If all else fails, a closet will work, too, but a bit more comfort can't hurt since most of the magical gestures (such as the assumption of god-forms) require a certain amount of room to move, just like dancing for certain invocations does.

Only those working in an angular tradition will need more furniture: an altar for the Worshipful Master, one table each for Senior and Junior Wardens, and an appropriate number of chairs. In the circular tradition, which will be our focus for now, the magician generally stands, while occasionally sitting or kneeling on the floor in a meditative position. He or she usually faces the east, but the furnishings should be flexible enough to allow work in other directions as well.

Another good "temple" is the outdoors. In particular, rituals dealing with the elements or nature gods are best performed outside, although we magicians of the Industrial Age are often quite restricted in this sense due to our densely populated surroundings, especially if we really don't want to be disturbed during the ritual.

The actual temple, however, is the magician's body, as already mentioned briefly in connection with the Lesser Banishing Ritual of the Pentagram. That's why "temple care" in particular refers to the proper care and treatment of your own body. It's about time that magic finally shakes off its dislike of the human body that's prescribed by Christianity and misinterpreted Eastern ascetic ideals (which are no better than Western prudery) and start viewing humans again as the unity of body and spirit without wanting to make one the servant of the other. In any case, the body first becomes a temple through mental magic, and in order to prepare for this you need to handle this central medium for magical energy in a sensible and healthy way.

No matter how you design and furnish your magical temple, whether it's a corner of the room, an entire basement, or even a pavilion, in any case you should make sure that no one enters without your permission or, in the case of a ritual corner of a room, that it can't be recognized as such. The temple should be something like your inner sanctum that can thrive without being bothered by outer influences, where you can charge your battery and store energy, peace, concentration, contemplation, magical power, and gnosis each and every time you begin working with (and in) it.

It won't always be easy to have such a fully equipped temple like the one we just described. But this challenge itself can often put awareness and power processes in motion, which are more valuable to a magician than gold. That's why you should put every effort into designing and furnishing your ideal temple (as well as other magical equipment) and not be sparing, making it as complete as possible even if it can't be done overnight.

PRACTICAL EXERCISES

This time we're only giving you two new exercises since you're probably still busy enough with the previous ones—at least you should be if you really practice until you're satisfied with the results. We recommend making a timetable for your magical training schedule so you don't lose track of things. Since this has to be adapted to each person's individual situation and needs, we decided not to give you a standard one here.

EXERCISE 13

TRAINING OF MAGICAL PERCEPTION (IV): WORKING WITH DICE

Get yourself a common die if you don't already have one, but it shouldn't be too small. You should be able to see it clearly on the table in front of you. You can get such a die at a toy store, for example.

Now look at one side of the die for a while (no less than three minutes) by using the 180° gaze. Close your eyes and try to see the image of the die in your mind's eye. If you're not an optical person, this might even take you a few months to achieve. However, for this exercise, it's important that you master this form of perception, so if necessary you should practice it for a very long time on a daily basis, if possible.

Then concentrate on two sides of the die in the same way as above.

If you're able to do this satisfactorily, then look at three sides of the die at the same time and proceed as above.

Now it's getting tougher. Try to see four sides of the die all at the same time without moving it—using the 180° gaze and then with your mind's eye. (The latter may even be easier for you than the former; that's completely normal and no reason to worry.)

You can imagine what's coming up next. Try to see five sides of the die all at the same time—again without moving it. By now you should realize that we're dealing with a form of "meta-seeing" in which your eyes are nothing more than symbolic aids. But it gets even worse.

Try to see all six sides of the die at the same time. Maybe you'll notice that you have to "squint" as though you were looking around a corner.

Once you've done this successfully, you can start looking at all six sides of the die and viewing it in its past, or as what it used to be. We're intentionally not going to tell you what this is supposed to look like—you should find it out for yourself!

The next step of the exercise is to view the die from all six sides at the same time (the present) in the current of its past and in its future form. Don't think this is impossible—you'll definitely succeed as long as you put yourself in the proper state of mind, which is the point of this exercise in the first place. Technically speaking, this is called multidimensional perception, and experience has shown that the mere attempt to do this often leads to an extremely powerful magical trance or gnosis.

Do this exercise for awhile (about six months) on a daily basis. Once you've gotten accustomed to it, it will only take you a few minutes and can even be done without great effort in the office during your lunch break, in the subway, or just before dinner. Such little effort—and such a powerful result, as you'll soon find out! Because by changing your form of perceiving reality, whole new universes will open their gates for you.

EXERCISE 14

SYMBOL TRAINING

Meditate in detail on the planetary powers and their characteristics as listed in this section. Memorize the descriptions before starting the next section, especially if you're not very familiar with astrology or planetary magic yet. For the next four weeks, take a different planet each day and pay attention to the manifestation of the planetary powers in your everyday activities. For example, on the day of Mercury you could pay attention to the aspect of communication around you or observe your own patterns of thought; on the day of the moon you could pay attention to your feelings and impulses, and so on.

It would be best to stick to the proper days of the week as well (as stated below) since these are often taken into consideration when practicing planetary magic. You don't need to memorize the formulas of the hexagram ritual just yet; these won't be explained until the next section. However, every morning just after getting up you should draw the invoking hexagram of the day's planet without the Hebrew formula, and then at the end of the day before going to bed draw the banishing hexagram. Do this physically and not mentally during the initial practice period at least.

The planets and the days of the week[1]

Sun—Sunday
Moon—Monday
Mars—Tuesday (French: *mardi*)
Mercury—Wednesday (French: *mercredi*)
Jupiter—Thursday (German: *Donnerstag*, "Donner" = Wotan; French: *jeudi*, "Iovis Day"
Venus—Friday (from the Germanic goddess of love, Freya)
Saturn—Saturday

Remember to note your impressions in your magical diary for this exercise as well. The long-term goal is to be able to express absolutely anything in terms of planetary energies—only then is true planetary magic possible.

THE SECOND BASIC FORMULA OF MAGIC

We'd now like to introduce the second basic formula of magic as developed by Pete Carroll and myself. But first we need to mention that such formulas are meant to illustrate a point and not scientifically "explain" it. These formulas merely look scientific, which has the advantage of being able to "soften" our rational intellect as well as our censor, which is strongly influenced by a scientific outlook on the world.

This second basic formula of magic is a qualitative—not a quantitative—depiction. This means that the formula is mainly designed to illustrate conditions and circumstances; there's little point in trying to substitute the individual factors with specific numbers since these cannot really be objectified in the first place. But first have a look at the formula itself, and then we'll explain it a bit further.

$$M \propto \frac{g \cdot l}{a \cdot r} \cdot p$$

Legend

M = magical act, magic

g = degree of gnosis

l = degree of the magical link to the goal/target person

a = awareness of the act

r = resistance against the act

p = coincidental probability of magical success

Chart 14: The second basic formula of magic

Please note that the variable "∝" denotes proportionality in our formula. The successful magical act "M" (or magic in general) is directly proportional to the degree of gnosis or magical trance applied, multiplied by the degree of the magical link to the goal or target person (when magically influencing others); "M" is reversely proportional to the degree of awareness of the magical act and the psychological resistance against this. The whole thing is then multiplied by the degree of coincidental probability of magical success.

Let's break down this formula to see what it means to magical practice.

The fact that magical success depends on the magical trance (gnosis) applied was already discussed earlier and should need no further explanation.

However, magical success is directly proportional to the degree of the magical link to the goal or target person. This is quite obvious in magic for influencing others. For example, if a magician wants to heal or harm the target person, one needs appropriate access to this person. This is usually determined by or based on the first law of practical magic. This doctrine states that, for example, an object that has been with another person for a long time assumes the qualities of this person, even becoming "one" with him or her in a sense; in this way, the magician can treat this object as though it were the person. This is why the old grimoires often tell the magician to collect personal things from one's target person such as nail clippings, locks of hair, blood, or other bodily secretions and fluids. The second law of practical magic is the law of transmission (also called "contagion") and forms the theoretical basis for actively working with an object in practical magic. If the magician has in one's possession a piece of hair (or even a photo) from the target person, one can proceed in any desired way and this will bring about the effect that anything done to this object will also happen to the target person as well.

The degree of such a link can vary greatly; it almost always depends decisively on how well the magician can find the rhythm of the energy field of one's target person. This is often a question of one's intuition and power of imagination and the tools needed to optimally perform one's magical act. Some magicians can magically adjust to a person just by knowing his or her name, while others may need more comprehensive information and stronger stimuli, for example by having seen, spoken with, or having touched the person, or by possessing a photo or other object from the target. In this we can see that the variable "l" can only be determined quite subjectively, which naturally applies to the degree of gnosis as well. In this context, we need to remember that in order to charge a talisman or amulet, a magical link needs to be established.

We can understand our "magical link" as the degree of empathy (unison) between ourselves and the target person or object. In a theoretical sense, the relationship between the magician and target person can easily be established as such, but even the most experienced magicians often have difficulties finding a "connection," for example to quench their desire for material or mystical success. In fact, "binding" basically means joining or even merging—what we're referring to here is our own centralization, which requires the line dividing our will from our magical goal be kept extremely fine or lifted completely. If our desire has become "organic"(as Spare would say), and if it's centered yet at the same time vast enough to integrate our goal completely into our overall personality, we can call this a strong magical link. Like a samurai warrior, the magician has to become one with one's goal in order to eliminate psychological failure mechanisms.

There is, however, a much more subtle aspect of the variable "l," namely the magician's actual suitability for the desired action, and there are indeed specialists in every field of magic, although every serious magician does one's best to develop one's skills as flexibly as possible. But the magician's suitability to achieve the desired goal plays a role here as well. A person who has an unhealthy relationship to money will rarely be successful in money magic; the same holds true for sex magic and magicians who don't have a grip on their normal, everyday sexuality.

The person who tends to perform magic for love or attraction instead of for healing will need to apply more effort (and more tools) for magical operations in this weak area, and less in his or her area of strength. After all, modern magicians feel that the act of obtaining an object for practical magic use is merely just one weapon for winning the battle, but an act that's often more significant than the actual result itself. The best magical link is surely a precise mental image of the desired goal or target person. Of course, "precise" in this case means emotional precision rather than physical. If a magician makes a doll to represent the target person, it doesn't matter if this image looks exactly like him or her in every detail like a photograph, but rather it's much more important that a strong identity is established between the puppet and the target person. The best state of mind for doing this is what Spare calls "noninterest/nondisinterest." Often dolls and other representative objects are made or charged for the sole purpose of steering the magician's concentration toward one's goal and increasing his or her focus on it.

The variables "a" and "r" reduce the prospect of magical success. The awareness of the magical act is one of the greatest stumbling blocks for the beginner taking the first attempts at walking on the magical floor. With "awareness" we mainly mean the censor's conscious mental linking of the magical operation with the magical goal. Let's stick with the example of making a doll. Although a strong magical link needs to be established between the doll and the target person, this identification needs to be "forgotten" during the actual magical operation.

If you're not able to detach yourself emotionally from the situation (we could call this intentional "disidentification"), the censor will do everything in its power to prevent success in order to avoid the possible dilemma of having a bad conscience ("I didn't want to do that," "I didn't mean it that way," "I actually didn't deserve that"), which often results in much more of a mental burden than magical failure would. Such self-consciousness could ruin everything. That's why it's absolutely necessary to thoroughly think through the situation beforehand, otherwise the consequences could be catastrophic.[2]

Rational, skeptical objections ("That'll never work!", "I can't do that," "How is that supposed to work?") can easily be eliminated through magical success, with few exceptions. So unless you happen to live by Palmström-Morgenstern's motto "And so he made it his creed/that nothing can be what it cannot be," your success will surely convince you soon enough that skepticism is not infallible and certainly has its limits.

The "other" variables include not feeling well physically or mentally ("lack of energy"), lack of motivation or boredom (which often occurs when performing magic for others!), absent-mindedness (too much focus on subjective magical tasks that are viewed as more important), and more. Since these vary from situation to situation, there's no general rule that applies to all.

The variable "p," or the coincidental probability of magical success, is often underestimated by beginners as well. This is probably due to the fact that the esoteric ideology of today treats the word "coincidence" like a pariah without even realizing what any person with a healthy degree of common sense already feels and knows, namely that our actions as a magician are subject to certain limits. These limits are surely much farther away than we often think or want to believe, but it would be foolish to view magic as a mere tool for fulfilling childish fantasies of playing God. Although it may theoretically be possible for a magician to make the physical planets Mars or Mercury explode by using one's magical arts, such considerations are usually nothing more than intellectual games that can be quite dangerous by leading to megalomania, which is in fact quite widespread among magicians. Let's take a quantitative example this time. Let's assume that the probability of a meteor crashing into a magician's temple in the next half hour is 1:1,000,000,000,000,000. Let's assume further that, with the help of intense gnosis, a high emotional affinity to the goal "meteor crashes into temple," an extreme low degree of awareness of the magical act, and low psychological resistance, the magician is able to "raise" this probability in his favor to 1:1,000,000,000,000 (three less zeros), or if he's a true master of his art maybe even to 1:1,000,000,000 (six less zeros). According to probability this is a great feat, and even from a scientific point of view it would be tremendous, but nonetheless magical success is still highly improbable.

Certainly one could object to plenty of things in this example. Firstly, the probability of such a meteor crash (or even of magical success in general) could never be seriously calculated so precisely based on our current level of knowledge; secondly, there's no way to determine how many "zeros" can be eliminated by magic; and thirdly, high probability or improbability can say nothing about whether a desired event may just happen anyway, because, as we know, statistics only deal with averages and not with individual or even subjective events, experiences, or impressions. Plus, the probability or improbability often cannot be determined until after magical success or failure has taken place (and sometimes not even then), depending on the way in which it actually happens or doesn't happen. For example, one could perform magic to ensure that an inheritance that's already certain is received as soon as possible; but there might be a dispute involved and instead one might unexpectedly win the same amount of money in the lottery or by playing roulette. Such "success on another level" often reveals the limits of such models of thought, explanation, and illustration.

Nonetheless, the basic statement of our formula is founded on magical experience—subjective as well as collective.[3]

This once again clearly shows how senseless it is to want to replace the variables in our equation with actual numbers. Always remember that even the power of a magician is limited to his or her sphere of influence. Charging sigils for world peace or to eliminate famine may give you a sense of paying a moral contribution, but this has little to do with common practice—at most it could pacify a bad conscience. Along these lines, we've developed the rule that you should even use magic for a goal that's highly probable to occur in the first place without magic, especially at the beginning of your magical career. If we persistently work our way up to more difficult tasks instead of trying to jump there all at once, we'll be able to deal with failure (which is inevitable sometimes) much better on a psychological level since we've learned to take one step at a time.

Let's summarize this in short

Ideally, the values below the line should be zero because then the values above it would be "infinite," although this is rarely the case in practice.

The greater the magical trance ("g") and magical link ("l"), the higher the success rate of the magical operation will be.

It's reduced by the variables "a" and "r."

When the psychological and rational resistance ("r") to the magical act or its goal is higher, the magical link or value of "l" is automatically lower because the magical will is not organic enough, and alienation between the magician and the goal occurs instead of absolute unity.

You've probably noticed that our variables cannot always be clearly distinguished from one another anyway. In this sense, a high trance value means—according to definition—a limited amount of awareness, while resistance could be due to an insufficient magical link, and so on. Other equations would be possible as well, for example the variable "r" below the line could be replaced by another variable such as "w" (for "magical will"). This is more than just an intellectual game since it creates many different psychological approaches to practical magic, so feel free to experiment with other equations as well!

THE MAGIC OF AUSTIN OSMAN SPARE

Spare's sigil magic, which we'll mainly be dealing with in this section, is based on a mechanism that plays a key role in the psychology of Sigmund Freud: psychological repression. Roughly summarized, Freud's thesis claims that the psyche represses certain trauma, impulses, fears, and other parts of the conscious mind into the unconscious or subconscious for various reasons. This can lead to pathological behavior such as compulsiveness, neurosis, or psychosis. In other words, through repression, these components of the soul remain active only in the subconscious, but in no way do they lose their effectiveness and, on the contrary, they can even force the conscious mind to behave in a seemingly rational manner that is, in reality, controlled by the subconscious.[4]

Spare's brilliant idea that he developed just after the turn of the nineteenth to the twentieth century—a time when Sigmund Freud's work was only known to a tiny group of specialists in England—didn't view this psychological mechanism as disturbing or undesired, seeking its elimination like the "father of psychoanalysis" did,[5] but rather recognized it in an entirely pragmatic sense as being predefined and therefore quite practical for magical use. Spare's contribution can be measured by looking at the history of psychoanalysis and depth psychology in the twentieth century and their tremendous influence on the thought patterns of our time. Freud's model was pathologically oriented through and through; he and his colleagues felt that repression was merely something to be rejected and even reversed in order to free the person from unconscious obsessions and fears and, in this way, to rid the patient of pathogenic disturbances ("illnesses"). Freud's students, followers, successors, and academics all took this approach—from Alfred Adler and C. G. Jung to Georg Groddek. Even William Reich was mainly concerned with the elimination and prevention of mental illness. Although nearly all of Freud's great students eventually followed different paths than their old master of modern psychology did—with some of these paths even crossing over into the realms of magic (such as C. G. Jung's)—the possibility of "reversely using" the psychological process of repression was never seriously considered. This was reserved for Austin Osman Spare, who developed one of the most economical and most effective disciplines of the Black Arts, namely "sigil magic" that we've already mentioned here quite frequently.

Spare's train of thought was thusly. If the psyche represses certain impulses, desires, fears, and so on, and these then have the power to become so effective that they can mold or even determine entirely the entire conscious personality of a person right down to the most subtle detail, this means nothing more than the fact that through repression ("forgetting") many impulses, desires, etc. have the ability to create a reality to which they are denied access as long as they're either kept alive in the conscious mind or recalled into it. Under certain conditions, that which is repressed can become even more powerful than that which is held in the conscious mind.

Such considerations almost automatically created the desire to constructively use this mechanism of psychological power instead of wanting to eliminate, reverse, or avoid it. Spare believed that intentionally repressed material would become enormously effective in the same way that "unwanted" (since not consciously provoked) repressions and complexes have tremendous power over the person and his or her shaping of reality. It was a logical conclusion to view the subconscious mind as the source of all magical power, which Spare soon did. In his opinion, a magical desire cannot become truly effective until it has become an organic part of the subconscious mind. This can definitely be understood in a physical sense as well, which is why Spare plausibly placed great importance on personal magical posture (mudras).

But it wasn't Spare's only achievement to develop a theoretical basis based on psychoanalysis for the process of magical action; his ideas also enabled this process (a) to be more thoroughly understood and (b) to be used much more efficiently than Western magic did previously up to the nineteenth century. In fact, he developed the technique of controlled repression that we know today as sigil magic.

Let's summarize this once again for clarity. Spare's system of making the desire "organic" can be defined as a technique of conscious repression. Each and every desire is repressed immediately and not allowed to stay in the conscious mind for any period of time. Once embedded in the subconscious, this desire acts like a complex, functioning independently while striving toward fulfillment.[6]

The magician who works according to Spare's method uses the repression mechanism of the psyche to one's advantage. By purposely repressing the desired goal, one takes advantage of the psychological fulfillment automatism and forces the subconscious to bring about the desired effect against the potential resistance of the conscious mind and censor. A process that Freud and his followers would probably call pathological now becomes an instrument for magical action that guarantees success for the most part.

It's vital that you understand this process clearly since this forms the basis of all laws of modern magic; we'll continue to find these ideas again and again in both theoretical and practical magic.

Of course, we don't want to make the false impression that Freud's thesis was intended for magic in even the slightest way. In fact, Spare borrowed many ideas from psychology and implemented some of these for developing contemporary magic, in the same way many other magicians in the twentieth century have done (such as Aleister Crowley, Dion Fortune, William Gray, William Butler, Israel Regardie, and others). Many old magical techniques are celebrating new triumphs today in the light of psychology without magic being reduced to merely a somewhat bizarre variety of applied psychology, which we'll realize again and again throughout our practice.

However, Spare's system in no way intends to prevent or demonize desire as such for moral reasons such as Buddhism and other ascetic doctrines do. Rather, the desire should be repressed in order to make it capable of being fulfilled. The demons of one's own psyche will take care of this fulfillment. However, after all that being said, it's obvious that such methods require a very robust psyche in the first place.

The subconscious reacts to suppression and prohibition/self-denial like a child desperately trying to get what he or she wants. Plus, this technique has the advantage that the intellect remains turned off (such as when charging a sigil) regarding the contents of the desire, and its fulfillment cannot be prevented by fantasies, rational thought, objections, figments of the imagination, daydreams, doubt, or genuine fear of possible success by limiting its means of manifestation right from the start. This is also another form of the Crowleyan demand to "be free of the desire for results," which can also be found in similar form in karma yoga and Zen, just to name a few more examples.

So when using Spare's technique of repression, the wish or desire must first be suffocated, then separated from the self and fed with energy so that it's able to carry out its job. There are authors who feel that the desire needs to be energized first, and that simply forgetting (repressing) it isn't enough to guarantee magical success. This can differ from magician to magician. Energizing occurs through the actual charging, for example by means of the death posture. However, one can often observe even among nonpractitioners of magic that the desires most likely to come true are those that often surface in the conscious mind for just a fraction of a subjective second, only to immediately disappear again and be covered up by other material of the consciousness. Surely you can think of a few examples of this process from your own experience, for example when you briefly thought about calling a certain person and forgot about it right away—and then the phone rang! You might want to call this telepathy, but this attempt at explanation wouldn't work for unexpected situations of "luck" (such as winning money, an unpopular colleague or superior being unable to work, spontaneous healing, sudden gifts or presents), which would very clearly seem to be dealing with the mechanism described above.

Now let's look at the magical technology of Spare's system.

It's based unconditionally on the so-called "neither-neither principle." This principle is based on the realization that there is no truth (and no wish, want, or desire) that's not balanced by an equally true opposite. Only our individual outlook and our material and psychological circumstances have the power to choose what will appear to us as "more true" for the time being. The neither-neither principle leads directly to a magical technique that Spare described as "free belief." We decided to integrate this technique into our training program, and you'll find a detailed description of it in the practical exercises of this section. With the technique of free belief, the magician can achieve an undifferentiated energy potential since it's separated from the original "meaning." We've already introduced this concept in Exercise 10.[7]

Sometimes this is also called "aleatory" (determined by luck) instead of "free" belief, for example when we perform this technique with the help of a die.[8] Of course, this technique of free or aleatory belief has more than just the one effect of eliminating restrictions: These beliefs offset each other and thereby create the metapolar energies that hold the true secret to any form of sigil magic.

CHARGING THE SIGIL WITH THE DEATH POSTURE[9]

Before we wrap up this first part of our special section on the magic of Austin Osman Spare, we'd first like to talk more about the techniques for charging sigils.

First of all, we need to clarify that charging a sigil doesn't mean charging it with magical energy, but rather it can be compared to installing a program on to the "central computer subconscious." The closer the sigil is to being machinelike—meaning the more it corresponds to the subconscious in terms of language and content—the easier it can be decoded; the program will then be activated in the background (multitasking), allowing the finished results to be delivered to the application program (everyday consciousness).

In Spare's system, charging generally occurs with the so-called death posture, which we already described earlier in-depth. But we'd like to expand on that a bit further. "The death posture is as much an act as it is a position. The wizard postures death [. . .] By forcing his ego to mimic death, the wizard can 'stand back' to see the powers that energize his own and others' actions and so learn how he can best work to carry out his will." It's therefore a method of magical objectivity.

"He will make his thought as still as his body by accepting all contraries, uniting opposites in annihilation." In fact, a feeling of annihilation actually does occur, as well as a feeling of power and its expansion. Hereby the mind should be stilled and kept in the state of "neither-neither." In this way, we eliminate every possible inner disunity by expanding our "self" to include absolutely everything. Only constant practice can lead to what Spare calls "the center of desire," which cannot be defined further with normal means.

In Spare's own words, the death posture is "a simulation of death by the utter negation of thought, i.e., the prevention of desire and the functioning of all consciousness through the sexuality." Because through sexuality we connect with Kia, as Spare described the Absolute.[10]

However, it's important to point out that the death posture has nothing to do with the actual physical death of the magician: "It is one thing to simulate a death agony, quite another to stimulate one." Although it can safely be accompanied by a bit of sweat and tears, anything that may be damaging to your health should be avoided.

1. In parentheses you'll find helpful notes, mainly from other languages, that will make the classical planetary allocation even clearer.
2. In Crowley's words, the magical act must correspond with the person's own "True Will," otherwise the magician would be violating the primal law of one's own universe and have to pay the consequences for irresponsible actions, which is usually quite painful. After all: "Thou hast no right but to do thy will."
3. Never forget that magic is an art that uses scientific methodology, but is not a science in the sense of the academic definition we're familiar with today.
4. For example, the strong dislike of one's father in combination with a strong bond to the mother as a child can lead to disturbances in sexual behavior when dealing with the female sex.
5. Freud: "Where It once was is where I will become."
6. This may explain the fact that people who meditate frequently in a state of empty mind often report no longer needing to practice active forms of magic—such as ritual magic—since their desires are fulfilled almost automatically without great effort.
7. Also compare our mnemonic phrases about belief as a technique and surgical tool.
8. From the Latin *alea,* "die/dice game; uncertainty."
9. Due to their exemplary clarity and precision, we'd like to examine a few quotations here from a book on magic by Stephen Mace called *Stealing the Fire from Heaven: A Technique for Creating Individual Systems of Sorcery.*
10. This Kia can be compared to the Tao of the Chinese, with a few differences, of course.

PLANETARY MAGIC (II)

INTRODUCTION TO THE HEXAGRAM RITUAL (II)

As already mentioned in the last section, the modern hexagram ritual borrowed elements from the Golden Dawn tradition, which is of particular significance in planetary magic.

We've already dealt with the theoretical basis of this ritual, so let's get on to the practice. The hexagram ritual (the "greater" as well as the "lesser") is usually not performed alone (like nearly all other rituals of the modern Hermetic tradition), but in conjunction with the Lesser Banishing Ritual of the Pentagram. We're now entering the field of practical planetary magic, although we'll just be sticking to the hexagram ritual for now since it makes more sense to practice this for awhile before introducing the whole system of planetary conjurations, which can be quite elaborate at times. But to get the general picture, here's a summary of the basic structure of a typical planetary ritual.

THE STRUCTURE OF A PLANETARY RITUAL

1. Lesser Banishing Ritual of the Pentagram
2. Meditation on the planetary powers
3. Lesser Ritual of the Hexagram (invoking)

4. Invocation of the planetary power (hymn)
5. Practical work with the planetary power invoked
6. Dismissal of the planetary power
7. Meditation (in some traditions: Lesser Ritual of the Hexagram [banishing])
8. Lesser Banishing Ritual of the Pentagram (with license to depart)

The individual steps of this framework ritual will be discussed later. For now, we're only interested in the hexagram ritual itself and its very simple form.

THE BASIC STRUCTURE OF THE LESSER RITUAL OF THE HEXAGRAM (INVOKING OR BANISHING)

1. Draw the hexagram (in the east)
2. At the same time, vibrate the planetary formula
3. Draw the planetary symbol in the middle of the hexagram
4. At the same time, vibrate the formula "Ararita"
5. Repeat the entire procedure in the remaining three cardinal directions

THE LESSER RITUAL OF THE HEXAGRAM OF THE SUN (INVOKING OR BANISHING)

As already mentioned in the last section, the invocation of the sun using the hexagram ritual is a special case. The basic procedure is the same as above except that all six planetary hexagrams are drawn, with the difference that the sun formula is vibrated each time and the sun symbol is drawn in the middle of each. Technically speaking, you actually perform six separate hexagram rituals by drawing the lines correspondingly (for the six planets except the sun), but overlapping everything with the sun symbolism.

In doing so, a certain traditional order is adhered to. Here's the proper traditional order:

1. Draw the hexagram of Saturn (in the east)
2. At the same time, vibrate the sun formula
3. Draw the sun symbol in the middle of the hexagram

4. At the same time, vibrate the formula "Ararita"
5. Repeat the entire procedure in the remaining three cardinal directions
6. Repeat 1–5 with the hexagram of Jupiter
7. Repeat 1–5 with the hexagram of Mars
8. Repeat 1–5 with the hexagram of Venus
9. Repeat 1–5 with the hexagram of Mercury
10. Repeat 1–5 with the hexagram of the moon

Although this may seem complicated at first in theory, in practice it's really quite logical and easy to understand. But you don't need to memorize the procedure for the hexagram ritual of the sun for now since we'll be working with the other planetary powers first. But first you need more preliminary practice like we've already begun in Exercise 14 from the last section. You'll find more instructions on this in the practical exercises of this section.

THE PLANETARY FORMULAS, THEIR PRONUNCIATION AND MEANING

Sun

Planetary formula/god-name: YOD-HE-VAUH-HEH ELOHIM
Common pronunciation: (Yod-heh-vau-heh [*or* Yeh-ho-vah] Eh-loh-ah vah-da'at)
Meaning: "God manifested in the realm of the spirit"

Moon

Planetary formula/god-name: SHADDAI EL SHAI
Common pronunciation: (Shaddai-asch-shai)
Meaning: "The almighty living God"

Mercury

Planetary formula/god-name: ELOHIM TZABAOTH
Common pronunciation: (Eh-loh-heem-tzah-bah-oht)
Meaning: "Lord of the hosts"

Venus
Planetary formula/god-name: YOD-HE-VAUH-HEH TZABAOTH
Common pronunciation: (Yod-heh-vau-heh [*or* Yeh-ho-vah] tzah-bah-oht)
Meaning: "Lord of the hosts" or "I am who I am, Lord of the hosts"

Mars
Planetary formula/god-name: ELOHIM GIBOR
Common pronunciation: (Eh-loh-heem Geebor)
Meaning: "Almighty God"

Jupiter
Planetary formula/god-name: EL
Common pronunciation: (ahl) (*sometimes* Aleph-Lamed)
Meaning: "God" or "ox (Aleph)—ox goad (Lamed) "driving force, cosmic dynamics"

Saturn
Planetary formula/god-name: YOD-HE-VAUH-HEH ELOHIM
Common pronunciation: (Yod-heh-vau-heh [*or* Yeh-ho-vah] Eh-loh-heem)
Meaning: "God the Lord"

The allocation of the Hebrew god-names stems from the Kabbalah. The formulas correspond to the appropriate sephiroths of the Tree of Life (or their god-names) that are assigned to the planets.

We've purposely excluded any complicated tables of correspondence listing things such as the corresponding incense mixture, and so on at this time. In the next section we'll be dealing with this subject in more detail; by then you'll already have enough experience with the Lesser Ritual of the Hexagram to make use of such correspondences meaningfully. Then the daily amount of practical training will be lessened slightly for awhile, which will create a training cycle with alternate phases of inner reflection and phases of frequent activity.

INTRODUCTION TO RITUAL MAGIC (IV)

THE MAGICAL ROBE

When magicians enter their circle (or cast it), they're protected from everything that might interfere with their work. This is their entrance into "another world," the realm of magical energies and entities.

When ordinary people enter "another world" within their everyday life, they perform certain rituals. They might take more time getting ready, perform washing ceremonies and anointments, and choose "festive" clothing—an evening gown, a tuxedo, or just their "Sunday best." This is a way of announcing to the outside world that a different, noneveryday state of being or consciousness is about to be entered.

The same is true in a magical ritual. Magicians document their entrance into the magical state of consciousness not only by ceremonial washing and anointment, but also and especially by changing their clothing. This technique generally takes on two forms: (1) Either the magician works completely naked, or (2) one wears clothing that's reserved only for magical work. There's not much more to say about item 1 except that it's not only a matter of taste, but may also depend on climatic or weather conditions. After all, the mere act of working "sky-clad" (as some Wiccans calls it) can lead to a state of altered consciousness, especially in group work.

If the magician works in a group, a uniform type of clothing will ensure the anonymity of all participants, which can be especially helpful to accept the others while working with magical invocations. For example, it's no longer your friend Carl Miller who suddenly speaks to you as Mercury, but rather an anonymous human vehicle for this planetary power—therefore, by working in a standard magical "uniform," you're robbing the censor of a possible target and the effect of this shouldn't be underestimated.

One important function of working unclothed or uniformed in a group has always been the elimination of any social contrasts because, during a ritual, all participants are equal within the framework of the individual role that they play.

If the magician works alone, however, which is usually the case, he or she can choose either option according to one's preference.

Aleister Crowley introduced a certain mechanism that, when varied slightly, can be applied to all magical equipment. On the one hand, he gave precise instructions for obtaining a magical robe, but on the other hand, he said that the magician can even work in a bathrobe just as effectively as long as it's only used for that purpose. As you see, it doesn't matter whether you adhere strictly "to the rules" concerning your magical equipment, as long as your subconscious is calibrated to associate it with your magical work.

A lot of nonsense has been written about the magical robe that does nothing but fill the beginner with uncertainty instead of explaining what this piece of clothing is actually about. First of all, this piece of clothing is quite simple, which can aid the magician's concentration in itself. The second purpose of the robe (which is equally important) is the protection it gives, although concentration and protection basically have the same function. This magical protection is understood as the elimination of undesired energies, while concentration is the elimination of undesired thoughts. Symbolically, the robe also stands for the magician's aura since it conceals oneself and his or her intentions, or concentrates them inside. With its help, the magician makes oneself invisible or unidentifiable to the profane outside world. This anonymity will guarantee that one's everyday ego (or censor) won't get in the way. The magician is usually naked underneath the robe because this symbol of the magical art is the only bulwark one has against obtrusive influences and the powers conjured that can be quite dangerous at times.

The robe is the most classical piece of magical clothing. It's usually tau-shaped.[1] The sleeves get gradually wider toward the cuffs, and their length usually reaches to the middle of the hand. The lower part of the robe should either reach to the middle of the calf or to the ankles. The robe should have no pockets. The simplest and most common form of the magical robe has no opening at the front and just slips over the head. A robe with a front opening, which usually runs vertically down the center, is technically called a magical coat. The opening can be closed with buttons or snaps, although some modern magicians even use Velcro. The coat is often used by magical lodges, but also in sex magic operations where the genitals need to be exposed but complete nakedness is not desired. For reasons of simplicity, we'll no longer make a distinction between the robe and coat since their function is the same.

Traditionally, the robe is made of pure black silk since black is the color of concentration and repellence and silk is a good insulator. For theonic and mystic work, a white robe made of linen (flax linen) is often used (generally without a hood), although most magicians usually only have one all-purpose robe that's not always made of silk—synthetic materials are fairly common as well. After all, pure silk is definitely not cheap so when the magician decides on the material for his robe, it's fine for him to take his wallet into consideration as well. Extremely ambitious magicians use different colored robes for various operations, for example a different color for each planet, but experience has shown that this is certainly not necessary. A silk robe has the advantage of being able to keep you either warm or cool as necessary, it's comfortable on your skin, it can be folded and stored easier, and it's more space-saving than most other cloth robes. Plus, depending on the type of silk, it doesn't weigh very much. Some dogmatic schools require the robe to be made of all-natural materials; in this case, it should be sewn with natural yarn.

The traditional robe also has a hood that's either sewn directly to the robe—which is usually the case—or is attached as needed by means of safety pins, snaps, or other types of fasteners. The hood can either be round or pointed and should extend well beyond the edge of the face when wearing it.

To cover the face, which is required sometimes in group rituals, the magician usually uses a veil that's attached to the front edge of the hood, or else a mask. Both cover the face entirely, usually just leaving slits for the eyes.

According to tradition, the robe should never be washed to prevent its "astral impregnation" from being lost. In fact, the scents that a robe naturally attracts during hard work (such as incense, sweat, anointing oils, and so on) can even help the magician enter a state of magical trance since they can trigger mechanisms of association in the subconscious mind; such associations can reduce the time required in preparatory meditation to a minimum, although at the cost of bodily hygiene (which is overly exaggerated in our society anyway).

Generally, the robe should remain undecorated, although the magician may prefer to decorate it with personal symbols or the grade of his magical order.

Most magicians keep their robe in a square or round bag, which, for practical reasons, is usually made out of the same material as the robe itself, sewn from remnants. The bag should be large enough to hold the hood, the belt, and the sandals as well.

But more important than the material and cut of the robe is the rule (according to Western tradition) that this magical item of clothing, as well as all other magical tools, should only be used for magical purposes. At first we can even use a piece of clothing that we already have, as long as we no longer use it for everyday wear. The purpose of this rule is to program your subconscious into associating the robe only with magical work and gnosis, which isn't easy to do if, for example, the robe is worn to a costume party right after a ritual like some initiates of the Golden Dawn supposedly once did![2]

THE BELT

The belt is wrapped around the robe and tied in a knot; usually it hangs down the side a bit (up to around the middle of the thigh or to the knee). The belt can be colored according to the magician's symbolism; for example, a white belt and black robe would be appropriate for magically working with the polarities of existence, or a red belt could be used for sex magic operations, or an appropriately colored belt could be used for planetary work.

It can be made of any material although cord is most common, but leather or silk is often used as well. Symbolic knots can give the belt an additional meaning, such as three knots for Saturn work or a knot for trapping or storing magical energies or states of consciousness.

One variation of the belt is the sash, which is usually made of silk and decorated with magical symbols. It often has a function similar to that of the headband and can serve to cover the solar plexus.

Another symbol of the belt or sash can be interpreted as "discipline," the discipline that's required of a magician in order for him or her to practice one's art, his or her unyielding will, and his or her centeredness are all represented by the belt, which is really a magical circle wrapped tightly around one's body.

THE HEADBAND

The headband protects or activates the magician's third eye, and can be viewed as a sort of "energetic burning glass." It can be made of any material; leather or velvet is most common, but silk is used occasionally too. The headband can be made of any color, such as the color corresponding to a planet for planetary work, but if the magician only uses one headband it's usually the same color as the robe.

It can also be decorated with magical symbols, such as the magician's personal sigil ("astral seal"), and sometimes precious or semiprecious stones or even small metal plates are used. The moonstone, for example, could be used for invocations of the moon and divination to strengthen visual perception. Mythical symbols can also be used on the headband, such as an Egyptian uraeus snake of pure gold. In the same way the belt tightens and disciplines the middle of the body, the headband does the same to the head, and therefore, according to Western symbolism, to the spirit and thought.

Whoever has ever worn a headband knows the feeling of security and concentration that it gives. Of course, it shouldn't be too tight but also not too loose. Light pressure should be felt, but it shouldn't be too uncomfortable or leave any deep impressions on the skin. (Among some native tribes, it's a common practice to use an extremely tight headband to reach a certain state of trance, but this requires a great deal of experience and careful observation, which is why we warn against such practices here.)

THE SANDALS

The sandals are actually quite "old-fashioned" magical accessories that are seldom used today. Most magicians prefer to work barefoot, which symbolically means that they literally have both feet on the ground and are utilizing the powers of the earth. Such grounding is occasionally frowned upon, especially in so-called "theonic"-oriented circles that are ultratraditional and dogmatic and are characterized by having an extreme aversion to their bodies and the material world, with their highest goal being to exalt the spirit and overcome the body. But this doesn't concern us, so we won't go into it any further.

Traditionally, sandals are usually made of leather and meant to symbolize a firm grip that the magician has in one's art, and they protect one's foot chakras from chthonic (subterranean) powers as well.[3]

On the other hand, they're also considered a symbol of Mercury and Hermes who were messengers of the gods and known to have worn winged sandals. In this sense, sandals can also be a symbol for the swiftness and mobility of a magician (or one's ability of astral travel).

This is just another example of how magical symbols can often be interpreted and used quite subjectively; only their basic structures are not arbitrary and are relatively fixed. This freedom of interpretation may confuse the beginner at first, but it offers the experienced magician a great deal of practical versatility.

PRACTICAL EXERCISES

EXERCISE 15

TRAINING YOUR CONCENTRATION AND ATTENTION

This exercise serves to improve your concentration and attention. Although we like to try to avoid exercises that seem to have no direct relation to practical magic, the importance of the following exercise shouldn't be underestimated. This exercise demands the magician's attention to seemingly meaningless details, which is important in the practice of magic as well.

Write a letter to any person. It can be a person who's either alive or dead, real or fictitious, or even an animal, a mythical figure or other creature. The contents of the letter are insignificant, so choose any subject you like.

There are only a few rules. Avoid using the words "the," "and," and "but," as well as the letters *a*, *l*, and *f*.

We don't want to reveal any more details since you should experience this for yourself. Pay very close attention to how you carry out this task and notice any states of consciousness you might experience. After writing and proofreading the letter, leave it alone for a few days. Then proofread it again.[4]

If you find the letter to be completely perfect with no errors when proofreading it the second time, the exercise is over. If this is not the case, keep repeating the procedure until you've obtained this result.

Just a hint—with this exercise, you can become aware of the tiniest little components of your reality that have no meaning alone, in this case the letters of your language. Such components influence our patterns of perception in all areas of life, even that which we consider to be true and untrue. As you know, "it's the little things that count" and this holds true in working with states of altered consciousness as well. Especially in the beginning, it's vital that you learn to recognize these countless components of your reality and their significance. Only then can we actually become "master builders" (as Freemasons say) of our reality, not overlooking the "little" details in our quest for finding overall correlations, and treating these just as carefully and respectfully as the entire thing.

EXERCISE 16

PENDULUM TRAINING (I)

If you don't already have one, get yourself a pendulum. Shape and size are unimportant for the time being; at first, you can even use a key or ring tied to a piece of string as long as the pendulum isn't too heavy. (A builder's plumb bob is usually too heavy.) You can find a wide variety of good pendulums in New Age specialty shops; spiral pendulums usually react most sensitively, are relatively light, and can be made of various materials (e.g., brass, copper, or sometimes even silver or gold). But the most important thing is that you find a pendulum that you like.[5]

Collect several photographs of men and women (clippings from magazines will work in a pinch as well). Only one person should be pictured on each photo. Place the photos facedown on the table and mix them up well enough so that you can't recognize them from the back side. To help you forget, you might even want to leave them on the table for awhile (even a few hours) before you continue.

Now sit comfortably in front of the pictures and rest your elbow on the table so that your forearm is vertically straight. Hold the pendulum between your middle and forefinger and let it hang about one to two inches above the first photo. Wait until the pendulum stops moving. Then ask the pendulum whether the person on the first photo is male or female. Let the pendulum swing freely but never try to help it along. If you really want, you can suggest to yourself that the pendulum should move, for example, counterclockwise for a female and clockwise for a male, but it's really better if you experiment and discover your own individual patterns of movement. Write down your successes and failures. Don't repeat this exercise too frequently or you'll get tired too fast; two or three times a week for fifteen minutes each is plenty for the start. Don't be disappointed if you don't get the best results at first. This form of subtle or magical perception often takes time and practice.[6]

EXERCISE 17

APPLIED PARADIGM SHIFTING IN PRACTICE (II)[7]

Take something that you're absolutely convinced is true; either wait until you can convince yourself of something, or take an example of a doctrine or belief that you're already convinced of. Then swear to yourself that the opposite is true until both have neutralized each other. It doesn't matter what kind of "truths" these are—you can work just as well in the fields of religion or philosophy, psychology or science, emotion or perception, partnership or sexuality, career or hobby.

Here are some concrete examples:

a) You completely believe in reincarnation. "Missionize" yourself until you completely reject any theory of reincarnation, believing it to be nothing but humbug. However, all of your contemplations should be rationally founded. Then proceed according to step c.

b) On the other hand, if you're completely convinced of the value of homeopathy, turn into an fanatic allopathist for a while (at least for a few weeks).

c) Then return to your original viewpoint and analyze it by using the new insights you've gained (or the fanaticism that you've just toiled to rid yourself of), and repeat this exercise until you're able to support any possible position at any time without your previous insistence of absoluteness.

Working with scientific truths requires a certain amount of background knowledge; at first you should stick to those areas you already know a lot about. These could even be trite things, or emotionally charged "truths" that usually seem more like habits than anything else. For example, a person who absolutely loves horseback riding might develop a temporary aversion to this pastime, or a person who's fanatic about the Japanese culture may concentrate on the negative aspects of it for awhile, while a determined heterosexual may focus on homosexuality, and so on.

We don't want to dictate exactly what areas you should choose for this exercise; even any time periods stated are merely recommendations. However, for the start it would be wise to stick to one certain paradigm for at least a week (if not longer) since frequent paradigm shifting from one day to the other (or, as practice sometimes requires, one second to another!) can cause certain difficulties for the beginner.

With the help of this exercise, you'll find it much easier to comprehend the hodgepodge of different symbolic elements that's typical to Western magic; for example, using kabbalistic formulas for the assumption of Egyptian god-forms while reciting Indian mantras and ancient Greek hymns. It will save you the trouble of first having to familiarize yourself with every single area these symbols are taken from.

That's why we recommend that you practice this exercise as often as you can and not a minute of your time will be wasted!

Make sure you write down any observations about your states of consciousness. Your goal is to achieve the undifferentiated (not fixed) energy potential, which is the source of all magic, as we've mentioned before.

EXERCISE 18

PRACTICE OF THE LESSER RITUAL OF THE HEXAGRAM (I)

Perform at least two Lesser Rituals of the Hexagram with various planetary powers. It would be best to start with Jupiter and then try out Mercury. (Try to find out for yourself why we recommend this!) In any case, avoid the sun ritual for now since it requires thorough experience with all of the other planetary powers first, as we'll discuss in the next section in more detail.

Follow the basic structure of the planetary rituals listed below, but leave out numbers 4 and 5 (which is why they're in brackets). Here's how you should proceed:

1. Lesser Banishing Ritual of the Pentagram
2. Meditation on the planetary powers
3. Lesser Ritual of the Hexagram (invoking)

[4. Invocation of the planetary power (hymn)]

[5. Practical work with the planetary power invoked]

6. Dismissal of the planetary power
7. Final meditation
8. Lesser Banishing Ritual of the Pentagram (with license to depart)

Feel free to meditate on the planetary powers in any way you like; at first you'll probably just be concentrating on memorizing their characteristics and qualities. That's just fine for this stage in your training.

Dismissing the planetary powers at this stage means just letting them fade away or saying a short word of thanks. Do this even if you didn't noticeably feel anything because these rituals often work in a very subtle way that's nearly impossible to sense at first.

Again, write down all of your impressions in your magical diary.

HARDENING OF THE MAGICIAN'S AURA[8]

Let's return to the importance of the magic circle. In the opinion of some modern authors, it's only necessary for extreme magical operations. Stephen Mace, for example, says it's only needed for (a) blood sacrifices and (b) the evocation of spirits and demons to the point of physical appearance. He feels that the protection of the magician's aura is more important here. If it's "hardened," the magician needs no other special protective ritual: "A bright, firm aura, hardened by years of regular banishing and blazing under the force of a wizard's words of power, is his best protection against obsession, possession, and psychic attack."

No matter how reluctant the beginner is, the key phrase to the above quotation is "years of regular banishing." Only after years of practice can magical protection become an automated process, which can often be seen in great magicians and shamans although they may no longer do any regular exercises anymore.[9]

However, the "passion," which is equally as important, can only be obtained through intense, dedicated practice. Not until magic has become a passion that's satisfying and fulfilling, and when you have no choice but to answer the question "Why do you do all that?" like Carlos Castaneda's Don Juan ("Because there's no other way to live"), only then can you expect magic to become an automated or integrated function that completely reprograms the censor, which turns magic into a daily matter of fact and tinkers within the same way magic is used to tinker with your profane reality.

But with passion we don't mean the overhasty enthusiasm of the beginner who's so thrilled with the new world that has suddenly opened up to him or her through magic that one often takes the tenth step before the first and scoffs at words like "patience" and "persistence"—and who often takes a hard fall just as suddenly as it all came, losing ambition as soon as it turns into hard work. It's not the short-lived spark but the roaring fire deep in your soul that will really make you progress in magic; it's the secret pounding of your heartbeat saying "I want, I want, I want" that makes you strive for more: for perfection, for mastery, and for completion, even if this is as far away as the end of our galaxy or our universe.

Regardless of these psychological considerations, there are a number of magical exercises that can be used for hardening the aura and constructing an automatic warning signal system. The first exercise that we're already familiar with is the Kabbalistic Cross, and the second is the Lesser Banishing Ritual of the Pentagram.[10]

The third is the Lesser Ritual of the Hexagram and the fourth is the IAO formula described later in this section along with its first practical application. Further recommendations are listed in the practical exercises section.

So even if it's a bit early to present the heretical idea that magical circles are "basically unnecessary" apart from a few special operations,[11] we don't intend to downplay your magical practice so far or cause mass confusion. But rather our intention is to give you a quick look into the future of what magical practice has in store for us as magicians and which course our ship should actually be taking.

The techniques alone are no guarantee for magical protection and successful magic. Only persistent practice itself could even come close to guaranteeing this. The fact that there are so many different magical systems in the world that are all equally effective just proves that it's not important what the magician actually does during one's training, but how and—last but not least—how long one actually does it. Nonetheless, even thirty years of training won't lead to any kind of success if the basic approach is wrong and magical perception is never developed.

---

1. Named after the Greek letter tau, which resembles a T form.
2. This rule is generally heeded worldwide with one exception—the Afro-American religions of Voodoo, Macumba, Candomblé, and Santeria, which occasionally use everyday items such as kitchen knives and plates. These religions work with the trance techniques of intentional possession and full trance—methods that Western magic tends to avoid since it's extremely difficult to control. In these religions, continual charging is neglected, which means that rituals are often held for days on end until the actual goal of the ceremony has been achieved.
3. Interestingly, these are the powers that shamans actually prefer working with. This example alone illustrates the strong ideological contrast between "primitive" tribes and "technocentric" cultures!
4. It might make sense to let a neutral friend proofread the letter once or twice since our goal here is to achieve objective and not subjective perfection.
5. Beginners, if you've never worked with a pendulum before for an extended period of time, you'll have to get accustomed to it first. Remember that the pendulum represents a direct link to your subconscious and needs to be trained. Instead of explaining the usual programming methods here, we prefer to get straight to the practice.

6. Not every magician is good with the pendulum. Some may be much better with a dowsing rod, for example. In this case, the magician could use any type of rod instead of the pendulum. But you should try working with the pendulum for at least a few months before moving on to another method.
7. This exercise continues where Exercise 10 left off and moves on from there.
8. The quotations in this section were taken from *Stealing the Fire From Heaven: A Technique for Creating Individual Systems of Sorcery* by Stephen Mace—a highly recommended book.
9. We can see the same in well-trained hatha yogis who only need to practice their asanas once or twice a month at best, whereas the average person usually requires many hours of daily training to stay in good physical and mental shape, and nonetheless will still never achieve the same degree of mastery.
10. Of course, all magical exercises contribute to this. We're only talking about exercises that specifically fulfill this purpose.
11. Angular ritual traditions, for example, almost always do without.

MANTRA MEDITATION (I)

INTRODUCTION TO MANTRA MEDITATION

Mantra meditation is understood as the teachings of the magical effects of linguistic sounds. The Sanskrit word *mantra* basically means "magical mystical phonetic formula," and has been a permanent part of the language of Western esotericism for a good hundred years.

Mantra meditation is a highly complicated subject that we'll be touching on again and again in the course of this book without ever possibly being able to exhaust it. However, if we can only understand the basic structure of magical mantras, we'll be able to effectively utilize the magic of sound in our work without any great deal of knowledge about religion and linguistic history.

Every mantra used magically serves mainly one purpose: to induce gnosis or a state of magical trance. For now we don't need to concern ourselves with the extremely complicated theories that characterize Indian and Hebrew mantra meditation. It's enough to remember that, in Hindu and Jewish traditions (but not only here), Sanskrit and Hebrew were considered to be among the "primeval languages of creation." Sanskrit in particular was considered to be a source of power in Hindu culture and its mastery was thought to make the magician divine. "In the beginning was the word"; this biblical quotation can be applied here quite well; the person who masters the subtle energies of such a sacral and ritual language can become a creator. Similar thoughts can be found in Hebrew and Latin, and at times such power has also been ascribed to the Arabic used in the Koran. This is the macrocosmic approach.

The microcosmic approach is more concerned with the effect that mantras have. Let's forget for awhile about the thesis of the "objective" power that mantras contain and experiment with the effects that can be achieved with certain mantras. We don't want to deny the fact that some literature on mantra meditation even warns against such "profane use" of mantras. But experience has shown that in such cases these sources generally support a dogmatic-religious perspective that has nothing to do with practical experience in magic.[1]

For now we're not interested at all in the "meaning" that a certain mantra might have.

Strangely, we even agree with the dogmatic-religious practitioners of mantra meditation when they say that the "holy" mantras have a meaning of their own that's entirely beyond the comprehension of the person who uses it.[2]

For now, the important thing to remember is that mantras are combinations of sounds used for the following purposes:

a) bringing about gnosis
b) bringing about magical effects

They have other functions as well, including:

c) blocking out disruptive external influences
d) increasing concentration
e) causing a state of empty mind
f) improving magical powers and perception

Some parts of a) automatically overlap with c)–f) but there's no need to go into detail on that right now.

In practice we'll notice that there's quite a difference whether we use Hebrew, Sanskrit, Tibetan, Arabic, or Japanese mantras—all of these languages have a unique, unmistakable energy quality and therefore cause different forms of gnosis. We'll have the opportunity to experiment with this soon.

Before we wrap up our first section on mantra meditation for now, we'd like to touch on the various ways of using mantras (called "japa mantra" in Sanskrit). In general, Indian tradition says there are three ways to intone mantras:

1) loudly
2) softly
3) silently

Silent or mental intonation is considered in many mantra schools to be the "highest" form, although this most likely describes the subtleness of the energy involved and isn't meant to be a moral evaluation. Logically, the type of intonation used should be chosen according to the purpose. The comparatively subtle energy achieved through silent or mental intonation isn't always desired, so we should think functionally and choose accordingly. As a rule of thumb, intoning mantras loudly can block out external impulses and enable a state of trance, while soft intonation is best for concentration and self-reflection; silent intonation, on the other hand, creates the spiritual-astral detachment from the physical body.

As we already know from sigil magic, the magician can create one's own mantras (or acoustic sigils) and "words of power." Although these mantras are created from one's common everyday language, they're abstracted in such a way that they no longer resemble it in the end.

To wrap up this theoretical section, let's move on now to the practice of mantric sigils, which will help us prepare step by step for our practical work with traditional mantras later on.

---

1. The religious cosmos isn't meant to be explored independently (that would be sacrilege) but rather it's meant to be tolerated and accepted—in this sense, it's also static. The magical cosmos, on the other hand, is dynamic and knows (at least ideally) no fixed laws and can only be explored through the magician's own personal experience. In a sense, this magical cosmos is even created this way in the first place.

2. In the same sense, it would be wise from a magical point of view to keep Latin as the language used in Catholic Mass, and many members of the church felt the same right up to the Second Council.

PRACTICAL SIGIL MAGIC (II)

MANTRIC SIGILS

Up until now, we've only learned the word method of sigil magic. Now we'd like to introduce the mantric sigil method. As opposed to the word method, mantric sigils are usually not charged or activated spasmodically, but rather through rhythmic, monotonous recitation.[1] This method has both advantages and disadvantages. Probably the most significant disadvantage is the amount of time required for the operation. Using spasmodic charging (the word and picture method), the entire magical operation takes just a few minutes, while reciting sigils can often involve hours or even days of work. Plus mantric sigils are more noticeable—at least when they're recited out loud and not silently, which is generally the rule. That's why they can't really be activated unless you have your privacy.

But there are advantages as well. Firstly, many magicians feel that mantric sigils are more "organic" and don't just "hit your head with a sledgehammer" like sigils charged with the word or picture method often do. Secondly, the monotonous repetition of seemingly meaningless mantras often opens some magicians' subconscious minds much further than the death posture does—which sex magic charging often achieves as well. Thirdly, mantric activation generally works well for magicians who already have some experience with methods of verbal suggestion or hypnosis, and auditory people such as musicians often have success with this method as well. Fourthly, remember that even mantric sigils are most effective when you forget what they're about. As opposed to other methods of sigil magic, reciting mantric sigils has the advantage that you automatically forget or repress its meaning after awhile.[2]

Furthermore, using only the vowels *I, A,* and *O* when intoning mantric sigils has proven most effective. For some reason it seems that the subconscious reacts better to these sound combinations.

Below you'll find a modern exercise that's based on the ancient gnostic IAO formula and specifically utilizes its effects. Maybe you should experiment with mantric sigils a bit by using different intonations for the same operation. For example, you could use the acoustic sigil "BILAKO" on the first day, "BALAKA" the next, and "BELUKO" the following day while paying attention to which vowel combination feels best. The order of the vowels *I-A-O* doesn't always have to stay the same; we can mix them up any way we like (e.g., *O-A-I, I-O-A, A-O-I*), which the ancient gnostics did as well.

THE IAO FORMULA

Lots has been written about the so-called IAO formula, although it's not always easy to define exactly what this means in a magical sense. The vowel combination *I-A-O* played an important role in late ancient gnosticism, and even Aleister Crowley liked to use it a lot.[3]

We don't want to get into the philosophical and symbolic meaning of the IAO formula just yet since personal experience and practice is much more important right now. Besides, we also want to prove that a majority of magical techniques will work automatically without a lot of ideological background knowledge or philosophical "facts" as long as the appropriate state of gnosis is reached.

Instead of making a bunch of philosophical-mystical statements here, I'd rather introduce a practical exercise that I designed myself and explain it in detail.

It's an energizing and protection exercise with effects similar to those of the Kabbalistic Cross, but not as complicated and in some ways even more effective. It's predominately used to "harden" the magician's aura, which in turn allows for optimal magical protection.

WORKING WITH THE IAO FORMULA

At first, the IAO formula should always be practiced while standing, but after awhile you should try other positions as well.

The I Formula

Stand upright with your feet together; you can face the east if you like. With your eyes closed (or half closed, if you're already experienced with this meditation technique), vibrate the vowel *I* long and sustained: "Iiiiiiiiiiiiiiiiihhhhhh."

At the same time, imagine a vertical ray of light entering your body at the top of your head, traveling through your body and exiting at your feet, disappearing into the floor. The current doesn't flow in any certain direction; however, with a bit of practice it will usually feel like it's flowing up and down at the same time in rhythm with your breath. This ray is a continuous current, so it's not like a single "lightning flash." Feel the strong flow of energy in your body. Often it will feel like a warm, prickling sensation or a feeling of power and might.

If you think you're up to it, try imagining this light ray in shimmering white right from the start. If you have trouble doing this, just practice for a few weeks without visualizing the color, and then try again.

This joins the macrocosm with the microcosm; the Chinese call this the "union of heaven and earth." It harmonizes your powers and creates a feeling of unison between your "above" and "below." This part of the IAO formula also supports inspiration and opens the crown chakra to your universe of information.

The A Formula

Still standing upright with closed (or half-closed) eyes, spread your arms out to the sides and vibrate the vowel *A* long and sustained: "Aaaaaaaaaaaaaaaaaahhhhhh."

At the same time, imagine a continual, horizontal current of energy penetrating your body horizontally and exiting from the left and right sides, shooting far out in both the directions it came from. The current doesn't flow in any fixed direction; it actually feels like it's moving from left to right and from right to left at the same time. Feel the strong flow of energy in your body. Often it will feel like a warm, prickling sensation or a feeling of power and might.

If you think you're up to it, try imagining this light ray in shimmering red right from the start. If you have trouble doing this, just practice for a few weeks without visualizing the color, and then try again.

This joins the left and right sides, giving and taking, doing and enduring; the Chinese call this the "union of yin and yang." It activates your powers and creates a feeling of unison between your "right" and "left." This part of the IAO formula is also used for creating and maintaining a spiritual and physical balance and opens the hand chakras to your universe of information.

This is inner centering and it's similar in function to that of the magical circle. It concentrates your powers and puts yourself in the center of your own cosmos.

The O Formula

Still standing upright with closed (or half-closed) eyes, let your arms hang to the sides of your body and vibrate the vowel O long and sustained: "Ooooooooooooooooooohhhhhh."

At the same time, imagine a continual current of energy shaped as a double circle of about five feet in diameter that surrounds your body vertically and horizontally. The current doesn't flow in any fixed direction; it actually feels like it's rotating to the left and to the right from above and below at the same time. Feel the strong flow of energy surrounding your body. Often it will feel like a warm, prickling sensation just above your skin or a feeling of power and might.

If you think you're up to it, try imagining this circular current in shimmering blue right from the start. If you have trouble doing this, just practice for a few weeks without visualizing the color and then try again. Now you can expand this double O circle to a diameter of about twenty feet regardless of how well you can visualize it at this stage.[4]

This is inner centering and it's similar in function to that of the magical circle. It concentrates your powers and puts yourself in the center of your own cosmos.

This part of the IAO formula is also used for creating and maintaining a spiritual and physical balance and a sense of security and confidence, and it reduces your magical vulnerability and makes you the master of your own universe of information.

You don't need to vibrate the letters real loud, but you should try to do it as powerfully as possible. With a bit of practice, you'll find the exact method that's just right for you (volume, pitch, length of vibration, etc.).

The IAO formula is used for magical protection as well as for centering and storing energy. It can also be used effectively prior to healing operations. We also like to use it before and after the Lesser Banishing Ritual of the Pentagram as well as after every strenuous magical operation that requires a great deal of energy. Furthermore, it can be used when working with your magical double or in magical operations for influencing others, and can be used by magicians who prefer it over the Kabbalistic Cross and can be used in its place as well as in other exercises for centering and storing energy. Plus, the IAO formula can be performed without risk at any time and as often as you want.

EXCURSION: A MAGICIAN'S VULNERABILITY (I)

The magician Gurdjieff dedicated his entire life to "the war against sleep," as he called it. This is, by the way, the title of a study on Gurdjieff by Colin Wilson that's well worth reading. He understood sleep to be something similar to what the ancient gnostics believed—living in the nonawareness of one's true destination. Searching for the answers to the three gnostic questions ("Who am I? Where did I come from? Where am I going?") means waking up from what Colin Wilson called "habitual neurosis."

In contrast to earlier times, only a handful of magicians still believe that there's a general answer to these questions or to the "meaning of life". People's thoughts and perceptions have become too sophisticated, the relationships in which they think and act too complicated, to conform without resistance to the seemingly simple explanations of the past. With this, we have no intentions of putting down the wisdoms of the past. On the contrary, if we look at these wisdoms a bit closer and more undogmatically, we just might realize that they're not that simple after all, but it was actually their unreflected and even silly interpretation that distorted our view of true versatility and flexibility for quite a long time. The heritage of the Renaissance and the Enlightenment didn't make a real impact on magic until late in our modern times, but that impact is the individual is ruthlessly placed in the center of one's own universe so that one finally learns to assume responsibility for his or her own life and image of reality instead of hanging on the skirts of some father or mother god, "divine" commandments, imposed morals and ethics, church, or community—only striving to become a perfectly functioning agent or slave to someone else's will in the hopes of getting a nice spot in the sun in the afterlife, of being forgiven of all sins, of "positive karma," or of social recognition—that have been luring "humanity" for thousands of years like carrots dangling in front of a donkey's nose so that it parries and tirelessly continues to plod into dead ends. Instead, modern magic wants everyone to have self-determination and be able to act on one's inner experience and wisdom, which in no way means one is immoral or irresponsible just because he or she won't let any church or secret order dictate one's ethics with a "monopoly of the truth."

Until this goal is actually reached, there's a long road ahead of us with lots of obstacles—and this surely applies to each and every one of us. A magician's vulnerability can be as individual as one's goals in life. This is why we can't possibly list all the stumbling blocks here; we can only list a few of the most common ones and give you tips on how to deal with them constructively. We'd like to take a closer look at one of these stumbling blocks: habit.

The Power of Habit

Sometimes we forget that everyday sayings and quotations can often be an informative lesson in the way of perceiving things. A phrase like "the power of habit" that we use daily—yes, almost habitually—without even thinking of its true meaning should actually make us suspicious. In fact, habit generally has such a great deal of power over us that (a) it can become a serious obstacle in modern magic when working with the important technique of paradigm shifting, but also (b) it can be utilized for intentionally acquiring new habits that can benefit our magic.

That's why it's also necessary to get an exact picture of our own habits and study them as thoroughly as possible until we find their source. None of this is half as easy as it sounds. The majority of our habits are anchored in our subconscious and therefore quite difficult to track down. We're often surprised when friends or acquaintances point out habits we never even knew we had. It's even more difficult to find out the cause of such habits since they're usually quite complex and can't be put into exact words—at best we might have a hunch about their origin. That's why we should start with habits that are more obvious, such as smoking, or needing that morning cup of coffee, or having to watch the news or sports every day, and so on. When searching for the causes, don't be satisfied with superficial explanations such as "I smoke because I like smoking." Maybe you like eating ice cream, too, but you'd never devour twenty to sixty ice cream bars a day for years on end or get all jittery when you don't have any in the house, unless you're really addicted! The line separating habit and addiction is often very fine, and one of the main characteristics of an addiction is the stubborn denial that it exists. If you've been convincing yourself for years that you "can quit anytime" if you set your mind to it, prove it by quitting, for example, for six months or even two years or even just a week, or smoking twenty cigarettes one day and just three the next, ten the next, one the next, and so on, until your smoking has become completely unpredictable. You can even use a die as a magical means of deciding how many to smoke that day.

We don't intend to encourage smoking in any way, nor do we want to condemn it—each person needs to decide for oneself if he or she's willing to accept the health risk involved or not. In any case, those old books about magic are full of nonsense when they claim that a magician absolutely should not smoke, drink alcohol, or eat meat and must remain sexually abstinent. The insignificance of such strict demands is pretty clear when we keep in mind that someone like Franz Bardon prohibited his aspiring initiates from smoking, but was a chain smoker himself!

Smoking is a good example though because it's widespread and gives us the opportunity to deal with it quite intensely as a habit and/or addiction. If you're a nonsmoker, try the same with an eating or drinking habit, sexual habit, or something similar. In the practical exercises section, you'll find more helpful hints on how to work with this theme.

From the above, it's also clear that the magician needs to put aside magic from time to time so one doesn't become addicted to the habit and turn into its slave instead of its master. But first, you need to build up at least one year of magic routine before that could ever happen.

---

1. Often called "chanting," which actually means to sing liturgically.

2. This holds true for words in general. Try mumbling the word "cheesecake" for a half hour straight, and it won't take long before you don't even realize what you're saying anymore—you'll have to consciously focus on reactivating this information.

3. To clarify things, we'd like to point out that the term "formula" is used in magic similar to the way it's used in mathematics or chemistry. The dictionary defines "formula" as "a series of letters, numbers, or words used to concisely describe a situation." Applied to magic, there's another definition: "A short sen-

tence or expression used to clarify a thought." Actually, magical formulas are often a combination of the two. Sometimes they're just letter abbreviations, such as the IAO formula described here, or our mathemagical structural formulas (e.g., the symbol-logical fuzzy relation), but at times they're made up of mnemonic phrases or words with a practical background, such as in the formulas "V.I.T.R.I.O.L.," "Thelema,, or "93/93" (a Thelemic greeting that combines the words "Thelema" and "agape" by using their kabbalistic numerical values).

4. These are merely suggested distances; in cases of doubt, always trust your own intuition.

PLANETARY MAGIC (III)

LEARNING THE CORRESPONDENCES (I)

Before we continue our introduction to planetary magic and the hexagram ritual, we'd like to discuss a few of the basic aspects of working with magical correspondences since these directly affect our ritual practice.

The word "correspondence" also means "allocation" or "conformity," but we'll stick to "correspondences" since this is the term most commonly used in magical literature. Instead of "correspondences" we could also say "analogies," which has been quite a popular word in more recent times. The latter basically means the same but gives it a slightly different slant.[1] "Analogy" means "similarity," but not necessarily equality or identity. With the help of correspondences, the magician structures his universe in such a way that helps him develop possible microcosmic solutions to macrocosmic problems—a process that will become clearer to you with practice. This is a reference to the so-called law of analogies, according to which similar or corresponding things exist in a subtle relationship of cause and effect.

Particularly in dogmatic magic, these correspondences have been used and abused, for example when they were understood as "objective" and therefore incontestable. A dogmatic magician, for example, would try to convince you that the metal lead only belongs to the planetary principle of Saturn and in no way to Venus or the moon. He would argue that if you would perform a moon ritual and use the metal lead, the operation would be destined to fail from the start. In this way he thinks similar to a chemist conducting a laboratory experiment—his image of the world prevents him from randomly substituting sodium with potassium or helium if a specific result is expected. Ramsey Dukes used a different example of a chemist looking at a little pile of table salt (sodium chloride); the chemist shook his head in disbelief and mumbled, "No one can tell me that there's chlorine in this stuff!" Dukes explains that it would be wrong to believe that the metal lead would in any way "contain" Saturn in the same way that sodium chloride contains chlorine.

Especially in such a scientific world like ours is today, it's of great importance that the magician not succumb to the temptation of mixing up the reference planes and correspondences by equating similarity with identity. This is not only unscientific thinking, but it also creates unnecessary problems that could stunt our magical growth by years and even decades, because, among other things, this disguises the subjective character of the correspondences.

The practical use of correspondences results less from the structure that they impose on the otherwise seemingly chaotic cosmos, but more from the wide variety of ways to apply them that they offer us. As Ramsey Dukes says in *LIBER SSOTBME*:

> *In Ritual Magic, we learn to form attributions both by meditating and observing, but instead of passively studying the state of affairs in order to prophesy—as does the diviner—we deliberately set up an unnatural concentration of appropriate factors in order to precipitate a desired event (a parallel with a laboratory experiment).*

Within certain (although strict) limits, the correspondences are principally random and arbitrary. Whether we allocate the metal lead (as in one of the many contradictory traditions)[2] or iron to Saturn is of no significance as long as we remain consistent and don't use lead once and iron the next time and then copper the next, because experience has shown that this will badly confuse the subconscious, which will lead to entirely unpredictable results. These limits shouldn't concern us right now since this would just increase the flood of information and possibly even distract you from your actual practice. More important, on the other hand, is the fact that the correspondences create an artificial one-sidedness during magical rituals that's absolutely necessary for carrying out our operations. For example, if we wanted to work with the planetary principle of Jupiter, we would banish everything from the temple that doesn't correspond to this planet or that may even negate or work against it. This is an act of symbolic concentration, which we can also observe in pathological form in hysteria—only that here it happens intentionally and in a controlled manner, which is why it leads to the desired success in the end.

You should always keep in mind that the correspondences need to be experienced and lived through practice if they're to be of any value. Simply stated, regardless of whether you adopt the fixed correspondences sanctioned through tradition or create your own, you need to bring them to life through your own practice if they're meant to be more than just intellectual games.

Once we've thoroughly spiritualized our system of correspondences, it has the advantage of enabling fast and flexible reactions. We don't need long to find the right tools and can act immediately since everything reflects a subjective meaning and can be put in relation to the whole without having to waste too much time on searching for reasons.[3]

I think Mace probably summarized the process of implementing correspondences most clearly: "[T]he wizard distinguishes many different types of available power, dresses each with its own symbol and name, and then calls them up when he needs them through the means of meditation, chanting (mantra), dance, and even sexual activity."

However, modern freestyle sorcerers don't attempt to structure the powers they work with into a universal, generally valid system. In fact, they generally don't use many traditional symbols at all, but only those that are a product of their own subconscious mind. But this process is usually a long, thorny path that we'd like to shorten for you with our information in the next sections.

In the next two charts, you'll find the most significant traditional correspondences of planetary magic that are especially relevant for ritual practice. For the most part, they were taken from the systems of the Golden Dawn and Aleister Crowley. After that, we'll be giving you more information on how to use these correspondences in practice by giving and explaining a sample ritual outline.

If you feel it's important that your training should include these traditional elements as well, then you should memorize these correspondences in the long run until they're stored deep inside and can be recalled automatically anytime. Only then can you ever hope to be able to apply these meaningfully and clearly for structuring your magical life in such a way that results in successful practice.

Please don't forget that the planets are correspondences themselves! After all, we're dealing here with the linking and expansion of analogies.

We also need to avoid misleading equations such as "planet = gemstone," "number = color," etc. that have unfortunately been used excessively in the past. Once again, we're not dealing here with mathematical equality or identity, but rather with analogous correspondences. Using an everyday example, we don't say that the color red is the same as "love" or the color black is the same as "mourning"—these colors merely reflect their individual correspondences! Not until we've thoroughly comprehended this are we able to fully take advantage of the symbol-logical fuzzy relation effectively and no longer need to waste our time with pseudo-scientific pseudo-problems such is what are the "true" corresponding plants for a certain planet or which frequency do they "vibrate" at.

Planet	Symbol	Number	Day of Week	Metal/Color/Gemstone/ Scent/Plant/Formula
Sun	☉	6	Sunday	m = gold c = yellow, gold g = heliotrope, topaz s = olibanum, cinnamon/ "all glorious odours" p = acacia, laurel, wine f = YOD-HE-VAU-HE ELOA VA-DAATH
Moon	☽	9	Monday	m = silver c = white, silver g = moonstone, crystal, pearl s= jasmine, ginseng/ "all sweet, virginal odours" p = damiana, mandrake, almond f = SHADDAI EL SHAI

Planet	Symbol	Number	Day of Week	Metal/Color/Gemstone/ Scent/Plant/Formula
Mercury	☿	8	Wednesday	m = mercury, brass c = orange (yellow) g = (fire) opal, agate s = styrax, mastic/ "all fugitive odours" p = moly, sage, peyote f = ELOHIM TZABAOTH
Venus	♀	7	Friday	m = copper c = green g = emerald, turquoise s = rose, myrtle/"all soft, voluptuous odours" p = rose, myrtle, clover f = YOD-HE-VAU-HETZ ABAOTH
Mars	♂	5	Tuesday	m = iron c = red g = ruby s = pepper, tobacco, dragon's blood/"all hot, pungent odours" p = oak, nettle, nux vomica f = ELOHIM GIBOR

Planet	Symbol	Number	Day of Week	Metal/Color/Gemstone/ Scent/Plant/Formula
Jupiter	♃	4	Thursday	m = tin c = blue (royal blue) g = amethyst, sapphire s = horsetail, saffron/ "all generous odours" p = olive, shamrock f = EL
Saturn	♄	3	Saturday	m = lead c = black, brown g = onyx s = asant, scammonia, indigo/ "all evil odours" p = yew, cypress, nightshade f = YOD-HE-VAU-HEH ELOHIM

Chart 15: The planets and their most significant correspondences

INTRODUCTION TO THE HEXAGRAM RITUAL (III)

In this section, you'll find the hexagram ritual embedded into a Mercury ritual. That should be sufficient to get you familiar with the practical application of the hexagram ritual, which is quite appropriate since it's generally used as part of a larger ritual anyway.

The only thing we'd like to explain before we start is why the sun principle shouldn't be dealt with until all of the other planets have been studied in-depth. Since the sun is not an ordinary planet, but rather the sum of all the others (although a size that's much larger than the sum of all its parts), thorough knowledge of its "parts" is required before dealing with the sun itself. This is why some older magic literature warns against practicing sun magic. For example, until we've understood the principle of Saturn, we won't be able to understand the old dictum "the core of the sun is Saturnic," or understand why the numbers 3 (Saturn) and 6 (sun) are closely related ("doubling" is not the answer). Not until then will we realize why "666" is the number of the beast, "333" is the number of the demon "Choronzon," or understand what this all means and how it can be used in practice.

The newcomer to magic—with certain restrictions based on one's individual horoscope—will generally find it easier to understand planets such as Mercury or Jupiter at first instead of Mars or Saturn for example, which is why we'd like to start with these principles before getting to the more difficult, "harder" ones.

The Ritual Outline

Although there's plenty of room for spontaneity in modern magic, this requires thorough knowledge of the material you're working with—only a magician who has truly mastered one's trade could ever hope to improvise effectively in an emergency or whenever one wants. Although I personally don't tend to be as overcautious as some magicians (predominately those from the old school) who prepare their rituals months or even years ahead of time with the fear that if the wrong correspondences are used, something might go wrong and the whole operation could be sabotaged.

But of course there are no objections to you thoroughly studying your trade. But you should never let despair prevent you from taking practical action.

The beginner in particular often has problems "styling" one's own rituals properly. Since one of the immediate main goals of a magical ceremony is "creating the right atmosphere" (which you should be well familiar with by now) or creating the proper ambience to promote the gnosis that's necessary for achieving your magical goal, you should take the same amount of care in planning a ritual as you would in planning a party (such as a housewarming party) for good friends. Admittedly, it's true that small accidents can tremendously liven up a party and unexpectedly create a very nice mood, and this applies to rituals as well. But since these happen often enough anyway unexpectedly, there's no need to plan for them artificially.

In the next chart, you'll find a sample outline of a planetary magic hexagram ritual that builds on the basic ritual structure that we've already given; this basic structure (with slight variations) will form the basis for most of our rituals for the time being. The following chart contains a complete example of such an outline for a Mercury ritual. If you want, copy Chart 16 (covering the header and footer) several times, once for each of the seven classical planets, and fill them out as time goes by, keeping them on the altar in your temple as a guide. One characteristic of rituals from the circular tradition is that they involve only a minimum amount of written preparation. The angular tradition, on the other hand, generally prefers much more elaborate rituals with a strict distribution of the various roles (usually three people are involved) that are planned right down to the smallest detail and include fixed ritual texts. Our rituals of the circular tradition, which will be the main focus of our interest for now, are designed for "household use" and can be performed without a great deal of effort or requiring outrageous tools and the memorization of long texts.

There's a certain philosophy behind all of this. In contrast to the angular tradition that's common to most magical orders where the magician is required to apply a maximum amount of external effort—from the elaborate temple equipment and paraphernalia up to the sometimes extreme baroque-sounding ritual texts and an often autocratic master of ceremony—and allowed to grow or even be forced "en masse" into a certain energy, the circular tradition concentrates on letting the magician find and develop the appropriate energies inside oneself on one's own.

Just to avoid any misunderstandings, I have no intentions of putting down the angular tradition in any way. In my opinion, it's usually just too complicated and strict for a beginner, as is any kind of related dogmatic magic.

Of course, you can also note the time and location of the ritual on the checklist, but that's not really necessary unless you want to use this means to inform a whole group of participating magicians and prepare them for the ritual.

Ritual Outline for a ________ Ritual

1. Setting up the temple/ritual site:

2. Equipment:
   a) Lighting:
   b) Correspondences
      Metal:
      Colors:
      Gemstones:
      Scents:
      Plants/incense:
      Other:

3. Ritual structure
   a) Preparation:
   b) Lesser Banishing Ritual of the Pentagram:
   c) Invoking hexagram ritual:
   d) Invocation:
   e) Concentration of the energy:
   f) Work with the energy:
   g) Word of thanks and dismissal:
   h) Lesser Banishing Ritual of the Pentagram
   i) License to depart:

Invocation text:

Chart 16: The ritual outline—checklist

Ritual Outline for a Mercury Ritual

1. Setting up the temple/ritual site:

__ Altar in the middle of the room

__ Foyer for dispute

2. Equipment:

a) Lighting: *8 yellow candles/spotlights*

b) Correspondences

Metal:	*Eight-sided brass plate*
Colors:	*orange, yellow; veil, headband*
Gemstones:	*opal*
Scents:	*ether*
Plants/incense:	*mastic and sage*
Other:	*fish, white wine, guncotton, winged sandals, dictionary, rap music*

3. Ritual structure

a) Preparation: *meditation on the intellect/language, solving of math problems/crossword puzzles, philosophical dispute*

b) Lesser Banishing Ritual of the Pentagram:	*as usual*
c) Invoking hexagram ritual:	*1. ELOHIM 2. TZABAOTH*
d) Invocation:	*see below*
e) Concentration of the energy:	*meditation, mantras*
f) Work with the energy:	*charging of a talisman, tarot reading, consumption of the offerings*
g) Word of thanks and dismissal:	*as usual*
h) Lesser Banishing Ritual of the Pentagram:	*as usual*
i) License to depart:	*as usual*

Invocation text:

Hymn to Mercury
High spirit of the intellect,
playful fool of thieves:
You give us the knowledge of knowledge itself,
in a nimble game of words and thought.
You've been invoked for ages
by the ancestors of our kind:
philosophers, magicians, and tricksters
constantly demanding your favor.
You give us your gifts with a mocking chuckle,
easy come, easy go:
Silvery, shiny Mercurius,
in just the blink of an eye
you break all patterns of static thought.
O share with me your clever ideas,
make me rich with your knowledge,
teach me to search and to strive—
and to slip through the cracks!

{then ring bell eight times}

Fra U.·. D.·.

Chart 17: Example of a ritual outline (Mercury ritual)

Comments on the Example Ritual Outline (Charts 16 and 17)

Using this example for all rituals of this type, we'd like to discuss the things you need to remember when designing a magical ceremony. Please view Chart 17 as a mere suggestion, or one example of many—it's not my intention to prevent anyone from designing his or her own ritual according to one's own ideas and needs!

Setting up the temple/ritual site

For most planetary rituals, the temple or ritual site is generally set up in the same manner. But for some operations a change might be necessary, for example traditional demon evocations that require a triangle outside of the circle. Group rituals require the room to be prepared in a certain way, too; after all, you don't want everyone to be stepping on each other's feet. Rituals from the angular tradition sometimes require pretty fancy choreography, and often a temple warden will even escort the participants to their seats.

Before beginning your work, you should always make sure that everything is in the right place; if you have to look for a tool while in magical trance, it can disrupt the ritual tremendously.

Equipment and ritual structure

Here you only need to list the equipment that's specific to this ritual, not the usual paraphernalia such as the robe, dagger, belt, and so on. Forgetful magicians, however, should remember to have a pen and paper ready on or next to the altar since you'll often receive important information during a ritual that you'll want to write down right away—it's something like dream work, in which immediate recording is the only guarantee for making progress.

The selection of specific equipment for the ritual depends on the magician's personal correspondences. That's why we'd like to point out once again that the chart shown is merely an example! The factor "lighting" is often overlooked, although this is a good way to create the corresponding atmosphere (especially in the form of colored candles or light bulbs). There may be some authors that reject any kind of electric lighting in the temple, but there are plenty of those who welcome it. In any case, modern lighting techniques can offer a number of possibilities to the experimental magician by creating the corresponding color effects that our ancestors surely would have envied—the theatrical effect of having the temple flooded with orange (Mercury) or green (Venus) light shouldn't be underestimated.

Of course, there's no limit to the number of correspondences that you can use in your temple, so let's just look at a few of the more common examples taken from the traditional magical analogies. The first item listed under 2b is an eight-sided brass plate—here you see a combination of the correspondences "8" and "brass," which is relatively common to practical magical thinking. In the same way, for a Mars operation we could use a five-sided iron ring with an embedded ruby that's decorated in blood with symbols.

The correspondences used don't need to be unique, meaning that they can be used several times in the same operation. For example, we could also put another eight-sided brass plate on a yellow- or orange-colored headband, decorate our belt with eight orange-colored, eight-sided pieces of leather, and attach an agate stone to the brass buckle. This may seem too time-consuming, or even too theatrical or kitschy, but we should always keep in mind that the subconscious mind reacts quite positively in its "childish" way to such a flood of impulses. It's well- known that nothing is more effective in magic than excess, or, as the saying goes, "The more the merrier." In this sense, it's impossible to overdo the correspondences, and any intellectual-aesthetic considerations need to be put on the back burner. In fact, many aspects of magic may seem tasteless to the aesthetically sensitive layman, but the main thing we're talking about here is functionality—just as in any other trade. If it's practiced consciously enough, it will develop a specific and autonomous aesthetic of its own that the observer needs to grow into in the same way he or she grows into the aesthetics of futurism or cubism.

The correspondences for fragrances and incense often overlap since one often takes the place of the other. In general, though, ceremonial magic differentiates between fragrances that are used as perfume or oil, and those that can be burned as incense. Knowledge of how to use them often results from practice itself. Even though fresh roses can smell sweet and remind you of Venus, dried (or even fresh) rose petals stink horribly when burned, and even the most experienced magician would have trouble associating this stench with "Venus" and "loveliness." And not every oil that smells good on the skin will smell good when it evaporates or is burned. And, to return to our example for Mercury, we definitely don't recommend trying to burn highly explosive ether—but when it's sniffed in small doses (without getting high!) it will definitely let you experience the vivacity of Mercury (but be careful with open fire—ether is highly flammable, so don't leave the container open unnecessarily!). In a similar sense, applying sage oil to your skin surely won't stimulate you intellectually (unless it occurs to you how exotic magic can be . . .), but will more likely remind you of a hospital room—but when this herb is dried and burned, it can surely have a cleansing, clearing effect.

We've summarized the so-called sacraments in the category "other" since not every ritual works with such offerings. Generally speaking, there are two ways of dealing with offerings (which applies to religion as well, by the way). The followers of the first prefer to destroy the offering after the rite (which can be done by burning or burying it), while the followers of the second prefer to consume it. The latter tradition, which I belong to myself, can again be divided into two subgroups: (a) magicians/mystics who elevate the offering, for example in Christianity where bread is equated with the body of Christ, and (b) magicians/mystics who elevate themselves to equality with the gods, who have earned the offerings and therefore consume them. The method in b) sounds most logical to me for invocations, but that doesn't necessarily mean that the other methods don't have their advantages as well: In principle, it's just a question of belief and/or temperament that each person has to answer for him- or herself. The theophagic (from the Greek *theos,* "god," and *phagein,* "to eat or devour") or "cannibalistic" method has certain advantages in a magical sense since it anchors the paradigm of taking power from the outside ("Spirit of God," "Mercy of the Highest"), which has quite a significant psychological value.

Of course, the winged sandals (which the magician most likely will have to make him- or herself) correspond to the typical form of Mercury-Hermes in his function as a messenger of the gods. The correspondences of fish (the swiftness and mobility of this aquatic animal) and white wine (the clarity and elated effect of this drink) are traditional. The dictionary is a logical correspondence if you think about the function of Mercury as a communicator (he corresponds to the ancient Egyptian god Thot, the inventor of the written alphabet). The less orthodox may think of correspondences like guncotton and rap music, but these are really just modern expansions of the traditional ones. Guncotton looks completely harmless and can be used like normal cotton fabric or absorbent cotton. But when it comes in contact with fire, it reveals its true (and quite dangerous) nature. Is there a better analogy for Mercury, who's also known as the god of thieves and rogues, tricksters and charlatans? Rap music, on the other hand, is characterized by the spoken word; lyrics and language are the main focus while the individual words are intertwined in clever symbiosis with the beats. This reflects the game Mercury likes to play with language, truth, and wit.

An important aspect of being able to magically work with correspondences is converting them into practical action. Experience has shown that this is especially effective when considered during the preparation of a magical operation. At first it may seem a bit "fake" if you start a philosophical dispute on command directly before a ritual (especially if it's with yourself!), but you'll quickly learn that such actions indeed contribute to (or even guarantee) the success of the operation. Creativity is not only desired, but is even an integral part of magic itself; only the consequent conversion of these correspondences into everyday actions and perceptions can bring them to life and enable them to share some of their power and energy with the magician.

In categories 2 and 3, there's plenty of room to add little reminders such as, in our example, the Hebrew ritual formulas. (We've left out the formula "Ararita," assuming that you've memorized it by now since it's the same for all hexagrams.) You can also note the direction the lines of the pentagram or hexagram are drawn by making little sketches, and so on.

For group work, it's important that each person knows their role in advance, which should also be noted in the ritual outline. (For example, you would write "Frater X" under 2 and "Soror Y" under 3, and so on.)

As you can see in our outline, the hymn or invocation text doesn't necessarily need to fill several pages. Although we'll occasionally provide you with examples of such hymns, you should get used to writing your own right from the start! That may be pure hell for those magicians who have little or no talent for creative writing, but the poetic value of the text doesn't really matter. After all, there are no literary standards you need to conform to and there's no need for you to strive for a Nobel Prize in literature. Plus, your hymns can be even simpler than the one I suggested; often just simply repeating the name of the planet along with "Come, come, come!" is enough to get the desired effect. In our example, you'll see that our hymn in Chart 17 mentions a whole bunch of correspondences ("spirit of the intellect," "playful fool of thieves," and so on). If you have difficulties wording your hymns poetically, then keep them short and concise and put all the more effort into assuring that your temple contains lots of correspondences.

However, you should remember the function that a hymn has in a ritual in the first place: In a way it's like a "telephone call" to finally establish contact with the desired energy. (In German, invocations are literally called *Anrufungen*, "calls.") In psychological terms, a Mercury invocation gives the subconscious mind the message that it should now activate Mercury's energies. That's why we shouldn't leave out such texts, especially in the first few years of our training, since they also represent articulations of our will (statements of intent). Later we'll be able to reduce the number of correspondences we use.

By using such correspondences regularly, our subconscious will be conditioned until it automatically associates "Mercury" with the smell of styrax or the color orange. Once you've achieved this, you'll only need to use a few correspondences to arouse the desired energy.

In any case, you should also study mythology parallel to working with planetary magic since it's usually pretty difficult to invoke a planetary god that you know nothing about. This is all a part of magical conditioning. In the Further Reading section, we'll recommend a few reference books on mythology that could be quite helpful when planning your rituals.

In the next section we'll be discussing the ritual function of incense in more detail.

PRACTICAL EXERCISES

EXERCISE 19

APPLIED PARADIGM SHIFTING IN PRACTICE (III)

These continue where Exercises 10 and 17 left off.

Make a list of your habits, trying to think of as many as possible—keep adding to this list every day for a week. You might try carrying a notebook with you at all times so that you can write down each habit immediately as it occurs to you. You can even ask friends, acquaintances, partners, and relatives about your habits that they might have noticed—often you'll be surprised at the answers!

After you've collected a fairly comprehensive list, pick one habit from the list and give it up for a week and a half. Pick a habit that you have no emotional relation to, such as taking off your glasses whenever you speak, scratching the back of your head, or eating only certain kinds of food at breakfast, and so on.

Every time you catch yourself submitting to your habit (usually "completely unconsciously and unintentionally," right?), you should give yourself a little reminder. Crowley required his students to cut their forearm with a razor blade for each transgression, which can be highly effective, but is something we definitely do not recommend for hygienic and health reasons. But the principle of "pay with pain" is not necessarily all that wrong since we've acquired many of our habits through pain (physical or psychological) in the first place, for example during our childhood. The "reminder" about your habit should certainly be unpleasant enough to encourage you to stick to your intention. However, with more and more practice you shouldn't have to rely on such tools.

For the next week and a half, try to acquire a new habit that's just as meaningless to compensate for the loss of the old one. In this way, you'll recognize how much energy is actually "eaten up" by such habits.

After a total of four weeks, start all over again with new habits. Do this for at least five months in order to really get the feel for this exercise.

In doing so, you'll learn how to free yourself from deep-seated habits by establishing and proving your independence from them—when this is achieved, you can consciously choose or reject them at will.

The preliminary goal of this exercise is for you to be able to give up a habit that's very important to you (such as smoking, morning coffee, characteristic sexual habits, evening walk, and so on) for a longer period of time without you feeling any longing for it or possibly even relapsing.

In this sense, a helpful question might be, "How would someone be able to recognize me if I were to wear a disguise/completely disfigured/invisible—for example, if I were standing in complete darkness?"

EXERCISE 20

PENDULUM TRAINING (II)

Proceed with Exercise 16 for a while until you're pleased with your progress. That might even take months, so take your time and work thoroughly before moving on to this exercise.

Get ten empty matchboxes and a piece of aluminum foil. Now hold the pendulum in the usual manner for a few minutes above the foil and pay close attention to its movements; try to keep your mind in a state of emptiness. You can even "ask" the foil which pendulum movement it has. Now put the foil inside one of the matchboxes and mix them up until you can no longer remember which box it's in. Line up the matchboxes in a row so that you can comfortably hold the pendulum above each without moving them. Of course, you can move your chair if necessary. Try to determine which matchbox contains the foil by using the pendulum as a guide.

Instead of aluminum foil, you can use any other object as long as it's small and light enough. Of course, you don't want to be able to recognize the object by its weight when you move around the matchboxes.

If you don't trust this method completely, or prefer to work with heavier objects, you can leave the room after first testing the pendulum's reaction to the object and have a friend or partner hide it in one of the boxes for you. However, we recommend that the other person leaves the room before you start with your experiment so that he or she won't influence you in any way, even if intentionally or unconsciously.

If you get good results (a success rate of 80 percent or higher would be excellent), then double the number of matchboxes—this increases your power of concentration while dowsing. Later you can also work with a combination of boxes and various different objects.

Make a note of when your success rate is higher than usual. Of course, the conditions surrounding the experiment should be as identical as possible each time. By learning to pay attention to such factors as weather, mood, planetary positions, previous or following rituals, and many other things, you're increasing your subtle or magical perception at the same time and learning how to monitor the results of your operations.

EXERCISE 21

PRACTICE OF THE LESSER RITUAL OF THE HEXAGRAM (II)

Perform at least two Mercury rituals by integrating the Lesser Ritual of the Hexagram as described in our example. Choose an object that corresponds to Mercury and charge it during every ritual with the energy of this planet by transferring it mentally through your hand.[4] This time, use the entire ritual structure given in Exercise 18 (including numbers 4 and 5). You'll be charging the object a total of eight times, just so you're mentally prepared. Concerning the rest, just perform it according to the instructions in Exercise 18.

EXERCISE 22

THE IAO FORMULA IN PRACTICE (I)

Perform the IAO formula as described in this section immediately after showering or bathing while your body's still wet.

Pay attention to your subtle perception, especially in your body. Where does the energy flow with each vowel? How do the three vowels differ in their effect?

Following the exercise, try closing your eyes and feeling the ball of energy with your hands. What do you feel?

Note all of your impressions in your magical diary.

After a while you can perform the IAO formula anytime you feel is appropriate, such as right after waking up or just before going to bed. It can also be used before and after the pentagram ritual, or before every magical ceremony.

FURTHER READING

At this time we'd like to recommend that the magician read some standard literature on mythology that will be of particular assistance when planning planetary rituals and magical operations involving traditional gods and deities.

BIBLIOGRAPHY

The quotations in this section (with the exception of Stephen Mace, see previous section) were taken from the following sources:

Ramsey Dukes, *LIBER SSOTBME*

Colin Wilson, *G.I. Gurdjieff: The War Against Sleep*

1. It's interesting to see what my German dictionary has to say about the word "analogy": "Latin: *analogica,* Greek: *analogía.* Resemblance, similarity, correspondence of relationships." It even contains the term "analogy magic": "magic intended to bring about a similar reaction through a certain action (e.g., burning human hair to weaken or even kill the person)."
2. This just happens to be the currently predominate tradition, but this certainly wasn't always the case.
3. If we run into a mishap four times in a row, we immediately "know" that we're dealing with some kind of interference in the Jupiter sphere (Jupiter = 4) and can take appropriate action to precisely find and eliminate this interference. Even if it's just our imagination, as materialistic psychology may want to convince us, it's only the effectiveness of the procedure that counts, and in this regard magic is no different than other disciplines dedicated to the study of the shaping of one's destiny (e.g., religion, psychology, or science).
4. This doesn't require any further explanation—just stick to the one basic rule of our training method: "Whenever something is not specifically explained, do it any way you like."

MANTRA MEDITATION (II)

MANTRAS AND MEDITATION

I've discovered an interesting correlation between the way a mantra is intonated and how wide the eyes are open during meditation—as far as I'm aware of, this has never been mentioned in literature before. You can meditate:

a) with open eyes

b) with half-closed eyes

c) with closed eyes

Mantras, on the other hand, can either be intonated (a) loudly, (b) softly, or (c) silently. Loud intonation is easier and more accessible; soft and especially silent intonation requires much better concentration skills and the ability to tune out external distractions. The same applies to meditation, but in the opposite order. Generally it's easier to meditate with your eyes completely closed, and more difficult when they're half-closed—and being able to meditate with your eyes open is surely a master skill! The following chart depicts this schematically.

Mantras	Meditation	DD
loud intonation	closed eyes	I
soft intonation	half-closed eyes	II
silent intonation	open eyes	III

Chart 18: Mantra and meditation techniques
(DD = degree of difficulty, increasing from I–III)

Since the quality of the energy is different in each case, we recommend that you try out several different combinations when working with mantras, for example with closed eyes while intonating softly, with open eyes while intonating silently, and so on. This will also keep you flexible in your habits.

Now we'd like to introduce some traditional mantras that you should get accustomed to working with. We'll explain how to use them later on in the Practical Exercises section.

TRADITIONAL MANTRAS[1]

OM MANI PADME HUM

("Behold the jewel in the lotus"—an invocation of Buddha.) (Tibetan)

The Tibetans pronounce "padme" more like "peme," but the pronunciation "padme" is widespread and acceptable as well among both Asians and Europeans.

OM

(According to Indian teachings, this is the "primeval syllable" of creation.) (Sanskrit)

Pronounced like a long, very nasal "aaauuuooommm."

HARE KRISHNA, HARE KRISHNA, KRISHNA KRISHNA, HARE HARE, HARE RAMA, HARE RAMA, RAMA RAMA, HARE HARE

(Invocation of Krishna and Rama.) (Sanskrit)

An old mantra with strong trance-inducing qualities that was popularized in the West by the musical *Hair* and the Krishna movement. (Also available on record and tape, which is a helpful way to get a feel for what it sounds like.)

OM NAMO SHIVAYA

("Holy is the name of Shiva.") (Sanskrit)

Used for Shivaistic meditation. Shiva, the third aspect of the Hindu trinity Brahma, Vishnu and Shiva, is not only the god of (constructive) destruction, but also the lord of the yogis and ascetics, as well as the master of meditation.

LAM VAM RAM YAM HAM OM

(The so-called seed syllables of the six lower chakras that can be used to awaken the power of kundalini.) (Sanskrit)

The uppermost chakra (sahasrara, the "1000-petal lotus") has no fixed single syllable, but uses a combination of all mantras.

OM HRAM HRIM HRUM

(Actually god-names or seed syllables, but described and implemented by many schools as being "meaningless.") (Sanskrit)

SO HAM

("I am He/That/The Infinite/God.") (Sanskrit)

Mainly used during meditation as a silent mantra.

HAM SO

(Sanskrit)

Same as SO HAM. (see above)

OM NAMO BUDDHAYA
OM NAMO DHARMAYA
OM NAMO SANGHAYA

(Seeking refuge with the Enlightened One [Buddha], with the Universal Law [dharma], and with the community of those seeking enlightenment [sangh]. (Sanskrit)

Generally vibrated loudly during *kirtan* (see below) and group meditation. Also used by the Buddhist for connecting to the group spirit for summoning the helping powers.

SHIKI FU I KU KU FU SHIKI SHIKI SOKU ZE KU KU SOKU ZE SHIKI

(Roughly: "Form is nothing but emptiness, emptiness is nothing but form, form is emptiness, emptiness is form.") (Japanese)

This mantra is recited frequently in Zen monasteries and originates from the *Prajna Paramita Sutra,* or "Great Textbook of Complete Wisdom," translated in Japanese as *Hannya Haramita Shingyô.*

LA ILLALAH (or: LA ILLALAHU)

("God is God.") (Arabic)

This Arabic mantra is widespread in the Sufi tradition, and every faithful Muslim is familiar with its recitation. It expresses the fact that the divine cannot be described in words (similar to the Chinese concept of Tao). Just like the Zen koan (a meditation riddle in the school of Rinzai Zen), it turns off your rational intellect by inducing a state of trance through paradox. In the same way, it's similar to the function of "I AM WHO I AM" (JEHOVAH/YAHWEH) in Judaism, although this Hebrew mantra is taboo for Orthodox Jews and it may never be spoken out loud.

ALAM	TASAM
ALAMAS	JAS
ALAR	KAHA JA AS
ALAMAR	CHAM
TA HAM	CHAM ASAK

These Arabic mantras are magic spells from the Koran and their meaning cannot be clearly defined. They are used in Sufism and Dervishism ("Turkish Freemasonry") and are integral parts of Rudolf von Sebottendorf's oriental-style "letter magic."

We've already mentioned that the recitation of mantras is called japa mantra in Sanskrit. If a mantra is sung loudly (in public), this is called kirtan, and is usually accompanied by music and dance. Knowledge of this special vocabulary is necessary if you want to delve deeper into the literature on this subject.

We'd like to leave it at that for now with this selection of traditional mantras since you're already familiar with a number of Hebrew formulas through your work with the two pentagram rituals and the hexagram ritual.

EXCURSION: A MAGICIAN'S VULNERABILITY (II)

Fear, A Dark Brother

Of all the human emotions, fear is probably the most dangerous, unpredictable, and most difficult to control. Fear can bind people in chains, strangle them, steal their reasonability, their self-esteem and self-respect, cause panic and hysteria, eat away at their organism, penetrate their dreams like a thorn, destroy their will, make them forget all of their duties and rights, blur their perception, stupefy their spirit—and it will constantly attack what it feeds on, attracting the dreaded, and begging for deliverance through stupefaction, through salvation, or through the desperation of just wanting to finally put an end to it all. Out of fear a friend may betray a friend, a mother her daughter, a son his father, a brother his sister; in war, fear is despised and may even be punished by death if the fearful person is an endangerment to the situation.

And yet fear is essential and may even be the most important of man's primeval instincts. Fear keeps the human organism out of danger, helps it avoid situations where it might fail and be injured, thereby ensuring the continuance of its species. Isn't this survival instinct just another expression for the fear of death, destruction, and extinction?

Consequently, it's in no way desirable to eliminate fear entirely—at least not until this instinct has learned to optimally perform its vital functions on another fear-free level without subjecting the organism as a whole to such tormenting fear to make it get out of the way of danger or render it harmless. But on the other hand, we owe thanks to the fear of freezing for architecture, the fear of starvation for farming and agriculture, and the process of food conservation and long-term food storage, and so on.

To become a fear-free person who no longer needs this alarm mechanism often involves long, hard work that could take decades or even an entire lifetime, without any guarantee of success. The magician is impatient and doesn't want to waste any valuable time (a lifetime is always way too short for magic!) waiting for this goal to be achieved. That's why the magician takes a pragmatic approach and utilizes fear where one can, in order to gain control of it little by little, so that one's finally able to decide freely which fears one wants to keep (for whatever reasons) and which ones to eliminate or convert into valuable energy. For some magical operations, fear is simply indispensable, e.g., during demon evocations and sometimes when working with the so-called "Holy Guardian Angel."

Therefore we should learn to respect fear without letting it control every aspect of our being. If fear already has control, we need to shake it off and put it back on its right course. Of course, this is much easier said than done. But the serious magician will encounter more than enough opportunities to turn the lead of fear into the gold of bravery and courage, of independence and fearlessness, and of security and composure that spring from the true love of one's self, the recognition of one's true will, and the acceptance of one's own power and might. Literally speaking, magic really has to do with growing up, and the final exam is fear itself and the way that one deals with it.

Unfortunately, there's no recipe that tells you how to do this. Usually we just work with old, time-tested methods that are often quite primitive, such as building up a counterbalance to fear by consciously experiencing things that make us afraid. For example, whoever has a fear of heights should slowly get accustomed to mountain climbing and riding elevators, and whoever is afraid of roller coasters should buy a pack of tickets and stick it out until one's fear is gone once and for all. This is a bit more difficult with psychological fears such as jealousy, fear of failure, or angst. The only thing that helps here is plenty of meditation and insight in combination with the specific and systematic building up of your self-confidence. After all, most fears are based on a lack of self-esteem, and once this is reestablished, the fears usually just disappear. Frequent meditation on death in connection with Saturn rituals and occasionally even experiencing a mystical or shamanistic death can lead to a healthier attitude toward the subject and relativize the fears and worries of everyday life.

Some fears are hidden deep down inside and are not all that easy to track down. Usually they betray themselves through unexplainable aversions and preferences, through dreams, or through "Freudian slips" that happen when you're directly and unexpectedly confronted with fear-causing things, people, or situations. Often only an experienced psychologist (meaning someone who understands human nature) is able to call these fears by their name.

Always watch for any fears that you may not have been aware of before, and expand on the knowledge you've gained in Exercise 1 by making a complete list of your present fears. Continue to add to this list whenever necessary and cross out the items once you've overcome them!

Always keep in mind that in magic, any fear you might have will attract it all the more. We can observe this especially well in our behavior with animals. If you let a strange dog know that you're afraid of it, you arouse its hunting instinct and it may even attack you. But if you face him with intrepid fearlessness, it will most likely succumb to your will or at least leave you alone.

Of course, you shouldn't overdo this work with your fears, but on the other hand it's usually fear that torments people the most and prevents them from reaching their goal of self-determination. The important thing here is to determine whether or not your fear is specific or general, and learn how to deal with the two types. In this sense, being afraid of riding an elevator is a concrete fear that can be eliminated with the help of an elevator. Angst, on the other hand, as we already mentioned, cannot be combated with such little things; it needs to be approached more thoroughly and offset with experiences of success, safety, and security until it loses its power (e.g., by building self-confidence).

LEARNING THE CORRESPONDENCES (II)

Maybe you've already asked yourself in the last section what we mean by such vague correspondences as "all glorious odours" and "all evil odours." We purposely didn't go into detail at the time, hoping that it would encourage you to think about these things on your own.

The beginner to magic usually prefers precise instructions, even concerning the exact amount and use. This is both a product of our inner insecurity and of the search for "objective" or at least tangible guidelines. Actually, such "unclear" descriptions as the ones above are usually much more useful than a specific list of herbs, ointments and oils. Categories, such as "all sweet scents" (Crowley), leave the final decision up to the magician him- or herself and support the fact that correspondences are always nothing more than "subjunctive," so that every magician is compelled to develop one's own personal system of correspondences as he or she progresses.

Our symbol-logical fuzzy relation can be applied analogously here as well. Too much precision would place more importance on the intellect and its characteristics of structure, categorization, and analytical thought, which would distract the intuition and emotion from its actual task with a flood of unnecessary, individual facts. Once again, the "science" of magic needs to step down and give the "art" of it the upper hand if it wants to achieve any kind of success. In this sense, please go back to the first section and reread our comments on this.

You'll find more information on this subject further along where we'll be discussing the function of incense in magic.

MAGIC AS A REALITY DANCE

In an article, English magician Ramsey Dukes touched on the problem of magic and the assertion of reality. People had asked him again and again "How come we Europeans with our overwhelmingly unmagical and rational view of the world and technology have been able to suppress for centuries the shamanic native peoples who supposedly have so much magical power?" Dukes' answer was unexpected yet extraordinarily insightful: "Because we're the better magicians." He explained further that magic principally means establishing a certain intentional reality and asserting it despite any possible resistance from the outside world. This is exactly what the European magician did, and in the meantime even the most remote shamans of the Amazon or the mountains of Nepal have accepted these values and try to live accordingly, for example by striving to possess technical devices such as radios, digital clocks, or guns.

If we think about this more carefully and what it has to do with our practice, namely that magic is actually "the production of reality," many things will now become clear that were previously much too indirect and complicated to explain using other models of thought. On the one hand, we can draw the conclusion that the selection of magical tools we work with is basically endless since magic includes everything that serves the purpose of creating reality—from the most insignificant everyday gesture right down to the most elaborate ceremonial spell. On the other hand, the meaning of the phrase "Magic is always the perception of magic" will also become clearer. We have to recognize (or, if necessary, "imagine") magic as such until it actually becomes "reality." Although we recognize the latter in the scientific paradigm mainly through the effects on a physical ("objective") level, magic is much more subtle. And in the end, we finally realize that we've always actively used magic to assert ourselves in life without consciously calling it that or recognizing it as such.

Such considerations inevitably lead to the question of what reality actually is—a question that both religion and philosophy as well as science and psychology have struggled to answer for thousands of years. For obvious reasons, we cannot provide a general answer to that just like the other systems cannot, but we'd like to point out that reality to a magician is not a rigid, inflexible constant, but more of a greatness that's constantly flowing and can never be clearly defined. Yes, it even goes so far to say that there are innumerable realities and that his or her main task as a magician is to take part in as many of these as possible in order to ensure one's own versatility and flexibility, therefore consequently and logically expanding one's own spectrum of action.

BIBLIOGRAPHY

Ramsey Dukes, *Blast your Way to Megabuck$ with My SECRET Sex-Power Formula: And Other Reflections Upon the Spiritual Path*

---

1. All mantras from the Sanskrit, Pali, and Tibetan languages should be recited nasally. If you're not familiar with this technique, try holding your nose for the first few times you vibrate them in order to develop a sense of what they sound like (but don't continue with this practice for too long!).

INTRODUCTION TO RITUAL MAGIC (V)

THE MAGICAL DAGGER

The magical dagger is one of the most important weapons of the traditional magician, yet at the same time it's the easiest to describe. It represents the magician's will and it is used for all important magical operations, from casting the circle to charging talismans and amulets, as well as in magical warfare and in the dissolving and binding of relationships. The dagger is used to banish and protect, and many magicians view it as their only weapon that's never allowed to be touched by anyone else.

It might be difficult for the beginner to understand how such a magical weapon can develop a life of its own, but here's an example about my own magical dagger. It's a letter opener of Mauritanian origin made out of silver that I found in Senegal. I had already been using it for quite some time when a person I knew stole it from me during a dispute we had. Without taking any magical action against the person, I just waited and swore that I would only use astral weapons from then on. After a few days of practice, I was able to do this satisfactorily and from then on I used them daily. Then about a week later, the aforementioned person gave me the dagger back voluntarily. The soft silver blade was bent and stained with blood: the result of a failed suicide attempt. I carefully took the weapon, bent the blade back into shape, wrapped it in silk, and put it in a safe place and continued to work for a long time only with astral weapons. Later, my careful actions paid off. As the dispute escalated into an all-out magical war, I could easily defend myself against my opponent and prevent or repel any further magical or physical attacks since I possessed some of his blood and was able to work with his photograph; constant failure, setbacks of both a physical and psychological nature, and magical backfiring (attacks that are not ignited properly and therefore ricochet back to the originator himself) caused him to finally give up his hopes of ever wanting to destroy me. In doing so, I no longer worked astrally, but rather I used the physical dagger along with the *mumia* (a vital force tied to bodily secretions or the secretions themselves) of my opponent.

The legend that circulates among my colleagues that I possess a dagger that "keeps coming back" is a bit exaggerated, but it's a fact that weapons of this kind often develop an individual personality and behave in ways that are completely unpredictable, and not just on a material level. That's all the more reason for a magician to handle them with care and protect them from the hands of the unauthorized—not because the weapons could lose power, which shouldn't really happen if they're charged properly, but rather due to the unforeseeable effects they might have on these people. For this reason, every experienced magician should ensure that their weapons are dealt with properly after their death.

The dagger, along with the pentacle or lamen (which we'll be discussing later), is the magician's most individualistic weapon and is a symbol of his or her magical will. Consequently, its shape and the material it's made of can be anything you like and the illustration here merely shows one of many possibilities.

We'd like to mention that some magical traditions prefer the sword instead of the dagger for banishing and the charging of objects, while others view the magic sword as a weapon that should only be used in a dire emergency and is therefore rarely used.

If the characteristic of "male/female" is considered, the dagger would represent the male principle, while the chalice, used for example in the Wiccan tradition, would represent the female; in the Hermetic tradition, the male principle is often represented by the wand with its phallic shape.

When choosing the proper weapon to use as a dagger or when making one yourself, make sure that it's easy to grip and lies firmly in your hand. The blade should be sharp and pointed, yet sturdy, firm, and free of any nicks. On the other hand, as in my case, it's possible that the right weapon just might find you (or that it "comes to life" for you) under unusual circumstances, although this may not be the ideal weapon as far as its physical characteristics are considered, you'll know if it's just right for you. In this case, always listen to your intuition and never force yourself to use a weapon that you don't really like. This applies to weapons that "speak" as well, such as a dagger that the magician may cut oneself on the first time he or she touches it, drawing blood, and so on. By the way, the things we say here about the dagger apply analogously to all magical weapons as well.

In some traditions of Western magic that are still popular today, the dagger is given less significance than in others. Crowley views it merely as a symbol of alchemistic mercury (whereby the scourge and chain respectively stand for sulfur and salt), but he prescribes that the blade be plated with gold and the handle be made or plated with this metal as well.

THE FUNCTION OF INCENSE IN RITUAL MAGIC

From the viewpoint of developmental history, our sense of smell is the oldest of all the human senses and is directly connected to the human brainstem. For this reason it tends to function on a subconscious level, which is why some scientists even claim that it's impossible to control it or to intentionally induce olfactory hallucinations. Magicians find this quite humorous, of course, since they're well familiar with systematically training their sense of smell to bring about such "hallucinations" in the first place. However, it's correct that most people have trouble controlling this sensory organ without the proper training.

In ceremonial magic, scents and smells play a vital role—and that's always been the case. Shamanistic cultures are familiar with the use of oils and incense as well, and even back in the ancient days there was actually an industry that specialized in manufacturing such sacral incense mixtures for use in private and communal ritual ceremonies. There's no Indian temple, no Buddhist pagoda, and no Shinto shrine that doesn't use joss sticks; the offering of incense may be one of the oldest human practices of all times.

In this sense, it's certainly not true (as some literature claims) that Western magic "borrowed" the ritual use of incense and similar practices from the Catholic Church—in fact, the church itself actually "borrowed" this practice from ancient pre-Christian traditions.

The use of incense has two main functions. It serves the purpose of cleansing on a physical and subtle level, and induces a certain state of mind that we call magical trance or gnosis. Since the memory of scents is often stored deep in the unconscious mind, this offers us the perfect opportunity to condition the psyche. For example, if we always burn the same incense (at least ten or twenty times) for every Mars ritual, the Mars trance will be much deeper than without such aids so that, finally, simply burning the Mars incense will be enough to induce the desired Mars gnosis.

It may disappoint you even more that magical authors can almost never agree on which scents correspond to which principles (or planets, in this case). In order to give you just one example of the numerous contradictory statements that are out there, we'd like to take a look at the incense correspondents for the planet Jupiter as given by four different authors of magical literature in the German and English languages:[1]

- Aleister Crowley: saffron; all generous scents.
- Franz Bardon: saffron alone or mixed with linseed, orrisroot, peony blossoms, betony leaves, birch leaves.
- Karl Spiesberger: saffron, ash seed, aloeswood, styrax, benzoin, lapis lazuli, mirror, peacock feather.
- James Sturzaker: ox-tongue, apple tree, ash, barley, red beech, carnation, maize, dandelion, lolium, cornus, elecampane, white fig, hazelnut, henbane, holly, horse chestnut, jasmine, nutmeg, oak, olive tree, peach tree, plum tree, poplar, grape, rhubarb, sage, wheat, agrimony, lavender.

We'll notice that at least saffron was mentioned by all three authors, although this isn't always true unless one author copies from another (which is often the case in occult literature), even if one's role model doesn't stick to the "traditional" correspondences. The word "traditional" is here in quotation marks because there really is no such thing when it comes to incense, although correspondences have often overlapped throughout magic's history.

We can therefore conclude that there is no objective list of correspondences in this field and that traditional authors often contradict each other considerably—and in our practice, we have to pay the consequences of this, meaning that every magician needs to find one's own correspondences as far as incense goes. This won't always be easy for beginners since they're not yet familiar enough with the planetary powers to make final decisions of this kind. That's why it's fine at first to buy prepackaged incense in the store that's usually mixed according to the instructions of certain authors or by other magicians who have the necessary experience.

Prepackaged incense certainly has its disadvantages as well. On the one hand, the magician creates a dependence on the suppliers and manufacturers, which could become a problem if one of these companies goes out of business or removes the product from its catalog. This is fairly common on the small (or even tiny) market for magical equipment. And once you're conditioned to a certain scent, it often requires a lot of hard work to get the same results with a new one. Plus, the passive act of buying a magical tool can lead to general passivity in other areas of magic. Last, but not least, good incense is not cheap.

On the other hand, if you decide to make your own incense you'll soon discover that this is no easy task and that it requires a fine touch and a good nose as well as patience and hard work. That's why some magicians prefer to work with as few ingredients as possible, and only with those that are easy to obtain. You can get such ingredients in a magic shop, pharmacy, or a store that sells church supplies. This applies in particular to resins. Herbs can be found in the same way; in fact, there are plenty of herbal and health food stores that sell quite a wide variety.

Some of the more traditional ingredients used in ancient times particularly in the Middle East include the following:

Styrax (or storax, liquid amber, benzoin)

This liquid balsam from the amber tree is often added to mixtures to make the smoke thicker. In liquid form, it's quite sticky and is therefore also used to bind dryer resins together, for example larger pieces of frankincense (see below). Often styrax is meant when the term "amber" is used (see "amber" below).

Galbanum (or mother resin)

A gum resin made of greenish-blue grains that plays an important role in the incense mixtures used in the Hermetic, angular tradition.

Olibanum (also frankincense)

After hardening, this milky juice from the North African Boswellia tree *(Boswellia serrata)*, whose name was derived by distorting the Hebrew word *lebonah* or "milk," turns into yellowish or brownish translucent tears.

Myrrh

One of the most commonly used gum resins, which consists of brittle, brownish tears. As a tincture, myrrh is also used in naturopathy.

Benzoin (or sweet asant, asa dulcis)

This resin of the benzoin tree is easily available everywhere and is used to season incense mixtures.

Asant (or asafoetida, devil's dung)

This gum resin was frequently used in the Middle Ages as a substitute for garlic and was an essential ingredient in every cake(!). Today it's almost solely used in veterinary medicine, which is why it's usually only obtainable in a very dirty state and therefore needs to be cleaned before use. When burned, asant causes thick clouds of penetrating smoke that stinks, similar to the stench of burning rubber or garlic, and it's mainly used for demonic operations or occasionally for exorcisms.

Ambra (or gray amber, ambergris)

A secretion from a sick sperm whale that's generally caught on the surface of the sea after storms. It's extremely rare and expensive, therefore not easy to obtain. Some authors understand ambra to include other pleasant-smelling substances as well, usually styrax (see "styrax" above). Bernstein is sometimes called "yellow amber" and may be used in incense mixtures as well as in ground form.

Balsam

This is a general term for pleasant-smelling, syrupy resins. Mecca balsam (or balm of Gilead, *Opobalsum verum*), for example, is the resin of the plant *Somiphora opobalsamum,* while sweet Peru balsam is made from the resin of the *Toluifera pereirae* tree and is also called "black Indian balsam." Tolu balsam (or opobalsam) is the resin of the *Toluifera balsamum* tree.

Ancient recipes for incense mixtures are often cause for confusion. Sometimes ingredients are confused, such as benzoin and benzoe, ambra and amber, and the various balsams, since they're translated from a number of languages and retranslated, and inaccurately written down and combined by those not having any great knowledge of the art. For example, one very old recipe for kyphi (Egyptian sun incense) is found in the Ebers papyrus. It reads: Dried myrrh, juniper berries, frankincense, cypress grass, mastic twigs, buckhorn, myrtle from northern Syria, raisins, styrax juice—grind together and form a substance. According to the recipe, women should add honey to it and cook everything together.

In Exodus 30:34, 36, you'll find instructions for an incense mixture as well that was revealed to Moses by Yahweh:

> *And the LORD said unto Moses: take unto thee sweet spices: stacte, onycha, sweet galbanum and pure frankincense, of each like much: and make cense of them compounded after the craft of the apothecary, mingled together, that it may be made pure and holy. And beat it to powder [. . .] let it be unto you holy.*

But he also warned Moses in Exodus 30:37–38 to not misuse and thereby desecrate this mixture that's reserved only for mass.

> *And see that ye make none after the making of that, but let it be unto you holy for the LORD. And whosoever shall make like unto that, to smell thereto, shall perish from among his people.*

Yahweh also gave instructions on how to make an anointing oil for consecrating the altar and the tabernacle, and for ordaining priests:

> *Take unto thee sweet spices: of pure myrrh five hundred sickles*[2]*, of sweet cinnamon half so much, two hundred and fifty sickles: of sweet calamite, two hundred and fifty. Of cassia, two hundred and fifty after the holy sickle, and of oil olive an hin. And make of them holy anointing oil even an oil compound after the craft of the apothecary* (Exodus 30:23–25).

This oil was reserved only for sacred acts as well, and violators were threatened with destruction.

Instead of resins, herbs (usually dried) are frequently used as incense as well and can be used alone or in mixtures. Shamans often use tobacco smoke for healing operations while some North American Indians prefer sage, which has become an established practice in shamanic groups in Europe as well.

In demonology or evocation, the goal is to conjure a spirit to "the consistency of thick vapors" (in Crowley's words) and make it materialize. This is sometimes taken literally. An incense burner is placed inside the evocational triangle and the demon is summoned to materialize in the column of smoke. Just a few hundred years ago, it was common practice to simplify this operation by using a prepared altar that was designed with a clever system of mirrors to project images on to the smoke as a sort of old-time "slide show." Surely this was seldom used as a means of intentional deceit, but the value of this practice as an imagination aid is still appreciated today. It's much easier to bring an image to life that already exists and can actually be seen moving on a flickering, rotating, and writhing column of smoke (projection), than to just wait until the right image materializes on its own (the so-called "eidetic" or crystal ball technique).

We should also mention that modern research has shown that the burning of certain incense (especially olibanum) causes the formation of so-called tetrahydrocannabinols or "hashish substances." In other words, incense makes you "high" in a sense, which definitely corresponds at least in part with our intention of inducing magical trance. Some ministers were even known to have an "addiction to incense," which resulted mainly from the chewing of incense, not just the inhaling of it. In addition, incense has a number of specific hygienic functions since it disinfects and keeps away bugs.

For your own practice, it would be advisable for you to first get accustomed to the elemental and planetary powers through ritual by either not using any incense at all, or by using a premixed, store-bought one. Once the magician has gotten acquainted with all of the planets, he or she should work with each one individually as the main focus until its correspondences are completely clear to him or her. Then one should make one's own personal incense mixture. You can see that this process can easily take years because after all, how many magicians can truly say that they understand and are familiar with all of the correspondences of a certain energy! In the end, the problem is purely theoretical as long as you always have enough of some kind of incense on hand that clearly contributes to the atmosphere of the ritual.

While in earlier times the incense was thrown into the sacrificial fire, today the preference is to smolder or vaporize it in an incense burner instead of burning it directly. This practice releases the aroma substances more gently and effectively. Most modern magicians use impregnated, self-igniting charcoal tablets that have a hollow on one side to hold the incense. For vaporizing liquid incense and oils, you can place them on a piece of metal (made of copper, for example) that rests on a tripod and light a candle underneath.

The Incense Burner

The incense burner is one of the most frequently used tools in ceremonial magic. In order to be able to read other literature on magic, it's important to know that the incense burner may also be called a "thurible" or a "censer." Crowley distinguishes between the two in his book *Magick* and uses two different burners at the same time.

Often the incense burner will consist of some kind of a bowl on a tripod. Kabbalistically and biblically oriented magicians prefer burners made of brass.

The act of burning incense is filled with much symbolism, so we'd like to quote Crowley on this matter:

> *Into the Magick Fire all things are cast. It symbolizes the final burning up of all things in shivadarshana. It is the absolute destruction alike of the Magician and the Universe* (*Magick*, p. 113).

It's the magician's will that ignites this consuming fire that destroys the old to make room for the new, and the censer is the container (or universe) in which this act of horrible destruction (e.g., undesired influences and distracting thoughts) takes place. But Crowley also warns against overestimating that which you might see:

> *In this smoke illusions arise. We sought the light, and behold the Temple is darkened! In the darkness this smoke seems to take strange shapes, and we may hear the crying of beasts. The thicker the smoke, the darker grows the Universe. We gasp and tremble, beholding what foul and unsubstantial things we have evoked!*

Yet we cannot do without the Incense! Unless our aspiration took form it could not influence form. This also is the mystery of incarnation (ibid., pp. 113–14).

Later on, he continues:

> *All these phantoms, of whatever nature, must be evoked, examined, and mastered; otherwise we may find that just when we want it there is some idea with which we have never dealt; and perhaps that idea, springing on us by surprise, and as it were from behind, may strangle us. This is the legend of the sorcerer strangled by the Devil!* (ibid., p. 116).

However, the old master of modern-day magic doesn't just mean the apparitions that we can visibly see in the clouds of smoke, but also our moral and religious concepts and ideas, as well as every single thought itself that's not analyzed and therefore kept at a distance so as not to identify ourselves with it, forcing us into the abyss of illusion.

Crowley gives a recipe of his own for incense: 1 part olibanum (the sacrifice of the human will of the heart, or his profane wanting), ¼ part styrax (the earthly desires, dark, sweet, and clinging) and ¼ part aloe (lignum aloes, which symbolizes Sagittarius, the arrow, and therefore the magical aspiration itself).

For Crowley (who is actually talking about the metaphysical significance of burning incense and the materials used, and not really about the censer itself quoted here), smoke also represents the astral plane, which surely needs no further explanation if you remember our statements about demon evocations.

Hanging incense burners are popular as well, especially for group rituals and when working in large rooms, and they can also be used to redraw the lines of the magical circle after it has been cast. This forms a column of smoke that provides the magician with additional protection; this column also resembles a veil that hides the magical operation from profane eyes and symbolizes the impenetrability of a good magician.

Of course, we shouldn't need to mention that the incense burner must be made of fireproof material. Although frequently, literature does fail to mention the need for sufficient ventilation to prevent the charcoal and incense from being suffocated. This of course doesn't pose a problem when an open burner is used, but sometimes a covered censer is preferred since it controls flying sparks and allows the oils and essences to vaporize underneath the lid. A covered burner should always have enough holes for ventilation in order to ensure optimal smoke development.

One variety of the burner is the smoke pan, which some magicians prefer. The pan is usually made of copper, sturdy brass (if brass is too thin, as in most cheap flowerpots, it will crack when heated), or even iron. It rarely has a cover. Due to its easy-to-grip handle, it's especially suited for initiations, for example when the candidate is fumigated with smoke in order to cleanse him or her with or connect him or her to the element of Air.

PRACTICAL EXERCISES

EXERCISE 23

ASTRAL MAGIC AND MEDITATION (I)

Contrary to other authors, we won't be starting our training of astral travel and astral magic by recommending that you learn to separate your astral from your physical body. Complete beginners with no previous experience in astral travel usually find the following technique much easier and are able to achieve equally good results in just a short period of time, which is why we'll be discussing the actual astral trip at a later time. Our technique trains the mastery of asana and body control as well.

Sit in an asana of your choice—preferably the god posture, dragon posture, or half-lotus posture—each day for at least fifteen minutes for several weeks. Collect your thoughts and just observe your breathing. If any thoughts come to mind (and they surely will!), don't try to force them away since that will only make them more stubborn—just let them pass without taking any notice of them. After awhile, let yourself and your body expand mentally with each breath. Do this little by little—at first maybe just two or three inches—and increase the distance each day you practice until you finally fill the entire room that you're meditating in (after about four weeks). Finish your meditation by making yourself get smaller again each time you inhale. You can combine this exercise with the following one as well by first working with mantras until you reach a sufficient state of gnosis before beginning with the actual meditation.

EXERCISE 24

MANTRA TRAINING

Practice one of the traditional mantras listed in this section each day for at least ten minutes. Or you can use a different mantra if you like as long as it comes from some entirely different language or culture other than your own. In either case, recite it out loud at first (whereby the volume is irrelevant) and save silent intonation for later practice. Pay close attention to the various types of energy.

EXERCISE 25

THE IAO FORMULA IN PRACTICE (II)

You need a partner for this exercise. If the person's not a magician and you don't want him or her to find out about your magical activities, just say it's a sound and energy exercise similar to those used in singing lessons or eutony training. Even the greatest doubter will soon realize how this exercise vitalizes one's whole body and stop asking questions.

Face your partner. Stretch your arms out in front of you, palms vertical and facing inward near the neck area of your partner—then vibrate the vowel *I* as powerfully as possible. Then hold your arms out straight in front of you, palms horizontal with fingertips facing outward and direct them toward the chest of your partner while vibrating the vowel *A*. Then spread your arms to form a circle with your palms facing the hip region of your partner (as though you were to give a hip hug) and vibrate *O*. You should never actually touch your partner since this could hinder your concentration and the flow of energy.

Now let your partner do the same to you. Repeat this exercise as often as you like, but listen to what your body says to prevent it from being overcharged—this usually feels like an extreme sensation of power. It's well suited for healing operations and in preparation for a ritual. It's important to make sure that the person doing the vibrating doesn't transfer any of his or her own energy to the other person, but rather should stimulate his or her partner's own personal energy and cause it to start flowing. Otherwise, the result would be a severe loss of energy. You can prevent this by concentrating on the vibrating.

EXERCISE 26

TRATAK

The practice known to Indian yoga and tantra called *tratak* consists of concentrating on an external object to obtain a state of empty mind or gnosis. Choose an object that you have no emotional attachment to; it can be any everyday object such as a fork, a disposable lighter, or a shoestring. Sit in your asana and look at the object without thinking about anything. You'll notice that this exercise is quite different than Exercise 23 above. Don't overdo it—just three or four times a week for ten minutes each is fine for the start. Don't try to think about the object, just be aware of it while applying your 180° gaze as long as you can look at it without your eyes burning. Don't make any judgments about the object or this exercise whatsoever—just write down any impressions in your magical diary afterward. Practice this exercise for at least three months as described above, because practice makes perfect here as well.

BIBLIOGRAPHY

Aleister Crowley, *Magick*

---

1. This list was taken from Georg Ivanovas' *Räucherwerk—Nahrung der Götter.*

2. Just for orientation, a sickle as listed in the Old Testament equals about half an ounce.

MYSTICISM OR MAGIC?

SUPREME BEINGS AND THE OCCULT

Stephen Mace points out the basic difference between faith and knowledge, prayer and magical ritual, or even between mysticism and magic is that prayer demands a lot of faith and devotion from the person praying, yet very little skill and talent. The magical ritual demands only little faith but all the more skill; devotion to a deity is substituted by perseverance and persistence.

This corresponds to the path that magic is taking today. If we take a look at its development over the last thirty years, we'll notice that it has been influenced by two qualitatively new characteristics, namely the abandonment of dogma and the emphasis on magical dexterity. Both factors naturally depend on one another and give the magical act an entire new quality, making it more effective as well.

Sometimes traditionalistic magicians will complain that this approach is too "unromantic" and "technocratic." This accusation is surely justified in a sense and should be taken seriously in more aspects than just this, although at the same time it points out a practical problem that magic geared toward success and efficiency is continually confronted with. It would be wrong to believe that this "new objectivity" and the related exposure of old occult bluffs (such as a secret cosmic master in the Himalayas, an astral leader of an order, and so on) could completely eliminate the basic interest of humanity in the mystic and the numinous, or "holy." Moreover, in a practical sense, it's questionable as to whether this would actually be desired in the first place. As we'll see again and again in conjunction with our practice of invocational magic, the temporary submission of a magician to some "higher" principle is often one of the basic requirements for magical success.

Since the practice of magic always requires working with the unconscious mind, images and especially myths play an important role as well. Surely modern magic in its need for iconoclasm and its rebellion against ancient, fossilized structures and dogmas has well surpassed this goal. But that's exactly what revolutions and radical change do, like a cleansing thunderstorm.

Let's take a closer look at exactly what happened in order to get a better idea of how to evaluate the question of the supreme or divine in relation to magic.

THE MAGICIAN AS A MYSTIC

If we take a look at magical authors such as Levi, Papus, Guaïta, Mathers, Waite, Crowley, Quintscher, Bardon, and Gregorius, and the history of magic from ancient times up to the modern-day present, mystical models have always predominated and the magical path has always been understood as the way to godhood—regardless of how this is defined.

Apart from a few early exceptions (by Crowley on occasion as well), it wasn't until the development of Pragmatic Magic and Chaos Magic that a departure from magical theism took place on a large scale, giving it mere philosophical value instead. This is all the more amazing when we remember the significant role that early Buddhism (which was nontheistic as well) played in Eastern philosophy since the end of the classicism and romanticism periods. Philosophers such as Schopenhauer or Nietzsche cannot possibly be understood without this influence, just like Kierkegaard and the much later field of existential philosophy.[1]

The occult was influenced strongly by Buddhism as well, and even Crowley referred to himself as a Buddhist for quite some time, writing essays such as "Science and Buddhism" and radically rejecting any kind of theism while representing a rather skeptical yet rational outlook on things before he finally became a Thelemic mystic by accepting the *Book of the Law* as a revelation that can be applied to the entire world. Both Theosophy and Anthroposophy, which were movements that had a significant influence on Eastern esotericism, spread Buddhist ideas (among others), although these were theistically disguised and closer to mahayana Buddhism than anything else.

In any case, Western esotericism almost always worked with some kind of theism, which even included monotheism. In this we'll recognize the strong and seemingly invincible influence that Judaism and Christianity have on our culture. This is inseparable from the opinion that there are "higher" and "lower" or "good" and "bad" spheres, and that religion is superior to magic in the end since it's supposedly more "true." There's no point in arguing about whether religion is the mother or daughter of magic since there are good viewpoints to support each side. Personally I tend to support the opinion that religion probably originated from magic, although the two certainly overlapped right from the start. But this is more of a factual consideration and there's no intention whatsoever to place more importance on one or the other with postulated "greater originality". In the end, it's all a matter of temperament anyway. Some people are more religious than others (probably the majority, in fact), and those who prefer the magical path generally won't submit to any kind of god other than themselves for a longer period of time.[2]

But mysticism and religion are surely not the same; in fact, just the opposite is true. Although the mystic considers him- or herself to be a representative of "true religion" in the sense of *religio*, or reconnecting with the origin of things, this outlook usually strongly contradicts religious orthodoxy. In this sense, the mystic is considered a threat to religion's carefully protected hierarchy because he or she's not dependent on it to establish communication with divine principles. Usually mystics are more or less ignored by Christian churches or, at best, just briefly mentioned without ever truly discussing their principles. Often the reason for all the skepticism surrounding mysticism is said to be the spiritual and mental health of the "average person" who supposedly wouldn't be able to deal with such concepts. Mysticism has sometimes even been condemned as being seriously dangerous, which is not surprising considering the fact that many mystics have entirely done away with any church dogmas, causing them to slip into the category of "self-idolization" due to its mystical union with the divine. (This still seems to be an aftereffect of the gnosis-shock caused by early Christianity.)

Nonetheless, mysticism and religion agree that there's some sort of divinity that humanity is subordinate to. For both, the goal of life is to make some kind of long-term arrangement with this divinity in order to realize religio.

Magic, on the other hand, is principally an ideological, neutral technique for influencing one's fate. Through its sociocultural and, of course, religious environment, it comes into contact with other systems and merges with them. This can be clearly seen in the development of Western magic, which was influenced at a very early stage almost exclusively by Jewish-Christian practices (with the exception of a few ancient pagan elements during the Middle Ages). In search of a model to explain how magic works, the predominate religion of the times was a natural reference since it claimed to be able to explain everything anyway, and this harmonized well with it's job of salvation. This is certainly not a phenomenon specific to the West since the same procedure can also be observed, for example, in the Islam and Hindu cultural regions. On the other hand, due to its active role in dealing with fate, magic paradoxically seems to be much closer to mysticism (which is generally described as being "passive") than to religion, which merely "tolerates" and follows predetermined revelations and "holy laws." And both rebel against external control by human authority figures: The mystic doesn't let him- or herself be prevented from accessing the origin of all things by clinging to some artificial system created by humans, and the magician isn't content with simply being a pawn in a game and a victim of fate, and therefore strives to master the powers that one sees controlling him- or herself and others.

In this sense, it's of considerable importance in a structural sense that most mystics receive their visions and information passively and rarely strive for them, making their rebellion more of an unconscious act instead of an intentional one. But their humbleness toward the divine shouldn't distract from the fact that it's basically a Luciferian spirit that's at work here (which the reaction of orthodox religions clearly proves) that wants to reach the highest but without the structure that others ("ignorant people" and therefore "subordinates") have built around it. From a practical point of view, both are also pragmatic while religion on the other hand is dogmatic since it's almost always lacking the dimension of experience, and therefore it can usually only base its belief (of something not experienced firsthand) on the hearsay of others, which in turn needs to be interpreted by others (priests).

Within Western magic, this development led to the adoption of monotheistic and mystic ideas that have hidden our view from their actual mechanisms for a very long time. Thus the magician is understood to be someone who will eventually have to give up magic in the end anyway. The separation between the so-called lower and higher magic that we often find in literature is merely an expression of such a fundamental viewpoint. "Lower" magic is considered to be everything that has to do with matter, including all types of practical magic—for money, love, health, harm, and death—and even the expression of one's own will in general. While matter is generally considered inferior, being able to influence it is naturally a preliminary step that needs to be mastered and then eventually left behind. "High" magic is more difficult to describe. Today we have two definitions: (a) the conventional description in which the magician eventually succeeds in establishing contact with transcendence, allowing oneself from then on to be guided by it ("Not my will, but thy will be done, Lord," and so on), consequently becoming a saint in a way; (b) the more modern version (although recognized in shamanism for thousands of years) that strives for independence from external means ("empty hand techniques are the mark of an adept" as Pete Carroll once wrote), or a direct form of magic for directly influencing fate without needing elaborate symbolic equipment and external exercises, and not having to rely on external factors. In the first definition, the magician is a theurgic mystic, while in the second he or she's a virtuoso technician who no longer needs any tools.

Last but not least, magic is directly related to knowledge and realization as well as to personal development and truth. Within the religious-monotheistic paradigm, the path can only run linear with hierarchical steps reaching from bottom to top, whereby the top (e.g., the spirit) is considered more valuable than the bottom (e.g., the body). Here the magician is understood once again as a searcher of the truth, in contrast to a person who merely strives for personal freedom and independence. Due to the patriarchal structure of this paradigm, hardly anyone ever considers the possibility that these two goals do not necessarily need to contradict one another, since the truth has already been preformulated by the predominating monotheism and could therefore only mean the submission to only one god.

What is often forgotten in this connection is the fact that the peak of this form of magic was certainly not in the Middle Ages, as often assumed, but rather during the Renaissance or the preliminary phase of the Enlightenment. During this era, there was a certain restlessness caused by the sudden questioning of the world's social and religious structures (and the first hidden form of atheism); the individual as such was rediscovered and, at the same time, there was great fear as to whether there would be eternal damnation as a result of such "ungodly" sin. In this midst, a curious mixture of self-assertion and submission to religion developed in magic that still causes us a lot of headaches today. Even comparatively modern authors such as Douval are still stuck in this old paradigm of inner contradiction, e.g., when the magician is instructed to practices of piousness and devoutness before performing an act of magic to harm someone, and even being told to call upon the powers of the Holy Trinity or the Son of God, Jesus Christ, and the heavenly hosts before performing an extremely unchristian act.

Even the many words of warning and caution that these authors like to decorate their writing with can be explained by a bad conscience because they're really not magicians at all, but mystics for the most part (and frustrated ones at that) who can't afford to or won't let themselves be freed from the shackles of orthodox religion and regard this as sober and structural as science does. Aleister Crowley was the only one to ever attempt to synthesize the "methods of science, the goal of religion," which corresponded to the broken perception of reality that was common to his era and that still applies to many of us today.

THE MAGICIAN AS AN ANTIMYSTIC

The course of spiritual development as described above was probably unavoidable considering the historical circumstances, but now there really seems to be no point in continuing to fight the current as contemporary magic does frequently enough anyway.

Even revolutions have eventually outlived themselves in the end. What remains—ideally—are their achievements. In our case, this includes the realization that magic is not only possible, but actually even more effective when it's freed from all religious and ethic burdens of the past. Through the changes that morals and ethics underwent during the twentieth century, the magician has learned to understand his or her art in a relativistic and yet less religious-dogmatic sense.[3]

In the same way science had to free itself from the choking grip of priori religions and philosophies before it was able to begin its march of triumph throughout the entire world, magic needs to do the same before it can develop into a technology that's geared toward efficiency. Today magic is generally understood as a mere tool or skill.

But if it's more than just this nonetheless, then the reason is that—in contrast to the disciplines of natural science—magic doesn't just deal with a tiny, restricted number of "subtle" natural laws, but rather with an entire life process in which, once again in contrast to science, the theory is perfect but the *operand* is not, as Ramsey Dukes once put it. The raw material of magic is the magician him- or herself since it always requires a living medium, and a truly skilled magician is always one who has carefully weighed every aspect of one's entire life. Now we're not referring to some kind of metaphysical "pact with the devil," but rather to the fact that our reality is the product of our state of awareness. And the magician needs to be able to utilize, change, and manipulate this in order to be successful.

We don't own the term "magician" and therefore have no right to swing the executioner's axe by distinguishing between who is and who isn't a true magician. That's why it should be sufficient to say that the majority of modern magicians (as long as they don't cling solely to traditional systems) welcome this rebellion against the kind of mysticism and religious dogmatism that have predominated for such a long time because it's this rebellion that allows the actual technical structures of magic to be worked out and defined in the first place. By restricting magic to one single technology and excluding all ontological questions and any talk of salvation, we create a greater degree of clarity about its effective mechanisms and can use these more efficiently—for mystical purposes as well!

In addition, modern humanity has recognized that by searching for the one, "objective" truth, they're only avoiding the actual problem, namely the creation of their own subjective truth. Maybe it would be more appropriate to describe the modern magician as an "antimysticist" instead of an "antimystic." The search for the answers to the three gnostic questions, "Who am I? Where did I come from? Where am I going?" is still common to our time, as it will always be. Only the methods of finding the answers have changed, and the glasses through which we view the world.

Probably the most important driving force behind the magical rebellion against orthodox religiousness and mysticism is the release from all fears and relief of bad conscience that they both promise. The latter plays a fatal role in magic since it paralyzes a great deal of our magical potential. A presumptuous and arrogant magician whose intentions are merely to do something "forbidden" or "ungodly," but who doesn't know how to utilize this fear for his or her work, creates a dynamic contradiction within oneself that can have devastating consequences, such as causing one's work to magically "backfire" like a boomerang.[4] But a person without any religious affiliation or dependence whatsoever can have a bad conscience as well, which can sabotage his or her own magic, and psychoanalysis has shown us the mechanisms that can cause such a reaction. On the other hand, by eliminating the restricting factors that we're consciously aware of (which is relatively easy to do), we can greatly improve our work.

So we're not encouraging anyone to do away with religion and mysticism entirely, especially since the search for religio seems to be inherent in humans. The magician who has deep ties to religion and/or mysticism will eventually have to combine it with one's magic, and that, too, is part of the Thelemic principle of "Do what thou wilt."

But in the interest of being successful in our practice, we'd like to remind you of a principle that we've discussed before: Magicians choose their beliefs like surgeons choose their instruments. When keeping this in mind, there's really no room left over in one's outlook on the world for any "absolute," soul-saving beliefs.

If you're not really interested in magical effectiveness or if it just doesn't play an important role in your work, then you're more of the religious-mystical type, and magic will never be any more to you than an intermediate step on the path to salvation.

---

1. Of course, with this statement we're not assuming that these thinkers were ever practicing Buddhists. Instead, they perceived Eastern Buddhism through their own "filter" made up of their own ideas and influenced by their own period in history. It's undeniable that Hinayana Buddhism in the nineteenth century was highly respected by scholars due to its rationalistic approach.
2. In order to avoid misunderstandings, we need to point out here as well that a mixed form is generally the rule in practice. Our simplification here is merely meant to help illustrate the basic positions in order to be able to understand the dispute better.
3. In this sense, it might be more accurate to say that magic pursues "the methods of science" and "the goal of art," with "art" referring to that of an engineer of fate.
4. The classical examples of this are failed attempts at money or sex magic because they're deeply rooted in puritan philosophies, which even affected old master Crowley in some ways as anyone who reads his biography and diaries can see.

PRACTICAL SIGIL MAGIC (III)

THE PICTURE METHOD

There's not much more to say about the picture method of making magical sigils according to Austin Osman Spare's system than what we discussed earlier. But maybe the advantages and disadvantages should be mentioned here briefly.

This method is generally preferred by people with artistic talent, such as painters, graphic designers, and architects, since it makes good use of their skills. It has a more "natural" effect on many magicians (similar to the mantric method of making sigils as well) since it doesn't need to take the detour through the intellectual or linguistic part of the mind, and it doesn't require use of a rational alphabet. Obviously this method is also more directly linked to the subconscious since it makes immediate use of pictures. Statements of intent don't need to be formulated in writing first, but can be converted directly into pictograms, which is this method's greatest disadvantage as well. As already mentioned in connection with the symbol-logical fuzzy relation, it's difficult to be very precise when using pictures and symbols. Therefore the picture method isn't very suitable for statements of intent and magical operations concerning exact numbers, dates, or measurements. If, for example, you want to meet a certain person on a certain day, you'd generally be better off using the word method instead of the picture method.

In addition, vague concepts such as "realization" or "happiness" are difficult to express in pictures. But if that doesn't seem to be a problem for you, feel free to work with the picture method for such operations.

In any case, it's time you started working with this method in order to expand your spectrum of sigil magic skills and be able to determine which method works best for you.

CHARGING A SIGIL THROUGH VISUALIZATION

Generally sigils are charged through a sex magic operation or by means of the death posture, whereby the latter can take on many forms. British magicians in particular like to work with a method of charging that's a mixture between visualization and the death posture.

Remember that the goal of the death posture is to eliminate all mental activity. Another version often used by Spare is to gaze at your own face in a mirror without letting the image blur. Since the human mind usually can't go any extended period of time without new stimuli, it will usually disfigure or add to the image, forcing a new meaning upon it. The face in the mirror will twist and turn into strange shapes, an ugly grimace, or some other form. Try it out yourself. Just gaze at a plain white or gray wallpapered wall for ten minutes without letting yourself see pictures or patterns in it. In the same way, you'll probably start hearing words and phrases in the meaningless static noise of a radio under normal circumstances.

If your reflection doesn't distort, it will assume that your mind is no longer active and will try to project patterns and information into it, which usually takes the form of a change in your perception. Once this has happened, you've successfully internalized the sigil through intense visualization, and you can then end the operation by laughing spasmodically.

In the Practical Exercises section, we've recommended a way for you to combine this technique with tratak, which you learned in the last section—all in the interest of developing your visualization skills of course.

The only disadvantage to visualizing sigils is probably the fact that concentrating on the image of the symbol for such a long time makes it difficult to forget. But this, too, is just a matter of practice.

The main advantage of this method is that it's an "empty hand" technique, meaning that you're not dependent on anything to hold the sigil, such as a piece of paper or the like. That could be of great use, for example whenever you need to charge a sigil without being noticed, such as in the company of other people, in the waiting room of a doctor's office, while traveling in a train or an airplane, or anywhere else.

EMOTIONS AND CHARGING SIGILS

Beginners are often shocked at the composed and controlled way magicians can work with their emotions and are able to use them at will for specific magical operations. Sigil magic responds especially well to the use of extreme emotional states; when a magician is able to take one's magical life seriously despite strong feelings of anger or fear and is able to use these emotions for magical operations, thereby never wasting any valuable energy, this is proof of one's inner freedom and unsentimentality. Besides, magic is always a bit of self-therapy anyway.

For example, if you're afraid of riding a roller coaster, you could rid yourself of this restricting fear and use it productively at the same time by charging a sigil right at the moment your fear climaxes—during a long ride, or several consecutive rides, you can charge the sigil again or charge several different sigils. Practice has shown that such operations are usually highly effective in both senses—effectively charging the sigil and effectively overcoming your fear.

This is another reason why it can be quite valuable to take the time and make an exact list of your fears and emotions. With a little bit of imagination, you can develop quite a wide range of possibilities for your practical work and eliminate a great deal of your fears along the way. Try visualizing a sigil during your first parachute jump, for example!

But don't make the mistake in thinking that magic can only work with such extreme states of mind, which is a misconception that too many magicians—the younger ones in particular—tend to believe. Rather, seeking out such extreme conditions is an integral part in the process of liberation or becoming whole that most magicians desire, and not as an end in itself or an indispensable component of magical technology. Nonetheless, there's surely some truth in the belief that emotional excess leads to the best magical results.

THE OMNIL FORMULA

The OMNIL formula was developed by the British magician William Gray, who wrote a number of excellent books. This formula is described in his book *Magical Ritual Methods.* The word OMNIL is a combination of the two Latin words *omnis* (everything) and *nihil* (nothing). Michael Gebauer summarized this as follows: "Out of the emptiness, out of the nothingness [. . .], everything [. . .] can develop, everything I can create. In this so-called 'phase zero', we experience the same distance to all forms of existence" *(Grundlagen der Zeremonialmagie I)*. The OMNIL formula is therefore a method for centering and for recognition at the same time; it serves to create a cosmic state of gnosis within the magician that represents the center of one's own universe. This universe (the "everything") is created out of the nothingness, and in between is where magic—and all of life itself—takes place. So the first thing we need to do is realize our "nihil" potential (called "chaos" in Chaos Magic) before we can start applying it to truly become gods, which is the goal of most magical systems. The first step in reaching "nihil" is to thoroughly banish everything that has no place in our universe—because the power of chaos can only develop fully and freely in complete emptiness. Therefore we have to start at zero if we want to turn our magical cosmos into reality, because if the remains of other cosmoses are still floating around, this will muddle our creation and it won't be entirely our own.

Gray described this quite clearly with the ritual question:

> "What is the most important of all?"
> "God."
> "What is more important than God?"
> "Nothing is more important than God."
> "Therefore let Nothing come before God."
> (*Magical Ritual Methods,* p. 27)

He continues: "We see now the esoteric significance of the injunction to: 'have no other Gods before Me.' That is not a command to abolish idols or other God-concepts than IHWH but a positive instruction to start from the Nil or Zero point before any concept of Deity whatever" (ibid.).

With his OMNIL formula, he gave us a tool that we can use to "zero ourselves," as he expresses it—quite similar to the state of "empty mind," or *samadhi* and *satori,* used in Eastern styles of meditation. In many systems of initiation, candidates are robbed of their entire previous identity—they're completely undressed, relieved of the "dirt" from their past by means of ritual cleansing, take on a new name, set a new goal in life, and so on. This often takes the form of ritual rebirth, a practice that can be traced back to the ancient mysteries of Eleusis right up to the current practices of Christian monasteries, Indian ashrams, and Western Freemason lodges, despite the fact that these all have quite different goals.

Optically speaking, the OMNIL formula closely resembles the IAO formula that we discussed earlier, and indeed there are even certain mixed forms that combine the two elements. But we'd like to concentrate on the pure form of this technique for now, as Gray introduced it. Although his explanations are quite sparse, it shouldn't be a problem to implement it into our practice with the knowledge of ritual magic that we already have.

THE OMNIL FORMULA IN PRACTICE

In a place where you won't be disturbed, stand facing the east or north and focus your attention on the supreme ("divine") above you and the life that exists below you. With the energy of your awareness now focused, draw a horizontal circle around yourself. Use your magical wand or dagger if you like—although this should only be necessary at the beginning. This circle is Zero-time.

Now draw a lateral circle starting at the zenith (the top of your head) to the right, continue to the nadir and then back up along the left side until you finally reach the zenith again. This is Zero-space.

Then draw a vertical circle starting at the zenith and down in front of your body, going back up your back until you reach the zenith again. This is Zero-event.

Make sure you draw all circles deosil (clockwise). Ideally you should draw or project all three simultaneously, which will become easier each time you practice.

After a bit of practice, the whole exercise shouldn't take more than a split second. It's extremely powerful, stabilizes the magical operation, focuses your concentration, and works on a symbol-logical level, which is basically what the Lesser Banishing Ritual of the Pentagram does in a more ritual sense. Gebauer compared its effect to that of the Kabbalistic Cross, but this doesn't cover all aspects of how you can implement the OMNIL formula. Try to determine for yourself the similarities and differences in the two.

USE OF THE OMNIL FORMULA

The OMNIL formula is rarely used alone, but as an introduction to a larger ritual, and sometimes even as part of the Lesser Banishing Ritual of the Pentagram. But since it can be performed easily anywhere, it can be implemented into your everyday routine, for example as a concentration aid before doing mentally demanding work, for centering yourself in emotional situations, and so on. The value of this exercise cannot be overestimated, and experience has shown that it also hardens the aura just like the IAO formula.

Michael Gebauer developed a mixed version of the IAO and OMNIL formulas. In his version, the vowels *I, A,* and *O* are vibrated respectively as each circle is drawn. But we recommend that you keep the exercises separate for now so that you can become thoroughly familiar with the various energy qualities of each before experimenting with the mixed form later.[1]

COMMENTS ON IMAGINATION TRAINING

Magical literature often starts off by focusing on the training of magical imagination, whereby visualization is usually meant, although we've repeated several times that magical perception doesn't necessarily have to be visual.

Now practice has shown that many people only have difficulties with visualization exercises when these are specifically designated as such, probably because this kind of training was (and sometimes still is today) overestimated by many authors. This creates a high pressure to succeed, which ends up being more detrimental to good imagination skills than it benefits them. In fact, everything we refer to as "the training of magical perception" is actually the training of your imagination, although our passive method is much more effective than an active approach when first starting out. In the future, we'll continue to avoid putting too much pressure on our apprentice magicians by keeping our training methods as simple as possible and by embedding our visualization exercises into practical work, such as we did right at the start with the Lesser Banishing Ritual of the Pentagram.

So don't worry that your imagination skills might be lacking—just trust in our system and get comfortable working with the techniques given here even though you're not yet a master of visualization or even magical hallucination. There are many paths leading to magic, and the example of sigil magic shows how little we often need to work effectively.

One characteristic of magical imagination is the fact that it often isn't consciously perceived as such. That's one thing it has in common with magical trance. While the magic of earlier days focused more on projection (active imagination projection), today we tend to concentrate more on active perception; the latter is considered more natural since its basic structure stems back to shamanic practices.

Even though many magicians may achieve good results with the projection method, my own personal experience has given me the strong impression that a focus on perception will bring about better results. Therefore it's not so important to visualize and project the image of a desired event as powerfully and with as much concentration as possible, but rather to perceive it as precisely as possible (even for just a short period of time) and to get a feel of its energy quality. After all, one of the insights of modern magic states that:

Precision is more important than power

This certainly doesn't undermine the importance of imagination; we're only saying that the second structural formula of magic seems to be qualitatively superior to the first. In practice, this difference isn't distinguished as strictly as it might seem to be in theory.

However, thorough imagination training is imperative for people who either have difficulty with magical perception (perceptional blockades) or who are overwhelmed with inner pictures (image flooding). In the first case, the person needs to train the ability of image/subtle perception in the first place, while in the second case, the person needs to learn to control and master it in order to prevent oneself from constantly drifting off into daydreams, which is fatal to magic most of the time.

This is why we chose a solid middle course for our training program that attempts to make imagination easier by making it controllable and manageable.

INTRODUCTION TO ASTROMAGIC

The field of astrological magic (more commonly called astromagic) is so comprehensive and specialized that it would be impossible for us to cover it in detail here. Those of you who already have sound knowledge of astrology as well as some experience in the field as well can just skim over this section.

We don't want to commit ourselves here to any certain astrological system since astrology is always subjective and purely a matter of personal experience. It doesn't matter if you work with classical astrology, or if you prefer the Placidus house system, the Koch (GOH) system, or maybe even the equal house system, or if you follow the teachings of the Hamburg School or Ebertins' cosmobiology, or represent the Hubers School or the Munich Rhythm School—the important thing is how you integrate astrology into your magic, if at all.

There are a number of magicians who prefer not to use astrology in their work at all, and there are good reasons for this. Astrology is meant to familiarize humans with the cosmic principles according to the Hermetic belief "As above, so below." With this information, humans are able to link the rhythm of the heavenly bodies to their own fate. It's a powerful instrument of self-knowledge and prediction that can be a valuable magical tool for putting the finishing touch on magical operations by coordinating them with favorable time periods by means of astrological knowledge.

But there's a catch to this. Whoever makes oneself so dependent on astrology that one can only work during certain planetary constellations, or always blames failure on "unfavorable" planetary influences instead of looking for the fault within, such as one's carelessness or lack of attention and concentration, and whoever ignores the golden rule that the stars can tilt something in a certain direction but can never force it there—such a person will never be a good magician. We can rarely pick the constellations we want anyway. If you absolutely need a Jupiter-Saturn trine to perform a certain ritual because your paradigm makes you dependent on it, you might have to wait for years until the right time comes along. And if it needs to be a transiting Saturn to put a certain aspect on your birth Jupiter, you might even have to wait for up to twenty-eight years. It gets even more complicated when you need a combination of several planetary aspects, e.g., if you need a conjunction of Mercury and Jupiter that at the same time forms a trine with Saturn and a sextile with the tip of your fifth house. . . .[2] Moreover, astrology can even become a real burden by making the magician dependent on it for one's predictions, thereby restricting one in freedom of choice (a problem that all divinatory systems pose), or when the magician's concept of oneself is only understood in astrological terms ("I can't really change anyway because Capricorns are like that . . .").

This is why we advise beginners against linking their magic too closely with astrology, although we have no intentions of downplaying its significance. It can be of great service to us, e.g., if we need to get a quick impression of a person's personality and his current daily cycle of activity, which can play an important role when working with clients. And it's certainly useful to take advantage of favorable planetary positions when they just happen to occur, such as for charging a planetary talisman or amulet or when attacking an opponent when he or she is weakest.

After all, astrology has always played a significant role throughout the history of Western magic, and in the interest of getting a general, comprehensive magical education, no magician should refrain from studying the subject thoroughly. In magical alchemy it's even a necessity, and it's also next to impossible to understand a great deal of magical literature without a good knowledge of astrology. Plus it's probably one of the most comprehensive yet fascinating fields of the occult sciences and could never be thoroughly exhausted in one lifetime. Furthermore it trains your magical perception and your ability to think in symbols, since its symbol-logic is often exemplary.

So that's why we'll be delving a bit deeper into astrology whenever it's of significance to our magic. For now, the exercises recommended at the end of this section should be enough.

---

1. This applies to all exercises in this book as well. We don't want to give you a strict set of instructions to follow exactly, but would rather encourage you to develop your own style, which can only happen if you eventually vary and adapt the exercises to fit your individual needs.
2. The essentials of this terminology will be explained in the next chapter, in Exercise 29.

INTRODUCTION TO RITUAL MAGIC (VI)

THE MAGIC CUP

The cup represents the element of Water, but also the female, receptive principle as well as emotion, intuition, dream, vision, and divination. Crowley equated it with understanding, although he didn't mean logical-rational, intellectual understanding, but rather the feeling that we know something "in our heart." Today we're more likely to use the term "instinctive knowledge," and indeed, such instinctive knowledge needs to be trained well.

Crowley wrote:

> *In the beginning the Cup of the student is almost empty; and even such truth as he receives may leak away, and be lost.*
>
> *They say that the Venetians made glasses which changed colour if poison was put into them; of such a glass must the student make his Cup* (*Magick*, p. 73).

These instructions should be understood metaphorically, of course. This is a good time to point out that simply making the magical weapons isn't enough. They not only stand for abstract elemental principles, but also reflect the magician's current spiritual stage of development. This is a good reason why you should never restrict the making of your magical weapons to a certain time frame.[1]

While the magician will probably have the least difficulty making one's wand or sword, it might take one many years until the cup is perfect. This isn't a question of technical skill, but rather of mental maturity and development of character. Basically, this is an alchemistic process; the external event (the making of a magical weapon) should reflect the stage of inner development, and the other way around.

The cup is therefore a symbol and tool of the magician's developed instinct and trained intuition. It's dangerous until it's perfect. "*This Cup is full of bitterness, and of blood, and of intoxication*" (ibid., p. 73). Having a subconscious that's too receptive, that accepting every foreign influence imaginable without criticism, is equal to having a defective censor. Delusions and a general loss of one's grip on reality are the most common results. The cup doesn't just receive, but it also gives shape—the water that's poured into it adapts to its form, but loses its shape just as soon as it's poured out again. In this sense, the cup can also be viewed as a symbol for shaped illusion: The images the magician receives require structure in order to become effective. If they remain without structure or form, they'll destroy their environment; wine becomes a corrosive acid and destroys the vessel.

Here are a few more quotations from Crowley that you should meditate on:

> *The Cup can hardly be described as a weapon. It is round like the Pantacle—not straight like the Wand and the Dagger. Reception, not projection, is its nature.* (ibid., p. 73).
>
> *Concerning the water in this Cup, it may be said that just as the Wand should be perfectly rigid, the ideal solid, so should the water be the ideal fluid.*
>
> *The Wand is erect, and must extend to Infinity.*
>
> *The surface of the water is flat, and must extend to Infinity.*
>
> *But as the Wand is weak without breadth, so is the water false without depth. The Understanding of the Magus must include all things, and that understanding must be infinitely profound* (ibid., p. 74).

> *The surface of the water in the Magick Cup is infinite; there is no point different from any other point.*
>
> *Thus, ultimately, as the Wand is a binding and a limitation, so is the Cup an expansion—into the Infinite.*

And this is the danger of the Cup; it must necessarily be open to all, and yet if anything is put into it which is out of proportion, unbalanced, or impure, it takes hurt (ibid., p. 78).

The cup can be of any shape (sometimes it's made to look like the female sexual organ), and the most common material used is silver, although sometimes copper or glass is used as well.

On a practical level, the cup is used to serve the sacrament during a ritual. Sometimes it's used in divination as a magic mirror—the magician asks a question and gazes into the liquid in the cup until one sees the answer in it (usually metaphorical). To do so, the water needs to be perfectly still, another symbol of the mental state required for performing such operations!

PRACTICAL EXERCISES

EXERCISE 27

THE OMNIL FORMULA IN PRACTICE

For four weeks in a row, experiment daily with the OMNIL formula as described further above. You can integrate it into your practice of the Lesser Banishing Ritual of the Pentagram or perform it in a manner similar to the IAO formula. But don't neglect the IAO formula completely since both exercises supplement each other quite well. For example, you could perform the IAO formula in the morning and the OMNIL formula in the evening. Again, record your impressions in your magical diary.

EXERCISE 28

ASTRAL MAGIC AND MEDITATION (II)

This exercise is similar to Exercise 23 in the last section with the one difference that you should concentrate on getting smaller each time you exhale. Start off slowly, step by step, and increase the exercise daily until after about four weeks when the exercise is over, you've reached the size of an atom. After each exercise, imagine yourself getting bigger with each inhaled breath.

EXERCISE 29

PRACTICAL ASTROMAGIC

If you haven't done so yet, get a hold of your personal horoscope. It doesn't matter whether you calculate it yourself or print it out on a computer. But in case of the latter, you only need an actual calculation and not an interpretation—computerized interpretations are utterly useless for a living human being since its method of calculation is rigid and stiff. If you decide to calculate your horoscope yourself, make sure to use serious tables (ephemerides and house tables) and not the "approximate" tables that you'll find in most cheap horoscope books since these are notoriously inaccurate.

In order to calculate a horoscope, you'll need the following information: date of birth (day, month, year); place of birth; exact time of birth (watch out for daylight saving time!). You may be able to find the exact time of birth on your birth certificate (unfortunately, this is not always the case). Otherwise, try enquiring at the local courthouse, or asking your parents or other relatives. Such information might not always be the most reliable, but we need to do the best we can with the information we have.[2]

Your horoscope should be calculated according to the classical method and should contain the following information:

planetary positions

houses (sometimes called "fields"; Placidus or Koch system)

aspects

For now, just the "larger aspects" are sufficient—conjunction (0°), opposition (180°), sextile (60°), square (90°), and trine (30°).

If you're a beginner to astrology, study your horoscope in detail with the help of reference books (see recommended literature at the end of this section). This is surely not the most intelligent and reliable method, but there's unfortunately no other way for the astrological layman but to plow one's way through. So if you know absolutely nothing about astrology, you'll have no other choice but to work your way into the material until you've thoroughly memorized its symbols and the choreography of their energies, and learned how to virtuously interpret their many possible combinations. Meanwhile, through your practice of the hexagram ritual, you should already have a fairly reliable feeling for the subtle planetary energies, which will help you quite a bit.

Also, start paying attention to transits, or the crossing of the planets over your own natal chart. If you don't have a lot of experience yet, concentrate on just two or three planets at first (e.g., moon, Jupiter, and Saturn). Note their aspects and positions in your natal chart, e.g., on which day Jupiter in transit forms an opposition with Jupiter in your natal chart, or when Saturn in transit forms a square with Saturn in your natal chart, or when the moon in transit forms a conjunction with the moon in your natal chart, and so on.

At the same time, pay attention to the effect that such transits have on your magical perception and your magic as a whole—if any, because as we already mentioned, not everyone reacts in the same way to transits. Do this for at least one year until you're thoroughly familiar with your horoscope as well as with your reaction to such transits. The purpose of this exercise isn't to make you dependent on such astrological factors, but rather to train your feeling for the link between cosmic energy and fate.

If you're completely new to astrology, be patient with yourself and don't expect too much at first. Through your previous practice of the planetary rituals, you should find it a bit easier to understand the planetary powers, but learning astrology involves its long-term study before you'll have enough knowledge to effectively be able to work with it.

If, on the other hand, you're already an experienced astrologer, you've probably already done these exercises in one form or another. In this case, just skip over this part unless you'd like to start integrating your astrological experience more closely with your magical practice, or begin monitoring the results of your magical operations by considering the astrological aspects.

By the way, it's a good idea to support your study of astrology with sigil magic operations.

EXERCISE 30

PRACTICAL SIGIL MAGIC (II)

Combine the Tratak Exercise 26 with sigil magic by using a sigil that you made according to the picture method as a focus for your concentration. Do this one or two times a week, or even more if you like. But don't use a sigil until you feel that you're quite good at the exercise already, which might even take a few weeks. You can also experiment by using the same sigil several times. Record the results in your magical diary.

FURTHER READING

Today there are so many excellent books on astrology available that it's difficult to choose just a few to list here. You can find more detailed information on astrological tables and charts (ephemerides, house tables, geographic position tables) in New Age bookstores. Classical astrology mainly works with Placidus house tables, but modern astrology often uses the system developed by Walter Koch (also called GOH, *Geburtsortshoroskop*, "birthplace horoscope").

When buying books containing ephemerides, make sure that they contain calculations for Pluto, which wasn't discovered until 1930. (Some books didn't incorporate this planet into their calculations until the early 1960s!) Today, for technical reasons, the midnight ephemeris is generally preferred over the midday ephemeris.

BIBLIOGRAPHY

Aleister Crowley, *Magick*
Michael Gebauer, *Grundlagen der Zeremonialmagie I, Thelema,* Issue 9, 1984, pp. 30–35
William Gray, *Magical Ritual Methods*
Stephen Mace, *Stealing The Fire From Heaven*

1. An exception to this rule is made by magical orders that offer a standardized training program; in their own interest, training is synchronized and standardized in order to ensure that the group as a whole remains clearly structured.
2. If there's absolutely no way to find out your exact time of birth, things can get pretty complicated. In this case, a respectable astrologer could backtrack and find out your time of birth based on the events in your life so far, and by cross-checking the results with future forecasts over an extended period of time, which could take years. That's a painstaking process that not every astrologer is capable of doing, and it surely wouldn't be cheap either. Many astrologers just assume for the start that the time of birth is around midday, but a person skilled in dowsing could also use a pendulum to determine the exact time.

THE MAGIC GAZE (I)

The famous "evil eye" (sometimes known by its Italian name, *malocchio*) has been one of the basic techniques used by witches and magicians for years. It was and still is feared from the North Pole to the South and ethnographers consider it to be the perfect example of "common superstition." But while ethnologists and anthropologists just scoff at the stories about this magic gaze, considering it to be nothing more than a fascinating remnant of prehistoric times, magicians take it seriously and practice it widely.

There have been many explanations for the way it works, but this phenomena is actually way too complex to describe in just a few sentences since it actually includes a great number of different "gazes." In other words, the magic gaze has a great deal of various functions and can be trained and applied accordingly. We'd like to dedicate several sections of this book to this topic since it will also help us train our magical perception at the same time and give us a powerful tool for magically influencing others.

You've probably heard the expression "If looks could kill!" Well, from a magician's point of view, they can—although only in rare cases—but they can also cause a lot of sustained damage. Nonetheless, it would be wrong to only consider the negative aspect of this practice because it can be used just as well for healing, clairvoyance, and calming down overexcited people or animals. The main reason why the magic gaze has such a bad reputation is probably due to the fact that its technique and function have basically been unknown for such a long period of time.

To make things more difficult, the "evil eye" is often used instinctively by completely untrained people with a natural talent. But such people are usually outsiders (just like most other sensitive people are, such as psychics, clairvoyants, and so on) that are often ridiculed for the fact that they're different, forcing them to use this gaze for destructive purposes in pure self-defense. After all, the bringer of bad news is often identified with the bad news itself and therefore punished for it. For example, if a seer uses the magic gaze and happens to see the death of someone that walks by him on the street, and he carelessly shares this information with other people, he's putting himself in a pretty dangerous position (during the Inquisition, this could even have been deadly). At best, nothing will happen and people will just laugh at him or brush him off as being "not quite right in the head." But if his prediction comes true, there will be plenty of sharp tongues who mix up cause and effect to such a severe degree that they'll end up blaming the seer and his magic gaze for the death of that person.

Since the eyes are considered to be the "window to the soul," magic has always worked with various eye techniques; these techniques are either used in magical operations or to disguise the eyes themselves (e.g., hiding one's thoughts). The eyes can reveal a great deal about a person's current state of mind, and usually they'll signify change well ahead of any change in the person's expression or gestures.

The best ways to use the magic gaze that we should concern ourselves with now are listed below. In order to save room, we've only given short explanations of each since most will become self-explanatory throughout the course of your work.

1) To concentrate the power of thought and focus on a specific thing: requires no target person (no "victim"), but serves as a technique for thought control in general.
2) To transfer magical impulses (commands) to a target person without one's knowledge in order to influence him or her: for use ranging from aura and chakra manipulation for healing purposes to the implantation of an exploding glyph in the person's aura.
3) To disguise one's own state of mind and intentions: disguising one's own eyes or putting on a fake expression (e.g., friendly instead of grim).
4) To perceive subtle energies and direct them as well as for clairvoyance: an extension of one's own range of perception for the purpose of manipulation or gazing

into the future (e.g., in the magic mirror or crystal ball).

5) To scan another person in order to determine other's strengths and weaknesses: determining and diagnosing a situation (e.g., in healing operations, magical warfare, etc.) before beginning a magical operation.
6) Extracting energy or information from a target person: aura and chakra manipulation by tapping the victim's subtle energies, causing him or her to weaken until (although quite rare) completely emptied of odic force; but also used for tapping undesired energies that cause an illness or in exorcisms; furthermore, for duplicating and "recording" conscious and unconscious information that's stored in the target person.

In contrast to the 180° gaze that we've already discussed, the magic gaze is a so-called fixation technique. Here, the eyes are not "defocused," but rather just the opposite—they're focused on a specific point.

While the 180° gaze (which, technically speaking, actually belongs to the wider category of "magic gazes") is mainly used for passive perception, or receiving subtle sensory impulses and expanding one's awareness, the magic gaze in general (with the exception of numbers 4 and 5) has the task of sending subtle sensory impulses and concentrating awareness and energy into one point of focus.

Its power is due to the fact that a person tends to pay particular attention to changes around the eye area when conversing with others, thereby receiving lots of other information from them that goes above and beyond the contents of the actual conversation itself—and often without even being aware of it. Often enough, all you have to do is refuse direct eye contact to make the other person nervous or even to make him or her mad for seemingly no reason at all.

Try it out yourself. Whenever you talk to people, gaze at the spot directly between their eyes (ajna chakra). Don't look into their eyes while talking, but keep your eyes "peeled" on them as described above and talk completely normal. This is also a good exercise for magicians who have trouble looking people in the eye. The clever point of this trick is that the other people can never see through you. You're not avoiding their gaze because they're looking directly into your eyes all the time, but they aren't able to see where they're focused (they can't "catch your gaze"), and their own uncertainty bounces right back to them with full force. The result is increased nervousness, uncontrollable wiggling, an undefined feeling of discomfort, or even hefty outbreaks of sweating or anger among people with less control over themselves. So if your boss is screaming at you for supposedly making a mistake, you can easily stand up to his or her tirade by applying this technique, and the more he or she loses inner strength and security, the more yours will grow. On the other hand, you should use this technique sparingly, otherwise the other person could get uncontrollably mad, which isn't always desired.

The following experiment will prove that the effectiveness of this gaze doesn't have to be limited to direct eye contact and that it cannot be explained with the tools of common psychology ("intimidating look"):

The next time you find yourself sitting in a movie theater, bus, streetcar, train, or airplane, gaze at the back of someone's head. The best spot to gaze at is the back of the neck, or "death chakra," located in the center just above where the backbone starts. Do this until your "victim" either turns around, scratches his or her neck, or wiggles around nervously. Then try it on a new target person.

Experiment with various distances, for example by first choosing someone in the next row directly in front of you, and then someone five or ten rows away. Of course, you can try this out in a restaurant as well to get the waitstaff's attention when they seem to be deliberately avoiding you.

Once you've mastered this technique to your own satisfaction, try looking right through the target people as though they were made of glass by staring through the same spot on the back of their neck. At first you'll be doing this with your eyes open, but later they'll be half-closed or even closed entirely. This method will be even more effective if you thoroughly train your eyes in the technique of fixation, which is imperative for further work with the magic gaze anyway. To do so, use the fixation circle pictured in Illustration 19 on page 243. You can use it in three ways:

1) Separate page 243 from the book and fold back the bottom so that you're not irritated by the printing.
2) Copy the page and cut out the middle part with the circle.
3) Draw your own circle by using our illustration as a guide.

In any case, we recommend that you color in the circle with pale yellow. Crayons will probably work the best. Afterward, make sure that the dot in the center is still clearly dis-

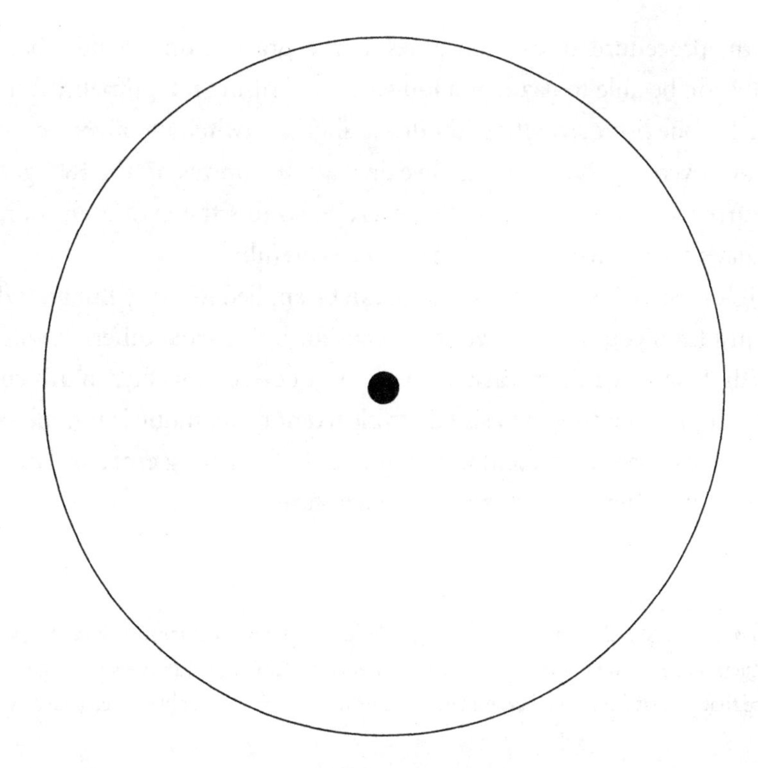

Illustration 19: Eye fixation chart

tinct since it's the most important part of the illustration. If worse comes to worse, you can always color over it again with a black marker.

Hang the fixation chart at eye level on a bare wall—the best is a pure white or black background with no patterns. If you don't have a suitable wall at home, you can hang up a white or black sheet to use as a backdrop. Sit five to six feet away on a comfortable chair in the god posture; if you have experience with the half-lotus, dragon, or lotus postures, you can sit on the floor instead.

With your eyes half-closed, breathe deeply for a few minutes—in and out. Now open your eyes all the way and gaze at the dot in the center of the circle. With your eyes stiffly open wide (without letting your eyelids twitch!) gaze at the dot until your eyes begin to water. Then close them and place the palms of your hands, slightly cupped, over your eyes and apply slight pressure to the lids by pressing (so-called "palming"). This relaxes your eyes so you can try again!

Repeat the procedure at least ten times. If you practice on a regular basis (daily is best), you'll soon be able to gaze for a longer period of time. Optimally, you should be able to gaze for one hour straight without the slightest twitching of your eyelids. But at first, avoid any overexertion to prevent eye damage. In contrast to the 180° gaze—which uses the blurred vision technique—this exercise strains the eyes even more and unequally at that, which is why it's important to be careful![1]

The skills developed with this technique can be applied to many things. It does much more than just train your magic gaze as a means for influencing others; it will also make working with the magic mirror easier, as we'll begin discussing later in this chapter.

Once again, we need to emphasize that this fixation technique is not the same as the 180° gaze! So please avoid accidentally slipping into the wrong exercise. For now, make a clear distinction between tratak and the magic gaze.

---

1. For this exercise, you should remove any seeing aids (especially contact lenses) since the eyes need to be trained in their natural state in order to be magically effective. If you're extremely nearsighted, just reduce the distance that you sit from the fixation chart accordingly until you're able to see it clearly enough.

INTRODUCTION TO RITUAL MAGIC (VII)

THE MAGIC WAND

The magic wand is a favorite tool of the stereotype image of a magician.

Actually, the wand represents the element of Fire in the Hermetic tradition of the Golden Dawn. As such, it's always been the subject of much discussion. Surely one of the reasons for this is the fact that the element of Fire stands for sexuality, among other things, and even in magical operations that have nothing to do with sexual themes or sex magic, certain aspects are often bashfully concealed or disguised, and sometimes even become the object of pompous, mystical speculation, such as the case with Aleister Crowley at times.

In this connection, however, we need to keep one important fact in mind: Every magician—and every generation of magicians—will treat the magical weapons with various degrees of importance depending on one's own individual preferences and insufficiencies. Crowley hardly even mentions the dagger, for example, while the wand seems to be the most important weapon of all to him. However, instead of dealing with it in connection with ritual work (his statements on the weapons are a great exception anyway), he wrote pages and pages about the importance of the Magical Will and Magical Oath, which will probably confuse beginners even more instead of enlightening them. Even Bardon called the wand "the most important tool in ritual magic" and pointed out that magicians have been depicted holding a wand since the beginning of time. Even modern-day stage magicians—whom we prefer to call "illusionists" (according to their own terminology) in order to avoid misunderstandings—want their audiences to believe that their magic wand can give them their seemingly supernatural powers to perform all kinds of miracles. Bardon, like Crowley (who owes much more to the former than his followers like to believe) views the dagger as a rather subordinate weapon. In fact, they both treat it as merely a miniature sword with no mentionable symbolism of its own.

The increased significance of the dagger in the few last decades is most likely due to the influence of the Anglo-Saxon Wicca tradition. With every right, this tradition claims that it has undergone a considerable paradigm shift since the end of World War II concerning the magic of Europe and North America, which—in my opinion—has never been mentioned in the relevant literature as of yet: the wand being replaced by the dagger in its function as the embodiment of the magical will. In the angular tradition today, the dagger is rarely used, and when so, only as a substitute for the sword.

If you read older literature on magic, you'll have to keep in mind that the wand is generally considered to be the main elemental weapon. It represents the magician's will and symbolizes one's power and might. On the other hand, Bardon, for example, works with several different wands with each being used for a different purpose or consecrated for a different sphere, but he uses only one single sword—although he considers the dagger and trident to be suitable substitutes as well, especially for demonic operations.

How does modern magic use the wand? As already mentioned, it's a symbol of the element of Fire. As such, it embodies vitality and the will, both in a biological sense as well as in a psychological and magical one. The analogy "wand = will" becomes clearer when we also look at the word "action" as its *tertium comparationis*. Essentially, the wand is an active weapon: a symbol for magical action and taking effect, the assumption and exercising of personal power. But since it also represents sexuality, it's sometimes depicted in phallic form, especially in older, patriarchal traditions. And this is exactly why the paradigm shift we mentioned inevitably had to take place in more modern times. The general departure from the phallocratic, patriarchal, male-dominated image of the world that early magicians held expressed itself quite unnoticeably in the gradual changeover from the wand to the dagger. Today, it's difficult for us to accept that a magician's entire will is embodied in only one element, namely Fire. The dagger, on the other hand, is not an elemental weapon, so in the lines of modern thought it corresponds better to the will, which is supposed to be the master of the elements and therefore logically cannot be just one of them. At least this is one of the arguments of modern magic that we should at least take into serious consideration, even though every person should decide for oneself whether or not one might prefer to follow the old tradition instead. In any case, we'll have to delve deeper into the symbolism and philosophy of magical thinking following our discussion of the ritual weapons so that we don't get stuck on the level of "lower" or everyday practical magic, regardless of how important this certainly is.

Nonetheless, the wand is and remains an important magical weapon, although today's versatile modern magician will certainly hesitate to claim that any single weapon is the "most important," even though one most likely will have a better relationship to some weapons than to others. All magical weapons are principally equal. Apart from their function or element classification, the only thing that differentiates one from the other is our own opinion about them. In the sense of a holistic, harmonic image of the world, it would be unacceptable to give one element precedence over another.

While the cup receives and gives birth, the wand becomes the manifestation of the will, or its executive body.[1] However, this is not the same as the complete identification of the will and the wand! Picture the wand as a sort of "right hand" of your own magical will. It embodies creation and action. While the cup is centripetal (moving toward centralization) and feminine, the wand is centrifugal (moving away from centralization) and male. When dipped in cold water, the hot wand will cause vaporization, thereby creating air: Thought itself is born out of the polarity of the sexes, and even earth is a child of this primeval union.

The wand is therefore power and driving force at the same time, but also the power of control over itself and control over the universe that it creates. But the wand doesn't create entirely on its own—it needs the cup. Blind action without firm intuition is a waste of energy and life. The lingam (phallus, wand) must unite with the yoni (vagina, cup); only the interaction between yin and yang can arouse the energy that leads to creation.

It is action that makes a magician truly a magician. Whoever just sits in a room speculating on the possibilities of magic without facing the bitter winds of practice will remain nothing but a bloodless theorist and never be able to force "Dark Brother Fear" to its knees. That's why the wand is also the symbol of fearlessness. On a practical level, it's used mainly to concentrate and transfer energy; in sex magic, it's substituted by the male magician's penis in the same way the female magician's vagina becomes the cup.

The wand can be of any form—it's often depicted as a phallus or as the staff of the Egyptian god Thot or Tahuti, who corresponds to Hermes and Mercury. The Golden Dawn prefers the Hermes staff with the double snake, while modern Chaos Magic developed the wand into a lightning bolt from the Chaos Sphere. It can be made of anything from carved wood to gold or iron. It can even be shaped like a fork and made of wicker if it's designed to double as a divining rod. Even if its symbolism is quite deep, the wand itself is the easiest weapon to make. A thick branch and a carving knife are all that you need to make a usable wand. It's rarely longer than a cubit (measured from the wrist to the elbow), although sometimes it can be as long as a walking stick, especially when the Egyptian form is used. In any case, it should fit firmly in your grip and not be too lightweight.

THE MAGIC MIRROR

Before you start working with the magic mirror—which is a fascinating and diversified field—you should already have a good deal of experience with the 180° gaze (defocusing) as well as with the magic gaze (fixation) described in this section in order to achieve optimal results. If you want to make your own mirror, you can train these eye techniques parallel to working on it. Goal for beginners: the ability to gaze for three to six minutes without any twitching of the eyes. Midterm goal: about ten to fifteen minutes.

Strictly speaking, the magic mirror is not a ritual weapon but one of your magical tools. However, in practice this isn't completely true since the magic mirror is really one of the best weapons in magical warfare, such as for influencing a target person from a distance, distant tapping of one's odic force, and so on. Most authors describe the magic mirror as a tool for divination and in this function it resembles the crystal ball.

If it is only used for divination and evocation, the magic mirror can basically be made of any shiny material: glass, crystal, gemstones, or similar. There are even "temporary" magic mirrors, for example, when the magician fills a bowl with water or dark oil that's poured out after the operation. Even a black-painted thumbnail can be used! Some magicians prefer to use their magic cup for divinatory operations instead of using a separate mirror.

However, the term "magic mirror" usually refers to a special tool that's often called a "black mirror" as well. The reason for this is obvious—it has a black surface. The surface is usually concave, or bent inward, and is either made of common glass or shiny rock, such as obsidian or even polished coal. Metals can also be used, preferably steel or silver, whereby the latter will turn "black" automatically through oxidation. Generally most modern magicians use a so-called clock glass mirror, which is why we've decided to deal with it in more detail here.

The easiest way to make such a mirror is by obtaining a clock glass that's about four to seven inches in diameter. The external, bulged side is then blackened. Theoretically this is easily done but there are a number of ways to do it wrong. In order to spare you from unnecessarily wasting your time, we'd like to list a few unsuitable methods here that beginners often attempt. After all, the wheel doesn't have to be rediscovered every day!

Practice has shown that common glass paint is not really suited for blackening since it doesn't actually get black enough. The glass remains too transparent. Using soot (e.g., by holding the clock glass over a candle) is problematic because the coating is easily scratched and scraped. If you wanted to frame the clock glass later on, which is recommended anyway and absolutely necessary if you used this method of blackening, you'd need to be extremely careful, otherwise you'd have to keep trying to cover up the scratch marks. Black wax, on the other hand, usually blisters just like synthetic plastic and sticks irregularly to the glass, giving it an undesired texture that will distract your eyes instead of focusing them. Plus, it's quite sensitive to heat.

The best method is to simply paint the surface of the glass with the kind of undercoating paint that's used for cars (available in automotive stores). (Gregor A. Gregorius recommends tar paint.) This will give you a smooth, opaque black color that's just perfect for your work with the mirror.

The magician can design the frame in any way one desires. Magic mirrors can have all possible kinds of frames: round, square, pentagonal, oval, and so on. The round form is the most common, and usually the frame is just made of plain, black-painted wood. Stained wood will distract your eyes because of the wood grain, but some magicians prefer this kind anyway. Generally, we recommend that you not press the clock glass into a synthetic plastic form since it will usually come loose after awhile. Instead, a skilled plastics molder could make the mirror and frame all at once, entirely out of synthetic plastic. Papier-mâché is sometimes used as well.

A more complicated method of making a magic mirror is to cut a flat slab out of a large, black gemstone and polish it, which any good gem cutter should be able to do. As already mentioned, the most common material for this is obsidian, but smaller formats are occasionally made of onyx.

In older magic literature you'll find many different ways to make a magic mirror. However, most of the books agree that after it's completed and consecrated, no other person than the magician him- or herself should be allowed to look into it. That's why the mirror should always be covered up when not in use and hidden from prying eyes. Traditionally, it's wrapped in black silk or velvet or sometimes kept in a closeable box.

The reason for this is both psychological as well as symbol-logical. Firstly, in older literature, the mirror is mainly used for divination and acts as a gateway to the magician's soul, or unconscious, and no unauthorized persons should be allowed to enter from the other side. That's why many fortunetellers never let their clients touch their cards or crystal balls. Secondly, tradition requires that all magical weapons only be handled by their owner, since an outsider could destroy the subtle energy that they've been painstakingly charged with through elaborate ritual procedures. The same applies to "touching with the eyes."

Thirdly, the conscious mind develops a sort of inner confidence when it owns objects that no other person is allowed to handle, which surely has to do with the fact that the subconscious then feels more comfortable (or "unnoticed") when it opens up, therefore enabling a state of trance to be reached.

REPORTS FROM MAGICAL PRACTICE (I)

With this little series, we'd like to round off our training by reporting occasionally on experiences from everyday magical work. All examples are absolutely authentic and originate either from my own practice or that of other magicians. They serve the purpose of showing and illustrating the basic principles of magic in such a way that we can only experience through practice. To protect the identity of the people involved, we didn't use the names of any living magicians; if an abbreviation of the name seemed necessary or appropriate for reasons of style, we disguised other characteristics and places in such a way that the people involved can no longer be identified. Only those examples that can easily be found in other literature that's available to the public haven't been changed.

Frater A. in D. discovered firsthand the importance of correctly formulating his statement of intent in sigil magic. He made a sigil according to the word method with the statement of intent "I will have 500 dollars within two weeks" and charged it by means of sex magic.

After about one and a half weeks, Frater A. visited a friend and sat down on his couch in the living room. After awhile, the friend began looking for his wallet and started getting nervous because it contained a large sum of money. Finally, they discovered that Frater A. had accidentally sat down on his friend's wallet. You can imagine how astonished Frater A. was when he found out that the sum of money in the wallet was identical to the sum he had charged a sigil for, right down to the last cent. What happened? Obviously his subconscious took the word "have" a little to literally.

The unusual thing about this incident is the fact that Frater A. tried a second time by rewording his statement of intent to make it more clear to his subconscious that he wanted to get the desired amount. Usually such "touch-up jobs" are rarely successful, especially if they follow just a short time after the failed operation. After all, this example shows us that we never need to give up hope and certainly should try another attempt.

When formulating our statement of intent, we should always remember the fact that our subconscious prefers the path of less resistance (at least that's how it seems to our conscious mind) when fulfilling a magical task. In Frater A.'s situation, it was surely easier to get someone else's money by sitting on it. But this example also points out a common problem of sigil magic and working with statements of intent: It's nearly impossible to completely eliminate all potential false interpretations (or to be more exact, "all too literal interpretations") when formulating a statement of intent. So there's really no other choice but trial and error with the goal of developing a certain sensitivity for the language that our own subconscious mind speaks. This can only be achieved through frequent practice and careful monitoring of the results.

The following episode is taken from my own practice. A female client asked me to apply my magic to make her husband agree to a divorce according to the terms that she stipulated. Although he principally agreed to a divorce, he only wanted to commit to a minimum in financial obligations for his wife and their three children, which caused quite a bit of dispute that even turned violent at times. The married couple had already separated and the wife wanted to keep the house and receive a certain monthly sum for alimony. Plus, she demanded custody of the children.

Using a recent photo of her husband, I influenced him magically by means of doll magic. About three weeks later, the husband paid a visit to my client and was completely changed. He was in an extremely good mood because he was looking forward to his upcoming vacation with his new girlfriend. Once again, the subject of divorce was brought up, but this time he agreed to everything that his wife had been demanding for months. Thrilled, she called me the next day to tell me what had happened.

However, after asking her a few questions, we realized that she had forgotten to get his consent in writing, not to mention not getting it notarized. In all her excitement, she completely forgot. I didn't want to discourage her, but I had the feeling that it wasn't over just yet. And I was right. When the husband returned from his vacation, he claimed that he never agreed to anything, and offered her even less than before.[2]

It took many more magical operations and nearly an entire year to get the problem under control until the couple was finally divorced in common consent and a relatively favorable solution was found for my client that she could live with. But this solution—even though it wasn't a bad one—was only a "second alternative" as compared to the original goal that she just missed by a thread.

With this example, I'd like to point out the fact that the effects of a magical operation are often fleeting. You need to recognize them with an alert eye in order to quickly snatch up the favorable opportunity, otherwise it will be gone in a flash and nothing but disappointment will remain. After all, magic is often described as "the art of illusion." But the actual art is being able to give substance to the "illusions" that are created by magic to make them lasting and allow them to manifest concretely and tangibly.

However, this requires that you do everything in your power even in a nonmagical sense to ensure success. A magician who uses one's art as a substitute for physical effort and alertness, for cunning and attentiveness, will constantly run into difficulties. Not that magic would never work under these circumstances, but in such cases the result is often delayed, success may occur on an entirely different level, or all kinds of situations may arise that seem to be the sheer expression of the "irony of fate."

PRACTICAL EXERCISES

EXERCISE 31

THE MAGIC GAZE (I)

Work actively with the magic gaze as described in this section. Work in a playful manner so you don't get tired of it, but also practice regularly and seriously (especially with the eye fixation chart) in order to get good results as soon as possible.

EXERCISE 32

THE MAGIC GAZE (II)

You need a partner for this exercise. In fact, you can even practice with children since they seem to like this exercise and often have extremely good results, as long as you don't force them to do anything they don't want to do. The purpose of this exercise is to develop a feel for receiving the magic gaze so that you notice when someone uses it against you—an important aspect of magical protection! You can do this exercise either indoors or outside.

The sender should sit comfortably on the floor since the optical sending perspective is better this way, although it will surely work from any position. Stand comfortably with your back to your partner no less than ten feet away from him or her, yet no more than twenty-five feet away for the start. According to my experience this is the average optimal distance, although it naturally may vary some. It would be best to close your eyes, breathe deeply and relax for a few minutes, then give your partner a signal with your hand so that he or she can start. If you're not a complete beginner, you can also work with your eyes open.

Now your partner will gaze at a certain part of your body, and your job is to find out what he or she's staring at. Rely entirely on your own intuition. In any case you should avoid rationally thinking about where you would gaze if you were the other person. Experience has shown that this exercise works best when your partner shuts off rational thought to the best of his or her ability. Your partner shouldn't try to "send" you anything, nor should he or she try to cause a certain sensation (burning, itching, or similar) or impatiently wait for you to shudder in fear. Ideally, the brief, firm intention of wanting to train your magical gaze is enough—the rest requires only forgetting and relaxing, just like with sigil magic. (Always remember the principle of "nonattachment/nonlack of interest"!)

For now, practice as the receiver for just five to ten minutes. Now exchange roles with your partner. If both partners still feel like practicing, you can do the exercise again, but more than that is not recommended since the unknown organ that we use for subtle perception gets tired quickly, which could impair the results (and therefore affect later results as well).

THE MAGIC GAZE (II)

Now we'd like to go into more detail about the actual use of the magic gaze. In order to do so, we'll discuss the individual points mentioned in the last section.

1) Concentrating the Power of Thought and Focus on a Specific Thing

This exercise requires no target person (or "victim"), but serves as a technique for thought control in general. We practice this gaze for the sole purpose of mastering the control of our thoughts and focusing our will.

Practice has shown repeatedly that a magical process is initiated in the subconscious by the mere focusing of one's gaze. Compare the death posture technique used for charging a sigil in which the eyes are focused to obtain the desired state of gnosis necessary for charging.

2) Transferring Magical Impulses (Commands) to a Target Person Without Target's Knowledge in Order to Influence Him or Her

By charging the gaze with a statement of intent or command (by making it the center of focus), the aura and chakras can be manipulated for healing purposes. However, this requires previous mastery of the gaze in order to work. We then enter a state of gnosis and transfer the command imaginatively and semiconsciously to the target person. This can even go so far as to implant an exploding glyph into a victim's aura. An exploding glyph is a sigil (designed either according to Spare's method or in any other way) that's designed to trigger a self-destruction mechanism in the target person. Figuratively speaking, it "blows up" the opponent's force field from the inside. Since most operations for magically harming others are designed to attack the victim's immune system, the exploding glyph should contain a corresponding command. The glyph is projected into the target person's aura where it's anchored and then activated—or caused to self-activate—by discontinuation of the gaze and distraction ("banishing"). This example points out once again how neutral the techniques of magic actually are, as the same gaze can either heal or make someone sick.

3) Disguising One's Own State of Mind and Intentions

"Looks are deceiving," or "the eyes are the mirror to the soul." If we want to effectively hide our moods and intentions from others, we need to be able to masterfully disguise our own eyes by feigning a deceptive expression (e.g., friendly instead of grim). This alone is enough for superficial contacts. However, if our opponent is particularly sensitive, the situation may require strict thought control so that the other person cannot "tap" our true intentions by means of telepathy. To do so, we recommend activating a distracting and completely irrelevant train of thought that will act as an interfering transmitter. In particular, strong emotions such as fear, anger, or happiness are quite difficult to disguise without practice. The literal "poker face" of a professional gambler is characterized not only by the complete control of facial expressions and face muscles, but mainly by a rigid "blocking" expression that allows no insight into what's going on inside. This procedure could also be called an "armored gaze." The mastery of such techniques can be of significant use, for example during difficult business negotiations.

4) Perceiving Subtle Energies and Directing Them as well as for Clairvoyance

Generally we use the 180° gaze for perceiving subtle energies, although some magicians prefer using the fixed magic gaze for this purpose. You need to find out for yourself what works best for you. The goal here is the extension of your own range of perception for the purpose of manipulation or gazing into the future (with a magic mirror or crystal ball, for example). Directing subtle energies, on the other hand, is almost always done in a focused state. Often the fixed gaze is used for perceiving subtle energies by turning off the psychological censor and creating a state of empty mind. Only when this is achieved should the magician switch to the 180° gaze.

5) Scanning Another Person in Order to Determine His or Her Strengths and Weaknesses

The fixed gaze can also be of use for determining and diagnosing a situation (e.g., in healing operations, magical warfare, etc.) before beginning a magical operation. First we sweep over the entire aura of the person using the 180° gaze in order to get a general overview where his or her strengths and weaknesses are, then we apply the fixed gaze to recognize more details. But here, too, an ounce of practice is worth a ton of theory. Practice scanning various things with your partner or any other person using both eye techniques and compare the results.

6) Extracting Energy or Information from a Target Person

By using our eyes like absorbing sponges, we can manipulate the aura and chakras of our target person by tapping his or her subtle energies, even causing the target to weaken until (although quite rare) completely emptied of odic force. But this technique can also be used for extracting undesired pathogenic energies, for exorcisms, or other similar purposes. Plus, we can also duplicate the conscious and unconscious information stored in a target person and transfer it into our own information memory. The technique of absorbing with the eyes as compared to using the palm of the hand or other tools—such as crystals—has the advantage of being less complicated and sometimes even less noticeable. During an exorcism, an extremely rigid gaze is generally applied that's focused directly into the eyes or onto the ajna chakra of the victim in order to break the resistance of his or her possession. The victim's eyes usually begin to twitch when this is about to happen. This is also the moment when the undesired energy or being withdraws from the victim, which is usually accompanied by deep, jerky inhalation. Depending on the severity of possession, it may take several attempts that often require weeks or even months of effort.

All of these practices are difficult to describe in detail and can only be hinted at. Our language is basically unsuitable for specifying such subjective procedures. But with the techniques that we've alluded to here along with your practice of mirror magic, you have enough information to try some experiments of your own. And don't ever forget that ultimately every magician develops his or her very own personal style of magic anyway. This book is designed primarily to help you along the way to finding your individual method of sorcery instead of trying to force you into a rigid system of specific practices.

Turn your eyes into control stations of power! Learn to play with your visual perception and see the spaces in between reality (and in between concrete objects as well)—perceive things receptively and learn to actively emit looks of power. For example, you can practice by projecting self-made word or picture sigils onto a neutrally colored background, either at home or in the company of other people. Experiments with animals are quite interesting as well since they often react quite sensitively to such eye techniques.

---

1. Just think about the caduceus or Hermes staff, or the staff of Asklepios. While Hermes is the psychopompos—or guide of the souls—in the Kingdom of the Dead, Asklepios is the god of medicine and therefore of life. The staff also symbolizes kundalini, or the power of the snake, and the essence of sexuality and all of life itself.

2. This is a common reaction to such a magical influencing operation after the first spell has been broken. It's nothing more than the common law of action and reaction—or *actio et reactio*.

INTRODUCTION TO RITUAL MAGIC (VIII)

THE MAGIC SWORD

Probably the most profound contemplation on the magical sword as a ritual weapon in a magical-philosophical sense once again comes from Aleister Crowley:

> *The Magick Sword is the analytical faculty; directed against any demon it attacks his complexity.*
>
> *Only the simple can withstand the Sword. As we are below the Abyss, this weapon is then entirely destructive: it divides Satan against Satan. It is only in the lower forms of Magick, the purely human forms, that the Sword has become so important a weapon. A Dagger should be sufficient.*
>
> *But the mind of man is normally so important to him that the Sword is actually the largest of his weapons; happy is he who can make the Dagger suffice!* (Magick, p. 86).

How should this be understood? Why does Crowley praise the magician who doesn't need a sword, calling him or her happy? Let's have a look at more of what he has to say first:

The Sword, necessary as it is to the beginner, is but a crude weapon. Its function is to keep off the enemy or to force a passage through them—and though it must be wielded to gain admission to the palace, it cannot be worn at the marriage feast.

One might say that the Pantacle is the bread of life, and the Sword the knife which cuts it up. One must have ideas, but one must criticize them.

The Sword, too, is that weapon with which one strikes terror into the demons and dominates them. One must keep the Ego Lord of the Impressions. One must not allow the circle to be broken by the demon; one must not allow any one idea to carry one away.

It will readily be seen how very elementary and false all this is—but for the beginner it is necessary.

In all dealings with demons the point of the Sword is kept downwards, and it should not be used for invocation, as is taught in certain schools of magick.

If the Sword is raised towards the Crown, it is no longer really a sword. The Crown cannot be divided. Certainly the Sword should not be lifted.

The Sword may, however, be clasped in both hands, and kept steady and erect, symbolizing that thought has become one with the single aspiration, and burnt up like a flame. This flame is the shin[1]*, the Ruach Alhim, not the mere Ruach Adam. The divine and not the human consciousness.*

The Magician cannot wield the Sword unless the Crown is on his head.

Those Magicians, who have attempted to make the Sword the sole or even the principal weapon, have only destroyed themselves, not by the destruction of combination, but by the destruction of division.[2] *Weakness overcomes strength.*

The mind must be broken up into a form of insanity before it can be transcended (ibid., p. 87f.).

The sword is therefore a critical authority—with its help, the magician can get a grip on one's feelings that distort one's perceptions and hide the nature of things. Needing to use it means being susceptible to the danger of self-deception and insanity. Because if the instinctive confidence of the cup is injured, there will be dangerous discord within the magician. But the sword is also an instrument of thought control and preciseness, and it represents the scientific ideal and emotionally neutral objectivity.

Hence every idea must be analysed by the Sword. Hence, too, there must only be a single thought in the mind of the person meditating.

One may now go on to consider the use of the Sword in purifying Emotions into Perceptions.

It was the function of the Cup to interpret the Perceptions by the Tendencies; the Sword frees the Perceptions from the Web of Emotion.

The Perceptions are meaningless in themselves; but the Emotions are worse, for they delude their victim into supposing them significant and true.

Every Emotion is an obsession; the most horrible of blasphemies is to attribute any emotion to God in the Macrocosm, or to the pure soul in the Microcosm.[. . .]

Even in instruments themselves, their physical qualities, such as expansion and contraction (which may be called, in a way, the roots of pleasure and pain), cause error.

Make a thermometer, and the glass is so excited by the necessary fusion that year by year, for thirty years afterwards or more, the height of the mercury will continue to alter; how much more then with so plastic a matter as the mind! There is no emotion which does not leave a mark on the mind, and all marks are bad marks. Hope and fear are only opposite phases of a single emotion; both are incompatible with the purity of the soul. With the passions of man the case is somewhat different, as they are functions of his own Will. They need to be disciplined, not to be suppressed. But emotion is impressed from without. It is an invasion of the Circle (ibid., pp. 90–92)

Crowley's admonitions—just like those of every shaman—point out again and again that the mind should never be our master, but rather our servant. But this isn't meant to be derogatory. Even this servant has an important and even vital function because without it, the door would be wide open for self-deception, paranoia, and megalomania.

The sword represents our guarantee against magical possession, which is why we need to apply at least the same amount of care in making and consecrating it as we would with all of our other weapons.

The sword corresponds to the element of Air in its characteristics that represent thought, communication, language, and the rational mind. It can be of any shape or form. The handle is usually made of wood[3] coated or set with copper, although solid copper is sometimes used as well.

There is usually a copper ball or disc at the pommel of the handle. The hilt is made of two crescent moons that represent its waxing and waning phases. In between these, round copper discs are attached.[4]

Together, the three discs or balls form an equilateral triangle. Crowley mentions that some magicians make the three balls out of lead, pewter, and gold; the crescent moons would then be made of silver and the handle filled with mercury, turning the sword into a symbol of the planets. But he also continues on to say that this is usually just a wild fantasy that's never followed through with.

The blade of the sword is usually made of stainless steel and should be straight and pointed, and sharp all the way to the hilt. If we look at the symbolism of the metal correspondences, it clearly tells us that this is a weapon that merges the principles of Mars and Venus. In this sense, Crowley wrote:

> *Those two planets are Male and Female—and thus reflect the Wand and the Cup, though in a much lower sense.*
>
> *The hilt is of Venus, for Love is the motive of this ruthless analysis—if this were not so the sword would be a Black Magical weapon* (p. 86).

The magician etches or carves glyphs, symbols, or god-names into the blade. The sigil of a magical name could be used, for example, and Crowley suggests etching the formula AGLA by using vitriol oil.[5]

In the ritual techniques we teach in this book, the sword will only be used for evocations, or demonic operations. But even in this case, it's always "a weapon of last resort." Just imagine it in a practical sense. If the demon in the triangle threatens the stability of the circle, the sword (the intellect, or rational mind) is called for. It's not only used to drive back or "destroy" the demon if necessary, but—if we think back on our model of paradigm shifting—the magician can also use it as a last resort to prevent possible possession by immediately shifting to a paradigm of "magic/disbelief" and declare the entire operation to be nothing but "superstitious nonsense." Of course, such an operation not only has to be learned, but it's also accompanied by a great deal of danger because it violates the magician's symbol-logic by practically voiding the entire magical operation, which could lead to serious negative conditioning every time one's in a state of trance. Reversing these effects can often take years, causing dry spells in which the magician doesn't seem to succeed at any kind of magic at all, causing a sense of desperation that can easily take the upper hand on things.

Strictly speaking, the sword should be used (without physical contact) before the operation since it's also the embodiment of the intellectual capacity to make decisions and the magician makes decisions (e.g., to perform or not to perform a ritual) only after carefully thinking about them beforehand. Afterward, he or she acts uncompromisingly on the decision one has made.

So here's the warning once again since it cannot be repeated often enough:

The magician who never needs to use one's sword is well-off!

With this, we recognize how deep the symbolism of ritual weapons goes, and—without wanting to exaggerate—it has hopefully become clear what we mean by saying that the magician creates one's own universe. In doing so, it doesn't matter at all that he or she adapts a whole heap of symbolic material along the way because the number one rule is always that each magician's individual system of symbols needs to be coherent—in other words, the symbol-logic needs to be retained. That's why the relatively simple, coarse system of symbols that the beginner uses today is certainly much better than the blind imitation of some of the fancy techniques used in earlier times. In any case, we need to give life to the symbols themselves if they're to be of any use, and by giving them the breath of life, we ourselves become gods!

THE CROWN AND THE HAT

Although the crown is rarely used today, there was a time when it was considered to be an important tool, for example in the magic of the Golden Dawn as well as in all magic systems with a strong Egyptian influence. Even Crowley has dedicated two pages to the crown in his book *Magick*, and as we can see in his comments on the magic sword, he feels that the crown is a prerequisite for using the sword.

However, modern magic generally prefers to use the magic hat (sometimes named the "wizard's cap") instead, and its function resembles that of the crown.

Crowley simply wrote: "The Crown of the Magician represents the Attainment of his Work" (ibid., p. 104). After that, he merely described various crowns and their symbolism. He basically recommends two types of crowns:

1) a crown with a band of pure gold with three pentagrams on the front (the middle one contains a diamond or opal) and a hexagram on the back, with the ureaus serpent entwined around it (a typical symbol of sovereignty and initiation;
2) the classical Egyptian ateph crown of Thoth, the god of magic, that's made of two ram's horns, one large and three small sun-discs, large feathers, and a stylized lotus.

A crimson cap is attached to the back of the gold band crown that falls to the shoulders. Since such crowns are rarely used today, as we already mentioned, this reference to Crowley's writings on the symbolism should be enough.

The hat, on the other hand, is usually cone-shaped and therefore symbolizes the subtle energy falling down upon the magician as he or she's standing in one's circle (a "power cone," so to speak). It's usually made of felt (supported by a wire frame), cotton, or even leather. It's often decorated with common magical symbols or the magician's personal sigil.

Apart from their symbolic meanings, both the crown and the hat mainly serve the purpose of increasing the magician's sense of personal power and greatness. This is a psychological aid that supports and strengthens the magician's ability to assert his magical will.

Anyone who has ever worn a crown or a hat during a ritual will know what I'm talking about. This head covering is a valuable tool to help the magician's concentration and focus, although it requires a temple with a fairly high ceiling since the hat can be quite tall sometimes. The suggested height of the magic hat is the measurement from the magician's belly button to the chin.

Rulers, magicians, shamans, medicine people, and sorcerers of all cultures have always worn some kind of head covering; not only does it aid the state of trance, but the mere visual extension of the head always seems to impress any observers. If the crown or hat is not too heavy, yet still noticeable when worn, just the mere wearing of it will cause the magician to stand up straighter and stronger, giving more strength to the arm movements and allowing one to physically manifest that which is demanded of him or her spiritually: preciseness, centeredness, and the focused will.

In group rituals, usually only the ritual leader (e.g., the high priest or priestess) will wear a crown or hat as a sign of dignity and power.

Even though not having a crown or hat as part of your ritual utensils isn't really considered a drawback, you still might want to try out the feeling of wearing some kind of tall headgear (even if it's just provisional) in order for you to at least get an idea of the potential value of such tools. But in the end, it's all a matter of personal preference anyway and we don't want to make the mistake of overestimating its importance here.

THE MAGIC NAME

All around the world, it's a common practice for magicians to give themselves a magic name. Even monks and nuns take on such a name when embarking on their spiritual or monastic way of life. It represents both a new identity and the departure from one's everyday personality. In magical groups and orders, it's also a means of retaining anonymity and preventing infiltration from outsiders.

The magical name is usually received in trance, although it's sometimes calculated kabbalistically or it may symbolize a principle that the magician feels closely linked to, such as Aquarius or Therion, just to name a few. Mythological or historical role models are popular as namesakes as well, such as Merlin, Kundry, Parsifal, or Cassandra.

In almost every case, the magical name represents the magician's motto in life, and quite often the name is the motto itself. My own name is a good example of this: U.·. D.·. is the abbreviation for UBIQUE DÆMON UBIQUE DEUS (Latin for "the demon is everywhere/in everything, the god is everywhere/in everything"). This represents my firm intention to always look at both sides of the coin and not always try to systematically categorize everything into good and evil. Other examples are Crowley's name "Perdurabo" (Latin for "I will persevere"), or that of William Butler Yeats, who as a member of the Golden Dawn, assumed the name D.E.D.I. (Demon est deus inversus), which is Latin for "A demon is a god turned upside down."

Sometimes fantasy names that are received in trance are used as well. In these cases, the actual meaning of the name may not be revealed until much later, or the original meaning may fade away with time and eventually be replaced by a new one.

The addition of "Frater" (Latin for "brother") for males, or "Soror" (Latin for "sister") for females is especially common in magical groups and orders, and corresponds to the Christian monastic tradition. But throughout the course of time, it has become commonplace to use this addition (especially in literary works or written correspondence) even without belonging to an order since the terms "Frater" and "Soror" can also be understood as "comrade" or "colleague."

By the way, numbers that are of certain significance (kabbalistic or otherwise) to the magician are often added to magic names as well (such as Abraxas 333).

Luckily there are no rules for acquiring a magic name. It's even quite common to have more than one. For example, a person who belongs to a magical order may have a lodge name as well as a personal one. Many magicians have another name as well that no other person knows and that's never revealed to another soul as long as the magician is alive. This represents the old magic belief that if a person's (or god's) "true" name is known, one holds the power over it. That's why the secret magical name represents the "last internal line of defense," or the place that protects one's identity—a sort of spiritual inner sanctum.

In its function as a motto of life, the magical name is reflected in the lamen, or pentacle, which we'll be discussing in the next section. While the lamen represents the current state of the magician's individual cosmos, or the present, the magical name symbolizes the future, or the goal that the magician is striving toward—one's desired future. This kind of name can be a blessing and a curse at the same time. Once it's assumed and accepted, it will constantly remind the magician of what one still needs to do. This conscious choosing of a name will become even clearer the less you've thought about the meaning of your real name that you received "by chance" throughout the course of your life.

Choosing a magical name can be a great, joyous moment of self-determination, but often it will become the first warning we receive. After all, while helping us maneuver around various psychonautic obstacles, it can serve as both a walking staff and a crutch. That's why the magician shouldn't just assume any old magical name without really thinking about it, nor should one drop the name without careful consideration.

Of course, it's quite common in magical tradition to document various levels of personal development with the use of various names. The wide variety of magic names that Aleister Crowley used, for example, ranged from Perdurabo to V.V.V.V.V. to Baphomet, right up to his most famous name, To Mega Therion 666.

On the other hand, a name is nothing more than a randomly chosen document of one's stage of personal magical development. When used frequently, the name will become a permanent fixture of one's magical personality, or "part of his or her aura," which therefore cannot just be easily shaken off at will.

Sometimes a magician may even choose a separate name for one single, usually long-term, magical operation that he or she may never use again. This can be compared to the costume or makeup of an actor, although it's also an expression of the emphasis of one certain aspect of one's personality or actions. In other words, the magician specifically creates a certain personality for some specific task that lies ahead.

In this sense, it could even be considered to be a sort of psychogon! But this is quite rare and is usually only done in magical warfare.

Each magician needs to decide for oneself whether or when one should take on a magical name (or maybe even several) if one hasn't done so already. If you just can't come up with the right name using these methods, try incubating a dream designed to reveal the right name (sigil magic would be the best method for doing so). This is the traditional way a shaman would do it. Also think about whether you want other people to know your name or not—after all, you'd be exposing a very intimate part of your personality and that requires mutual trust.

INTRODUCTION TO THE PAN RITUAL

Here we'd like to make a suggestion on one possible way to perform a Pan ritual; the ritual given here has been used by various magicians a number of times.

The Greek figure Pan has always played a large role throughout the history of European magic. The meaning of his name is unclear; some believe its origins derive from the Sanskrit language, while others think it's just a babbled word like "mommy" or "daddy." Not until much later did the word "Pan" receive the meaning "all, everything" that's still connected with it today (in its interpretation as "whole"), and is reflected in modern words such as "pan-Arabic friendship," "pansexuality," or even "panorama" ("whole view"). Pan as an omnipotent god wasn't mentioned until Nero's time.

Pan was thought to be the son of Zeus and a nymph. Right from the day of his birth, his entire body was covered with hair, and he had the horns and legs of a goat. According to tradition, he hunts the nymph named Syrinx who begs her sisters (or the Earth Mother, Gaia, in other versions) to change her into reed. Saddened, Pan sinks down into the reed and a lamenting sound rings out. He cuts a few pieces of various lengths and binds them together with wax, making the shepherd's pipe or pan flute. He later loses this flute and makes a new one out of reeds so that he can play at Dionysos' spring festival. He even challenges Apollo to a musical competition, but loses.

Pan made his home in Arcadia. He was a typical god of shepherds and goats and was worshiped for his fertility—he would "mount" one goat to make the whole herd fertile. But even in early times, he was considered to be at least part human, and therefore didn't have the pure form of an animal.

He can scare man and animal by suddenly appearing, for example while they're resting in the midday heat, but he's also playful and enjoys making jokes and drinking wine.[6]

Pan is in no way just after all the beautiful nymphs—he even likes little boys and even in early times he was considered the epitome of sexuality as such. Pindar mentions him as a companion of the Great Mother, which is reflected in modern-day witchcraft and Wicca where he's honored as the "Horned One" or "Great God." He appears in many shapes and forms and was later merged or equated with other deities such as Dionysos, although his lineage is a bit confusing as well. He's also related to the Roman Fanus, just as Saturn and Faune are often viewed as embodiments of Pan.

It was Christianity that made a devil out of Pan and equated him with the Bible's Satan. This is a clear sign of the demonization of pre-Christian heathenism, and soon afterward images of the devil were automatically given the features of a goat. In this sense, Pan is often merged with Saturn, whereby older Egyptian elements probably played a role as well (Set—Satan—Saturn). As the herald of physical sensuality, Pan became the reincarnation of evil to Christianity since this religion preaches the hatred of one's own body. Concerning Pan's kabbalistic correspondences, I'd like to quote here and in the following some of the passages from my *Versuch über Pan* ("Essay on Pan," see Bibliography at the end of this chapter):

> *In his book LIBER 777, Aleister Crowley assigns the numbers 0 and 13 to Pan—which I feel is quite correct. Omnipotent god and devil in one—what a tremendous step well beyond the awkward dualism of Zoroastrian and Manichaeus systems—not to mention that of Christianity, Mosaism and Islam! With this, Master Therion naturally follows the best of syncretic and gnostic tradition.*

The word "panic" is derived from this deity as well because Pan is not just generous and kind, he can also cause horror and fear, especially to those who have sexual and virile inhibitions. This brings us to his magical functions, and these are quite varied:

> *Pan appears to some as nature personified that could be categorized as spring and the ecstasy of awakening; others, on the other hand, see in him the abyss of existence, the principle of totality, ecstasy and even death. After all, there's a good reason why Pan corresponds to the planet Saturn (in LIBER 777 and other sources), which also carried the stigma of being "devilish" for quite some time.*
>
> *For me personally, Pan is the ultimate symbol of ecstasy—namely the ecstasy that's expressed in the merging of the mystic with his god, as well as in the thundering dance of creation, the cycle of life, death and rebirth, and in the rapture of the spirit and the senses. Pan is the ONE and ALL. In this sense, he has qualities similar to those of CHAOS, even though he more strongly embodies its more creative, ecstatic aspect.*

When called and if he comes, Pan almost always brings something luxuriant along with him, but also something sudden and excessive:

> *Pan just loves giving someone that one extra scoop of soup in the bowl that makes it overflow, or overfilling the glass until it spills—and being able to deal with that is one of the most important prerequisites for magically working with the Pan principle. When he comes, he comes all the way. A friend of mine once told me that he always made new friends after a Pan ritual—in fact, he made so many new friends that it just got to be too much. So whoever asks Pan for something specific (although he'll gladly stop by during a ritual "just to say hello") should keep in mind that he can be a real joker sometimes who likes to tease and play tricks on his servants. Magicians without a sense of humor wouldn't stand a chance with him, and he'd turn their life into hell—which brings us right back to the subject of the devil.*
>
> *Of course, Pan is also sensual pleasure and ecstasy, so that he particularly likes to show up when his festivals have an orgiastic nature. That's when he breaks all bounds [. . .], because the One and All won't let himself be imprisoned in our tiny little nutshell of ideas and structure. I highly recommend this method to whomever wants to really find out in a theurgic way what boundlessness and panic [. . .] can be like. Pan is "devilish"*

in the way that he terminates old, well-loved, routine opinions—he separates us from our illusion and leads us to a new ecstatic unity. In the process, it's possible that some feathers might be shed, but once you let yourself get caught up in the unleashed current, you'll soon realize that the things you had to discard along the way were nothing but a burden anyway.

Pan is a god that will allow you to have as much an insight into his principles as you can handle. Although he'll gladly give you one more ounce on top of that, my experience has shown that this is usually a mere quantitative figure. In this sense—despite all the racing around—he's actually a mild god, and a mischievous comrade who will not obey any rules.

So if you'd like to try your hand at the Pan principle, alone or in a group, feel free to do so. Pan can probably sweeten up your magic more than any other god since he's the epitome of cheerfulness. Magically and therapeutically speaking, he can rid you of any type of sexual problem ranging from impotence to frigidity, and he can help fight depression and increase your zest for life, revive your spirits, or help you obtain a lover—or a sexual partner, to be more specific.

After a Pan ritual, you should pay close attention to any changes in your life, such as omens in your everyday routine, new acquaintances, and so on.

Pan often gives his friends some kind of identifying sign to use if they want to contact him again: perhaps a melody, or a certain word or gesture, etc. Of course, this sign should always be used in the future any time you want to contact Pan. This can even be done mentally in everyday situations (in the car, the subway, at work—practically everywhere). "The more the merrier"—you'll certainly know when you've had enough. Or at least Pan will make sure you do . . .

But seriously, once you've truly had enough of Pan's effects, just let them fade away and of course avoid any social events for awhile. Since Pan is humanitarian (although not necessarily in the sense of the Red Cross or Salvation Army), he'll (almost) never force himself on you unless you ask.

THE RITUAL STRUCTURE

We start with an introductory protection and banishing ritual, followed by a short meditation; then music is played, preferably by the magicians or participants themselves. (It doesn't necessarily have to be "beautiful," just as long as it is halfway powerful and ecstatic!) Now Liber A'ash from Aleister Crowley is recited—if it's a group ritual, it should be accompanied by live music as well. Then to heighten the moment, recite the Hymn to Pan (several times as well); this should be done as ecstatically as possible also (see text below). Then music, dance, invocations/mantras such as "IO PAN!", or just plain cheering and screaming (with several participants, this should happen simultaneously with reciting the hymn).

By this time at the latest, Pan should have noticeably "entered" every participant and will take over the course of the rest of the ritual himself until he's dismissed. Depending on the mood, this could either be meditative or orgiastic, or sex magic could be performed as well.

After another phase of final meditation, the offerings are consumed. For group rituals, make sure to wipe off those long faces! Pan loves laughter and even a dirty joke now and again. When it's all over, there's another short meditation, followed by a word of thanks, the closing banishing ritual, and the license to depart.

The following checklist is just a suggestion to give you some ideas; it certainly can and should be adapted to your own needs.

The Pan Ritual

Participants: The ritual can be performed alone or with several people (it's especially suited for group rituals, even for beginners).

Time: any time, but especially in the early spring or summer.

Clothing: the usual robe, which can be taken off during the ritual.

Ritual Outline

1. Setting up the temple/ritual site:

    a) preferably outdoors, otherwise in the temple

    b) altar in the middle

    c) plenty of room to dance

2. Equipment:

a) Lighting: appropriate to the location (candles, torches)

b) Further correspondences

Metal: none

Colors: Arcadian, country colors (shades of brown)

Gemstone: possibly onyx

Scents: tangy oils

Plants/incense: tangy, sensual scents

Other:

- Offerings to be consumed after the ritual (olives, white bread, goat's cheese, dry white wine/Retsina, onions, garlic, lemons, and so on)
- Music instruments (pan flute, cymbals, drums, rattlers, woodblocks)

3. Ritual structure:

a) Preparation: laying out the offerings, etc.

b) Lesser Banishing Ritual of the Pentagram: yes

c) Invoking hexagram ritual: no

d) Invocation: yes

e) Concentration of energy: singing, dancing

f) Working with the energy: orgiastic or sex magic, followed by consumption of the offerings

g) Word of thanks and dismissal: yes

h) Lesser Banishing Ritual of the Pentagram: yes

i) License to depart: yes

Invocations (see below):

- Liber A'ash
- Hymn to Pan (several times)
- Mantra: IO PAN!

LIBER A'ASH VEL CAPRICORNI PNEUMATICI

SUB FIGURA

CCCLXX[7]

0. Gnarled Oak of God! In thy branches is the lightning nested! Above thee hangs the Eyeless Hawk.
1. Thou art blasted and black! Supremely solitary in that heath of scrub.
2. Up! The Ruddy clouds hang over thee! It is the storm.
3. There is a flaming gash in the sky.
4. Up.
5. Thou art tossed about in the grip of the storm for an aeon and an aeon and an aeon. But thou givest not thy sap; thou fallest not.
6. Only in the end shalt thou give up thy sap when the great God F.I.A.T. is enthroned on the day of Be-With-Us.
7. For two things are done and a third thing is begun. Isis and Osiris are given over to incest and adultery. Horus leaps up thrice armed from the womb of his mother. Harpocrates his twin is hidden within him. SET is his holy covenant, that he shall display in the great day of M.A.A.T., that is being interpreted the Master of the Temple of A.·.A.·., whose name is Truth.
8. Now in this is the magical power known.
9. It is like the oak that hardens itself and bears up against the storm. It is weather-beaten and scarred and confident like a sea captain.
10. Also it straineth like a hound in the leash.
11. It hath pride and great subtlety. Yea, and glee also!
12. Let the Magus act thus in his conjuration.
13. Let him sit and conjure; let him draw himself together in that forcefulness; let him rise next swollen and straining; let him dash back the hood from his head and fix his basilisk eye upon the sigil of the demon. Then let him sway the force of him to and fro like a satyr in silence, until the Word burst from his throat.

14. Then let him not fall exhausted, although he might have been ten thousandfold the human; but that which floodeth him is the infinite mercy of the Genitor-Genitrix of the Universe, whereof he is the Vessel.
15. Nor do thou deceive thyself. It is easy to tell the live force from the dead matter. It is no easier to tell the live snake from the dead snake.
16. Also concerning vows. Be obstinate, and be not obstinate. Understand that the yielding of the Yoni is one with the lengthening of the Lingam. Thou art both these; and thy vow is but the rustling of the wind on Mount Meru.
17. How shalt thou adore me who am the Eye and the Tooth, the Goat of the Spirit, the Lord of Creation. I am the Eye in the Triangle, the Silver Star that ye adore.
18. I am Baphomet, that is the Eightfold Word that shall be equilibrated with the Three.
19. There is no act or passion that shall not be a hymn in mine honor.
20. All holy things and all symbolic things shall be my sacraments.
21. These animals are sacred unto me; the goat, and the duck, and the ass, and the gazelle, the man, the woman, and the child.
22. All corpses are sacred unto me; they shall not be touched save in mine eucharist. All lonely places are sacred unto me; where one man gathereth himself together in my name, there will I leap forth in the midst of him.
23. I am the hideous god, and who mastereth me is uglier than I.
24. Yet I give more than Bacchus and Apollo; my gifts exceed the olive and the horse.
25. Who worshippeth me must worship me with many rites.
26. I am concealed with all concealments; when the Most Holy Ancient One is stripped and driven through the market place, I am still secret and apart.
27. Whom I love I chastise with many rods.
28. All things are sacred to me; no thing is sacred from me.
29. For there is no holiness where I am not.
30. Fear not when I fall in the fury of the storm; for mine acorns are blown afar by the wind; and verily I shall rise again, and my children about me, so that we shall uplift our forest in Eternity.
31. Eternity is the storm that covereth me.

32. I am Existence, the Existence that existeth not save through its own Existence, that is beyond the Existence of Existences, and rooted deeper than the No-Thing-Tree in the Land of No-Thing.
33. Now therefore thou knowest when I am within Thee, when my hood is spread over thy skull, when my might is more than the penned Indus, and unresistable as the Giant Glacier.
34. For as thou art before a lewd woman in Thy nakedness in the bazaar, sucked up by her slyness and smiles, so art thou wholly and no more in part before the symbol of the beloved, though it be but a Pisacha or a Yantra or a Deva.
35. And in all shalt thou create the Infinite Bliss and the next link of the Infinite Chain.
36. This chain reaches from Eternity to Eternity, ever in triangles—is not my symbol a triangle?—ever in circles—is not the symbol of the Beloved a circle? Therein is all progress base illusion, for every circle is alike and every triangle alike!
37. But the progress is progress, and progress is rapture, constant, dazzling, showers of light, waves of dew, flames of the hair of the Great Goddess, flowers of the roses that are about her neck, Amen!
38. Therefore lift up thyself as I am lifted up. Hold thyself in as I am master to accomplish. At the end, be the end far distant as the stars that lie in the navel of Nuit, do thou slay thyself as I at the end am slain, in the death that is life, in the peace that is mother of war, in the darkness that holds light in his hand, as an harlot that plucks a jewel from her nostrils.
39. So therefore the beginning is delight, and the end is delight, and delight is in the midst, even as the Indus is water in the cavern of the glacier, and water among the greater hills and the lesser hills and through the ramparts of the hills and through the plains, and water at the mouth thereof when it leaps forth into the mighty sea, yea, into the mighty sea.

***Hymn to Pan*[8]**

Thrill with lissome lust of the light,
O man! My man!
Come careering out of the night
Of Pan! Io Pan.

Io Pan! Io Pan! Come over the sea
From Sicily and from Arcady!
Roaming as Bacchus, with fauns and pards
And nymphs and satyrs for thy guards,
On a milk-white ass, come over the sea
To me, to me,
Come with Apollo in bridal dress
(Shepherdess and pythoness)
Come with Artemis, silken shod,
And wash thy white thigh, beautiful God,
In the moon, of the woods, on the marble mount,
The dimpled dawn of the amber fount!
Dip the purple of passionate prayer
In the crimson shrine, the scarlet snare,
The soul that startles in eyes of blue
To watch thy wantoness weeping through
The tangled grove, the gnarled bole
Of the living tree that is spirit and soul
And body and brain—come over the sea,
(Io Pan! Io Pan!)
Devil or god, to me, to me,
My man! my man!
Come with trumpets sounding shrill
Over the hill!
Come with drums low muttering
From the spring!
Come with flute and come with pipe!
Am I not ripe?
I, who wait and writhe and wrestle
With air that hath no boughs to nestle
My body, weary of empty clasp,
Strong as a lion, and sharp as an asp

Come, O come!
I am numb
With the lonely lust of devildom.
Thrust the sword through the galling fetter,
All devourer, all begetter;
Give me the sign of the Open Eye
And the token erect of thorny thigh
And the word of madness and mystery,
O Pan! Io Pan!
Io Pan! Io Pan! Pan, Pan! Pan,
I am a man:
Do as thou wilt, as a great god can,
O Pan! Io Pan!
Io Pan! Io Pan, Pan! I am awake
In the grip of the snake.
The eagle slashes with beak and claw;
The gods withdraw:
The great beasts come, Io Pan! I am borne
To death on the horn
Of the Unicorn.
I am Pan! Io Pan! Io Pan, Pan! Pan!
I am thy mate, I am thy man,
Goat of thy flock, I am gold, I am god,
Flesh to thy bone, flower to thy rod.
With hoofs of steel I race on the rocks
Through solstice stubborn to equinox.
And I rave; and I rape and I rip and I rend
Everlasting, world without end.
Mannequin, maiden, maenad, man,
In the might of Pan.
Io Pan! Io Pan Pan! Pan! Io Pan!

Concerning the deeper symbolism of Crowley's ritual prose—and this is certainly a typical example of his style—we'd basically like to leave it up to you as to whether or not you decide to reflect on it for awhile. Which is why we'll just give you a few tips here to help those of you who aren't all that familiar with the Kabbalah yet.

The Hebrew word A'ASH means "creation," and its numerical value is 370. In *777*, Crowley writes the following about this number: "The Sabbatic Goat in his highest aspect. This shows the whole of Creation as matter and spirit. The material 3, the spiritual 7, and all cancelling to Zero." That's why we have the phrase "pneumatic Capricorn" (from the Greek *pneuma,* "spirit"). Therefore it's a logical conclusion to connect this goat aspect of transcendence with the principle of Pan.

REPORTS FROM MAGICAL PRACTICE (II)

This time we'd like to illustrate two magical operations where some common problems occurred that could easily happen again in everyday situations.

Two magicians, P. and W., had an ongoing dispute with their landlord that seemingly never wanted to end. They lived together in a secluded house in the woods and their landlord terrorized them constantly; one morning they even found him standing unannounced in the living room holding an electric drill!

Even after threatening to take legal action didn't help one bit, the magicians felt compelled to turn to stronger means. They created a psychogon to curse the landlord and make him leave them alone. In doing so, they used the technique of imagospurius as described by Bardon that we'll discuss later. The operation took an entire month. Every evening they charged the psychogon for two hours and then let it loose on their victim.

A few days after the operation was over, the landlord's small child was run over by a car, seriously injured, and later died. The problems stopped after that, but P. and W. decided to give up the house and move to a more comfortable place. Even today, the two are still tormented by a bad conscience. For quite a long time, they were uninterested in any kind of magical warfare whatsoever (even, as in this case, in self-defense).

Basically, this is a real good example of the "magical ricochet" that often causes big problems in magical warfare and other operations intended at hurting or killing someone. The magician attacks a certain target person but someone else who's close to the target person gets hit full force instead. Usually it hits relatives or lovers, but can even hit colleagues or neighbors too. How can this happen?

There are several possible explanations that we'd like to take a closer look at. First of all, we'll most likely think of the symbol-logical fuzzy relation that we discussed earlier on. The precision of the symbols that we work with in magic is not the same as we know and expect from science. It's common knowledge that especially in magical warfare it's often quite difficult to find just the right dosage of force to carry out an attack and apply it accurately to the target. It's not uncommon for a magician to hit a seemingly "innocent" third person instead of the intended target. But this doesn't automatically have to be considered a "failure." The loss of his child possibly affected the landlord much more than if he were to fall ill himself, or possibly even die (which the magicians surely didn't intend). In any case, what remains is the undeniable fact that the magicians hit a person that they didn't consciously intend to hit. At best, this was "success on another level"—a phenomena that can be observed again and again in magic.

Another explanation could be that the target person was protected so well that everything bounced right off him, hitting his child instead. Such cases are common as well. If you've ever tried to magically influence a drunk person, or someone who's extremely down to earth, or simply insensitive or extremely skeptic when it comes to magic, then you'll know how hard it can be. This is called "the hardening of the aura," which often happens entirely unintentionally. In such cases, the energy of the attack is automatically deflected, especially when the target person is in the best of health. Or, sometimes, it can even be unconsciously thrown back at the attacker.

Most magicians forget to test the hardness of the target person's aura before initiating an attack. When in doubt, the magician can always perform an operation to soften the aura (e.g., by implanting an exploding glyph) before proceeding with the actual attack. However, such operations known as "acidic magic" require superbly trained skills in magical energy perception—the mirror magic is especially well suited for this.

But it's also possible that the actual cause of failure lies with the magician. Whoever reacts on a psychological weakness instead of proceeding with a clear head usually lacks the necessary precision. By the way, I think this is the most likely explanation in this case. The magicians' anger didn't just take place during the ritual; that's just where it was concentrated. The commandment of "nonattachment/nonlack of interest" was broken repeatedly, which probably affected the quality of the magical operation right from the start. Whoever considers the opponent to be superior for any length of time starts fighting with one's back up against the wall, making him or her weak and his or her opponent strong.

You can compare it to a desperate teenaged boy wildly lashing out at everything around him. He builds up such an enormous amount of force that sometimes half a dozen strong, full-grown men are needed to tame the raging youth; but he's rarely accurate since he wastes most of his energy on unintentionally smashing up completely harmless objects or people instead of focusing on his real opponent. His coordination is impaired as well. However, he's still dangerous due to the amount of force he releases and his unpredictability. And in the same way such a furious person can accidentally hit an innocent bystander, a magician who can't control one's own anger can miss his or her target just as easily. Of course, the force of anger shouldn't be underestimated, and it can be splendidly used for a magical operation, but it has to be controlled—in a state of trance, for example—and it's imperative that it be thoroughly banished afterward.

Finally, we need to mention the technique of thought control that's absolutely necessary for any kind of magical attack, or any kind of concentrative magical work in general. Because if the magician's thoughts wander even for a split second while directing this kind of energy, the powers can quickly develop a mind of their own, and that can have unpredictable consequences.

The following operation was a bit more accurate. Married magicians T. and C. had difficulties with their landlord as well, who also happened to live in the same house. By the time the two finally magically intervened, the whole situation had escalated to such a degree that the first operation had no effect at all. They finally chose the path of least resistance and decided to move out. But since a legal dispute was imminent, they left behind several exploding glyphs and a curse fetish made of parchment that were well hidden in various spots in the house. These were concealed in the floorboards and walls and remained unnoticed when the couple moved out.

During the court hearing that took place later on, the landlord—who was also the plaintiff—suddenly broke down and started to cry, "These people ruined us. Since they moved out, we can't find anyone else to rent the apartment. My wife is in psychiatric care and I feel like I'm on the brink of death myself." This didn't bother our two magicians one bit, even though the landlords attempted to defame their character in the face of their new landlord and practiced nightly telephone harrassment. The legal accusations were entirely unfounded, which I was able to convince myself of as well. On moving day, the landlord and his family even got physically violent without being provoked in any way, until the police were finally called.

This is a case of successful magical revenge. Regardless of what you think about such kinds of operations, they're a good example of the subtle and lasting effects that magic can have. It's also typical that the actual success took place after the magician couple moved out. It physically fulfilled the requirement of "nonattachment," which surely gave the magical operation a push start. The failure of the first attempts (one of which I participated in myself) can be explained as in the first example with the fact that the magicians were too involved in the situation and lacked the inner peace and centralization required.

This is why I highly recommend every magician to magically protect one's abode from undesired disturbances right from the day he or she moves in, even though there may be no immediate danger. In an emergency, the magician can then build up on this existing form of protection instead of having to dig up lines of defense at the last minute. "De-oding" (or removing od from) the apartment by dowsing it in incense and performing an appropriate ritual, possibly supported by an operation of sigil magic, will prevent or deflect the worst. In the case of an actual threat, you can mentally cast a protective circle, such as a belt of light, around the whole property. This is also recommended to protect against theft and fire and can be done mentally as you're leaving the residence. But in doing so, don't forget the laws of symbol-logic: When you return home from work and break through the circle as you enter the dwelling, you'll naturally have to cast a new one.

PRACTICAL EXERCISES

EXERCISE 33

THE MAGIC GAZE (III)

If you've already practiced the tratak exercise for three months, you can now combine it with the magic gaze by using the eye fixation chart from the last section. Now the idea is to alternate practicing the 180° gaze and the magic gaze. (This is a combination of Exercises 26 and 32.) Alternate using the two gazes every few minutes and change a bit faster each time you practice until finally you're able to switch every fifteen or even five seconds. At first, don't practice for more than six to eight minutes at a time—later you can even shorten the practice sessions.

By the way, this is also an extremely good eye exercise.

EXERCISE 34
THE MAGIC GAZE (IV): GAZE PROJECTION

Take an everyday object made of metal (such as a spoon, a ring, or similar object) and stare at it using the 180° gaze. Try determining its temperature by gazing at it. (Of course, this is a subjective temperature that can't be measured in degrees!) Once you've done this to your satisfaction, use the focused magic gaze to project heat into the object, first on to its surface, then a bit deeper, and finally deep into its core. Make it get hotter and hotter and stop when you feel you've reached your goal.

Practice this exercise at least 500 times (!) without actually checking to see if the object's temperature has changed. This rule is extremely important. If you want to achieve such physical results, you have to release yourself from all pressure to succeed. So just leave the object alone for awhile after the exercise to let it cool off before touching it again or continuing.

EXERCISE 35
THE MAGIC GAZE (V): CHARGING VIA GAZE PROJECTION

Later on, after you've practiced the previous exercise at least 100 times, you can practice the charging of normal tap water (not carbonated mineral water). Place a glass of water on the table in front of you, take a sip, have a quick look at its aura and overall state with the defocused 180° gaze, and then switch to the focused magic gaze. Try looking right into the "core" of the water. Then taste the water again and see if you notice any change in taste. Experiment with and without special imagination techniques—often all you have to do is gaze at the water intensely enough to cause a change in its taste. Therefore it won't be necessary to project any kind of command into the water to make it change its taste. When you're all done, try turning the taste back to its original by using the same method.

You can practice this exercise with one or more partners. For example, take two glasses of water and use your gaze to charge one of them while your partners wait outside. When you're done, they should try to determine which of the two glasses you charged by tasting it. Don't try this, though, until you've practiced enough on your own.

EXERCISE 36

WORKING WITH THE PAN PRINCIPLE

Whenever you like, perform the above Pan ritual either alone or with others. You can even do it when you're not feeling all that well since Pan is the ultimate symbol of vitality.

Experiment with the Pan principle during various seasons of the year. What does this god feel like in the spring, summer, fall, and winter? Do you prefer performing Pan rituals outdoors, at home in your temple, or maybe even in a cave? You don't need any special occasion to perform a Pan ritual—do it if you just want to see him again, or are simply curious, or even if you're not quite sure of your intentions yet. However, avoid constraining Pan in any way—once he's inside of you, let him run his full course. Quite often you'll be sexually excited after such a ritual, which is why it's not a bad idea to perform it with your partner.

BIBLIOGRAPHY

Aleister Crowley, *Magick*

Frater U.·.D.·., "*Versuch über Pan,*" Thelema 7 (1984), pp. 4–9

1. Shin is the Hebrew letter for spirit; Ruach Alhim is the breath of the spirit or of the gods; Ruach Adam is the breath or spirit of man.
2. The ambiguity of the word "destruction" has been the cause of much misunderstanding. "Solve" is destruction, but so is "coagula." The aim of the magus is to destroy his or her partial thought by uniting it with Universal Thought, and not to make a further breach and division in the Whole.
3. Yew is often used, which is the typical "magician's wood."
4. Sometimes small, smoothly polished balls of pure rock crystal are preferred, but these are usually quite difficult to make since such constructions are generally not very stable.
5. The formula V.I.T.R.I.O.L. is a kabbalistic notaricon for: Visita Interiora Terræ Rectificando Invenies Occultum Lapidem. A free translation would be: "By venturing to the center of the earth and examining and investigating everything along the way, I discovered the philosopher's stone." This is an alchemistic call to be persistently thorough and critical.
6. Dionysos—later the Roman god Bacchus—was also the god that liked Pan the most when he was introduced after his birth on Mount Olympus.
7. By Aleister Crowley.
8. Ibid.

INTRODUCTION TO MONEY MAGIC (I)

"MONEY MAGIC—GREENBACKS NEED LOVE TO MULTIPLY"

Years ago I wrote an article on money magic for the German magic magazine, *ANUBIS*. Since this magazine is long out of print, I'd like to reprint that article here.[1]

Wenn Ahmed keine Drachmen hat	*If Ahmed's out of drachmas*
lutscht traurig er am Dattelblatt (. . .)	*He'll chew sadly on a date leaf (. . .)*
Hat der Svenson keine Öre	*If Svenson's out of öres*
elcht von dannen seine Göre.	*He'll mooch a few off his chicks*
Nimmt man mir den letzten Schilling	*If you take away my last schilling*
hab auch ich ein schlechtes Feeling.	*I'll be gettin' a real bad feeling.*

Taken from the song "Geld oder Leben" ("Money or Life") from the German band, Erste Allgemeine Verunsicherung, EMI/COLUMBIA.

The magician's relationship with money has been strangely controversial for centuries, and not just in Western countries. Many people consider it to be an ultimate act of black magic if you try to improve your household budget through ritual, regardless of whether you just conjure to win the lottery or for the opportunity to conjure for others for cash on your way to becoming a magic mercenary. This "yucky" attitude is common among Eastern traditions as well, and some gurus, yogis, and meditation teachers might warn you about messing up your karma with spiritual marketing. Usually such tirades are accompanied by sentences such as "Down with spiritual materialism!" "Knowledge is a right of birth," "The truth is always free," and so on.

The supporters of this type of money-making, however, claim that although knowledge and wisdom may be free (which is a thought that just might not occur to everyone), this in no way applies to its transfer and that Enlightened Ones have to earn their bread and butter too . . .

Surely there are plenty of magicians who are just interested in making a fast buck and won't even lift a finger until they're paid in gold (or at least silver) in advance, and there are a number of naive ones as well who think that everything should be free nowadays in this New Age, the Age of Aquarius. Now it's certainly no surprise that everyone in the New Age and magic scenes seems to be getting itchy about money—this subject has occupied humanity since day one of their existence. After all, even the earliest societies that traded and bartered probably showed signs of commercialism as well.

It's pretty clear that the roots of money usually lie in contempt, and to most people it's the ultimate symbol of materialism. Cultures such as the Indian, with its inherent hatred of the here and now, and the Christian, with its late Egyptian cult of the afterlife, can hardly tolerate the fact that the masses go about the task of making money with such pleasure instead of piously looking toward heaven or *moksha*—which certainly never stopped the priest castes of all times from readily taking advantage of the privilege of hoarding money either. "Give me the money, it'll only make you rotten," said Lupo to Lupinchen, two German comic figures, and these words accurately reflect the opinion of most religious hierarchies when it comes to their often quite pecuniary believers.

How on earth could something as useful and migratory as money make you rotten? Of course, it can be addictive just like many other conveniences in life, and it's no coincidence that the same kind of people tend to vehemently curse alcohol, sex, and all other pleasures as well. And those who control money-making also control the lives of the masses themselves, at least for the most part. Even today, radical Islamic banks are prohibited from charging or paying interest (the sheiks often turn to cleverly designed cooperative models for the distribution of profit and loss), and in the Christian Middle Ages, only Jews were allowed to do pure business with money (especially lending on interest), for which they were sometimes even stoned nonetheless—this was, by the way, one of the main causes for the start of European anti-Semitism. This could also be called an exercise in the "systematic cultivation of scapegoats," and one that was even encouraged by the New Testament, as the supposedly mild youth of Nazareth was suddenly not so innocent when he chased the money-changers out of the temple—a gesture that thrilled the hearts of Marxists everywhere.

This leads us to another contemptuous ideology toward money. When it comes to private ownership and making money, socialism and communism (at least in theory) often behave quite similar to the past mendicant orders of the Albigens era. By the way, the more you study this subject in detail, the more surprised you'll be to discover how much energy is put into rejecting something (at least pro forma) that none of us could do without, and—as already mentioned—that has enormous practical value. Or, as Douglas Adams says so well about our planet in his famous novel, *The Hitchhiker's Guide to the Galaxy*: "Most of the people on it were unhappy for pretty much of the time. Many solutions were suggested to this problem, but most of these were concerned with the movements of small green pieces of paper, which is odd because on the whole it wasn't the small green pieces of paper that were unhappy." How true, how true!

Let's have a look at this problem from another point of view by using the symbolism of the tarot as an example. Today it's generally common to allocate the pentacles (still often referred to and depicted as coins) to the element of Earth, probably because money (if we stick to the ancient analogy "pentacles/coins" instead of the euphemistic term "discs") was considered the epitome of material property. But strangely this is a development that didn't occur until the nineteenth century, during a time in which "property" was associated more and more (and almost exclusively) with "real estate." Back then as in other times as well, the merchant risked dealing with movable ("airy") goods, but made sure to quickly "invest" profits in static ("earthy") valuables such as property, buildings, and entire estates. But oddly enough, in the same century we can find a much older interpretation that allocates the coins to the element of Air, namely by no one less than Papus in his *Tarot of the Bohemians!* Personally, I can understand this allocation[2] much better for several reasons. First of all, money is essentially moveable—it thrives off the fact that it's transferred from one place to another and from owner to owner. Only then can it truly fulfill its purpose, which is why it seems absurd to want to hoard it. (In economically more stable times, banks hoarded significantly less cash and much more precious metals and property!) The merchant is principally of Mercurial ("airy") nature: He or she thrives off of transportation, communication, and mobility, and takes advantage of the surplus at one location and the demand at another by skillfully maintaining a balance (the Libra principle) between the two, although only temporarily. This is exactly the function that money has.

The second reason that supports the allocation of "coins" to "air" is the fact that money is an abstract concept (principle of Air) of the first degree. It's not edible and has no other purpose than to refer to other nonmonetary values[3] or act as a mediator (Mercury/Hermes = messenger of the gods).

The third reason naturally seems to be the most important to me because it directly touches on the psychology of money. By categorizing money in the element of Air and viewing it as something nonstatic, it loses a great part of its threatening nature—unless of course you're still crawling around in ontological diapers, scratching your head, and lamenting over the fact that change is the only thing that's certain in this world. But who on earth is capable of both understanding money as something light-footed and ephemeral, but also appreciating it when one doesn't have it? In my opinion, being stuck in financial difficulties (which I have been in many times!) is the perfect time to take the first step and start viewing money as a toy or the cosmic expression of the dance of creation, the embodiment of the continuously changing and alternating energies of yin and yang, of light and darkness, and so on.

Now what does this all have to do with magic? Quite a bit, I think. Not just because magicians are pestered with financial problems sometimes too. (Interestingly enough, this seems to be the rule. Magicians who are rich in money and material goods are the absolute exception. Maybe they find their way to magic as a result of financial difficulties in the first place in the hopes of being able to resolve them by these means. Who knows?) It's probably more likely that these magicians (who really should know better) have been affected by the negative connotations surrounding "the multiplication of our currency" just as well, and have developed an incredibly bad conscience when it comes to money magic. And that can have devastating consequences in practice.

Many of my colleagues (myself included) have either had no luck whatsoever in money magic operations, or they resulted in just the exact opposite, or "success on another level," which I'll explain shortly.

There's not all that much to say when a magical operation fails entirely. There are too many factors that could have played a role, including those that I'll discuss later on. If the magician achieves "negative success," on the other hand, the whole thing becomes clearer. Aleister Crowley referred to this phenomena in his internal O.T.O. documents relating to sex magic. Here's a general paraphrasing. A magician conjures up a spell to get ahold of, say, $5,000 and three days later she causes an accident that costs exactly this amount; or the sheriff unexpectedly knocks on the door (maybe even unjustly, which would be relatively harmless, e.g., if the local tax office mixes up your taxpayer's account number) and kindly asks for the five grand or else he'll let his underlings loose to watch over your every move. This has happened to plenty of magicians and not just in connection with sex magic (which is why I feel this phenomena can't just be ascribed to this discipline)—they often "received" exactly the specified amount, just with a minus sign instead of a plus sign in front of the sum. As the saying goes, you could "hear God laughing." And just like any joke made at our expense, it takes a great deal of distance and self-irony to be able to laugh right along with God—an excellent technique that I can't stress enough, for psychological as well as magical reasons. (Don't forget: "Laughter banishes!") Psychologists, as clever as they are, have a nice explanation for such experiences as long as they're willing to draw an analogous, causal relationship between ritual and negative success in the first place, such as "Repressed feelings of guilt and behavioral patterns of self-punishment could have reversed the intended statement of intent." It's hard to find arguments against this because by denying it ("No, I don't!"), psychoanalysis pulls its standard trick out of the bag and says, "Oh no? You sure do! They're *unconscious!*" And since by definition alone there's no possible way to make any conscious statements about the subconscious, at least not directly, the buck is passed right back to you. Nonetheless, I don't want to deny the fact that this explanation may hold some truth; at least it seems to be a plausible explanation when such instances happen quite frequently, and it might make the magician take a good look at his or her overall relationship with money.

However, the third possibility gets really interesting—"success on another level." This phenomena occurs quite often and I could list a zillion true stories from my own practice and that of magician friends, but one example should be enough. A few years ago, I was in financial trouble up to my neck so bad that I had no idea how I'd survive the next month. I decided to take a trip into the Earth tattwa (still the analogy of "money = earth") and received a ritual from the "authorities" there that I was to perform over a period of several days. (Such information could be called a "revelation," "announcement," or "message from the subconscious," but that's unimportant here.) Instead of winning the lottery or receiving unlikely gifts of money, I received five job assignments all at once just a few days before completing the ritual, and all were extremely urgent. Since I couldn't afford turning down even one of them (and follow-up assignments were foreseen as well), I had to work sixteen hours a day for several weeks until I was thoroughly wiped out, although I at least didn't have to starve. That was the "Earth" I asked for!

But there are plenty of other variations of "success on another level," such as the fact that even after many years of practice, many magicians often find it disproportionately easier to conjure up tangible objects and valuables instead of the cash that would be necessary to buy them. In this sense, a friend of mine needed a bicycle but didn't have the money to buy one. Shortly after the money ritual, someone just "happened" to give him a bike. . . . So whoever has trouble conjuring up cash should try this method instead, and it just happens to take a considerable amount of the strain off your nerves as well.

Principally, it doesn't really matter what technique you use for money magic. Sigil magic has proven to be quite effective, but planetary magic works just as well. For the latter, I'd recommend first doing a Jupiter ritual to "create the general mood" (although Jupiter is responsible for wealth and abundance, it usually expresses itself in bountiful luxuries such as champagne by the cartload or buckets full of caviar, and not really in lottery winnings or cash) before targeting a specific action with Mercury. If you want to give the whole thing a bit more stability and permanence, you can top it off with a Saturn ritual. Traveling into the tattwa spheres (which is basically a primeval shamanic technique) generally works quite well, too, as long as you ask to receive a ritual that you can perform on a physical level since this will, in a sense, anchor the operation in the material world. (After all, what's the use of a silly astral dollar?) Sex magic is excellently suited for money magic operations as well if that happens to be your taste.

Once you've completed your money magic operation, it's a good idea to open a few channels so that the money can actually flow and find its way to you, for example by going against your habits and playing the lottery or making wild bets, and so on. On the other hand, even though this principle of opening channels is theoretically correct, I actually don't recommend gambling or playing the lottery in this connection because it makes forgetting the operation (one of the most important prerequisites for success according to Austin Osman Spare) quite difficult. Whether you want to admit it or not—once you've got that lottery ticket in your hand, you'll get more nervous with every day as the drawing gets closer. It would probably be a better idea to just keep your eyes open and take advantage of any opportunities you might have to win something, to do business, and the like.

Casinos can truly be hell if you're not familiar with the atmosphere there. Let's take the example of roulette. If we want to take a magical approach, there are plenty of questions that will arise: Should we try influencing the ball's movement (telekinesis), or try guessing/foreseeing the upcoming number, color, and so on (which, by the way, applies to all kinds of gambling). Most people will find it more difficult to do the former than the latter, but there are certainly no fixed rules for this. But even the roulette magician should take one thing to heart: Good gamblers—and most certainly pros—never play more than twenty minutes a day because they can't maintain the necessary disassociation trance for much longer than that. And if you risk $50 and end up with $55 a half an hour later, don't turn up your nose at this! Where else can you walk off with 10 percent interest in such a short period of time (with a real winning chance of 48 percent)?

The fact that it's usually easier to conjure up objects or work or the like instead of cash and inheritance money may have to do with the fact that our subconscious (which is responsible for magic according to the psychological model) doesn't know how to deal with abstract concepts such as money, but is much more interested in getting lots of colorful objects, just like a child would be. After all, the likelihood that someone else around you wants a bicycle at the same time is much less than would be the case with money, so that the energy image of "bicycle" can find its way more easily and start moving like a taxi right toward the person who waves at it.

We're not doing ourselves as magicians any favor by putting too much importance on it. The truly deciding factor in money magic is our attitude toward money itself and the way we handle it. In my opinion, it's much more effective and certainly more healthy to approach the subject of money magic in a playful manner, for example by stroking a large dollar bill every day and whispering with a sly smile "Go and get your friends!" instead of stiffly casting the circle and desperately trying to evoke a demon into the triangle with the hopes of him eventually sending a little cash your way. It can also be quite amusing to write your particular pecuniary statement of intent (maybe as a sigil) in ballpoint pen on the sole of your shoe, so you can literally "walk your way" to its fulfillment. This is especially a good method for those people who think they always have to work hard for their money and it resembles the technique of the Tibetan prayer wheel. As Rev. Ike once put it so well: "If you love money, it will love you." Let's take a look at it in a personified sense as the shamans would do. Why would a creature named "Money" appear to a person who actually hates and despises it deep down inside? If we were in that position, would we do it if we had a choice? And money does have a choice, believe me! The doors are open to money day and night, and everywhere it's welcomed and cherished with warm hearts—and spent again. Back in the days as a college student, I got in the habit of giving the biggest tips when I had the least money. And I have to admit that this kind of money magic was more effective than any attempt to acquire it by force or hoard it. Money is airy and playful; it's not happy when it's locked up in musty dungeons and silly piggy banks, and it will take the next convenient or (usually) inconvenient opportunity to get the hell out—just like we would do!

Money wants to have fun, just like every good entertainment artist does too. And if we allow it to have its fun, such as by decorating the altar during a Mercury ritual with stuffed wallets and colorful banknotes from all over the world, or by stroking and caressing it but also by giving it its freedom without hesitation when it wants to leave, then, and only then will it stop controlling us when we don't have it, or enslaving us and making us dependent on its materialistic aspect (which it most certainly has). This certainly is true. Money itself doesn't stink, but it can make everything else stink. But as already mentioned, don't overestimate it! It's the lifeblood in our economical veins and it always was; it's necessary for life but it's merely one necessary part among many others. It would be silly to pretend that blood is the most important of all. Without a heart (as a motor) and the liver or kidneys (for cleansing), blood would stop flowing, thicken, and clot, eventually clogging the veins and clogging life itself. And that's exactly what the money magician should take to heart: Money is motion and needs air because it's the embodiment of air itself! Being rich means "having riches" and that doesn't necessarily have to do with money, even though it can be a magnificent indicator of our personal magical success. Money is like electricity, and like magic, it's a completely neutral force or energy that can be applied for either good or evil, and the magician who has not only understood this concept but who has also internalized it will discover a very special secret kind of magic, that giving is more blissful than taking—but this doesn't exclude the possibility of receiving either . . .

We'll be dedicating more time to practical money magic in the next section, but recommend that you already start doing a few practical exercises based on the above article.

---

1. The contents of this article haven't been changed, only printing and style errors have been corrected.
2. Some might raise an eyebrow at first to the fact that he chooses the swords to represent the element of Earth, but if you consider that this French tarot deck also assigns the swords to the suit of spades (spade = shovel), you can clearly see his reference to Earth.
3. Compare Georg Ivanovas' excellent comments on the coins in the tarot deck in "Das Münz-As—Anmerkungen zu den Kleinen Arcana," in UNICORN, Booklet X/84, pp. 146–148.

INTRODUCTION TO RITUAL MAGIC (IX)

THE PENTACLE

Before we discuss the functions of the pentacle and the lamen, we'd like to mention something that has led to quite a bit of confusion in modern magic literature. In such texts, these two tools are often confused with one another or merged into one, but we'll be discussing each of these magical weapons individually in the traditional sense. For now, it doesn't matter why contemporary authors just mention the pentacle since they don't state the reason themselves either. Let's just keep in mind that the older magical tradition (starting with Crowley and before) makes a clear distinction between the pentacle and the lamen, which is no longer the case today with all authors. In this section, we'll just be dealing with the pentacle, but the lamen will be discussed later.

The pentacle is the fourth and last elemental weapon that we'll be discussing. As the wand is to Fire, the cup to Water, and the sword to Air, the pentacle is associated with the element of Earth.[1]

Once again, Crowley's statements on the pentacle (or "pantacle") summarize it best:

As the Magick Cup is the heavenly food of the Magus, so is the Magick Pantacle his earthly food.

The Wand was his divine force, and the Sword his human force.

The Cup is hollow to receive the influence from above. The Pantacle is flat like the fertile plains of earth.

The name Pantacle implies an image of the All, omne in parvo; but this is by a magical transformation of the Pantacle. Just as we made the Sword symbolical of everything by the force of our Magick, so do we work upon the Pantacle. That which is merely a piece of common bread shall be the body of God!

The Wand was the will of man, his wisdom, his word; the Cup was his understanding, the vehicle of grace; the Sword was his reason; and the Pantacle shall be his body, the temple of the Holy Ghost.

What is the length of this Temple?

From North to South.

What is the breadth of this Temple?

From East to West.

What is the height of this Temple?

From the Abyss to the Abyss.

There is, therefore, nothing movable or immovable under the whole firmament of heaven which is not included in this Pantacle, though it be but "eight inches in diameter, and in thickness half an inch."

Fire is not matter at all; water is a combination of elements; air almost entirely a mixture of elements; earth contains all both in admixture and in combination.

So must it be with this Pantacle, the symbol of earth.

And as this Pantacle is made of pure wax, do not forget that "everything that lives is holy."

All phenomena are sacraments. Every fact, and even every falsehood, must enter into the Pantacle; it is the great storehouse from which the Magician draws (Magick, p. 95).

Crowley's reference to the pentacle needing to be made of pure wax (beeswax) and exactly "eight inches in diameter, and in thickness half an inch" is rarely heeded today. Nowadays plenty of other materials are used, ranging from metal to clay, and stone to wood. That was surely the case in the past as well.

The pentacle should represent an image of the magician's personal universe. Everything that one's cosmos contains must be reflected symbolically in the pentacle. This is why the pentacle is also the most difficult elemental weapon to make. Not because it poses a technical problem in actually making it, because just the opposite is true. It's not difficult at all to press or melt wax into the shape of a disc and to engrave it with symbols. No, making the pentacle also requires a fine sense of personal symbolism, but above all it requires that the magician thoroughly understands the depths of one's own soul. And the pentacle is surely not a static magical weapon. On the contrary, it's an extremely dynamic, versatile weapon that's a document of our entire life.

> *This Pantacle therefore represents all that we are, the resultant of all that we had a tendency to be. [. . .]*
>
> *The Pantacle is then in a sense identical with the karma or kamma of the Magician.*
>
> *The Karma of a man is his ledger. The balance has not been struck and he does not know what it is; he does not even fully know what debts he may have to pay, or what is owed him; nor does he know on what dates even those payments which he anticipates may fall due.*
>
> *A business conducted on such lines would be in a terrible mess; and we find in fact that man is in just such a mess. [. . .]*
>
> *Now consider that this Karma is all that a man has or is. His ultimate object is to get rid of it completely—when it comes to the point of surrendering*[2] *the Self to the Beloved; but in the beginning the Magician is not that Self, he is only the heap of refuse from which that Self is to be built up. The Magical instruments must be made before they are destroyed* (ibid., pp. 98–99).

Aleister Crowley also gives some ideas on how to design the pentacle:

> *All Pantacles will contain the ultimate conceptions of the circle and the cross, though some will prefer to replace the cross by a point, or by a Tau, or by a triangle. The vesica piscis is sometimes used instead of the circle, or the circle may be glyphed as a serpent. Time and space and the idea of causality are sometimes represented; so also are the three stages in the history of philosophy, in which the three objects of study were successively Nature, God, and Man.*
>
> *The duality of consciousness is also sometimes represented; and the Tree of Life itself may be figured therein, or the categories. An emblem of the Great Work should be*

added. But the Pantacle will be imperfect unless each idea is contrasted in a balanced manner with its opposite, and unless there is a necessary connection between each pair of ideas and every other pair.

The Neophyte will perhaps do well to make the first sketches for his Pantacle very large and complex, subsequently simplifying, not so much by exclusion as by combination, just as a zoologist, beginning with the four great apes and man, combines all in the single word "primate."

It is not wise to simplify too far, since the ultimate hieroglyphic must be an infinite. The ultimate resolution not having been performed, its symbol must not be portrayed (ibid., pp. 97–98).

But he also makes it clear as to how difficult it is to make the pentacle:

How few there are who can look back through the years and say that they have made advance in any definite direction! And in how few is that change, such as it is, a variable with intelligence and conscious volition! The dead weight of the original conditions under which we were born has counted for far more than all our striving. The unconscious forces are incomparably greater than those of which we have any knowledge. This is the solidity of our Pantacle, the karma of our Earth that whirls a man will he nill he around her axis at the rate of a thousand miles an hour. [. . .]

It is very difficult then in any way to fashion this heavy Pantacle. [. . .]

We cut a figure on the ice; it is effaced in a morning by the tracks of other skaters; nor did that figure do more than scratch the surface of the ice, and the ice itself must melt before the sun. Indeed the Magician may despair when he comes to make the Pantacle! [. . .]

And so—beware! Select! Select! Select!

This Pantacle is an infinite storehouse; things will always be there when we want them. We may see to it occasionally that they are dusted and the moth kept out, but we shall usually be too busy to do much more. Remember that in travelling from the earth to the stars, one dare not be encumbered with too much heavy luggage. Nothing that is not a necessary part of the machine should enter into its composition.

Now though this Pantacle is composed only of shams, some shams somehow seem to be more false than others.

The whole Universe is an illusion, but it is an illusion difficult to get rid of. It is true compared with most things. But ninety-nine out of every hundred impressions are false even in relation to the things on their own plane.

Such distinctions must be graven deeply upon the surface of the Pantacle by the Holy Dagger (ibid., pp. 100–101).

Therefore, making the pentacle requires the thorough examination and recognition of ourselves.

In this sense, it will always remain the most imperfect of our magical tools—one that we need to work on for our entire lives without ever completing it. It's the most individualistic of all weapons—and the greatest challenge of all.

THE ALTAR

By now at the latest, the time has come to finally start thinking more seriously about the magical altar that you use for your ceremonial work. Up until now, we haven't paid much attention to this piece of temple furniture; it basically served the purpose of just holding our various utensils.

Most modern magicians no longer bother making an elaborate altar, as the altar has become a purely functional piece of furniture. Usually a simple table or dresser is converted to an altar, and that's all. Of course you can do this too. But before doing so, you should at least take a few minutes to meditate on how you want your temple to look when it's all done. Remember that ideally the temple is a tiny little universe in itself. In the same way that you as a magician want to shape the great edifice of life and fate yourself, this should be reflected externally in your temple as well.

The magic of the nineteenth century was primarily responsible for drowning in symbolism absolutely everything the magician did, owned, and surrounded oneself with. Modern folk often perceive this—as well as many of the styles of painting, literature, and music from back then, by the way—as too extravagant and superfluous. The fact that magic can adapt to the external style of the times is proven by modern Chaos Magic that, for example, sometimes uses neon lights instead of candles, or mantras played from a computer recording.

We don't want to stipulate any rules for making a "proper" magical altar. The following ideas are merely examples of how we can approach the subject. Develop your own point of view, because that's the ultimate goal of this book in the first place.

For magicians following the tradition of the Golden Dawn, the altar should be a double cube. Why this? Because the altar is, as Crowley writes, "the solid basis of the Work, the fixed Will of the Magician; and the law under which he works." But the double cube is a symbol of the Great Work, since the doubling of the cube—like the squaring of the circle—was one of the great problems of antiquity. In this sense, the altar documents the magician's knowledge of the laws of nature, which are also the laws of magic through which one works.

The altar should be the height of one's navel, which is then used to calculate its dimensions. (The height from the floor to the navel divided by two results in the edges of each cube.) "Double cube" is not necessarily to be taken literally—the altar can certainly be one solid piece and you don't need to stack two cubes on top of one another. But in this case, the altar should at least be painted to retain its double cubic nature by painting each cube a different color. The colors could be black and white, for example, to represent the duality of our perception as well as our effort to always see both the light and the dark. We could also use silver (the moon) and gold (the sun), or green (for Venus) and red (for Mars). And we could also symbolically color each of the four sides of the top cube according to the four elements. For this, Crowley uses John Dee's categorical system. According to his system, the side facing the east would represent Earth, while the west side would represent the element of Water, and so on, just like in the pentagram ritual. The top surface could either be assigned to the element of Ether or Spirit, or used to represent our magical will, for example with a personal name glyph or sigil. We could just as well paint or engrave it with the seven planetary symbols. So you see, there are countless ways to design your altar, and every magician should develop one's own individual altar symbolism.

The top surface of the altar can be covered with gold and then engraved or—if using more reasonably priced gold leaf—painted with the kabbalistic Tree of Life.

The altar is generally made of wood, and oak is often used as a symbol of the stubbornness and rigidity of magical law, but acacia is sometimes used as well as a symbol of resurrection. This is surely a question of what you can afford, and many magicians today prefer more reasonably priced wood or veneer.

In practice, this kind of altar unfortunately poses a few problems. If the magician doesn't just happen to be a giant, using the navel as the basic measurement for an altar is pretty impractical, despite its symbolism. The surface is simply much too small to hold more than just the most necessary weapons, and if you want to set your magical diary or a few candle holders on it, too, you'll most likely run into problems. After all, you don't want to keep knocking things over during a ritual because you don't have enough room!

One solution would be to use a side table as an addition to your altar, although this will take up more temple space that's usually scarce to begin with. Many magicians prefer to use a cabinet-type altar that has a few shelves or drawers to store at least some of their tools. The cabinet doors (or curtain) can also be decorated with symbols.

Just try to find a symbol-logically nice but practical solution, so take your time to really think about your altar. Since you already have enough ritual experience now, you're more able to determine the demands that your altar needs to meet then you were at the very beginning. That's why we didn't discuss it until now.

MAGICAL OATHS

Similar to the magical name, the magical oath also represents an obligation that the magician enters into for various reasons. In this sense, Crowley wrote:

> *Word should express Will: hence the Mystic Name of the Probationer is the expression of his highest Will.*
>
> *There are, of course, few Probationers who understand themselves sufficiently to be able to formulate this Will to themselves, and therefore at the end of their probation they choose a new name.*
>
> *It is convenient therefore for the student to express his Will by taking Magical Oaths.*
>
> *Since such an oath is irrevocable it should be well considered; and it is better not to take any oath permanently; because with increase of understanding may come a perception of the incompatibility of the lesser oath with the greater.*
>
> *This is indeed almost certain to occur, and it must be remembered that as the whole essence of the Will is its one-pointedness, a dilemma of this sort is the worst in which the Magus can find himself.*

Another great point in this consideration of Magick Vows is to keep them in their proper place. They must be taken for a clearly defined purpose, a clearly understood purpose, and they must never be allowed to go beyond it.

It is a virtue in a diabetic not to eat sugar, but only in reference to his own condition. It is not a virtue of universal import. Elijah said on one occasion: "I do well to be angry"; but such occasions are rare.

Moreover, one man's meat is another man's poison. An oath of poverty might be very useful for a man who was unable intelligently to use his wealth for the single end proposed; to another it would be simply stripping himself of energy, causing him to waste his time over trifles.

There is no power which cannot be pressed in to the service of the Magical Will: it is only the temptation to value that power for itself which offends.

One does not say: "Cut it down; why cumbereth it the ground?" unless repeated prunings have convinced the gardener that the growth must always be a rank one.

"If thine hand offend thee, cut it off!" is the scream of a weakling. If one killed a dog the first time it misbehaved itself, not many would pass the stage of puppyhood.

The best vow, and that of most universal application, is the Vow of Holy Obedience; for not only does it lead to perfect freedom, but is a training in that surrender which is the last task.

It has this great value, that it never gets rusty. If the superior to whom the vow is taken knows his business, he will quickly detect which things are really displeasing to his pupil, and familiarize him with them.

Disobedience to the superior is a contest between these two Wills in the inferior. The Will expressed in his vow, which is the Will linked to his highest Will by the fact that he has taken it in order to develop that highest Will, contends with the temporary Will, which is based only on temporary considerations.

The Teacher should then seek gently and firmly to key up the pupil, little by little, until obedience follows command without reference to what that command may be; as Loyola wrote: "perinde ac cadaver."

[. . .] It is always something to pluck up the weeds, but the flower itself needs tending. Having crushed all volitions in ourselves, and if necessary in others, which we find opposing our real Will, that Will itself will grow naturally with greater freedom. But it

is not only necessary to purify the temple itself and consecrate it; invocations must be made. Hence it is necessary to be constantly doing things of a positive, not merely of a negative nature, to affirm that Will.

Renunciation and sacrifice are necessary, but they are comparatively easy. There are a hundred ways of missing, and only one of hitting. To avoid eating beef is easy; to eat nothing but pork is very difficult (ibid., pp. 63–65).

Were you puzzled when you read that Master Therion himself—the greatest preacher of all of free magical will—places such value on obedience? In these modern times marked by democratic and even anti-authoritarian ideals, this is a pretty touchy subject. It cannot be denied that Crowley as a person wasn't exactly the best example for the exemplary embodiment of the principles of command and obedience.

Voluntary self-discipline doesn't mean putting on any old random straitjacket, but rather it's a prerequisite for certain experiences that would be difficult or even impossible otherwise. In this sense, self-discipline is the conscious and intentional establishment of certain experimental conditions in the same way a scientist would, for example, if he wanted to sterilize a medium for cultivating certain cell cultures. After all, "concentration" also means eradicating the unnecessary in favor of the desired, or separating the chaff from the wheat.

It has become fashionable to counter every kind of compulsion with suspicion, with "Staying Cool" as the motto, and there's no place for self-restraint and asceticism. We, too, have blown this horn a number of times and proclaimed the great freedom that magic should lead us all to. After all, it was necessary (and surely still is today) to create a counterbalance to the rigid ascetic and self-chastising ideals of Christianity misunderstood that even today in modern magic still occasionally lift it's ugly Gorgon's head. For way too long, the fact has been overlooked that magic can and should be fun—that humans will progress much faster and more thoroughly when they're motivated by pleasure and fun.

But this doesn't mean that things such as discipline and constant practice—and consequently the self-discipline to counter all objections of idleness and fear, sluggishness and indolence—have become unnecessary. On the contrary, we need to find a middle course between cheerless, blind obedience and the structureless, entropic mess of conflicting, self-neutralizing desires and ephemeral passions and cravings.

For the magician who works independently and self-sufficiently, the obedience that's meant here refers to the obedience of one's own oath. To prevent a rosebush from rotting, drying up, and dying off, it has to be intentionally trimmed from time to time. Although it may hurt, it will prevent worse from happening.

When you take a magical oath—and that's something you most certainly should do at least a few times in your magical career—keep in mind that although you're limiting yourself in a sense, on the other hand it will enable you to accomplish much greater things than just the mere satisfaction of your temporary state of comfort.

> *The Magician must build all that he has into his pyramid; and if that pyramid is to touch the stars, how broad must be the base! There is no knowledge and no power which is useless to the Magician. One might almost say there is no scrap of material in the whole Universe with which he can dispense. His ultimate enemy is the great Magician, the Magician who created the whole illusion of the Universe; and to meet him in battle, so that nothing is left either of him or of yourself, you must be exactly equal to him.*
>
> *At the same time let the Magician never forget that every brick must tend to the summit of the pyramid—the sides must be perfectly smooth; there must be no false summits, even in the lowest layers.*
>
> *This is the practical and active form of that obligation of a Master of the Temple in which it is said: "I will interpret every phenomenon as a particular dealing of God with my soul"* (ibid., p. 68).

> *The statement that the Probationer can resign when he chooses is in truth only for those who have taken the oath but superficially.*
>
> *A real Magical Oath cannot be broken: you think it can, but it can't.*
>
> *This is the advantage of a real Magical Oath.*
>
> *However far you go around, you arrive at the end just the same, and all you have done by attempting to break your oath is to involve yourself in the most frightful trouble.*
>
> *It cannot be too clearly understood that such is the nature of things: it does not depend upon the will of any persons, however powerful or exalted; nor can Their force, the force of Their great oaths, avail against the weakest oath of the most trivial of beginners* (ibid., p. 72).

It's therefore good practice to view the magical oath in a functional way. An oath is more than just a resolution intention—it's a voluntary bonding. So only bond yourself where you really want to. For example, you could start with a smaller "oath" to do your magical training exercises regularly in the next month regardless of what external factors of resistance may arise. Then you could make an oath to get up every morning a half an hour earlier to perform a certain ritual. Making oaths (and of course, keeping them) is a useful exercise to strengthen your willpower that can even improve your omen interpretation and subtle energy perception since these are automatically sharpened considerably through the required alertness, and soon you'll begin to observe how the whole universe is helping you with your Great Work just as soon as you've set the first truly serious impulse yourself.

Of course, you should avoid "oath inflation." Use this powerful magical tool carefully and you'll surely be able to enjoy its tremendous advantages. But it's the truly serious oaths that will have a long-lasting, deep impact that can change your entire life.

The above text passages quoted from Crowley contain an example that has meanwhile become quite popular. Whoever endeavored to take the magical oath of Master of the Temple in his order (A.·.A.·.) was immediately promoted from the grade of neophyte right up to the highest grade—but, as mentioned, such oaths can be quite dangerous and should be thought over very carefully.

REPORTS FROM MAGICAL PRACTICE (III)

Frater G. from K. was a highly creative, although sometimes quick-tempered, person who often applied his magic in an uncontrolled manner as well. The fact that he's now much more careful is a direct result of the following experience that he told me about once, and in my opinion it's a perfect example of magical symbol-logic as we're continually confronted with in practice.

Frater G. was extremely angry with a man who caused him a great deal of problems both in his job as well as in private matters. He felt this person had tricked, deceived, humiliated, and taken advantage of him. At the time, he wasn't aware that this is not a good basis for magical warfare, which generally requires emotional coldness or artificial feelings that are immediately banished afterward. So he decided to perform an extremely drastic act of magical warfare. He wanted his victim to get testicular cancer!

To do so, he worked with the principle of Fire and the archangel principle of Michael—the actual technique he used is not important here.

But, at first, instead of watching his victim get sick, he was only disappointed to see that nothing was happening at all. Then about a month and a half later, Frater G.'s own testicles swelled up to enormous size within just a few hours until they were nearly the size of apples and he suffered excruciating pain. He was rushed to the hospital just in the nick of time, as the doctors said if he had waited just a few more hours he certainly would have died.

Frater G. didn't have testicular cancer as he initially feared, but he did have to undergo surgery and suffered from the aftereffects for quite some time. But he felt that the following synchronicity was even more significant: The doctor that treated him was named "Dr. Cancer" and his assistant was "Dr. Michael"!

"You can imagine the look on my face," he told me, "when I realized that the goal of my magical operation and the archangel principle that I applied were reflected in the names of my doctors after I was affected with a problem of the same body part that I aimed at on my opponent! Since then I've gotten much more careful when it comes to magical warfare and I only use it in dire emergencies in true self-defense."

This is a perfect example of the magical boomerang phenomena. The energy that this magician released bounces right back to him and causes the exact same thing to happen to himself that was actually intended for his opponent.

Such phenomena happen quite frequently and are certainly the reason that "black" or destructive magic has gotten the reputation of being dangerous to the operator. However, it would be wrong to want to interpret this as an automatic, moral-ethical means of punishment of "divine" origin, as though "evil" would always fall back on its initiator. This may or may not be true on a cosmic (or karmic) level (after death), but it's surely not the case in the practice of everyday magical warfare.

The explanations we discussed in the last section for failed operations of magical warfare could apply in this case as well. However, another factor comes into play that's quite common in such cases of magical backfire as this: the magician's bad conscience itself. We surely don't need to explain again that having personal reservations about a magical operation will deem it to fail right from the start; whereby the degree of failure is usually directly proportional to the intensity of the reservations. Frater G., just like

Fraters P. and W. from the last section, was at best only able to temporarily bundle his power of anger during the ritual; he reacted instead of acting and, in doing so, he chose a method that may have corresponded to his characteristic nature, but not to his inner ethics. This is reflected in the close link of ritual symbolism ("testicles," "cancer," "Michael") and event symbolism in this operation since it shows the extent to which G. had projected or (to his own disadvantage) objectified his magical energy. If just a little accident had happened with no apparent relation to his magical operation, it would have required a certain degree of paranoia to causally link one thing with another. But in this case, the magic symbolism manifested quite clearly in an external sense, so it would be foolish to deny that such a link exists.

It's extremely important to pay attention to such relationships. This is also the actual reason why Frater G.'s example is listed here in the first place: To be able to evaluate the results of a magical operation, an extremely fine touch and sharp intuition are required, but one must also remain rational and realistic enough to prevent from falling victim to insanity or a persecution complex. If you want to be able to evaluate the success or failure of a magical operation objectively, as only a person with a firm grip on subjectivity can do in the first place, you primarily need to consider its symbol-logic.

Unfortunately, there are way too many magicians that get utterly whiney and paranoid the minute an accident occurs after any kind of operation. Suddenly magic is to blame for everything, or there must be an evil, conjuring opponent to blame in order to distract attention from one's own stumbling blocks. "Trust in Allah, but tie up your camel first" is an Islamic proverb. There must always be a certain degree of external clarity before a magical operation can truly be evaluated. Wild guesses, hysterical hunches, suspicion, and distrust are not enough: Usually these are only confused with intuition and distract us from our own incapability to observe ourselves and our actions with a certain inner distance.

Therefore, heed the following advice. Always take the blame yourself and never blame magic in general or another person. This surely isn't always easy because many of our stumbling blocks are invisible. A bad conscience is often only unconscious. Only through constant self-observation and repeated compulsory actions that cannot be otherwise explained might it become clear to us that we're dealing with some kind of inner blockade. That's why self-recognition is the main task of every magician, even practical magicians who don't pursue any further transcendental goals with their art. To them it's a technical tool that's absolutely necessary if they want to avoid continual, self-caused failure.

Materialistically speaking, if we assume that the subconscious mind represents the magician's "raw material," exact knowledge of the material is a part of working successfully. What are we dealing with? What does it look like? Which laws is it subject to?

The following example comes from England and is quite a few years old. Frater John was unemployed and decided to perform a Mercury ritual to solve his financial problems. His goal was to improve his financial plight and general prosperity.

Shortly after he performed the operation on the same day, he left the house and found a credit card on the steps that someone must have lost. Now Frater John was faced with a moral dilemma. Should he ignore the card or turn it in to the police? Or should he view the event as an omen, a successful result of his ritual, and use the card without permission? After all, magic demands that you seize the moment of opportunity that success brings before it slips away. Frater John took this axiom to heart. Up until the weekend, he lived the high life with the credit card he found; he forged the signature of the lawful owner and bought all kinds of things. This was fraud, of course, although he decided to stop the following Monday at the latest since the risk seemed too great. After all, credit card companies supply their contract partners regularly with a list of cards that were lost or stolen, and often require them to call back for verification, especially for large transactions. On that Sunday, he discussed the situation with a friend. The friend had a different opinion. After all, it was the Christmas season with lots of hustle and bustle—the card loss surely wouldn't be processed for at least two weeks, so he could use the card for at least another week without having to worry. Carelessly, Frater John heeded this advice. On Monday he was arrested while trying to buy a stereo system with the card.

This example characterizes one of the main functions of the Mercury principle. Mercury is also known as the god of thieves and pickpockets. If you're planning to rob a bank, you'd be better off working with the Mercury principle instead of Jupiter; although Jupiter is "great fortune"—*fortuna major*—it also represents justice, and it never takes anything away from others, it only gives. The fact that the loss took place on a Monday (moon = loss) is a picture-book example of symbol-logic.

But the story continues. Frater John was sentenced to one and a half years in prison for credit card fraud. He was put in a fairly liberal correctional institute. In prison, he was able to get skilled training in electronics. After he was released, the computer boom was just getting underway; Frater John took advantage of this and entered the electronics business—and today he's a millionaire!

In this sense, we could view the operation as both (a) a direct success and (b) "success on another level." The direct success was the short-term gain and prosperity, although through deceitful means; the success on another level was the long-term advantage that our magician took the opportunity of while in prison by being "forced" to learn a professional skill.

"Basically, it was the best thing that ever happened to me," says Frater John now. "I got the wealth and prosperity that I wanted, although the procedure was quite complicated. But without my experience in prison, I'd probably be still unemployed today and poor as a church mouse."

Now ask yourself what you would have done in Frater John's situation if you found that credit card right after the ritual. Before immediately reacting with an indignant "I'd never do that!", please think about what we said about the Mercury principle. I can only stress once again that the real problem with magic is not whether it works, but that it works!

Surely you feel as well that it's not all that desirable to gain magical success through crooked or even criminal means. But this is a question of magical (not symbolical!) precision and experience. Understand magic as also being an opportunity to gain insight into your own ethics, and to recognize the course you want to take in life—and what your true desires really are.

Regardless of the moral-ethical debate here, I'd like to take this opportunity to point out that Frater John was probably only able to become truly wealthy and prosperous after his release from prison because he was always willing to take risks in the first place—including criminal ones—in order to allow his magical will the opportunity to become true. Regardless of whether or not we condone his actions, the fact that magic was able to help him become so successful was due solely to his uncompromising nature.

In the end, this example also teaches us that we shouldn't evaluate the results of a magical operation too soon. Sometimes what seems like an absolute catastrophe may turn out to be a true blessing years later. Of course, this is not only true about magic, but about life itself in general. The magician is an artist—a true master of the art of living—on several levels all at the same time. He or she steers coincidence in the right direction, creates opportunities where the normal person would only see the bitter hand of fate, prefers to be the perpetrator instead of the victim (but if one has to be the victim, one at least wants to bully oneself and not let others do it). And he or she consciously assumes the sole and complete responsibility for one's actions every minute of the day. Ideally, his or her life is truly self-determined. If one wants to follow the ethics of society, if one wants to assume standard moral norms, one does it only because he or she freely chooses to do so and not because one's unconsciously succumbing to the pressure of the majority. He or she can be a thief and a benefactor, a trickster and a paragon, a devil and a god, because he or she has recognized that everything originates in oneself. He or she doesn't blame fate or a punitive god for mishaps, as he or she constantly accounts for one's own actions and lives according to the motto of the French Revolution, *ni dieu ni maître* ("Neither God nor master [reigns over me]"). If one does decide to submit to a god, one does so voluntarily as a conscious act of mystic insight, and not as cowardly submission in heteronomy or out of fear of punishment after death.

The road to becoming this kind of ideal magician is a long one—maybe the goal will always remain just out of reach, but we should always keep it in sight when the journey seems toilsome and we're tempted to give in to despair when confronted with our own insufficiencies and the external resistance that we'll always run into occasionally. Utopias are not necessarily there to be realized, they should be viewed as goals to strive for in the sense of the Zen saying "The path is the goal." The path to becoming the ideal magician is more important than actually achieving that state in the end; the work on oneself is more significant than the trials and tribulations of the travels. But along the way, we should never forget that this work must go hand in hand with pleasure as well.

PRACTICAL EXERCISES

EXERCISE 37

PENDULUM TRAINING (III)

This exercise is connected to the following two as well. Before we go in depth into the theory of making amulets and talismans, it would be a good idea to familiarize ourselves with the principle of the magical or subtle charging of objects in practice. Exercise 39 will give you the opportunity to monitor your results and combine this with your pendulum training as well.

If you haven't already done so, get seven pieces (or discs) of metal that correspond to the seven planets. For gold, a finger ring or medallion will work fine, too, as long as it's not engraved and doesn't contain any stones.

In their raw state (the way you got them) place each piece of metal on the table in front of you on a black surface; a piece of black silk would be best since, according to tradition, it's a good insulator. Now hold your pendulum the way you learned (see Exercise 16) over the metal and notice the way it swings. Note your observance on a piece of paper or in your magical diary.[3]

Do this with all of the metals. You don't have to do this all in one session; you can do this exercise over a period of several days, but if you do so, make sure to carry out the work at regular intervals and always at the same time of day.

Now hold the first metal under a cold stream of water for about ten minutes while imagining that all undesired energies are being expelled and washed away. This is called de-oding. Afterward, dry off the metal without touching it with your hands (e.g., by wrapping it in a towel) and place it still untouched on the black surface. Repeat the procedure with the pendulum and observe the difference, which you should write down as well. If you cannot observe any difference in the swing of the pendulum, you need to keep de-oding the object until you do. When you are finished, wrap the de-oded piece of metal (still untouched) in a small piece of black silk and put it aside until you start the next exercise.

Now do the same with the other metals.

EXERCISE 38

PRACTICAL TALISMAN MAGIC (I)

Take one of the pieces of metal from the last exercise and perform a planetary ritual that corresponds to this metal. The goal of the ritual is to charge the metal at ritual climax with the planetary power invoked. Place the metal on your altar (still don't touch it!) after it's de-oded. Then hold both hands directly over the metal and transfer the energy with each powerful exhalation. This is called odic charging. Then perform the next exercise. You can do this during the ritual, but it would be better to close the ritual first.

Repeat this experiment with other objects as well; rock crystal and gemstones are particularly suited for this, but so are water, rock salt, table salt, and stones of all kinds. This doesn't necessarily have to be done during a ritual; the only important thing at first is that you alter the energy quality in some way and then monitor the result with the following exercise.

EXERCISE 39

PENDULUM TRAINING (IV)

Meanwhile, you should have enough practice with the pendulum so that you can now expand your experiments to another field.

This exercise is designed to check the odic content of an object. On the basis of your previous experiments in Exercise 37, you now have control values that you can use for this exercise as well. Proceed in the same manner as in Exercise 37 above when you first tested the odic force of the metal; observe the swing of the pendulum and observe how the energy quality of the od-charged object has changed. If you cannot observe any change, you'll have to repeat the oding procedure until you do.

These three exercises are the first steps in making amulets and talismans. Your od-charged planetary metals are not just practice objects. They're already simple planetary talismans and from now on you can place the corresponding metal on the altar for every planetary ritual. The degree of their odic force will grow each time, and this will make itself noticeable in a stronger swing of the pendulum. But don't make the typical beginner's mistake and reach for your pendulum after every ritual to monitor the change in odic force. Just do this every three or four times, and later you won't need to do it at all anymore.

BIBLIOGRAPHY

Aleister Crowley, *Magick*

Frater U.·. D.·., *"Geldmagie, oder mit Dreck fängt man keine Mäuse,"* *Anubis*, 1/85, pp. 13–21

---

1. From our statements on money magic in the previous section on the classification of the pentacles/coins/discs in tarot, we know that the allocation "pentacle = air" is actually the older, original version. But the Golden Dawn, which most magic of today still thrives on, allocates the pentacles to the element of Earth. This has become an established practice and to my knowledge was never changed in any of the modern magical systems that focus on the elements, which is why we'll stick to it here as well.
2. To surrender all, one must give up not only the bad but also the good; not only weakness but strength. How can the mystic surrender all, while still clinging to one's virtues?
3. Count the movements from the time it starts moving until it stops; that might take a little while. Pay attention to the type and frequency of movement. Your entry could read: "17 circles to the right, 3 ellipses to the left, 4 circles to the left." Try several times until you get the same result every time.

INTRODUCTION TO MONEY MAGIC (II)

DEALING WITH DEBTS

In the last section we discussed some of the basics of practical money magic. Now we should start thinking about concrete ways to apply this in daily magical life.

Once again we need to point out that—according to our experience thus far—the sole deciding factor that determines whether or not one's money magic will be successful is the magician's attitude toward money itself. Not because money magic is just a playful aspect of money psychology, but because no other field of magic (with the possible exceptions of astral magic and visualization) is affected in such a significant way by unconscious psychological factors that could systematically prevent success. Even sexuality, which is often burdened with all kinds of fears and inhibitions, is much easier to apply magically than efforts toward financial wealth. Even when working with sigil magic, which is extremely powerful due to the fact that it can evade nearly all unconscious obstacles, our money magic will only be successful if we have thoroughly recognized and banished all psychological barriers in advance.

Maybe you can understand the problem better if you think about the fact that most magicians usually wait until the last minute to perform a money magic operation when it's actually too late. A person who's in a position of destitution (or even "poverty," which, of course, is quite subjective) and wants to change one's situation magically has pretty unfavorable starting conditions. His or her subconscious is already conditioned to financial failure, and now in the moment of deepest despair, magic is suddenly supposed to correct everything that has often been done wrong for years. This can be compared to the situation with nonmedical practitioners, naturopaths, and spiritual healers whose patients usually only come after all other attempts of orthodox medicine have failed. Since personal money problems are rooted so deeply in the human psyche, a great deal of patience is required to solve them, and in doing so we need to accept the fact that the only way to start is by working with certain things that may seem to have no apparent, direct connection to the principle of money.

Even in less dramatic situations, e.g., when the magician just wants "a little spare cash," old patterns of failure and guilt play an important role. There's a helpful equation that we should take to heart right from the very first step we take on the way to becoming successful at money magic.

Debt = Objectified Feelings of Guilt

This equation mainly refers to personal, pressing debts ("problem debts") of the kind that we often think "just came up unexpectedly." It's a slightly different story with "external financing," such as receiving a bank loan for starting a business, which is usually only granted after real (although sometimes fictitious) securities are deposited; this type of financing is basically necessary in today's society in order to ensure a smooth ("lubricated") course of business. Plus we'd like to point out that the above equation doesn't mean that debts in general are bad and need to be avoided at all costs. On the contrary, the ability to deal properly with debts is a great aid because it's often necessary or helpful in money magic operations to take a certain financial risk in order to give the magical task more thrust.

Besides, having debts is really not a negative quality, and it would be helpful to point out a few things in this sense: (a) no one has ever died from a lack of money; (b) all of the money that we've ever spent was at our disposal at least briefly and has therefore become an integral part of us that no one can ever take away (just like memories and everything else that we've ever experienced); (c) the value of money is in no way objective, but rather is based on somewhat random arrangements that are at least theoretically revocable at any time, and a "minus" or "plus" of the amount in question cannot and may not in any way have such a degree of power over us that would cause us to psychologically perish.

Even if you have to take on high debts due to an accident or an unlucky inheritance for which you receive no recognizable material equivalent, you should still ask yourself why you (unconsciously) chose to be in this situation and/or what you wanted to learn from it! It won't always be easy to find the answer to this question, but the pursuit of these answers will help us break away from the deadly, paralyzing paradigm of being a helpless "victim of circumstance" and a pawn in the game of fate—and whoever has trouble fighting such attitudes will never achieve any degree of success in any of his or her magical endeavors.

Once, when I was having financial problems, one of my friends who was a millionaire recommended to me, "When you're completely broke and have no other funds to fall back on, take out a loan for $50,000. Then you'll never live a normal life again. Either you'll make it, or you'll go under." This advice is in no way as absurd as it might seem, because the fact is that we often live under internal and external pressure that we've created ourselves. In particular, freelancers and self-employed people who have no regular unemployment or retirement benefits can sing you a song about how the pressure to earn double that of what their salaried or civil service colleagues make inspires their creativity, imagination, and boldness. The true trick of the trade, however, is not to fall victim to the illusion that earning lots of money always involves hard work. Even if our personal experience often speaks against it. Closer observation of the esotericism of the money principle reflects the following rules.

- Hard work is not the key to wealth; it merely contributes to the development of a sense of being poor and the triggering of money-related complexes and problems.
- Money only comes to those who love it and treat it well.
- The more we hate money, the more it will hate us.
- The more we love money, the more it will love us.
- Money is not just the means to the end; it's a unique creature with an individual life of its own—or at least we should treat it that way.
- Money magic always involves leading a self-determined life and overcoming psychological fears and barriers.
- Since the value of money is fictious, the magician needs to find out for oneself how important it actually is.

Chart 19: Rules of the esotericism of the money principle

Of course, these few sentences are merely a sampling of the overall complexity of money magic. For now, let's put aside all theoretical concepts for the time being and see what practical consequences we can derive from the above statements. Of course, there's no use in giving precise and therefore limitable exercises here, but rather we prefer to suggest general recommendations that we should integrate—even more than usual—into our everyday life. Until this takes place, and until we've successfully eliminated all psychological resistance, most money magic operations will most likely fail. If your experience is different, then good for you; but as a general rule, you usually won't succeed in money magic until you've internalized the basics of proficiently dealing with money.

We therefore recommend that you examine your own attitude toward money, life, and material goods before attempting any kind of money magic operation. It's easy to say "The magician is the master of matter," but to what extent do we really take this seriously and to what degree do we retain our magical assurance and self-confidence when it comes to financial problems?

- Learn to take a sensual approach to money.
- Determine how significant money has been in your life up to now.
- Determine how significant money will be in your life from now on.
- View money as a real living being and develop a loving relationship to it.
- Determine mistakes you might have made in the past and how you can do better in the future.
- Design a concrete training schedule based on the recommendations in the last section for developing a "healthy attitude toward money" and apply it to daily practice.
- Don't practice any money magic until you're absolutely sure of what you want to achieve.

Chart 20: The principles of money magic operations

In connection with the statements in the last section, these words of advice should be self-explanatory. Here's a little tip for sensibly dealing with money. We recommend treating money the same way you'd treat a well-meaning spirit helper. Stroke it sometimes, meditate on its shape and color, its history, and, above all, on what it really means to you. Are you really interested in money itself, or do you really just want to own things, or have material security, love, health, luxury, power, independence, etc.? Think about what we said in the last section. In the majority of cases, it would be a better idea to apply magic directly to your actual goal instead of conjuring for money as a mediator, or a "means to the end." Along the way, we'll also learn to recognize what we truly want as opposed to what may just be the spontaneous copying of assumed behavior. In the practical exercises section, you'll find an exercise that can help you create the basis for successful money magic operations.

PRACTICAL EXERCISES

EXERCISE 40

MAGICAL MONEY TRAINING (I)

Get an overview of everything you own. Calculate exactly how much money you already have by converting the value of every object you own, from a privately owned home right down to the last spare button in the button jar. Be realistic. Since it's usually pretty tough to sell buttons individually, you'll only be able to write down a few cents; when in doubt, check prices at a flea market. Don't leave out anything, not even the slightest little thing. Count borrowed money and debts as well, because that's money that was at your disposal once. (And if you have a million in debts, it means that you're worth at least a million to someone in this world!)

When you're all done, add everything up and meditate on your current objectified wealth.

EXERCISE 41

MAGICAL MONEY TRAINING (II)

Get an overview of everything you own. Make an exact calculation of how much money has actually passed through your hands in your lifetime, including everything you've ever made, inherited, received as a gift, or obtained otherwise. Count borrowed money as well.

When you're all done, add everything up and meditate on the amount of money you were able to obtain in your lifetime thus far. (A million can be made quickly in just a few decades.)

For both exercises, it's fine to just meditate on the results. At this stage, don't attempt to correct a financial plight with a magical operation just yet—just keep working on your awareness of money.

THE MAGICAL WILL AND THE PRINCIPLE OF THELEMA (I)

Ultimately the Magical Will so identifies itself with the man's whole being that it becomes unconscious, and is as constant a force as gravitation (Crowley, *Magick*, p. 65).

In Cairo, in the year 1904, Aleister Crowley "received" his Book of the Law (more specifically, *Liber Al vel Legis*) that he viewed as being a revelation of the supernatural authority called Aiwass. Now we don't want to go into detail about the exact circumstances of this revelation and Crowley's interpretation of it. The important thing for us here is merely the fact that this "Law of Thelema" has found its way into modern magic. The Greek word *thelema* basically means "will."

The complete Law of Thelema reads as follows:

Do what thou wilt shall be the whole of the law,
love is the law, love under will.

Since our book has no intentions of being sectarian, we'll treat Crowley's system just as neutral and value-free as the systems of other magicians, granting it just enough space to provide a general understanding. To the Crowleyites or Thelemites reading this, please forgive us for not delving into every little ramification and detail of the Law of Thelema, but a general overview is quite sufficient enough for clarifying its basic principles. However, we should keep in mind that no other concept has given modern magic such powerful, fruitful impulses, with the possible exception of the magic of Austin Osman Spare and contemporary Chaos Magic.

Crowley's concept assumes that everyone has a "True Will" as opposed to the mere wants or desires of the everyday ego. We can compare this True Will (or Thelema, as we'll call it from time to time) to one's "calling" or "purpose" in life, with the goal of reaching a state of self-realization (Crowley doesn't mention this process in more detail) without having to rely on a god or other transcendental authority to do so—however, this doesn't exclude the possibility of such an authority being there from the start.

According to Crowley, the goal of each magician is to recognize one's own Thelema and to realize it. This is certainly not as obvious as it may first seem. On the contrary, it can be extremely tedious and painful, especially if you've been living in opposition to your own True Will for a longer period of time (e.g., decades). Then it's not just a matter of restructuring your thinking—it may also require you to throw off a lot of dead weight that you even may have learned to love over the years. If, for example, after thirty years of working as a coolly calculating businessperson you realize that your True Will means repenting in sackcloth and ashes, indulging in asceticism and performing unpaid jobs of charity, you're definitely going to have problems with your family and environment—ranging from the taunting and teasing of your business colleagues who are certain that you've fallen victim to the "midlife crisis," to the complaints of your family about the "deterioration of their standard of living," right up to the "friendly" letter from the bank or savings and loan association when you're no longer able to pay off your debts because you've written off your income to some charitable organization. This may sound like a pretty unlikely and exceptional case, but experience has shown that the fallout usually is much worse!

Nonetheless, Crowley's dictum reads "Thou hast no right but to do thy will." And that's the way it should be, because if we assume that life is mainly about being happy or achieving the goals we set for ourselves, it will become clear in a magical sense as well that everything else is unimportant.

Crowley's system also applies the premise that we'll have the support and motivating power of the entire universe behind us once we've recognized our True Will and begin to live it out. It can be compared to swimming in a river—since Thelema always exists in harmony with the overall will of the entire universe, living in harmony with one's own True Will means swimming with the current of it all instead of fighting against it. If we take a closer look at this concept, we'll see that it resembles the Way of Tao, and indeed Taoism and Thelema have quite a bit in common.

Many Crowleyites are often not aware that Aleister Crowley surely wasn't the first person to assert the primacy of the individual's will. From the *fac quid vult* of Father Augustinus von Hippo (354–430) up to the *fayce que voudras* of François Rabelais in the second volume of his novel printed around 1532–1564 called *Gargantua et Pantagruel* (which mentions an abbey "Thélème" as a sort of utopian antimonastery and symbol for humanistic freedom ideals), we realize that free will is not a new concept, and even the influence of philosophers such as Bergson (whose sister Moina was the wife of Mathers, the leader of the Golden Dawn), Schopenhauer, and Nietzsche can be unmistakably seen if we study the Book of the Law in more depth. A strong influence is also reflected in the well-known magic of Abramelin, which we unfortunately cannot deal with here in more detail.

The magician's greatest difficulty is being able to unequivocally recognize one's Thelema because the power of illusion is strong, the flesh is weak, and the spirit is in no way always willing. This is the ultimate goal of magic as Crowley understands it, in the same sense that the goal of the magic of Abramelin is to establish contact with one's own "Holy Guardian Angel," which we could also understand as a personification of our individual Thelema. Similar concepts can be found in shamanistic magic and the magic of tribal peoples, such as with the so-called totem or clan totem.

Crowley's system stops being magical there and turns into pure religion—the principle of Thelema becomes a dogmatic doctrine in which the concrete-magical aspects that directly influence fate are pushed into the background and belief itself and/or transcendental utopia seize predominance. We'll be examining this later on in more detail in connection with his doctrine "Every man and every woman is a star." We have no intentions of disparaging the concept of Thelema, but in this aspect the subject goes well beyond the intentions of this book as defined in the very first section.

On the other hand, it's very important that the aspiring magician understands this concept, otherwise one may have trouble understanding the works of Aleister Crowley. These works are not really written for magical everyday practice, but rather for religious transcendental mysticism within Western occultism, following the example of Eliphas Levi. We'll discuss this in more detail as well.

As a preliminary summary, it's sufficient to say that "Do what thou wilt" in no way means "Do whatever you currently want to do," but rather "Do what is your True Will." Crowley understood this to be the recognition and pursuit of one's own *daimonium*, and Thelema is both a vocation and an obligation that has absolutely nothing to do with the continual fluctuation of the wishes and desires of our tiny everyday ego. To Crowley, the magician is always a mystic, or a person who strives for the "highest truth" regardless of whether or not this may violate the norms of common civil ethics and morals. Despite his undeniable contributions to magical practice, Crowley's main intention was to found a new world religion; he admitted this himself a number of times, and this intention was also reflected in the 1928 Weida Conference where he attempted to have himself proclaimed "World Savior" by the German Pansophic Movement, which in the end led to the disintegration of this magic crème de la crème of German occultism and, among other things, also led to the founding of the Fraternitas Saturni. Even the subtitle of his magazine, *The Equinox*, clearly reflected this, namely "The Method of Science—the Aim of Religion." Nevertheless, there are a great number of Thelemites who would in no way describe themselves as Crowleyites. We'd like to examine the reason for this and the relationship between the two in the next section.

INTRODUCTION TO RITUAL MAGIC (X)

THE LAMEN

As we already mentioned in the last section, modern magic literature seldom differentiates between the lamen and the pentacle. But tradition views this differently and makes a clear distinction between the two, which is why we've chosen to discuss the lamen here separately as well, in order to be as thorough as possible.

Crowley complained about the fact that Eliphas Levi didn't distinguish between the lamen and the pentacle either, and many other older authors even confuse the two.

The lamen is a breastplate worn by the priests of the Old Testament as a tunicle for divination (see Deuteronomy 38:15–30). The modern lamen, however, is just a simple metal plate worn over the heart. To Crowley, the lamen is a symbol of the sephira, Tiphareth, which is why it should express the harmony of all other symbols united into one.

But there's also another type of lamen that the magician uses to evoke a spirit. In this case, the lamen containing the symbols of the spirit or demon is placed in the triangle and worn on the magician's chest—so actually there are two identical lamens. If the magician only works with one lamen, which is generally the rule today if used at all, it should represent the goal of one's Great Work. In this sense, Crowley wrote:

In this Lamen the Magician must place the secret keys of his power.

The Pantacle is merely the material to be worked upon, gathered together and harmonized but not yet in operation, the parts of the engine arranged for use, or even put together, but not yet set in motion. In the Lamen these forces are already at work; even accomplishment is prefigured.

In the system of Abramelin the Lamen is a plate of silver upon which the Holy Guardian Angel writes in dew. This is another way of expressing the same thing, for it is He who confers the secrets of that power which should be herein expressed (*Magick*, p. 111).

This strange uncertainty and vagueness is surely the reason that the lamen has nearly become extinct. On the one hand it should serve as a symbol of faith and invulnerability, but on the other hand it's basically a sort of demonic talisman used to evoke spirits.

Whenever the lamen is used today, it's usually used to protect the heart chakra. In addition, it gives the magician a certain sense of security and strength, especially when it's fairly heavy and its weight can be clearly felt on one's chest.

On the other hand, modern demonology generally doesn't use the lamen anymore since there are easier ways of evocation than making two identical laminas per demon.

If you decide to make a lamen for yourself, make sure you truly understand the difference between it and the pentacle; and of course you should also know what purpose your lamen is meant to fulfill.

THE MAGIC RING

Most authors of magic literature treat the ring quite carelessly, or don't even bother to mention it at all. This is quite amazing since the magic ring is one of the most common instruments in the history of magic, and nearly every practicing magician has at least a small (but often quite large) selection of them.

However, the ring is not an elemental weapon and does not stand for any specific symbolic principle; sometimes it acts as a fetish, or as a talisman or amulet, and occasionally it serves as a mark of identification (e.g., in a fraternal order) or the emblem of a certain grade—in short, it's a universal instrument of magic like no other that complies with the magician's intentions and can be used in an endless number of ways.

In this sense, it becomes clear that the ring cannot be forced into a rigid structure of rules, which may be the reason why (mostly older) authors are so hesitant to discuss it. However, we feel that the magic ring is one of the most important magic weapons of all, for both practical as well as theoretical reasons.

In a practical sense, the ring is lightweight and easy to use, and generally not too difficult or expensive to make. It's not easy to lose as long as it fits firmly on the finger, and it can also be designed to be inconspicuous (which, of course, may not always be the case), since even a simple gold or silver band can be magically charged and worn without attracting too much attention. Since the great majority of magical operations involve some kind of movements of the hand and fingers, it can be a good idea to enhance this by equipping the hand or fingers with an appropriate "weapon."

So it's quite common for a magician to make (or have made) at least one ring to document one's magical identity. For example, this could be a simple, wide band made out of a suitable metal engraved with the magician's personal motto in the form of a sigil, or one that contains glyphs that represent the powers (e.g., elements, planets, or demons/angels) that one predominately works with or has concluded a pact with. You could make a ring for constructive as well as destructive operations, which is charged through frequent use. However, we prefer working with at least one ring that unites both sides, light and dark.

The design of the ring is completely up to the magician oneself. One could integrate certain gemstones (e.g., for planetary powers), use a mixture of metals (e.g., gold and silver to represent the "Chymical Marriage," or the union of opposites), engrave the surface, or conceal engravings/decorations under a layer of metal (gold plating)—there are no limits to one's imagination when it comes to the design.

Since a ring, as already mentioned, can also function as a talisman or amulet, a magician might also make one to wear only on certain occasions or for certain operations, such as a ring charged with healing energy or money magnetic properties, a ring for evocations or for protection in magical warfare, and so on. In ancient Egypt, rings with images of the gods were often worn that served as a link to the corresponding energies.

Lodge rings are the identification marks of fraternal orders, but can also declare a general bond to a certain principle.

THE MAGICAL WILL AND THE PRINCIPLE OF THELEMA (II)

Thelemites, but not Crowleyites—how can that be?

"I am the Magician and the Exorcist. I am the axle of the wheel, and the cube in the circle. 'Come unto me' is a foolish word: for it is I that go."
Liber Al, II, 7

In the last section, we already saw that Crowley wasn't the first person in the history of the occident to deal with the concept of True Will, although he was surely one of its most radical and uncompromising representatives, putting him at least from an ideological point of view among the ranks of the Marquis de Sade or Gilles de Rais, both whom he highly regarded, by the way.

But even outside of Europe we'll find similar concepts, which we already touched on earlier. To illustrate this point further, we'd like to state one more example. We're talking about the "vision quest" that plays a significant role in cultures with a shamanic influence, such as with the Native American Indians. Typically the apprentice shaman (or any young man about to be initiated as a full adult member of the tribe) ventures out to have a vision. Along the way, he may go through a phase of physical deprivation (fasting, sexual abstinence, isolation, self-inflicted pain), either in preparation or as an integral part of the actual vision quest itself. Sometimes after a long period of fasting, the person is given a fever-inducing drug and sent out into the jungle to receive a vision as a dream or daydream that will show him the further course of his life. If the vision reveals to him that he's destined to be a warrior or shaman, and that he should leave his village and move to a foreign place or lead a war against a neighboring tribe, this is both a guidepost and obligation for the future. The statement "I will follow my vision" is considered to be an incontestable justification to the other members of the tribe, but it's obvious that such statements cannot be taken lightly, otherwise the protective spirits or the gods would punish it as sacrilege.

There are a number of stories about such people who were unable to have a vision on their quest. Even after several tries, they returned unsuccessfully, which often resulted in terrible ostracism by the tribal community. This logically aroused the suspicion that the person sometimes "cheated" to avoid such a situation. The main reason we've mentioned this is because it shows that even in today's romanticized esotericism, those oh so highly regarded Native American cultures often have difficulties with subtle perception, too, and can even be incapable of having visions!

Whoever wants to become a Catholic priest needs to "prove" that this is his "destiny," his "life vision" as a pastor. This is at least one small way of examining whether or not the candidate's choice to enter priesthood truly corresponds to his Thelema, or whether it might only be a passing flair or the result of a temporary crisis.

In this sense, Crowley's concept is in no way new as he himself liked to claim. Our example is in no way intended to devalue Crowley's statement, but in order to have an objective perspective of magic, we need to put it in the right context. In this way, we recognize that being a Thelemite certainly does not automatically mean being a Crowleyite as well. This is important in this respect because the Crowleyites—as all representatives of charismatic religions of revelation and salvation—often claim to have a monopoly on the definition of Thelema, which in our opinion can be justified neither by Crowley's *Book of the Law* itself nor by the historical Thelemic context.

And the relevant literature on the subject rarely mentions the various possible ways of interpreting the concept of "Thelema." Most Thelemites seem to assume that one's own personal Thelema is a fixed concept that you discover once and that never changes afterward. Such a concept has quite a bit in common with the so-called "clockwork paradigms" of earlier days when the cosmos was understood as a huge gear wheel machine (e.g., Newton's physics). However, due in part to the discoveries of modern particle physics, such models are beginning to lose their foothold, resulting in the fact that modern magic increasingly turns to relativistic ideas, and even some elements of the philosophy of critic rationalism (Popper), structuralism (Lévi-Strauss, Barthes, Lacan) and skepticism in general. Such a relativistic, skeptic magician will view Thelema as a "temporary vision," or a variable that's subject to change just like everything else in the universe and, as a result, needs to be rediscovered and redefined again and again—if its entire spectrum can even be recognized at all.

But this is not the time to get into the speculative aspects of magical philosophy—practice comes first! Only through continual personal experience will the magician be able to develop a sound opinion on such things; anything else would be nothing but assumptions and hearsay.

MAGIC AND FREE WILL

"I am alone: there is no God where I am."
Liber Al, II, 23

Before we return to more practical things, we should first spend a few minutes thinking about the highly disputed subject of "free will." The range between the statements of determinism ("everything is predetermined, one is unfree and dependent on nature, divinity, and fate") and those of free will ("everything is open and impressionable, one is free and can influence nature and life/fate at will") is quite large, and in between there has been a bitter ideological struggle for several hundreds of years. Magic was affected by this as well. On the one hand, we'll find statements of both Western and Eastern origin that support the idea that the magician should submit and adapt to the structure of the whole, because only then will one be able to truly influence things and become a master builder who contributes to the Great Work. On the other hand, some believe that the magician takes over control once he or she begins to worship oneself, recognizes one's own power, accepts it, and uses it according to one's will.

The beginner is often confused by the fact that such contradicting statements are frequently used by the same magician; Aleister Crowley is a perfect example of this, but even authors such as Levi, Papus, Quintscher, or Bardon seem to cultivate this apparent confusion. Often it seems like an attempt is being made to establish a middle path for postulating a more mild form of free will by recognizing and accepting certain inherent (and transcendental!) constraints. That doesn't come as a surprise since the extreme form of both opinions cannot hold ground to real experience: Neither can it be irrefutably proven that man has ever possessed any kind of free will at all, nor can we convincingly support the extreme opposite, namely that one has all freedoms at his or her disposal. On a pragmatic level, we usually take the middle path anyway. Two examples can illustrate this:

1) A criminal offender is held responsible for his crimes by the community because he has the freedom of choice to refrain from detrimental behavior. Perhaps he could plead for milder punishment if he had acted out of a desperate situation ("restricted free will") that obviously overtaxed his powers and abilities. (A person dying of starvation could care less about the ownership claims of rich grocery stores.)

2) Despite one's power of will, she remains dependent on a number of natural, inherent constraints, such as the need for oxygen and water for survival, and the fact that she cannot grow wings for flying, just to name a few.

Basically, the claim of free will is nothing but a positive utopia. For example, even if humans still haven't been able to grow wings, it doesn't automatically mean that they never will.

The magician is confronted with this problem on a daily basis because one constantly bumps into limits on one's ability to act, but at the same time one also sees broken barriers that previously seemed unbeatable, which resulted in the expansion of one's scope of maneuverability. In this sense, he or she often finds oneself balancing on the thin line between having absolutely no self-esteem whatsoever (when expressed positively = humbleness) and being equally absolutely megalomaniac (when expressed positively = self-confidence). But the realistic magician needs to maintain this inner and outer balance on this dangerous journey between Skylla and Charybdis and not sway from the middle path.

To wrap thing up, let's have a look at how Crowley handles this problem. The text passage quoted here is one of his more explicit statements on the subject:

> *But even though every man is "determined" so that every action is merely the passive resultant of the sum-total of the forces which have acted upon him from eternity, so that his own Will is only the echo of the Will of the Universe, yet that consciousness of "Free Will" is valuable; and if he really understands it as being the partial and individual expression of that internal motion in a Universe whose sum is rest, by so much will he feel that harmony, that totality. And though the happiness which he experiences may be criticised as only one scale of a balance in whose other scale is an equal misery, there are those who hold that misery consists only in the feeling of separation from the Universe, and that consequently all may cancel out among the lesser feelings, leaving only that infinite bliss which is one phase of the infinite consciousness of that ALL. [. . .] It is of no particular moment to observe that the elephant and flea can be no other than they are; but we do perceive that one is bigger than the other. That is the fact of practical importance.*

We do know that persons can be trained to do things which they could not do without training—and anyone who remarks that you cannot train a person unless it is his destiny to be trained is quite unpractical. Equally it is the destiny of the trainer to train. There is a fallacy in the determinist argument similar to the fallacy which is the root of all "systems" of gambling at Roulette. The odds are just over three to one against red coming up twice running; but after red has come up once the conditions are changed.

It would be useless to insist on such a point were it not for the fact that many people confuse philosophy with Magick. Philosophy is the enemy of Magick. Philosophy assures us that after all nothing matters, and that "che sarà sarà."

In practical life, and Magick is the most practical of the arts of life, this difficulty does not occur. It is useless to argue with a man who is running to catch a train that he may be destined not to catch it; he just runs, and if he could spare breath, would say "Blow destiny!" (*Magick*, pp. 66–67).

Here the old master worded things quite pragmatically and austerely. And in the end, practice and experience are much more important than any speculations about determinism and free will anyway. In any case, it's much more effective and satisfying to ignore the so-called "limits of fate" and live according to the principle that we are the masters of our own lives. On the other hand, though, there's little sense in overtaxing oneself with childish delusions of omnipotence, only to put the blame on magic in the end. That's why in the same context Crowley stresses the importance of "magical understanding," which the magical will requires to thrive.

INTRODUCTION TO RITUAL MAGIC (XI)

THE MAGIC BELL

Apart from the fact that many magicians like to implement the use of sound in order to highlight certain phases or sections of a ritual, the magic bell has a great deal of symbolical significance, just as all other ritual weapons do. It's considered to be a sort of "astral bell" that's used to announce the establishment of contact to "another world," literally "ringing it in." It therefore serves as a tool for both capturing attention and warning, but also for celebrating majestic passages of a hymn or intensifying the communication with the invoked powers, and can therefore also be used as an instrument of ecstasy. In addition, the ringing of a bell marks the interruption of profane time in the magician's universe while it conforms to one's will for this one eternal moment.

Crowley's description of a magic bell is not much different from that of a cymbal with a clapper hanging from a leather strap that's strung through the middle hole of the cymbal and knotted firmly on the other side. He requires the bell to be made of electrum magicum, which is an alloy of the seven planetary metals that played a significant role in medieval alchemy as well. The individual metals should be melted together one after another during favorable planetary constellations—gold and silver are melted first during a favorable aspect of the sun and moon, then tin when Jupiter is favorable, and so on in the same manner.

In practice, Nepalese or Tibetan cymbals that can be bought in Asian stores are most commonly used. Although these are often claimed to be made of electrum (which the layman cannot prove, of course), the most important thing is their beautiful sound. Cymbals are generally bought in pairs, with the two disks being connected by a leather strap. They are played by lightly striking the edges of the disks together. By slowly separating the cymbals after they are struck, interesting sound effects can be created (ranging from a "whimpering" to a subtle rumbling sound), which can help induce a state of trance as well.

However, we'd like to point out that most modern magicians no longer use the bell in a symbolic sense. Although they do indeed still use bells, cymbals, and other resonant instruments, they are usually nothing more than ritual accessories with no symbolic power.

THE MAGIC LAMP

In Crowley's system, the magic lamp is a metaphysical symbol and instrument of immense complexity which has led cynics to say that his directions for making one are just about as easy as telling a student to make a light bulb with one's bare hands. However, Crowley never really gave any recommendations on how to make one; on the contrary, the lamp is a ritual weapon that the initiate in his order (A.·.A.·.) is encouraged to make even without the permission of one's superior and it requires no approval from others. This is because the lamp symbolizes to him the "light of the pure soul," the "image of the Most High," and is comparable to Moses' vision of the burning bush. It's the eternal light of enlightenment that hangs above the altar and is nourished by the element of Ether alone. Its light is "without quantity or quality, unconditioned and sempiternal," Crowley writes (*Magick*, p. 102). He continues:

> *Without this Light the Magician could not work at all; yet few indeed are the Magicians that have known of it, and far fewer They that have beheld its brilliance!*
>
> *[. . .]*
>
> *Whatever you have and whatever you are are veils before that light.*
>
> *Yet in so great a matter all advice is vain. There is no Master so great that he can see clearly the whole character of any pupil* (ibid., p. 103).

The lamp is therefore a symbol of entry to the ether plane, and it embodies the illumination of the magician and one's link to transcendence. Its actual secret is that it doesn't need any kind of physical manifestation. Technically speaking, the magic lamp can be described as a nonmaterial ether weapon.

From what we've said here, it's obvious that it would be impossible to give any kind of instructions for making one. That's why every magician should find the way to one's own magic lamp oneself.

STRUCTURES OF MAGICAL TRANCE (I)

THE INHIBITORY MODE

Pete Carroll, the founder of Chaos Magic, is credited with drawing our attention as magicians to the significance of magical trance (which he defined as gnosis), while clearly breaking it down into various categories at the same time. Let's have a look at these categories here and explain them in more detail. After all, it's about time we start delving deeper into this subject since it just may be the most significant field of modern magic today.

Carroll basically distinguishes between two types of gnosis in his book *Liber Null*, namely the inhibitory mode and the excitatory mode. Schematically, this looks as follows:

Inhibitory Mode	Excitatory Mode
• Death posture	• Sexual excitation
• Magical trance concentration	• Emotional arousal, e.g., fear, anger, horror
• Sleeplessness	• Pain, torture
• Fasting	• Flagellation
• Exhaustion	• Dancing, drumming, chanting
• Gazing	• Right way of walking
• Hypnotic or trance-inducing drugs	• Excitatory or disinhibitory drugs • Mild hallucinogens • Hyperventilation
• Sensory deprivation	• Sensory overload

Chart 21: Forms of magical trance (according to Pete Carroll)

First we'll be taking a closer look at the inhibitory mode since you're already familiar with some of its elements from the practical exercises in this book. But first we'd like to point out the fact that the two basic principles of magic, namely the "spiritual blazing of a fire" and the establishment of "spiritual peace as deep as the ocean," are both reflected in this trance structure. The type of trance chosen depends just as much on the temperament of the magician as on the goal of one's corresponding magical operation.

THE DEATH POSTURE

We've already discussed the death posture here in depth, so there's no need to mention it again. This forced state of empty mind is and will always remain one of the most vital keys to unlocking magical powers and skills, and there's no way of emphasizing just how important it is that every magician practice it.

Concentrations Leading to Magical Trance

1. Object concentration. This includes tratak, among other things. Of course, this form of concentration can be expanded on in numerous ways.

2. Sound concentration. The magician concentrates on acoustically perceptible, articulated, or imagined sounds, usually mantras, in order to block verbal thoughts from intruding while at the same time developing the key to words of power and the skill of spell casting. (It's sort of a ritual exercise in rhetoric.)
3. Image concentration. The magician concentrates on images or symbols, such as a circle, square, or cross. More complicated image sequences can also be used. This is the key to mental magic and working with the magical double, as well as to creating psychogons and charging sigils through staring. Even demonology relies heavily on this technique.

With these three forms of concentration, the magician can gain control of the parts of one's mind that are responsible for both pictorial as well as verbal thoughts.

Surely if we focus on a magical statement of intent, this becomes an extremely powerful magical technique, provided that we can at least maintain—or better yet, improve—the state of trance reached in the meditation exercise.

As opposed to many earlier authors, we prefer not to work with visualization techniques alone in practical magic since experience has shown that the results of such techniques are insufficient and sporadic. In cases of doubt, a closer look will reveal that all three forms of concentration are actually used in every successful magical operation

From what we've already said about the structure of the psyche and the laws of forgetting, as well as symbol-logic and the fuzzy relation, it should be clear by now that this form of magic is much more effective and thorough than mere mental autosuggestion techniques that work mainly with concepts and rarely with images and sound.

This is reflected in the fact that thought concentration—which used to be an integral part of the magic of the past—is rarely used today in modern magic. Back then, this usually took the form of concentration on the magical goal, the magician's desire, or on one's statement of intent. This form of thought concentration has been replaced by the use of the state of empty mind technique (which is probably a result of Eastern, in particular Tibetan, influences); after achieving this state during a magical operation, a symbol of the magician's magical will is disguised and implanted into the subconscious. This is especially clear in sigil magic, but we'll be encountering other disciplines (such as doll magic) that use this technique as well.

But in your practice, please don't forget that although the techniques listed here can lead to gnosis, they alone do not yet represent trance.

Sleeplessness, Fasting, Exhaustion

With the help of these techniques, everyday reality is "softened" and the magician becomes more receptive to subtle perception since the censor weakens with time. Described by Pete Carroll as "old monastic favorites" (*Liber Null,* p. 34), these inhibitory techniques are still part of the standard repertoire of all shamans and nature magicians today. The trick is for the magician to be able to turn the confused state of consciousness that these three techniques will eventually produce into a true and powerful magical trance in which one retains enough control to impregnate oneself with the magical will. In simple, exaggerated terms, there's no point in fasting until you pass out unless you're able to charge your magical will at the moment you lose consciousness.

However, overexaggerated self-deprivation is useless; it's much wiser and more effective to find a moderate level of sleeplessness, fasting, and/or exhaustion that custom fits the magician's natural (and trained) gnosis ability. But this is a matter of personal experience and is difficult for an outsider to judge, even though many magicians and shamans are able to develop a feel for the trance ability and depth of a person and therefore help one accordingly in order for one to achieve optimal results. This is exactly what the participants in a group operation demand of a ritual leader since he or she's responsible for activating, storing, impregnating, and directing the energies of each participant on an equal level to reach a common goal.

Theoretically, the sign of a true master is the ability to synchronize each and every one of the participants of a group ritual (even under unfavorable circumstances) to create the desired level of gnosis while at the same time—in trance—keeping an eye on things and being able to respond if a participant seems to be losing control. If you work frequently with experienced magicians of the Black Arts, you'll surely observe this quite often.

Unfortunately, there are exceptions to this rule as well. For example, magicians who work with the Eastern paradigm of *wu-wei* ("action through nonaction") generally prefer to focus on the overall quality of the group's work instead of on each individual's success or failure at achieving the proper state of trance. Of course, in these cases we often observe that such masters harmonize or balance out these released energies either unconsciously through the sheer power and quality of their own force field, or by consciously eliminating any dissonance on the subtle energy level in a subtle way, which usually only the experienced eye will be able to see.

Gazing

We've already discussed this subject thoroughly in connection with the "magic gaze" so that no further explanation is necessary here.

Hypnotic or Trance-Inducing Drugs

Regardless of the legal aspects associated with this subject, the use of drugs for magical purposes is generally not recommended. This applies in particular to the beginner, especially for those who have already experimented with many types of drugs and still do so on a fairly regular basis. A trip is a far cry from a ritual! Although a ritual can (but does not necessarily) lead to states of altered consciousness that strongly resemble those induced by the use of drugs, it doesn't work the other way around, meaning that drugs do not necessarily lead to magical ritual. The main problem is that drugs not only cause the loss of the mental and physical control that's required for a magical operation, but they also blunt the sharp will. This is often overlooked, especially by young magicians who like to imitate Crowley's drug escapades, but in his case (which is also overlooked as well) these drugs were often medically prescribed (e.g., he was originally given heroin to treat his asthma attacks), and eventually led to a lifelong addiction that he was victim to on and off right up until his death.

But even during his addiction, Crowley was able to maintain his strength of will and a stable personality that most of his young admirers today fail to do. A later friend of Therion's once told me how he had an asthma attack in the middle of a conversation three years before his death; his face turned blue and he was just barely able to stumble over to the dresser to grab his heroin injection that was already prepared and ready to go. Afterward, Crowley made his friend promise never to touch or obstruct him in any way if this ever happened again since this injection was his last lifesaver. At the time, Crowley's doctor had already started drastically reducing his heroin prescriptions, which the old magician had quite a hard time adjusting to since he was already accustomed to such a high dosage of the drug. But at least he had enough willpower to always keep at least one injection on reserve in case of a dire emergency of suffocation. How many junkies today would be able to do that?

Although shamans often use drugs to stimulate trance, this is done in an entirely different sociocultural context, and to the shamanic community, this use of drugs is considered a sacral act so that any abuse would surely be punished just as severely as in our culture today.

Some of the hypnotic and trance-inducing drugs include alcohol in large amounts, cannabis, sleeping pills, and tranquilizers, as well as a number of psychopharmacological drugs. When administered by a true expert, it's indeed possible to induce a useful magical trance, but the disadvantages surely outweigh the advantages. The only time the use of drugs should be considered is if the magician has severe inhibitions that prevent one from achieving a state of trance (which is occasionally the case with completely untrained beginners), and in extremely visionary operations and those that work with "soft" group energies; the latter is occasionally the case in sex magic.

Sensory Deprivation

The technique of sensory deprivation was and still is used among monks and hermits alike, along with occasional practices of seclusion. Its goal is to reduce the number of external impulses that affect our rational thought as much as possible, which will eventually cause it to paralyze due to the lack of stimuli.

During a ritual, we create sensory deprivation by using blindfolds, hoods, and the element of darkness. Experience has shown that due to the "shock effect" it causes, it's much more effective to shut out external stimuli for just a short period of time instead of banishing it entirely over a longer period. Long-term sensory deprivation is usually more suited for mystical practices.

The "Samadhi Tank" (or "Meditation Tank") is an excellent modern machine designed by consciousness explorer John C. Lilly for working with this type of gnosis. In this tank, a person floats atop approximately two inches of brine with an extremely high salt concentration (similar to the Dead Sea); the door and walls of the tank block out all optical stimuli and external noise. Even after just a few minutes, the person will lose all sense of time and will experience an extraordinarily deep feeling of relaxation since the high propelling force of the brine supports the entire weight of the body, taking all pressure off of the muscles. Such tanks can be bought in stores, but they can also be found in therapy centers in most larger cities. Whoever hasn't had this experience yet should certainly try it out.

As already mentioned, it strongly depends on the personal preferences and goals of the magician as to which form of gnosis one should choose. It's obvious that an aggressive operation of magical warfare would be easier to perform with an excitatory trance than with inhibitory gnosis. On the other hand, such an operation could be aimed at breaking down the opponent or his or her situation, which would surely benefit more from a sort of "corrosive inhibitory trance."

But within both of these two categories, there are fine differences that each individual magician will most likely express in a completely unique way so that no fixed rules can be given. Ideally all methods should lead to the same level of gnosis, but in practice there certainly are differences that are probably related to the fact that the magician almost never induces a full trance with complete loss of consciousness since this would make him completely subject to the will and influence of others.

Every magician should be thoroughly familiar with the various energy qualities of the methods introduced here so that one's able to form one's own educated opinion about their advantages and disadvantages. Plus, it's a good idea to always have several techniques on hand in case it's too difficult or impossible to perform one method for some reason or another. For example, it would be pretty difficult to induce true sensory deprivation in the subway, but magic gazing or sound concentration would be much easier under such circumstances.

It's important to master and not just achieve a state of trance, otherwise it can lead to just the opposite of what the magician actually intended. That's why persistent practice in this field is a high priority for all types of modern and shamanic magic.

REPORTS FROM MAGICAL PRACTICE (IV)

Aleister Crowley once told a story about a magical operation with strange effects that has meanwhile become quite well-known. Once he was waiting for an urgent letter from a certain person that lived several thousand miles away. Finally he decided to perform a ritual to force the letter to arrive. In fact, the letter actually did arrive a few days later—but it had been mailed more than a week before. Below is a commentary on this event taken from the column "Tante Klaras Kummertempel" in the German magic magazine *ANUBIS* (it is no longer in print).

> *There have been several suggested models of explanation for such occurrences. The easiest and probably most common explanation due to its simplicity says that this was a case of divination: The magician intuitively senses that a certain event is imminent and acts instinctively in order to "bring it about.'"*
>
> *The question is, however, whether the desired event actually would have occurred without the ritual even though it had already been triggered. (The letter could have gotten lost, for example.) There's no way to test this, of course, but some magicians recommend performing a ritual even for things that have already been achieved before the operation! This would at least be a way to finally wrap up the matter using the symbolic language of the soul, and a religious person might even turn this ceremony into a ritual thanksgiving.*
>
> *Modern magic is concerned more and more with getting to the bottom of this problem of "retroactive conjuring," as this phenomena is technically called. After all, we modern conjurers live in a world of science fiction and stories about travels through time in which even physicists calculate time "backwards." If magic were actually just a way of directing information (and many things support this theory, which is how the word "cybermagic"—derived from the word "cybernetics," or "the science of control systems"—has recently developed to describe a modern form of magic that's currently evolving); if information exists beyond the limits of time and space and can be transferred beyond these limits as well (which would make the whole theory of incarnation unnecessary!)—after all, it doesn't have any mass and possibly no energy as well—, we see a possible future model of explanation rise above the horizon which would make any poor old lady's head spin. Because then the question would be "Can we change the past with magic? Can we—afterwards, mark you!—shift the switches of time?" Honestly I'm still hesitant to propose such a profound, reality-shattering claim. But if, and I repeat, if it really is this way, then retroactive magic would be dealing with "memories of the future," making the space gods and UFOs of Charroux and Daniken seem like nothing but wimps in comparison. If the magician—as often*

claimed and repeatedly confirmed by us practitioners—actually can change reality, if his reality exists beyond time and space, and if we should succeed in giving this claim a theoretical and practical, applicable, examinable foundation, then it probably wouldn't be exaggerating to say that we, within magic (and not only there) are about to make the largest spiritual quantum leap in the entire history of mankind.

[. . .] I'm truly sorry that I [. . .] have only been able to answer by posing a number of further questions, and maybe I've even made the whole thing even more unclear and incomprehensible than it already was. But don't take it too hard—our time isn't up yet and if the current development within the magic scene even lives up to just half of what it promises, by the turn of the millennium, the kind of magic we call our own will surely be one that mankind has never known before. Then we just might be able to conjure retroactively—specifically and consciously—to make our space-time continuum shake and tremble! The first steps have already been taken, and some of our best minds (a few dozen, after all) have already taken on the challenge and are examining how to make the best out of this situation. In this sense, we live in highly exciting and interesting times—which, according to a Chinese saying, is actually a curse. But who cares, we'll survive one way or another . . . There's nothing better than a true pioneering spirit —à l'hazard, Kybernautikos!. (*ANUBIS*, #8, p. 51–53).

The above statements raise the question of the fictitious "morphogenetic fields", where earlier generations are considered to have left their magical skills, or where "ancient" brotherhoods can be rediscovered—is this actually an attempt to influence our current reality by turning time backward? This example has purposely been given without providing any possible answers in order to show that there is still plenty to discover in modern magic, and that we can never really be sure about our pattern of reality and time—it's just important to think about these problems of magic from time to time.

PRACTICAL EXERCISES

EXERCISE 42

SYSTEMATIC TRANCE TRAINING (I): INHIBITORY GNOSIS

Develop your own systematic exercise plan based on the techniques in this section in order to familiarize yourself with the various forms and methods of inhibitory gnosis. You should practice at least four times a week, although short periods of about fifteen to thirty minutes are usually sufficient.

BIBLIOGRAPHY

Pete Carroll, *Liber Null* (the official training manual for the I.O.T.)

STRUCTURES OF MAGICAL TRANCE (II)

EXCITATORY MODES

Sexual Excitation

As already mentioned in connection with sigil magic, sexual excitement is one of the most powerful tools the magician has. During the state of sexual excitement, the censor is blocked by up to 100 percent,[1] the path to the subconscious is wide open and the magician is free to implant in it anything one needs for his or her operation.

Sexual excitement can be obtained by any method the individual prefers—but the magician should on occasion also use methods that are not necessarily one's favorites. Cases in which this could be of benefit are: (a) operations that require particularly strong energy; (b) when sex magic practices have become extremely routine; or (c) in cases of sexual oversaturation.

Pete Carroll mentions (*Liber Null,* p. 33) that sexual excitement is especially suited for creating independent beings (psychogons), and when working with a partner, this partner could invoke and materially embody a certain principle or deity, followed by sexual union with the invoked principle—a practice common to sexual-mystic and tantric operations. Prolonged orgasms through *karezza* (repeated stimulation without orgasmic climax) and repeated orgasms can lead to trance states that are useful for divination, whereby the latter generally leads to an exhaustion trance in most cases instead.

However, this can also lead the magician to Crowley's highly praised state of "eroto-comatose lucidity," which we'll be discussing in more detail later on in connection with sex magic. Of course the magician should also make sure that one's usual sexual habits are not dominated by constant thought associations and fantasies, otherwise this could lead to an undesired intermixing of symbols.

Emotional Arousal

In principle, all emotional states can be used magically. However, experience has shown that rage, fear, and horror work most effectively. Even on a physical level, all three of these emotions can lead to the release of unsuspected skills; just think about the unbelievable sheer physical power of someone who is raving mad, or about the perseverance and physical power of people in panic situations. The effectiveness of these three emotions is certainly just as strong as that of sexual excitement, but they have the disadvantage that they're quite difficult to arouse without a great deal of effort. Although systematic training can help remove some of the obstacles along the way—and every magician should undergo such training—it remains nonetheless quite difficult to get a fit of rage on command and then use it magically.

Initiation through others is a different situation. In ancient as well as in modern times, the power of fear and horror has been used effectively, and "initiation through fear" is an appropriate, well-known phrase.

Pain, Torture, and Flagellation

This method of trance is the complete opposite of sleeplessness, fasting, and exhaustion. While the latter calms and inhibits, the former ignites body and spirit. Extreme, unbearable pain always climaxes with either unconsciousness or lust because the human organism can only handle lasting pain through ecstatic acceptance. The penitent practices of the Middle Ages with their jumping processions and self-flagellation, the fakir practices of Hindus and Christians in Sri Lanka and the Philippines—these are all examples of access to ecstasy by paralyzing the intellect and the censor and sharpening the spirit to the same degree that a magician requires for his magical operations. Of course, these methods have the great disadvantage that they can lead quickly to ineffective and highly damaging excess. Because even if the human body is supposedly quite insensitive to pain naturally or through conditioning, the stimulus threshold gets higher and higher until eventually only self-mutilation will be able to achieve the desired effect. This is why we strongly warn against excessive use of this practice.

Dancing, Drumming, Chanting

It's a different story with dancing, drumming, and chanting. Practiced alone or in a group, these techniques can quickly lead to a quite usable excitatory trance. The magician's musical and gymnastic skills (or lack thereof) are of no importance whatsoever, although group work certainly requires more coordination than when working alone in the temple. In particular, African and Afro-American religions (Voodoo, Macumba, Candomblé, Santería) make use of these methods, as does shamanism throughout the world, ranging from the Tunguska region in Siberia to the Sami of Lapland, to the Native Americans of North and South America to the Aborigines of Australia. Chanting includes mantras and ritualistic songs, exaltation through lyricism (hymns), the telling of myths and "barbaric names of evocation," or magic spells and words of power. When supporting a magical operation with music, distinct rhythm and a certain monotony (the effect of repetition) are important. Experienced drummers usually begin with a heartbeat rhythm that the instinctive nervous system will automatically adapt to after swinging with it harmoniously for awhile. When the rhythm gets faster, the participants' heart rate will automatically adjust to a certain degree.

Magical Walking

Magical walking is a technique that's related to Zen walking, but goes well beyond this. This involves walking for long stretches while using the 180° gaze, whereby the hands, fingers, and arms should be held in unusual positions. Experience has shown that pressing the thumbnail sideways into the top of the sensitive pinky is quite effective. This creates a certain pain that's completely harmless as long as the skin is not damaged. Eventually, thinking will cease and the mind will become totally absorbed in its environment. From this description, it's clear that this technique is not really suited for conducting a specific magic operation (with the exception of charging a mantric sigil), but can be used quite effectively for training such states of consciousness. The technique of hyperventilation (see below) can be used here in addition as well.

Excitatory or Inhibitory Drugs, Mild Hallucinogens, Hyperventilation

Please remember what we've already said about the use of drugs in magic. Basically, there's not much more to say. Excitatory or inhibitory drugs and mild hallucinogens (remember, it's the dosage that counts) include alcohol in small amounts, cocaine, small and moderate doses of cannabis, as well as LSD, mescaline and psilocybin, along with some modern designer drugs, and, of course, stimulants (amphetamines). Tea (usually hot) made from galangal root is milder yet still quite effective. This is a legal substance, by the way. But even black tea, coffee, and tobacco can have an excitatory or inhibitory effect, although the price of one's health must be paid. This is why we'd like to emphasize once again that for the reasons mentioned we strongly warn against the use of drugs!

Hyperventilation is induced by fast, powerful panting over an extended period of time (generally from five to fifteen minutes, sometimes longer) and causes an excess of oxygen in the brain that can cause real hallucinatory effects. If you have health problems that affect your heart or respiratory system (lungs, bronchial tubes), you absolutely need to consult your doctor or nonmedical practitioner before attempting such techniques. In fact, due to the catatonic cramps that often occur, this practice should only be done under expert guidance in the first place. This also applies to people with general circulatory problems, as well as asthmatics and epileptics.

Sensory Overload

While monasteries and hermitages serve as special places to experience sensory deprivation, a state of sensory overload can be experienced nearly everywhere. To do so, several techniques are used all at once in order to stimulate all sensory organs simultaneously or in succession in order to induce a state of excitatory gnosis. Inhibitory methods can be used here as well since they can achieve the opposite effect when embedded in a cycle of excitation. For example, one of the classical methods of tantric training includes keeping the candidate awake over an extended period of time while his eyes are blindfolded (sleeplessness), then subjecting him to flagellation (painful torture), and, afterward, giving him hashish and taking him to a cemetery at midnight where he copulates with his *gurini* (female guru) atop a corpse to unite with his divinity. The Western methods of today include the use of the most modern technology, for example by causing stimulus overload with the help of stereos, radios and televisions (all on at the same time) until the mind enters a state of ecstasy/gnosis.

To wrap up this discussion on the basic structural principle of gnosis, let's summarize everything with a quotation from *Liber Null:*

> *The pinnacle of excitation and the cave of absolute quiescence are the same place magically and physiologically. In that hidden dimension of one's being hangs the hawk vulture of the Self [. . .], free of desire, yet ready to hurl itself into any experience or act.*

---

1. The fact that this is not the same as blocking the conscious mind is often forgotten or overlooked!

PLANETARY MAGIC (IV)

MOON MAGIC

Sometimes you'll hear about a male initiate who claims to be "a moon magician at heart." What does that mean? It would be impossible to list absolutely everything here that has made the moon (including the goddess Luna and her pantheon relatives) the ultimate symbol of magic throughout the course of the 10,000-year history of Western and Eastern occultism. We already mentioned the expression "sublunar" world that was used during the Middle Ages and the Renaissance to describe all earthly things as well as (and in particular) all magical and enchanting aspects of life itself.

The moon's influence on our earthy lives has been the subject of intensive research for quite some time. For example, we're aware that the rhythm of the tides is indirectly caused by the moon's gravity; the menstrual cycle of a woman lasts about one-moon month; bar owners claim that their guests seem to drink more at the full moon, and psychiatric clinics often report that their patients are particularly restless during the full or new moon; some statistics have shown that the number of car accidents and suicides increases significantly during these same phases as well (although this is somewhat controversial); the reproductive cycles of many sea creatures, such as sea urchins, scallops, and the palolo worm, are closely linked with the moon's phases, as are those of humans and many plant types. And, of course, we've all heard of somnambulists, or sleepwalkers (called "moon addicts" or *Mondsüchtige* in German)—in this state of slumber, one often does astounding things, such as balancing on the rooftop of a house with closed eyes. Although not all aspects of the moon's influence have been thoroughly researched, science can no longer deny the fact that there's a lot of truth to the old sayings and customs about the moon.

It, then, should come as no surprise that the moon's significance has grown so much over the years, and that many cultures (such as modern Islam) even base their calendar on it instead of the sun.

But the equation "moon = female principle" is not as fundamental and unchangeable as many magic circles seem to think; in many languages (such as German), the moon is considered to be "male," and ancient moon gods such as the Egyptian Thot/Tahuti (who was later associated with Mercury) were male as well. But it's not our intention here to delve into these quite complicated and confusing developments and peculiarities; after all, since the time of Agrippa and Paracelsus, Western magic has basically only known a female moon principle. Since the moon works in mysterious ways, e.g., by controlling the "juices" that we could equate today with hormones; since it swells up in the sky, grows, bulges, and gradually shrinks again until it finally disappears completely during the new moon (sun conjunction); and since it can make the night brighter or darker depending on its illumination, it has become a symbol for mystery, intuition, and the deepness of the soul, and rules over the authority that controls magical powers and makes them effective.

Magicians that have a stronger relationship to the sun instead of the moon almost always tend toward mysticism and religion. Although sun magic is truly a serious magical practice, the place where magic has always thrived and prospered is within moon cults; sun cults generally result in priesthood and organized religion that often bind anarchic, individualistic magic in chains with the intention of wanting to "civilize" it through monopolization. The classic example is the Christian Church that denies or rejects all magical practices (which they refer to as "sacraments," or even "miracles of God" on a rare occasion) unless performed by a priest acting as "God's servant," while emphasizing prayer and intercession.

When we as planetary magicians begin studying the lunar principle, we should be aware of the tension between the two poles formed by the sun and the moon. Of course, a good planetary magician will always take both aspects into consideration when planning an operation in order to combine the two energies into one constructive force instead of letting them fight each other head-on.

The secretiveness of the moon, however, has a dark side as well that's often perceived as threatening; this dark aspect is symbolized by the new moon (or "black moon"). The question as to what came first, the association of the moon with the female principle (and fear thereof) or the fear of the female principle and the resulting projection of this fear on to Earth's satellite as well, can probably never be answered. But surely this contempt for the moon, which has no light of its own (as opposed to the sun) and "merely" reflects, has helped create the symbol-ideological superstructure for the suppression of the woman and everything she stands for and represents. This is certainly related to the instability and changeability that the moon constantly demonstrates. "Sublunar" also means "variable, inconstant," which is why the moon was usually considered to be the "evildoer" in classical astrology.

In contrast, the principle of the sun is based on rational and efficient calculability. After all, the sun doesn't "die" every month, and despite the biannual solstices to mark its "death" and "birth," the sun's nature is basically constant. For this reason alone, sun cults are automatically forced to fight against such individualistic lunar magic that threatens every status quo. Because while the sun principle embodies the raison d'état and "collective common sense," the moon ecstatically destroys all of reality's limits and exposes the fiction of a predictable world over and over again. In this sense, the often bloody conflict between male priests and female witches—which is a sort of battle of the sexes—is something indispensably natural.

Let's not forget, however, that both are united androgynously in the Mercury principle (which is usually quite inconspicuous in the sky as well as in the horoscope) and therefore able to grow above and beyond this basic polarity. But here, too, it has always been the moon cults that have embraced this androgynous ideal as opposed to the sun religions that are only fixated on imperialistic, collective thought.[1]

Another difference between the solar and lunar principles is something that any planetary magician should recognize: The sun is centrifugal, while the moon is centripetal. This means nothing more than the old rule that the male is expansive while the female is contractive, although it would be quite helpful for modern people to get used to these other descriptive terms as well. Centrifugal means spinning away from the center or axis—along the way, very few foreign things are assimilated permanently and most everything burns up in its own fire (decentralization). Centripetal, on the other hand, means moving toward the center or axis—along the way, many foreign things are assimilated permanently and combined in a sort of melting pot where it eventually becomes an integral component of the whole (centralization). This also embodies the phallic and vaginal principles, or "lingam" and "yoni" in Eastern terminology or "extroverted" and "introverted" in Western terms, giving and taking, aggressiveness and passivity, and so on. This should all be nothing new to you, although it might be a good idea to think about how and where this is expressed concretely and practically in everyday life—and of course in your own magic as well.

Even today, many magicians work according to the principle that constructive operations should only be performed during the waxing moon, with destructive operations taking place during the waning moon. Although this general rule of thumb has proven effective, our level of knowledge today demands much more from us than just working in such a mechanical way. The fundamental idea behind this system is surely correct: that humans and everything else alive are subject to natural microcosmic and macrocosmic rhythms.[2] But there are also justified objections to this. For example, a magician's personal experience will surely reflect deviations from this norm that, in our opinion, can be better explained by the differences in each magician's individual biorhythm instead of the actual influence of the moon itself, which is without a doubt quite significant as well. In this sense, many magicians can observe in themselves phases of energetic highs and lows that often shift without any recognizable pattern. For example, you might always seem to experience your magical, energetic high during the full moon, and feel dull and weak during the new moon,[3] but after several years of practice, this could easily change, minimally or even quite drastically.

Being a moon magician also means being aware of your own personal moon rhythms and cycles. So this is the first step in our moon work as well. Begin by systematically observing the phases of the moon, your own levels of energy at various times, your world of dreams, visions, and success in divination work, and so on. According to the knowledge of modern rhythmic researchers, women are not the only ones who get their "periods"; men also have phases when they are gentler, more receptive, and more sentimental, but also more sensitive and susceptible than usual—and phases when they seem full of power and energy, and when everything they lay their hands on seems to succeed, when their mental and physical stamina seem to be at their peak.

One example of this daily rhythm principle is the fact that magical attacks and healing operations work best around 4:00 am, local time. This is the time when most target persons experience a daily biorhythmic low,[4] which makes them extremely susceptible/receptive. Yogis and mystics love this time of the night and recommend it for meditation since the mind is then open to subtle perception and energies. This shows us how important it is to pay attention to rhythmic cycles of all types—daily rhythms, weekly rhythms ("blue monday," weekend phases), as well as monthly (menses), yearly, and even life-cycle rhythms (childhood/youth/old age, menopause). The moon as the epitome of all rhythmic processes not only affects all kinds of cycles, but is also an excellent indicator that can help us practice and implement rhythmic thought and action that is so vital on the symbolic level. Plus, rhythm is something like "structured time" that can grant us access to this all-controlling yet nearly impalpable dimension. Let's stick to Solomon's wise advice since he's always been considered one of magic's earliest forefathers:

> *For everything there is an appointed time, and an appropriate time for every activity on earth: A time to be born, and a time to die; a time to plant, and a time to uproot what was planted; A time to kill, and a time to heal; a time to break down, and a time to build up; A time to weep, and a time to laugh; a time to mourn, and a time to dance. A time to throw away stones, and a time to gather stones; a time to embrace, and a time to refrain from embracing; A time to search, and a time to give something up as lost; a time to keep, and a time to throw away; A time to tear, and a time to mend; a time to keep silent, and a time to speak; A time to love, and a time to hate; a time for war, and a time for peace. What benefit can a worker gain from his toil?* (Eccl. 3:1–9)

Since we've already dealt with ritual structure in detail, and we can therefore assume that you're familiar with this, we're not going to repeat this information each time we discuss an individual planet in connection with ritual magic. Instead, we'd like to give you some hints and suggestions in the form of traditional correspondences and associations which, of course, every magician can and should adapt to one's own practice. In this sense, please view the following information as mere suggestions and not as strict rules and regulations!

We'll follow several structures at the same time. First we'll break everything down into the five "classical" disciplines of magic, just as Chaos Magic does: divination, evocation, invocation, sorcery, and illumination.

Afterward, we'll list a few suggestions for the practical application of the principles of moon magic. Under "Concrete Application" we've also included the category "Mysticism." This includes all those applications that were previously summarized under "Illumination."

MOON MAGIC IN THE CLASSIC DISCIPLINES

Divination (clairvoyance)

Work with the magic mirror for seeing into the future and for clairvoyance on a spatial level; incubation of clairvoyant dreams

Evocation (creation/conjuration of spirits)

Psychogons for self-intuition and causing confusion among opponents; healing psychogons

Invocation (activation/assumption of a spirit principle)

Anima work; recognition/change of macrocosmic/microcosmic rhythmic; healing magic

Sorcery (practical magic)

Seducing sexual partners; camouflage magic; telepathy; dream influencing; temporary increase of money in small amounts; settling third-party disputes; healing

Illumination (enlightenment and self-development)

Recognizing one's own rhythmic cycles in life; work with the Goddess

Element: Water
Zodiac: Cancer, Scorpion, Pisces
Sephira: Yesod
Tarot card: II The High Priestess

Here's a more specific list of possible ways to apply this information:

CONCRETE APPLICATION (EXAMPLES)

Healing Magic

Gynecological problems; rhythmic disturbances; blood cleansing; harmonization of hormonal "juices"; bladder problems

Magical Warfare (defensive)

Sharpening one's attention; sensing the opponent's actions and intentions; protection against attacks; counteracting and unmasking the opponent's disguises and camouflage

Magical Warfare (aggressive)

Confusion tactics; psychological and material destruction; sexual warfare psychogons (sexual de-oding); disruption through undesired love and attraction magic; distraction tactics; weakening the opponent's concentration

Sex Magic

Tantra; experiencing one's own femininity; work with succubi and incubi

Mysticism

Yoni cult; contacting the primeval mothers

Now you'll find two moon hymns that I wrote myself that are meant to encourage you to write your own. In my own ritual practice, I like to repeat these hymns nine times.

Hymn to Luna
(Hymn to the Full Moon)

lady moon, great mother, mine
sister charm illuminate
you adorn your waters with silver
hair glistening, sparkling with dew

you conjure circles that fade at their height
and gently, softly climb towards the light
noble wise woman, no more plight

for your animals and your sisters
picture tomorrow and yesterday
seen through your magic mirror
let the images dance and play
through dreams of the broken seal

lady moon, bright friend of time
foggy wife of the sun
adorn the veil of your hidden world
o wild and tender one

lady moon, hear my song of devotion
lady moon, sing a song of praise
shimmering moon help me interweave
my desire with your ways
silvery full moon splendor
milky radiant beams
your breasts dance in desire
o raise me into the deep!

be my one and precious love
and be with me when I win
the gifts of your horn of plenty

o you were never loved so much!
o you were never loved so much!

Fra. U.·. D.·.

Hymn to Hekate
(Hymn to the New Moon)

black moon, lilith, dark sister
the powers of hell in your hand
your strengths and your weaknesses
put me at your command

show me the darkness in my soul
and the gloomy woman in me
whether I do the suffering or the tormenting
drink your dark dew of the sea

bleeder of the starry forests
you unite with your own fire
die in the splendor of vast fields
of a new and ancient empire

you die and reveal the mirror
dull and tarnished in the forest
when the sun burns down hot
steals and grabs—never rests

black moon, lilith, dark mother
you bore child of darkest earth
gave it life and nourishment
thunder, nightmares and horses' hooves
and dreamy songs of divine birth

lady moon, dead one, listen to me!
lady moon, dark one, caress me!
lady moon, gloomy one, strangle me!
lady moon, severe one, overthrow me!

throw me into your deepest depths
that have tempted and beckoned me
lured me since the beginning of time
and put me under your magic spell
with a single kiss of your iron hand
while sand trickles through my veins

and barren is your fertile land!
and barren is your fertile land!

Fra. U.·. D.·.

EXCURSION: KARMA AND MAGIC

The question of karma has occupied Western esotericism since the time this Eastern term was introduced by Theosophy and used and expanded on by so many of its successors, followers, and even opponents. So much nonsense has been written about this subject, and this entirely un-Western thought principle has also been so fundamentally misunderstood and "Christianized." But although nowadays many New Agers at least say that karma is not a "sin" in a Christian sense, but rather a law of cause and effect, in practice this is an entirely different story. Karma is often exalted to a sort of de-Christianized sin, with the main goal being to collect as much "good" karma as possible while avoiding "bad" karma at any price, and the most banal everyday problems—as well as extreme hardships, birth defects, and illnesses—are blamed on sins from "past lives" with such uncritical naivety that it reminds a person of one of Thomas Mann's not so flattering essays on metaphysics. Gautama (the historical Buddha) is partially to blame for this since he tended to use this method to discipline his students. What irritates modern magicians the most today is the constant claim of self-named "wise men" (who usually have no idea about practical magic whatsoever) that any kind of magic can bring about the worst karmic results—an unequalled form of demonization with the reverse side being the bigotry that continually flares up, because in reality these apparently "informative" media attacks against "satanic cults" and "devil worshippers" have occasionally destroyed a magician's existence with completely groundless, unproven accusations.

One of the sharpest critics of this faulty development surely is and remains Aleister Crowley, which is why we'd like to quote him here in depth.

> *This idea of Karma has been confused by many who ought to have known better, including the Buddha, with the ideas of poetic justice and of retribution.*
>
> *We have the story of one of the Buddha's arahats, who being blind, in walking up and down unwittingly killed a number of insects. [The Buddhist regards the destruction of life as the most shocking crime.] His brother arahats inquired as to how this was, and Buddha spun them a long yarn as to how, in a previous incarnation, he had maliciously deprived a woman of her sight. This is only a fairy tale, a bogey to frighten the children, and probably the worst way of influencing the young yet devised by human stupidity.*
>
> *Karma does not work in this way at all.*

In any case moral fables have to be very carefully constructed, or they may prove dangerous to those who use them.

You will remember Bunyan's Passion and Patience: naughty Passion played with all his toys and broke them, good little Patience put them carefully aside. Bunyan forgets to mention that by the time Passion had broken all his toys, he had outgrown them.

Karma does not act in this tit-for-tat-way. An eye for an eye is a sort of savage justice, and the idea of justice in our human sense is quite foreign to the constitution of the Universe.

Karma is the Law of Cause and Effect. There is no proportion in its operations. Once an accident occurs it is impossible to say what may happen; and the Universe is a stupendous accident.

We go out to tea a thousand times without mishap, and the thousand-and-first time we meet some one who changes radically the course of our lives for ever.

There is a sort of sense in which every impression that is made upon our minds is the resultant of all the forces of the past; no incident is so trifling that it has not in some way shaped one's disposition. But there is none of this crude retribution about it. One may kill a hundred thousand lice in one brief hour at the foot of the Baltoro Glacier, as Frater P. once did. It would be stupid to suppose, as the Theosophist inclines to suppose, that this action involves one in the doom of being killed by a louse a hundred thousand times.

This ledger of karma is kept separate from the petty cash account; and in respect of bulk this petty cash account is very much bigger than the ledger.

If we eat too much salmon we get indigestion and perhaps nightmare. It is silly to suppose that a time will come when a salmon will eat us, and find us disagreeable.[4]

On the other hand we are always being terribly punished for actions that are not faults at all. Even our virtues rouse insulted nature to revenge.

Karma only grows by what it feeds on: and if karma is to be properly brought up, it requires a very careful diet.

With the majority of people their actions cancel each other out; no sooner is effort made than it is counterbalanced by idleness. Eros gives place to Anteros.

Not one man in a thousand makes even an apparent escape from the commonplace of animal life (*Magick*, pp. 99–100).

It's about time that we as magicians finally de-demonize this concept of karma and free it from this childish burden. If you punch some guy in the nose, the only "karma" involved is that the person's nose will hurt, and that's all! The fact that he might punch you back is a secondary result of your victim's pain, or his anger about his own inability to recognize your aggressive intentions and move his head in time.

But better than the naive, ill-considered burden of the old "guilt and repentance" complex would be the psychological approach that propagates avoiding any kind of karma at all, otherwise it might lead to a moral conflict that could even go as far as to cause psychosomatic illnesses. In this sense, it would be psychologically a good idea to only do what you really believe in with your whole heart—a completely rational wording of Crowley's motto, "Thou hast no right but to do thy will." Whoever sticks to this principle surely doesn't need a lesson in reincarnation—although we're certainly not claiming that this belief is principally wrong and misleading, just because we don't happen to represent it.

REPORTS FROM MAGICAL PRACTICE (V)

The effect of love spells is an interesting element when it comes to monitoring the results of a magical operation. Strictly speaking, most so-called love spells are really binding spells. Generally, the intention is to cause the target person to form an emotional attachment to the magician or his or her client and to take advantage of this. The problem with such spells is that they usually bind the magician or the client much stronger to the target person than the other way around. The success of the magical operation soon becomes an obsession until nearly nothing is left of the familiar principle of "nonattachment/nonlack of interest." On the astral/imaginative level, the target person can even take on the form of an incubus or succubus (an extremely energetically charged and powerful astral sexual partner or demon) that requires a great deal of experience and self-control in order to deal with properly, otherwise it could result in an extreme loss of energy that could even lead to near complete de-oding and the related consequences. The same applies to demonology as well. Therefore experience has shown that it's always a better idea to perform a general love spell instead of aiming for a specific target person. In other words, you should conjure for "a lover" without specifying who. Then the magician or the client still has the choice of seizing the resulting opportunity or not.

Such an opportunity is nearly impossible with binding spells. For example, if the target actually reacts to the spell as intended, he or she may "cling" to the magician/client to such a degree that it would take a great deal of effort to rectify (after all, the attraction was an act of magic) and such a situation often results in a catastrophic crisis.

The following two examples are taken from my own experience. A good female friend of mine once asked me to charge a love talisman to help her find a partner. Although she had already had several relationships, some even parallel to one another, the situation was unsatisfying in the long run and she now wanted a stable relationship. Surely she was also curious as to how such a talisman would work for her, because apart from a few rituals we did together, she had very little experience with magic.

I decided to make a Venus talisman according to the traditional principles. First I calculated an election, or an astrologically suitable time to perform the operation based on my client's horoscope. Shortly before the ritual, I engraved the sigil of the planet Venus (according to Agrippa) on to a round copper plate, and on the other side I engraved my client's personal sigil that I designed according to the principle of Aiq Bekr. Finally, I added the three geomantic symbols, Puer ("boy"), Puella ("girl"), and Conjunctio ("union"), which I felt were well suited for such an operation because of their name symbolism. Then I held the Venus ritual (alone), in which I first performed an invocation and then guided the activated energy into the talisman. The client received the charged talisman along with a short written explanation on how to use it, including the instructions to first wear it on a Friday (Venus day) at sunrise (Venus hour) following a fifteen-minute meditation after putting it on a green velvet ribbon that she obtained herself, and to wear it for at least seventy-seven days. She followed these instructions carefully and exactly.

About ten days later, she reported the first success. My friend/client had received half a dozen love letters from various men. Some were former lovers, but some were mere passing acquaintances. At first this was frustrating because the wide selection confused her. But there was also a letter from the man that she actually wanted, which she didn't tell me until afterward. This man later became her partner, so the operation can be considered a success.

The second situation, which I've also mentioned briefly in my book *Secrets of Western Sex Magic,* happened a bit differently. One day a man came to me and asked for a talisman "for love, relationships, contacts, and you know what else" (original quotation!). After a long conversation, we decided on a Venus talisman that I made and charged quite similar to the method used above. (Note the use here again of Puer, Puella, and Conjunctio, since this is related to what happened later.) But the client didn't follow the written instructions. He took the talisman impatiently out of the envelope after it was delivered by mail (interestingly, it was a Tuesday, or Mars day) and put it on right away. Two weeks later he called me, completely depressed. The talisman was supposedly causing strange things to happen—he nearly crashed in an airplane and an important business deal was suddenly cancelled. In short, he felt that the talisman was bringing him bad luck instead of good luck. My queries revealed that he didn't follow the instructions when activating the energy of the talisman, which was already the first problem. We agreed that the situation with the airplane crash was certainly not an effect of Venus, but rather of Mars—plus, there was still the objection that the catastrophe actually didn't happen and was avoided. The planned business deal proved to be a project that was unstable right from the start. Although some business matters can be attributed to Venus (trade), I didn't see any reason to link this with the talisman, because the talisman wasn't charged with the Venus principle in general, but rather specifically with love-related things. Plus, in order to bring about such negative reactions, the talisman would have to be charged demonically (with few exceptions), which wasn't the case.

This example shows how important it is to make a clear distinction between the various correspondences. This is especially important for magicians and clients who have a lot of fear or superstitious beliefs since they're often based on a lack of self-confidence or conscious/semiconscious feelings of guilt.

A good three and a half years later (!), my client called again about the same matter and asked if it were possible to decharge the talisman that seemed to be still causing him problems such as nightmares. At our next meeting, he finally told me the true reason of his discomfort: The client was homosexual and had a stable relationship with another man. He originally wanted to use the talisman to be able to cheat on his partner on occasion since the relationship was getting to be too "close-knit"—but he was extremely self-conscious and shy. Since he got the talisman, he sometimes had heterosexual nightmares, while the relationship with his partner grew even stronger and more loving—no sign of cheating. He admitted that he was "actually" happier than ever before in his relationship.

What happened here? I have to admit it was my mistake that I oversaw my client's homosexuality. Even though he hid it from me, I should have seen it in his horoscope, or noticed it otherwise. In my opinion, this shouldn't happen to a good magician. Even today, I still cannot find any indication of his homosexuality in his horoscope, which is still no excuse for my mistake. On the other hand, the talisman did indeed bring about all of the Venus-like effects that one could expect under normal circumstances: intensification of an existing love relationship, (hetero)erotic dreams (remember the geomancy symbols that were used!), happiness. If the client would have revealed his homosexuality to me, or if I had guessed it otherwise, I certainly wouldn't have recommended a Venus talisman, but rather a Mercury one instead since the androgynous Mercury principle is also responsible for homosexuality, among other things.[5]

A Mars talisman would have been possible as well since this would emphasize the purely sexual nature of the magical desire; on the other hand, Mars is much more aggressive, while Mercury is responsible for a variety of diverse contacts.[6]

Instead of Puella, I should have used Puer twice.

After our conversation, I offered to decharge the talisman for the client, but he wasn't interested anymore and admitted that he actually did receive what was best for him.

This is perfect proof that the popular psychological "placebo effect" explanation doesn't always apply in the case of talismans and amulets. Since the client believed that he was getting the "right" talisman, it should have worked anyway, at least according to the placebo effect explanation; after all, he had no knowledge of magic whatsoever and was therefore unable to interpret the symbols that were used to find out how it was truly charged. Instead, he got the effect that I intended.

I'd like to conclude with a few words about the "honesty" of clients wanting love spells. Practice has shown again and again that a great degree of thoroughness and sensitivity is required of the magician in such operations; because most clients conceal the most important details, either because they're ashamed to be so open, or because they don't realize the importance of the information, or for other reasons.

Often clients don't even really know what they want or why they have problems in the field of eroticism, and often they'll put the blame on external factors (especially popular: "black magic") or on a blow of fate—only self-criticism falls either entirely too short or is exaggerated to such a degree that it takes the form of auto-aggressive behavior.

The magician should always pay careful attention to the psychological state of one's clients and have an extensive conversation with them in advance in case one needs to coerce important information out of them that they may either consciously or unconsciously be concealing. This isn't because the magician has a voyeuristic interest in the private life of one's clients, but is rather an effort to truly help them as best as possible. Because a magician's professional ethics (especially when working for a client) require one to always do one's best, and in order to do so, one needs as much information as possible in order to get a good overall impression of the whole situation. If the client doesn't trust the magician, however, and intentionally withholds embarrassing details, I would recommend the magician to not take on the job at all, since there's only hope of success when the client consciously and unconsciously is willing to cooperate. This, of course, applies in the same sense to all magical operations performed for others.

PRACTICAL EXERCISES

EXERCISE 43

SYSTEMATIC TRANCE TRAINING (II): EXCITATORY GNOSIS

Develop your own systematic exercise plan based on the techniques in this section in order to familiarize yourself with the various forms and methods of excitatory gnosis. You should practice at least four times a week, although short periods of about fifteen to thirty minutes are usually sufficient.

EXERCISE 44

PRACTICAL MOON MAGIC (I)

Develop your own systematic exercise plan based on the techniques in this section in order to familiarize yourself with the moon principle. This should occur on all levels: on an everyday level where you can, for example, observe how the various phases of the moon affect your organic rhythms; from the menstrual cycle of female magicians to the psychological mood swings of their male counterparts; the effects of alcohol, dreams, visions and intuition; and finally the degree of magical power itself and the corresponding effectiveness of every—not just lunar—ritual. Develop a ritual moon cycle that you perform for one or more months, for example by drafting and performing rituals for each major moon phase—full moon, new moon, and the two quarter moons. The ritual charging of a moon talisman, a magic mirror, a rock crystal for healing, or a tarot deck can be integrated superbly into such a "lunar opus," as well as exercises in the field of dream work, astral magic, and divination.

EXERCISE 45

PRACTICAL MOON MAGIC (II)

This exercise can be combined with the above one after you've performed the latter alone in its entirety at least once. Try to recognize your own female principle (anima)—whether you're a man or woman. Let yourself be guided by the information collected and the knowledge gained in the first exercise—we purposely don't want to give you any strict rules to follow and are keeping this vague and general. If you don't feel ready for this exercise yet, just postpone it to a later date—but don't forget it completely since it represents a very important milestone on your magical development! You may even want to repeat this exercise several times throughout the course of your life in order to develop your anima principle even further.

BIBLIOGRAPHY

Peter J. Carroll, *Liber Null* (the official training manual for the I.O.T.)
Aleister Crowley, *Magick*

Samurai Creed

I have no parents: I make the heavens and the earth my parents.
I have no home: I make awareness my home.
I have no life or death: I make the tides of breathing my life and death.
I have no divine power: I make honesty my divine power.
I have no means: I make understanding my means.
I have no magic secrets: I make character my magic secret.
I have no body: I make endurance my body.
I have no eyes: I make the flash of lightning my eyes.
I have no ears: I make sensibility my ears.
I have no limbs: I make promptness my limbs.
I have no strategy: I make "unshadowed by thought" my strategy.
I have no designs: I make "seizing the opportunity by the forelock" my designs.
I have no miracles: I make right action my miracle.
I have no principles: I make adaptability to all circumstances my principles.
I have no tactics: I make emptiness and fullness my tactics.
I have no friends: I make my mind my friend.
I have no enemy: I make carelessness my enemy.
I have no armor: I make benevolence and righteousness my armor.
I have no castle: I make immovable mind my castle.
I have no sword: I make absence of self my sword.

---

1. To illustrate this, all you need to do is have a look at the androgynous episode in *Satyricon* by the late Roman author and "fashion pope" Gaius Petronius Arbiter, which was also the subject of a Fellini film of the same name.
2. Which, by the way, is also the first serious theoretical explanation of astrology that goes beyond the mere claims of empirical, factual material—in our opinion, this is a very significant and convincing argument.
3. Usually there's a fluctuation margin of plus or minus three days, which applies when scheduling practical work as well.

4. By the way, this is another reason why you shouldn't eat too late in the evening since digestive functions are generally limited during the night.
5. This is an association that probably only an experienced magician would make since Mercury is not necessarily related to sexual things, such as Mars or Venus is.
6. A sex magic Mars talisman, for example, would be more suited for practices in the field of sadomasochism, but would also work as an amulet to protect against rape.

THE PARADIGMS OF MAGIC

In magic, we work with a number of magical objects, use words such as "charge" and "uncharge," and talk about things such as "storing" power.

In order to understand such concepts better, it would be a good idea to first take a look at the various models of magic of the past and present, especially since this will also play a significant role when we later discuss the use of talismans and information or cyber magic. When reading the following, please keep in mind that the categories listed here are merely meant to help illustrate our point and rarely occur in the simplified, pure form stated here—a mixture of the various forms is generally the rule.

THE SPIRIT MODEL

Surely the oldest paradigm of magic is the spirit model. With this model, we assume the existence of real supernatural beings (spirits, demons, helpers, etc.) and the magician can communicate with them, get to know them, become friends with them, or submit to them as their servant. Here, the magician acts as a mediator between life on earth, or everyday reality, and the world beyond. This model is still characteristic of all types of shamanism, and most laypeople (including journalists and theologians!) base their opinions of magic on it as well. In Western Europe, this model enjoyed its greatest popularity during the Renaissance, and is still used by many traditionalistic magicians today.

In this day and age, it can be found in the magic of Bardon and Gregorius, while the entire Golden Dawn system and a great part of O.T.O. teachings are based on it as well, just as the majority of German occultism of the 1920s. Aleister Crowley used a mixed form, as we'll see later on.

In the spirit model, the goal of the magician or the shaman is to obtain access to the world of creatures that we'll describe here as "magical entities." This world has its own set of laws that the magician must learn in order to survive and to utilize the powers and the entities there. Each entity has its own name and formula and displays a specific, unmistakable character, and can therefore be considered an individual personality that has strengths and weaknesses.

With the help of trance, the magician travels to their realm where one can either make friends with them or have them serve one's self, provided that one has enough knowledge and power to do so. Such relationships can even be quite dangerous at times, since some spirits, such as demons, may not be all that eager to serve the magician and/or just might not like him or her. And they often charge a high price for their services, which could even require a blood sacrifice or something similar. A well-known example of this is the pact that Dr. Faust made with the Devil ("selling one's soul in return for material and intellectual success").

Although the exact terms of such a pact are a matter of negotiation, there's always the danger (just as with humans) of a breach of contract, a new interpretation of the agreement, or other difficulties, so that the magician needs to be continually alert—unless of course one only works with "good" spirits with a moral integrity that one can trust completely. From what we've said above, it's clear that spiritualism (which originated in America in the mid-nineteenth century and is still popular all over the world today, now often called "channeling" by New Agers) is an excellent example of the spirit model, even though it generally focuses on divination and prayer instead of on actual magical operations.

Once the magician has secured the assistance of "one's" spirits or demons—either with a friendly pact or through force—one uses it in one's magic in the same way one would use the assistance of a common human helper as well. But since these entities are immaterial, they can work on levels that common servants cannot, such as on the astral plane. Plus, most spirits are "specialists" that are generally superior to the magician in their field of expertise. For example, a magician would summon the Mercury demon Taphthartharath to achieve magical goals that are related to the Mercury sphere, while the Mars demon Bartzabel would be summoned to destroy an opponent or to learn the art of warfare. Or, one could use a planetary intelligence such as Yophiel (Jupiter sphere) to improve one's state of prosperity. The shaman generally has certain spirits of one's own that are specialized in certain areas (e.g., healing illnesses, making rain). For example, instead of sending healing power to a sick person from a distance, the magician can send one's spirit helper directly to the patient.[1]

Spirits and demons want attention, or want to be "fed," and can even rebel or demand a "pay raise." And they're not infallible. Just because they're experts doesn't mean that they cannot make mistakes or fail; but in general they can expand the magician's scope of action considerably although the quality of one's magic depends on the amount of control one has over such spirits.

So those are the basic concepts of the spirit model. It requires the magician to explore an already existing world and to learn and follow its rules right down to the last detail. For example, if one doesn't know the "true name" or the "correct formula" that gives power over such transcendental entities, all of one's efforts to gain control of them will be in vain. Even the means of communication with these entities—or their magical language—needs to be learned, and much of this knowledge is guarded secretly and only passed on directly from master to apprentice. Therefore, thorough training is generally required before magical operations can be performed.

THE ENERGY MODEL

With the triumphant march of mesmerism around the end of the eighteenth century, the Western conscious mind began to focus on internal bodily processes and energies. Although Mesmer basically only rediscovered ancient healing methods (hypnotism, suggestion, healing sleep), he made them socially acceptable in a culture that had made a clear distinction between the body and spirit for centuries. Suddenly, it was sensational news to learn that the mind can influence the body and even make it sick or heal it. For Mesmer, the means for all healing was "animal magnetism," a vital force that cannot be more closely defined in scientific terms. The concept of "vril force" developed by Bulwer-Lytton, who was a Rosicrucian and a magician himself, as well as the odic teachings of Reichenbach, are both proof of the impact that this change in awareness had, which significantly influenced Hahnemann's homeopathy as well (which was a predecessor of cyber magic, as we'll soon see). And Bulwer's friend, the extraordinarily influential magician Eliphas Levi, caused quite an uproar in the occult scene just about fifty years after Mesmer's death with his concept of "astral light." This made a significant impact on magic as well. Although the Golden Dawn still principally remains loyal to the old spirit model even a century after Mesmer's death, it has been strongly "softened" by psychological-animistic elements such as those taken from Indian yoga (e.g., teachings of chakras and prana).

But the energy model didn't actually celebrate its climax until after World War II, or more specifically during the occult renaissance of the 1960s, that mainly took place in England. This was surely aided by the strong influence of psychoanalysis, which didn't make its big breakthrough until after the war, even though magicians such as W. B. Yeats, Austin Osman Spare, and Aleister Crowley began integrating the concepts of psychoanalysis into their magical practice at a relatively early date.

In general, the energy model in its pure form rejects every kind of spiritual thesis. The magician is no longer a conjurer of spirits, but more of an "energy artist." The focus is on subtle perception, and the magician must be able to perceive, polarize ("charge"), and direct energies. If, for example, one senses a lack of energy in the kidney area of one's patient, one would transfer charged healing energy to the affected kidneys, possibly by placing one's hand on them and/or by using special crystals or gemstones. Talismans and amulets (which of course are used in the spirit model as well) are examples of artificial "objects of power," or tools that the magician ceremonially calibrates in which one stores certain specific energies for immediate or later use.

When the magician wants to transfer power (and that's the main focus of the energy model), one either has to have enough power to do the job his- or herself, or one needs access to one or more power sources. In the first case, the magician becomes a walking battery, while in the second the magician becomes a channel or medium for "higher" or at least "other" powers. And power isn't always just power. Depending on the system of magic used, the spectrum ranges from a complicated web of "positive" and "negative" energies to the "neutrality thesis" in which the magician his- or herself is responsible for "polarizing" the naturally neutral energies. With the latter, there's always too much or too little desired or undesired energy (for example too much fire in the kidney area: infection); the equation of "positive = good" and "negative = bad" (which is usually denied in theory, but often found in practice nonetheless) generally doesn't apply here, and the only important thing is the ability to direct the energy to its proper place.

Depending on the amount of power required, the magician might even be too weak to act. In magical warfare, the stronger magician always wins (not the "good" one), unless the weaker one can compensate for lack of power through speed and skill. The magician must be able to rely on oneself or, at best, on physical colleagues who might help, and there's no use in summoning a "higher authority"—although one can try using a "stronger" energy than one's opponent.

Power centers such as the chakras or acupuncture meridians often play an important role in the energy model, and the charging of objects such as talismans is done through the power of imagination. For example, the magician might imagine a colored beam of energy that one bundles with a certain gesture or spirally projects into the object to be charged with hands, dagger, or wand; for a Jupiter talisman, one might imagine a blue beam, for example, while green would be used for Venus. When attacking an opponent, the magician either sends an excessive amount of destructive or corrosive energy (e.g., Mars or moon power), or one draws off the opponents' energies and weakens them. In doing so, the magician usually doesn't summon the hierarchy of angels and demons ("princes of hell") of the individual planets or kabbalistic spheres. Instead, one generally activates a planetary principle through magical trance and then uses this energy to do everything else instead of sending some kind of being or entity to do the job.

Just as the hierarchies of angels and demons are greatly reduced in the energy model (or even eliminated completely by the pure "energy dance"), other external authorities lose significance as well. The job of the "master" is now done by a "teacher," and the strictly obedient "apprentice" has become a "student." The independence that results from this is strongly noticeable in the individually anarchistic and pragmatic systems of modern magic that place more importance on the personal experience of the magician instead of on the power and might of tradition.

This naturally demands higher performance from the magician as well. One must be able to do just about everything without any external help (including help from "beyond") and needs to have a very high level of personal energy since the self mainly functions as a power battery. When one is weak and tired, the quality of magical operations will suffer, and the effectiveness of one's magic depends directly on the amount and quality of one's own energy. Plus, one also needs to have excellent, well-trained, and reliable skills in subtle perception.

THE PSYCHOLOGICAL MODEL: A MIXTURE

The impact that Mesmer and his successors made on the eighteenth century is comparable to that of Sigmund Freud and Albert Einstein in the twentieth century. Freud and Einstein were revolutionary pioneers of a fundamental, radical change in thinking that drastically shook up the mechanistic view of the world until it eventually burst.

In a certain sense, Freud's theses were derived and developed from Mesmer's concepts, and it's no coincidence that the founder of psychoanalysis originally focused on the study of hypnosis and hysteria. What Mesmer publicly demonstrated in Europe just before the French Revolution with displays and exhibitions is what Freud and, in particular, Georg Groddek (the founder of psychosomatic medicine) tried to prove scientifically a good hundred years later, the realization that many, if not all, illnesses have mental causes, and that the mind is able to affect and influence the body.

Since we have no intention of going into the comprehensive details here, this brief information will have to suffice. Mainly, it's meant to illustrate the effect that this development had on magical practice. The first two well-known magicians to apply psychological or psychoanalytical thought to a greater degree were Aleister Crowley and Austin Osman Spare. Crowley toyed with the psychological model for quite some time, especially in his middle-age years, although he later became a firm supporter of the spirit model, even though he was moderately skeptical at times. Spare, on the other hand, went just the opposite direction—some of the theses in his magical writings seem to be taken from a textbook on psychoanalysis.

Strictly speaking, the psychological model is just an empirical "mixture" since it doesn't really go beyond the spirit and energy models, but instead strengthens the homocentrism of the latter while disputing the basis of the spirit model by denying the existence of spirits in an objective, external sense—but not in a subjective, psychological one. In addition, it doesn't explain magic with new or different mechanisms, but instead it just relocates its place of origin—namely deep inside the psyche—without really explaining the way it works. Of course, such a claim needs to be proved.

According to the psychological model, magic is merely an animistic phenomena. Everything that the magician perceives or does while performing one's art takes place inside the psyche where a certain mechanism (that's never more closely defined) causes the desired (or even undesired) results. The authority responsible for magic is the unconscious mind (or, according to Spare who uses Freud's terminology, the subconscious)—this is where all magical activity takes place. The supporters of this theory (and these include nearly all modern-day authors of magic) never mention a word about how the subconscious actually performs this "miracle." But above all, with this model, the magician becomes a psychonaut. While one used to be a spirit trader and later an energy traveler, one now becomes a "journeyer to the soul." By exploring the internal realm of the psyche and cartographically mapping it out, one learns the laws that can help take magical control over one's own life and the world around.

This approach—which is doubtlessly not perfect in theory—does have considerable advantages that explain its current popularity. First of all, it's formulated vaguely enough to avoid getting tangled up in pseudoscientific debates about things such as "Does od really exist or not?" and "Can it be measured?" It leaves this up to parapsychology. It cannot really explain magic, but instead it simply and pragmatically asserts that the manipulation of the psyche can lead to magical results, and it is content to accept this observation as an "explanation" instead of focusing on the question as to how such manipulation can actually be induced and controlled.

This corresponds to the modern-day utilitarian way of thinking that's much more interested in the "how" instead of the "why," as Crowley once put it as well. In a relativistic world where the inhabitants can no longer be sure of any kind of "truth" whatsoever, whether referring to religion, politics, science, or magic, the magician who supports the psychological model is a personification of the spirit of the times. Plus, magic explained in psychological terms has the advantage of being easier to comprehend by many people who have grown up with and are already familiar with such psychological models of thought, as compared to the belief in spirits and demons that has suffered quite a few cuts and bruises inflicted by scientifically based atheism.

The mixed-form nature of the psychological model can be recognized by the fact that—as practice has shown—it can be superbly combined with the other two models that we've discussed so far, which is indeed done quite frequently. We've used this model again and again throughout this book as well, and will continue to do so in order to illustrate certain aspects of magic. Some "variations" include magicians who add an animistic aspect to the spirit model while still communicating with spirits, demons, and angels, but seeing in them mainly "projected images of the soul" (which, of course, has proven to be quite ineffective when it comes to demonology); and magicians who apply the energy model without taking it too literally, and refer vaguely to "the power of the subconscious."[2]

The literalness applied to the exact wording of pacts with demons and the devil throughout tradition and even by many magicians today (and such pacts are often worded by the demons themselves) is a reference to the psychological mechanisms involved in this process, or to the "scene of the crime" being the psyche. After all, it's common knowledge that the subconscious often understands things quite literally, which we'll encounter again and again in sigil magic. But the psychological model also has the advantage of being able to make things much more easy to understand than its two predecessors, even though we generally use its explanations as supplemental information rather than as an independent thesis.

THE INFORMATION MODEL: CYBER MAGIC

Since cyber magic (the most recent branch of magic) is still in the developmental stages, it's too early to categorize it historically. Much of what currently seems to be quite promising might turn out to be nothing but an overoptimistic fallacy in the near future, although some aspects might become stronger and even more convincing. The essential features of cyber magic were developed in mid-1987 by myself along with the help of a few colleagues, and since then a number of magicians have been focusing on its further development.

Cyber magic is based on the information model, which is currently concerned predominately with physics. The term "cyber magic" is derived from "cybernetics" (control theory, from the Greek *kybernetos*, "the pilot"). The thought behind this concept is that all energy, in order to be effective, requires information to "tell" it what to do. The magician doesn't assume the energy directly, but rather the information matrices (or "blueprints") that control it, and is therefore able to influence the energy much quicker, more thoroughly, and with less effort than before. Plus, it's easier to overcome the limits of time and space since, according this model, information has neither mass nor energy and is therefore not subject to as many restrictions as these.

In addition, the magician doesn't have to rely on a good relationship with spirits or other subtle entities, or on one's own energy level. Once one has mastered the technique of downloading, transferring, and finally redownloading the information for activation, one no longer needs any imagination or concentration aids. According to the current state of research, one may not even need gnosis to perform magic effectively! But before you get too excited about this, let me warn you that practice has clearly shown that thorough training is still required, at least the field of controlling subtle energies (e.g., kundalini, activating one's own cell-memory), before you can ever hope to achieve any kind of useable results with cyber magic.

At first it seemed logical to explain the effects of cyber magic with the concept of morphogenetic fields as introduced by biologist Rupert Sheldrake; but this no longer seems necessary, although the term "information field" is still sometimes used for better illustration (after all, specific terminology for cyber magic has not yet been developed). This can occasionally pose problems, however, since we're not dealing with the kind of energetic field that we're used to in the sense of physics.

A historical prototype of the information model can be found in homeopathy. This system is known to work with dilution or "potentiation." In contrast to the allopathic principle that chemically higher doses of a medicine achieve better results, the homeopath prescribes chemically smaller doses in order to achieve a better healing rate under specific circumstances (appropriate clinical picture, activation by shaking). The idea behind this is based on the theory by Paracelsus that states that it's actually the "spirit" of a medicine that causes healing and that this works even stronger when the "like" interacts with the like, and is best when the spirit of a healing substance is "extracted" through distillation, which is exactly what occurs during the dilution/potentiation process.[3]

This "spirit" is fully comparable to the modern term "information," just like cyber magic or pure "high magic" as a whole, but of course without their ideological, mystical, and transcendental aspects. This comparison becomes obvious when you consider the fact that a cyber magician doesn't need to rely on a lot of paraphernalia, as he or she doesn't even practice "mental magic" because the actual act of cyber magic isn't an act of the imagination.

When working with cyber magic, it's particularly important to keep in mind that all of our models already existed in one form or another long ago. So this isn't a strictly hierarchal, chronological, stepped pyramid of development, but rather a shift in the focus that follows a circular or spiral pattern of movement. In the same sense, tradition has told us that old masters have always practiced some kind of "empty hand magic." In no way does this mean that an entirely new path has been forged on a practical level. Instead, certain aspects have been filtered out of older systems, put in a different context, supplemented by new ideas, and carefully—but not necessarily less revolutionary—developed further.

In a sense, this is even a traditional development since magic has always been "stripped" and redefined throughout the course of its history. This adaptability could even be viewed as its greatest strength since this has prevented it from suffering the fate of disappearing from the face of the earth, as many old traditions have.

Let's now take a look at magically "charged" objects (ritual weapons, talismans, amulets, fetishes, etc.) according to the four models of magic in order to explain them on a practical level as well. To do so, we've again used a schematic diagram. A few unfamiliar terms listed here will be explained later on in this book, such as in the next section on practical talisman magic.

Spirit Model		Energy Model
Gateway to and tool of the spirit world brings entities to life	Magical tool Talismans, amulets, fetishes	Stores energy Directs energy Transfers energy Absorbs energy
Means of projection Association aids Triggers complexes	Power objects	Information memory Data carriers Program generators Programming commands
Psychological Model		Information Model

Chart 22: The four basic paradigms of magic using the example of "charged" magical objects

You'll probably notice that we sometimes refer to one model and sometimes to another in order to explain or illustrate magical procedures. However, the word "explain" is hardly possible anymore in this context. Fact is that we can describe fairly precisely how magic works, but we still don't really know why it works. This, of course, is a fundamental problem of our four-dimensional existence in which we apparently can only observe the effects, but never the causes. We'll have to delve into this problem more deeply when we discuss Chaos Magic; for now it will have to suffice when we point out that none of the earlier systems that claimed to offer a "true explanation" were able to stand up to a thorough investigation based on the most current state of information. This, however, doesn't have any effect on the practical effectiveness of these systems.

This requires the modern magician (who is virtually compelled to relativism) to play with one's paradigms and choose the ones that correspond best to one's needs and promise the most success. But we don't want to dictate any dogmatic relativism here; our intention is merely to advise you to experiment with various paradigms in your practice, especially if you're still not sure which models of explanation you personally prefer in the first place. This approach will intensify the more you become familiar with the various paradigms.

In the next section we'll be discussing practical talisman magic, which will give you the opportunity to play around with the various models of illustration that we've introduced here. You'll find more suggestions on this in the practical exercises at the end of this section.

THE FOUR MODELS OF MAGIC USING THE EXAMPLE OF AN EXORCISM

Principally, each of the four paradigms of magic that we've discussed here can be applied to any magical sphere of activity whatsoever. We've chosen the example of an exorcism in order to illustrate the various theoretical and practical approaches according to the corresponding paradigm. Technically speaking, an exorcism is the reestablishment of a desired mental-spiritual state of normality using magical means. Although this can be interpreted and handled in many different ways depending on the magical paradigm applied, common language usage understands an exorcism to be the expulsion of spirits or demons. Let's have a look at this phenomena using our four models of magic since this will also help us learn to distinguish between the various ways of thinking.

Exorcism According to the Spirit Model

Case history/diagnosis: The client/patient is a victim of possession. Strange spirits and/or demons have taken possession and control of him. He's unable to get rid of them on his own, and often may not even realize the gravity of his situation. The magician evaluates the case, and begins proper treatment.

Therapy: Treatment requires the magician to make the spirits/demons leave the host's body. This could be done with threats, force, or cunning: (1) The magician conjures the annoying spirits in the name of a superior authority (e.g., the hierarchy of the princes of hell) that he makes, or already has made, an agreement (or so-called pact) with, threatening them with retaliation if his demands to leave the client are not met; (2) The magician applies controlled force such as hitting, torturing, or starving the host or the spirits themselves (e.g., astral warfare) and expels them; (3) The magician lures the spirits with promises, etc. out of the host and banishes them into a so-called "spirit trap."

Exorcism According to the Energy Model

Case history/diagnosis: The client/patient is a victim of unbalanced energy. Foreign energies or excess energies of his own have taken control of him, destroyed his energetic balance and are now in full control. He's unable to reestablish this balance on his own, and often may not even realize the cause of his suffering. The magician evaluates the case, and begins proper treatment.

Therapy: The magician extracts excess energy from the client's organism and banishes it (especially in cases of aggressive energies directed at the client by an opponent) into an energy storage medium (spirit trap). When energy is lacking, he transfers some to the client. Basically, he harmonizes the organism's balance of energy.

Exorcism According to the Psychological Model

Case history/diagnosis: The client/patient is a victim of a psychological disturbance. Repressed dark sides of his psyche have taken control of him in the form of projections, have destroyed his psychological balance and are now in full control; this can even take the form of split personalities. He's unable to reestablish this balance on his own, and often may not even realize the cause of his suffering. The magician evaluates the case, and begins proper treatment.

Therapy: The magician treats the client psychotherapeutically (e.g. shock therapy, mimicry of the client's behavior, ritual death initiation, or the like) with magical means in order to help him withdraw his magically effective projections and/or banish them. In doing so, he may apply a symbolic projection storage medium ("spirit trap"). In addition, he ensures that the client is now able to express previously repressed drives and desires in order to prevent a relapse.

Exorcism According to the Information Model

Case history/diagnosis: The client/patient is a victim of confused information. His energetic balance is thrown off course due to inherent or externally induced faulty circuits within his biocybernetic memory, which can result in a total loss of energy, as well as in hallucinations, psychosomatic problems and personality disorders. The client is unable to restore the functionality of his biocybernetic memory on his own, and may often not even realize that his condition is abnormal. The magician evaluates the case, and begins proper treatment.

Therapy: Treatment consists of a three-part operation: (1) By means of information transfer, the magician activates his client's physical and mental defense mechanisms as well as the ability to completely restore the memory; (2) He implants an infomagical "DELETE" command into the client in order to delete the destructive information and defect memory; (3) He establishes (also by means of information transfer) an infomagical, preventive alarm system to help recognize undesired information as soon as it's received so that it can be deleted or rendered useless by means of an activation block (so-called "information traps") or mutilation.

These four approaches reflect the great diversity of modern magic. In this sense, we could even mention a fifth paradigm of magic, namely the synthetic model that unites all four previous (and possibly later ones as well) models in a pragmatic sense ("the truth is what works"). We'll mention that again when we discuss the paradigms of magic in more detail.

SPIRIT TRAPS

Apart from cyber magic, which—as already mentioned—doesn't require any paraphernalia, all paradigms of magic use the so-called "spirit traps" for exorcisms as mentioned above. These are magically charged objects that represent a sort of prison for undesired spirits/energies/projections. This is based on the idea that it's not a good idea to simply rid the client or patient of these spirits/energies/projections. Instead, they should be banished, or bound and brought under the control of the magician's will so they're no longer able to get free and cause more damage.

The spirit trap often functions as a channel or entranceway that's used to transport the undesired spirits/energies/projections into another sphere (e.g., "into chaos," "into the sun", etc.), with the intention of either destroying them there or distracting them and sending them into exile.

Due to its concave form, the magic mirror is particularly suited for absorbing. Usually it's round as well, and in any case it's enclosed in a frame that makes it the perfect trap in a symbol-logical sense. This is why a magic mirror is often attached to the client's body, or at least pointed in one's direction; then the magician can extract the undesired spirits/energies/projections by means of will and imagination.

In both the spirit model and the psychological model, it's generally necessary to talk to and negotiate with the possessing spirits or externally manifested projections. That's why it may take a great deal of cunning and promises before the magician can coax them out of the patient's body and lure them into the trap. From what we've said, it's obvious that exorcism operations require a great deal of experience, skill, and even courage on the part of the magician, and one must be willing to risk one's own physical and spiritual health, and even one's life as well. Because in the same way the human organism is capable of performing incredible magical things when properly instructed and trained, one can also mobilize unimaginably damaging powers if one loses control, which might be caused, for example, by a specific external influence (e.g., magical attack designed to hurt or kill) or an "internal short circuit" (e.g., mental disorders, which on the other hand could also be a result of a magical attack as well). In a sense, an exorcism can be compared to magical warfare; the magician should therefore approach it accordingly.

Once the spirit trap is "filled," the question arises as to what the magician should do with the spirits/energies/projections that it contains. The answer depends on which model one uses. Spirits are usually either banished, as already explained, or the magician tries to make them submit so that one can use them for one's own purposes. Energies are usually stored, especially when dealing with offensive energies from a magical opponent, since these are particularly suited for defensive operations or retaliation, because no healthy person is immune to one's own energies. But often these energies are magically neutralized and returned to the general cosmic energy flow.

Only in exceptional cases are the spirits/energies/projections kept trapped inside the magic mirror permanently; after all, the mirror should be able to fulfill its "normal" purpose again after the exorcism. It therefore serves mainly as an instrument of extraction and intermediate storage, and after a successful operation the captured spirits/energies/projections are put into a final prison, such as a stone or preferably a rock crystal (which is highly appreciated by some practitioners due to its great storage capacity). Ordinary table or rock salt can also be used in an emergency as a temporary solution—which is why the magic circle is often reinforced with salt, such as in Voodoo, or why salt is added to holy water by the Catholic Church, and why many traditional witches refuse to consume any kind of salt at all. Since salt is strongly hygroscopic, meaning that it absorbs water and will dissolve (e.g., in rain), it can only be used as a temporary prison.

A common way to bind spirits is to trap them in a bottle. This is where the term "genie in a bottle" came from. We know several magicians who are specialized in capturing spirits and energies in bottles and storing them this way. In doing so, the important thing to remember symbol-logically is to always keep the bottle sealed tightly, and using ordinary cork is not enough—an additional seal of beeswax is generally used and engraved with the corresponding seals and sigils of defense.

---

1. This, of course, doesn't exclude the possibility of transferring power additionally. This is just one example of the simplification mentioned at the beginning of this section.
2. This also includes pseudo-energy models such as Couéism and positive thinking.
3. Paracelsus' frequently quoted concept of *similia similibus curantur* is often incorrectly translated as "identicals are cured by identicals." However, the correct translation is "likes are cured by likes," which is an interesting parallel to sympathetic magic and the correspondences!

PRACTICAL TALISMAN MAGIC

TALISMANS, AMULETS, AND FETISHES

One of the oldest fields in the application of practical magic is the making of talismans and amulets. We've mentioned these utensils several times throughout the course of this book and now want to deal with them in more depth. The layman usually uses the terms "talisman" and "amulet" interchangeably, and makes little or no distinction between the two. The modern magician is different.[1] As we've already seen, the magician uses specific vocabulary in order to describe one's art in all aspects as precisely as possible, and therefore makes a distinction between various charged objects according to their corresponding function. This is why you should memorize the following common definitions as well:

> Talismans: Magically charged objects used to fulfill a specific purpose or achieve a certain goal.
>
> Amulets: Magically charged objects used to prevent a certain condition or situation.
>
> Fetishes: Magically charged and activated objects used for storing energies and in operations of magical influence.

Now let's have a look at each of these magical tools individually. To put it short, a good way to describe them is to say that talismans are "for" something and amulets are to "prevent" something. For example, we could make a talisman "for good health," and charge an amulet "to prevent sickness." A fetish, on the other hand, can assume both functions, but is generally used as a magical battery or psychogon, which we'll discuss in more detail shortly.

In general, talismans, amulets, and fetishes can all be charged with any type of energy, for all purposes, and using any preferred magical technique that's suitable. But let's use planetary magic (Venus energy) as our first example to illustrate this.

THE VENUS TALISMAN

A Venus talisman is an object charged with Venus energy that's utilized to achieve Venusian goals (energy model). Let's stick to the most common correspondences based on the Golden Dawn (and, in part, on much older sources). According to these, a Venus talisman would ideally be made of a piece of copper and engraved with the sigils of Venus. This piece of copper would then be charged ceremonially during a Venus ritual. The Venus talisman should be heptagonal, and the engravings should be green. It should be made on a Friday during the hour ruled by Venus.[2]

During charging, the magician usually enters a Venus trance during a Venus ritual.

At the climax of the ritual, the talisman (already engraved and marked with, for example, a sigil of a statement of intent) is charged by the magician who spasmodically projects a green ray of light into the material basis (also called *materia prima* or "MP") by using one's hands (which, of course, will only be done imaginatively at first), and then by drawing the traditional Venus glyphs over it.

According to the usual procedure, the magician will concentrate on the intended goal while charging it, although contemporary Chaos Magic recommends not thinking about the goal at all while charging. But good results can certainly be achieved with the traditional method.

Once it's charged, the talisman is either worn for a while on the body or always kept at hand. Another technique is to put it away in a safe place and forget about it.

THE VENUS AMULET

A Venus amulet is an object charged with Venus energy that's utilized to prevent Venusian influences. Everything said about the Venus talisman applies here as well, but we need to add one important thing. Although the Venus amulet (like every other kind of amulet) principally has a negative goal (such as avoidance, prevention, blocking, and so on), the statement of intent must be formulated positively when charged (e.g., with a corresponding sigil). For example, if you want to use a Venus amulet to prevent a relationship from breaking up, you wouldn't say "This amulet is to prevent my relationship with X from breaking up," but rather "This amulet will protect my relationship to X from breaking up" or something similar. In the field of magical warfare, the necessity of amulets becomes even clearer. After all, you could also protect the relationship to X from external disturbances. And this fact is exactly the reason why many authors even today still confuse talismans and amulets.

THE VENUS FETISH

Experienced magicians might sharpen their ears when they hear this term since the old Western tradition never mentions it. We're usually only familiar with fetishes in connection with so-called "primitive" cultures, and ethnologists generally view "fetishism" as an animistic nature religion. But the basic concept of a fetish is not at all as "un-Western" as it might seem at first.

The word "fetish" is derived from the French word *fétiche* and the Portuguese word *feitiço,* and merely means some type of magical object. In general, fetishes are typically animated objects that are charged specifically to serve the magician as semi-autonomous entities. In contrast to psychogons, or artificially created magical creatures that mainly work on the astral plane but are tied to the material plane through their physical consistency, an external fetish object is a true source of a certain power, deity, entity or something similar. At the same time, however, they are identical. A fetish also needs to be fed, cared for, and talked to. This continuous procedure actually helps charge them in the first place. Some magicians report that they can even develop a personality and life of their own throughout the course of time. For example, poltergeist activities might occur in their presence, or the fetish may independently "take a trip" on its own and reappear entirely unexpectedly (and just as unexplainably as it disappeared) in unusual places.

Although fetishes are embodiments of certain powers, they're rarely animated for very specific, personalized purposes. In this sense, general healing fetishes are common, but they're rarely created for healing a specific person. Instead, they continue to live even after the patient is healed and can then help others as well. In this sense, the fetish is tied to a certain purpose, not to a certain person. It can be compared to a common battery.[3] A Venus fetish, for example, would be comparable to a general Venus talisman, or—even better—to a Venus pentacle. Like the pentacle, the Venus fetish could be used for every Venus operation in order to intensify the energy without actually having to be physically present or specifically directed at the target. From now on, we'll be referring to planetary fetishes as pentacles, and use the general term "fetish" for all other appropriately charged tools. Please keep in mind that we're not talking about the Earth pentacle that we mentioned earlier! This type of pentacle is more similar to the lamen, except that it's not worn on the chest—it's more of a mixture of the two as we'll often find mentioned in literature. If necessary, reread the sections of this book that explain these things to make sure the difference is truly clear.

In addition to the techniques already mentioned, a fetish is usually animated with blood, sperm, menstruation blood, or other bodily secretions of the magician as well, and is almost always made entirely by hand. It will often resemble a human or animal, but there are also fetishes that are completely abstract and have no recognizable shape and form. African fetishes often resemble a feather duster but can be made of various materials ranging from wood and leather, to metal, wax, rags, or straw.

The fetish can be used to charge other objects, or can at least help in doing so. In Western ceremonial planetary magic, this function is fulfilled by the pentacle (once again, we don't mean the earth pentacle!), which we've mentioned quite frequently already. To charge objects (generally talismans and amulets, but also brand-new magical weapons), they're placed on the pentacle to help charge them according to the principles of sympathetic magic.

Both talismans and amulets are often made for other people, while fetishes are generally used only by the magician oneself (of course, with the exception of charging one for a client). In practice, you'll soon understand the difference between these three categories of magical utensils, and in the practical exercises at the end of this section you'll find more recommendations on how to work with these.

A FEW TRADITIONAL TALISMANS AND AMULETS

In the course of our lesson on practical talisman magic, we don't want to restrict ourselves to just planetary talismans and amulets according to the Golden Dawn. For this reason, we'll discuss some traditional examples that you'll run into again and again in magical literature.

a) ABRACADABRA. This is one of the oldest talismans known. It was even mentioned back in ancient times. The gnostic Quintus Serenus Sammonicus recommended it for conjuring good spirits and as an amulet to prevent fever in his book on medicinal home remedies that was used throughout the Middle Ages. The meaning of the word itself is still disputed. The range of interpretations includes "a mutilation of the Gnostic god-name Abraxas" and "an acrostic (notaricon) of the Hebrew phrase AB BEN RUACH AKADOSH" ("Father, Son, Holy Spirit"). But even the Temurah rearrangement of the letters to read "ABRA KAD BARA"("fever") might be possible, just as "ABRA KADABRA" could be interpreted to mean "sickness disappear," while another theory sees it as a distortion of "ABBADA KEDABRA" ("disappear like this word"). Since Greek amulets usually spell the word as "ABRACADABPA," it's possible that the original word was pronounced as "abrasadabra." We should also mention that Aleister Crowley made it his "Word of the Aeon" after changing it to "ABRAHADABRA" in order to give it the significant gematric value 418.

b) Kabbalistic amulets from Rabbi Hama. Agrippa wrote:

"But Rabbi Hama in his book of speculation delivereth a sacred seal more efficacious [than the Abracadabra amulet] against any diseases of man, or any griefes whatsoever, in whose foreside are the four squared names of God, so subordinated to one another in a square, that from the highest to the lowest those most holy names or seales of the Godhead do arise, whose intention is inscribed in the circumferential circle, but on the backside is inscribed the seven-lettered name Araritha, and his interpretation is written about, viz. the verse from which it is extracted, even as you see it here described. But all must be done in most pure gold, or Virgin Parchment, pure, clean and unspotted, also with Inke made for this purpose, of the smoke of consecrated wax lights, or incense,

and holy water; The actor must be purified and cleansed by sacrifice, and have an infallible hope, a constant faith, and his mind lifted up to the most high God, if he would surely obtain this Divine power."

c) Old Testament symbol-logic. One such example has the front side containing the first letters of the first five verses of Genesis, while the reverse side contains the last letters of the same verses, which together are a "representation of the creation of the world." Please pay close attention to the elegant symbol-logic applied here. The First Book of Moses is the same as Genesis, which contains the biblical story of creation, so that the entire "creation of the world" is actually represented here for magical use with just ten letters. This kabbalistic amulet grants that the wearer "shall be free from all mischiefes, if so be that he firmly believeth in God the creator of all things" (Agrippa). It protects "against the affrightments and mischief of evil spirits and men, and what dangers soever, either of journey, waters, enemies, arms."

d) Christian "victory" or success talisman with the well-known symbol for Christ's name (the Chi-Ro) and the Latin words "in hoc vince" ("In this [symbol], conquer"). This type of talisman was often imitated by Hebrew amulet makers.

e) Pentagram talisman with the inscription "igíra," which basically means "healthy," or "for good health." The frequency of Bible quotations—generally Hebrew, but occasionally taken from Vulgar Latin—contained on amulets and talismans in ancient times, Middle Ages, and the Renaissance is not just due to the predominance of the Christian church, but more so to the fact that the Bible was viewed as an excellent example of a talisman/amulet/fetish itself, such as the Jewish Torah, the Muslim Koran, and even the ancient Egyptian Pert-em-hru. Since such scriptures of revelation are considered divine—and therefore magical—by definition, it's logical to view them as a treasure chest of surefire formulas. Often the "Good Book" itself was used as a magical defense simply by holding it up at unruly spirits and demons in the same way Christian exorcisms do with the cross, which is also a type of fetish in a magical sense.

ENGRAVING TALISMANS AND AMULETS

To wrap things up, here's a practical tip. Metal engravings can either be made manually or by using special engraving tools of various sizes, and even electric engraving tools can be purchased in certain craft stores. Electric tools have the advantage of requiring considerably less physical strength to use them, although it takes practice to learn how to draw clear lines. This kind of tool actually makes a dotted line (if not drawn too deeply) that's made up of lots of tiny, little dots. The tip of the tool is often interchangeable, and by attaching a diamond tip, you can even engrave glass and other especially hard objects (e.g., semiprecious stones). It would be best to purchase a few cheap copper plates (such as those used for enameling) at the craft store as well so that you can practice engraving for a while.

Another relatively simple means of inscription is etching. This is done by first covering the surface of the metal with a coating of shellac or thick wax. After the coating is dry, the desired symbols are carved into it. The carvings, of course, must be deep enough to go through the entire outer coating, but not scratch the surface of the metal. Afterward, acid is poured over the surface.

The disadvantage of this method is that the etched lines are usually blurred and unclear, depending on the adhesiveness of the coating. Plus, working with acid can be dangerous and cause unpleasant odors, which is why most magicians generally prefer the method of engraving.

PRACTICAL EXERCISES

EXERCISE 46

APPLIED PARADIGM SHIFTING IN PRACTICE (IV)

Do you remember Exercises 10, 17, and 19? Now it's time to delve deeper into what we've already learned and apply it to our practical magic. This will help increase your flexibility and expand your scope of action. Plus, this continually hammers the psychological censor until it gets "soft" and finally gives up, so that it no longer wants to contradict everything and search for explanations.

It would be best to combine this exercise with the following (the making of talismans and amulets), but you can use any other magical operation as well. Thoroughly study one of the first three paradigms described in this section; it would be best to choose one you're not that familiar with yet. You won't be able to use the fourth paradigm, or the information model, until later when we'll provide more information on its practical application. But if you're already familiar with cyber magic from other sources, feel free to use this model now as well. Shift to a different paradigm (e.g., from the energy to spirit model, or from a "mixed" form to a "pure" paradigm) for at least two weeks (reference value that should be viewed as a minimum, although more practice is actually desired), and observe all of your magical activities from this new point of view. Try as best as you can with the means you have available (knowledge, tools) to perform several magical operations that you're already familiar with, but by applying this new paradigm. For example, if you've already charged a Mercury talisman using the energy model, try doing the same with the psychological model, and then with the spirit model as well. Of course, this means that you'll have to make quite a few changes to your ritual practice. It's entirely up to you how to do this since you should understand enough of the subject by now, although you may have to page through some reference books on occasion for help. But in any case, it's up to you how long and how frequently you want to perform this exercise. Of course, it would probably be better and easier to do this exercise over a shorter period of time and practice more often, but if you prefer to work in a three-month cycle, you're free to do so as well.

Keep careful, precise records of your observations, and you'll surely make a few very new or even astonishing experiences that could speed up your magical development considerably.

EXERCISE 47

PRACTICAL TALISMAN MAGIC (II)

Over a period of no more than seven months, charge seven planetary fetishes (or planetary pentacles) that you should make according to all the rules of the art that you're familiar with. It would be best to use metal plates (since these are most durable) that correspond to the appropriate planets and cut with the appropriate number of sides. Engrave the traditional planetary sigils (see *Practical Sigil Magic*) on the front side, and the sigils of the planetary intelligence and demon on the back. Using the principle of the "Kabbalah of the Nine Chambers" (Aiq Bekr; described in the workbook *Practical Sigil Magic* by Frater U.·. D.·.), design a sigil to represent your magical name and engrave it in the middle between the two others. Charge these talismans during a planetary ritual, or the corresponding number of planetary rituals (three times for Saturn, seven times for Venus, nine times for the moon, etc.), anoint them with the corresponding planetary oil, and hold them in the smoke of the planetary incense until you're satisfied with their charging. You can check this with your pendulum.[4]

Use these talismans for every planetary ritual by placing them on the altar like the pentacle (which they really are, technically speaking); you can also use them to charge other planetary talismans or amulets by placing the object to be charged on top of it.

EXERCISE 48

PRACTICAL TALISMAN MAGIC (III)

Obtain a ring of any type of metal and charge it during seven separate planetary rituals with the corresponding planetary powers. Engrave into the ring the sigil of your magical name that you created using Spare's word method; it's up to you whether you engrave the sigil on the outside or inside of the ring. You can even engrave the ring with planetary sigils, affix the corresponding gemstones, and so on—just use your imagination.

After charging is completed, you should wear the ring daily for at least six months. This doesn't have to be twenty-four hours a day, which might not be possible anyway, so just a few hours are enough.[5] Afterward, wear this ring for every planetary ritual and make sure it doesn't fall into the wrong hands.

BIBLIOGRAPHY

Frater U.·. D.·., *Practical Sigil Magic*

Hans Biedermann, *Handlexikon der magischen Künste*

E. A. Wallis Budge, *Amulets and Superstitions*

---

1. Older authors, especially before the 1900s, often confused the two as well.
2. If these correspondences are still unclear, you should review the section on the correspondences!
3. There are many different types of batteries that are designed in various shapes and forms for various usages. But regardless of the type, all batteries must be able to perform certain general functions.
4. Remember to check the pendulum's swing before charging the object, and record this—along with the pendulum results after each charging—in your magical diary.
5. You can also use a completely neutral metal band that looks like a common wedding band or jewelry ring.

INTRODUCTION TO CHAOS MAGIC

"ONE'S COUNTENANCE IS LOST IN THE CHAOS"

Chaos Magic, which we've already mentioned on numerous occasions, is growing in popularity and has become a permanent fixture in modern magic. It's relatively young, officially founded in the year 1978 by Peter J. Carroll upon publication of the first edition his book *Liber Null.*

This book hit the British magic scene literally like a bomb. Following the somewhat amateurishly designed first edition of just 100 copies that was only available as an internal publication of the I.O.T., a second edition soon followed that quickly achieved the status of a cult book, and a third edition was soon after released by Sorcerer's Apprentice in Leeds. Later, the book was published in America by renowned occult publisher Samuel Weiser in combination with the sequel *Psychonaut,* first published in 1983 in England, and soon afterward the books reached more conventional distribution channels of the book trade. Meanwhile, Chaos Magic became a household name in England and the USA, and nearly every magazine reported on it at least occasionally for a while. As far as popularity is concerned, Chaos Magic bumped the Wiccan religion off the top for quite a while in England, and more and more authors felt the need to have a closer look at it.

In Germany, Chaos Magic made its debut in the year 1982 when a German-language edition of *Liber Null* was published by Edition Magus, which was originally founded just for this purpose. This edition was quite small as well, as only 150 copies were printed, of which about 130 actually made it in to stores. Later, a third German edition was published (on license from Weiser publishers), while the German sequel *Psychonautik* was published in 1984 in a total of two editions. (Both German titles are now out of print and no longer available from Edition Magus.)

But a wide number of magazine articles published mainly in England and Germany were probably even more significant than these two books concerning the number of readers they reached, and they certainly helped popularize this current trend within the tradition of magic.

I myself published one of these first articles in the year 1985 in my article "*Im Chaos hat man kein eigenes Antlitz—Die Chaoistische Magie und ihre Wurzeln*" in the magazine *Unicorn*, which is out of print. Since this article is no longer available to the public, I've taken the liberty to cite a few relevant passages:

> *A new paradigm? Well, Carroll's Chaos Magic ideas aren't really all that new, and most contemporaries should be familiar with a few of its direct predecessors. Those would include the so-called "Discordia Movement" that's closely linked to the scene around Robert Anton Wilson and Robert Shea, whose trilogy "Illuminatus!" (1975) paved the road for discordant, or Chaotic, thought. The "bible" of the Discordians (who often praised, heralded and—although not dead seriously—even worshiped) this Roman goddess of strife, or her Greek counterpart Eris, is most certainly the book* Principia Discordia or—How I Found Goddess And What I Did To Her When I Found Her. Being The Magnum Opiate Of Malaclypse The Younger, Wherein Is Explained Absolutely Everything Worth Knowing About Absolutely Everything, *that appeared in the late 1960s and has meanwhile become an absolute cult book in the true sense of the definition. Whoever the true "Malaclypse the Younger" (the author of this magnum opus) may be is the topic of a number of clever and brainy speculations that would be pointless to discuss here. This is surely in part a remnant from the late hippie and yippie movement, which should be sufficient information to put this in historical context. Robert Anton Wilson continued to weave the web with his* Cosmic Trigger *and other works, continually expanding the plot. There are also con-*

nections to the SMI2LE scene centered around Timothy Leary and other vitamin mystics as well.

Of course, Carroll and his colleague Ray Sherwin [. . .] didn't just limit themselves to unfolding new facets of the Vietnam War protests, including more or less humorous and abstruse historical misrepresentations, parodies of world conspiracy theories and intentional misinformation, in order to prolong and stabilize them for an indefinite period of time. They're not so interested in a "guerilla ontology" that would replace or expand the class struggle with a struggle of thought patterns—they're more interested in trying to convert the relativistic, and therefore gnostic and existentialistic, ideas contained in these sources (but not these alone) into a practical form of magic. [. . .] So in Chaos Magic, we'll discover ideas that can also be found in existentialism, structuralism, critical positivism, and a much older source—behaviorism. Even elements of nihilism, Nietzsche's reception and the awareness games of Romanticism can be found here without a problem.

[. . .] In the sense of the Anglo-Saxon spirit of pragmatism, the development of theories here [. . .] occurred at a comparatively later date. While Liber Null *is mainly a practice-oriented book that contains just a minimum of ideological and philosophical background material,* Psychonaut *is the attempt at creating a large-scale superstructure—a process that is in no way complete. [. . .]"*

Well, let's start with an introduction taken from *Psychonaut* itself.

THE CHAOETHERIC PARADIGM

The manifest universe is just a tiny island of comparative order, set in an infinite ocean of primal Chaos or potentia. Moreover, that limitless chaos pervades every interstice of our island of order. This island of order was randomly spewed up out of chaos and will eventually be redissolved into it. Although this universe is a highly unlikely event, it was bound to occur eventually. We ourselves are the most highly ordered structure known on that island, yet in the very center of our being is a spark of that same chaos which gives rise to the illusion of this universe. It is this spark of chaos that animates us and allows us to work magic. We cannot perceive Chaos directly, for it simultaneously contains the opposite to anything we might think it is. We can, however, occasionally glimpse and make use of partially formed matter, which has only a probabilistic and indeterminate existence. This stuff we can call the aethers.

If it makes us feel any better we can call this Chaos, the Tao, or God, and imagine it to be benevolent and human-hearted. There are two schools of thought in magic. One considers the formative agent of the universe to be random and chaotic, and the other considers that it is a force of spiritual consciousness. As they have only themselves on which to base their speculations, they are basically saying that their own natures are either random and chaotic or spiritually conscious. Myself, I am inclined to the view that my spiritual consciousness is random and chaotic in an agreeable sort of way (pp. 192–193).

This is Peter Carroll talking to us, who's also responsible for the fact that Chaos Magic joined close forces with the Zos Kia cult of Austin Osman Spare. Carroll and Sherwin assumed some of Spare's terminology, such as the "spark of chaos" quoted above that's described as "Kia." In Sherwin's *Theatre of Magic,* Kia is described as "soul; individuality without ego" (p. 32), while *Liber Null* defines it as "nascent energy seeking form" (p. 60), or as "Great Desire," "Life Force," or even "Self-Love." "It can be represented by Atu (trump) 0, the Tarot Fool, or the Joker. Its heraldic beast is the vulture, for it ever descends to take its satisfaction among the living and the dead" (ibid.). "Kia cannot be experienced directly," Carroll explains in another passage, "because it is the basis of consciousness (or experience), and it has no fixed qualities which the mind can latch on to. Kia is the consciousness, it is the elusive 'I' which confers self-awareness but does not seem to consist of anything itself. Kia can sometimes be felt as ecstacy or inspiration, but it is deeply buried in the dualistic mind. It is mostly trapped in the aimless wanderings of thought and in identification with experience and in that cluster of opinions about ourselves called ego. Magic is concerned with giving the Kia more freedom and flexibility and with providing means by which it can manifest its occult power" (p. 28).

Kia therefore is impersonal—which is an important fact—and it has nothing to do with the common, Christian-based definition of the "soul." Although we can recognize parallels (which Carroll incredulously mentioned himself) to the Tao of Chinese philosophy and the early Buddhist concept of the incarnation of karma (but not the individuality of the living being), and even to the Paramatman of Hinduism and the "cosmic consciousness" of some yoga and Jnana schools, one should avoid getting carried away with comparisons—a mistake that even Aleister Crowley made in one of his first commentaries on Spare's *Book of Pleasure* that he later regretted as he reread through it. Kia just isn't the exact same thing as Tao, Kamma, or Atman, although it may be related to these. The Egyptian concept of Ka comes closer yet, and may even resemble it more than any of the others, but it's still not the exact same thing. Carroll stresses that such terminology is purely random and, at best, has merely a functional value.

Kia is the point of intersection between chaos and the matter it created for its own "amusement." Chaos Magic doesn't recognize an individual soul that's given to a person at birth, or one that may continually incarnate whether it wants to or not. In this sense, it resembles Gurdjieff's system, which also assumed that man has to earn his soul. In *Psychonaut,* Carroll wrote:

> *A curious error has entered into many systems of occult thought. This is the notion of some higher self or true will which has been misappropriated from the monotheistic religions. There are many who like to think that they have some inner self which is somehow more real or spiritual than their ordinary or lower self. The facts do not bear this out. There is no part of one's beliefs about oneself which cannot be modified by sufficiently powerful psychological techniques. There is nothing about oneself which cannot be taken away or changed. The proper stimuli can, if correctly applied, turn communists into fascists, saints into devils, the meek into heroes, and vice-versa. There is no sovereign sanctuary within ourselves which represents our real nature. There is nobody at home in the internal fortress. Everything we cherish as our ego, everything we believe in, is just what we have cobbled together out of the accident of our birth and subsequent experiences. With drugs, brainwashing, and other techniques of extreme persuasion, we can quite readily make a man a devotee of a different ideology, the patriot of a different country, or the follower of a different religion. Our mind is just an extension of the body, and there is no part of it which cannot be taken away or modified.*
>
> *The only part of ourselves which exists above the temporary and mutable psychological structure we call the ego is the Kia. Kia is the deliberately meaningless term given to the vital spark or life force within us. The Kia is without form. It is neither this nor that* (p. 164).

Only the absolute lack of meaning of everything that exists can give the Chaos magician true freedom and make him a god, relatively speaking of course. [. . .] Belief is understood as a pure technique (as again borrowed from the Zos Kia cult, but also from late ancient gnosticism), but not as ontic reality—relativity is the trump, everything is random, with true freedom no more absolute barriers exist, but nor does a right to statics or pseudo-absolute structures such as power, domination, or hierarchies. Through this, Chaos Magic (surely influenced by the individual anarchy of Max Stirner and Nietzsche) almost incidentally gains an immense political, lifelong characteristic: If the magician truly wants to be free, he has to free himself from all chains. These chains include patterns of thought, behavior and belief as well as imbedded emotional structures and urges. This process, of course, is deeply amoral: Since there is nothing absolute in the conventional sense of the word, the initiate has the entire world at his feet. Here we can see a clear point of contact with the Discordia Movement as well, whose motto, attributed to the assassin boss Hassan ben Sabbah (the "Old Man of the Mountain," reads: "Nothing is true, everything is permitted." A sentence, by the way, that didn't first appear with Robert Anton Wilson and his followers, but actually much earlier with pre-hippie author William S. Burroughs of the beat generation (pp. 12–16).

This overview of the basic philosophy behind Chaos Magic should suffice for now. These self-descriptions are often worded quite apodeictic and absolute, but in practice, it's usually much more moderate. In fact, a Chaos magician can be a Crowleyan Thelemite or even a practicing Christian, Odinist, reincarnationalist, or transcendentalist. But Chaos Magic developed out of the above-mentioned ideological movements, and many modern magical techniques and practices stem from them as well. But first the old monuments need to be removed in order to prevent their shadows from permanently smothering the growth of creativity, originality, and technology as well as philosophical progress. The magical order called the Illuminates of Thanateros, which developed around Chaos Magic and is now officially known as the Magical Pact of the Illuminates of Thanateros (or "The Pact"), quickly became an active melting pot of international magical talent.

By 2001, the Chaos Magic movement has experienced struggles and separation. New impulses seem to be lacking, the majority of practical work is not available to the public (in contrast to the 1980s), and it can no longer be considered a "wave."

BIBLIOGRAPHY

Peter J. Carroll, *Liber Null* (the official training manual for the I.O.T.)
Ray Sherwin, *The Book of Results*
Frater U.·. D.·., *"Im Chaos hat man kein eigenes Antlitz.—Die Chaoistische Magie und ihre Wurzeln"*, *Unicorn,* Issue 12, 1985, pp. 12–19.

INTRODUCTION TO CYBER MAGIC

PRINCIPIA CYBER-MAGICA: (PROVISIONAL VERSION)

1. All movements of energy in the entire universe are controlled by information.
2. Information has no mass or energy. It is therefore nonlocal by definition and can spread/move faster than the speed of light.
3. With the help of cyber-magical techniques, it is possible to manipulate information, meaning that it can be retrieved, transferred, copied, deleted, and activated. This occurs through the manipulation of the central information memory in human, animal, mineral, and mechanical organisms.

Since information has no mass or energy, it cannot be stopped by material barriers from being spread or transferred. The only way to cause such a hindrance is to specifically influence the information's transmitter or receiver.

In this case, the transferred information itself remains unaffected by the hindrance; instead, an error code is emitted that will cause erratic results.

This transfer of information is similar to the copying of one data memory into another. In contrast to the energy model, no energy is lost (e.g., by the transmitter) since the information is merely duplicated. In this way, information about, for example, a foreign language can be transferred from A to B without either of the participants having to exert any significant amount of energy. The only thing required of both organisms is a minimum level of energetic performance, which is necessary for survival anyway (so-called "back-up generator"). If this condition is fulfilled, nothing can prevent the transfer of information when trained properly.

Let's take healing, for example. According to cyber magic's oldest model of explanation, the healer generates a morphogenetic field where the patient is healthy and lets this field do the job of "establishing" the patient's recovery. According to the current state of knowledge, it would be even more effective for the healer to project/copy the command or (to be more exact) the concept of "health" into the patient's memory.

If this is done successfully, the cyber-magical transfer of information to the patient creates a new energy matrix that assimilates its own energies as well as foreign ones that enter from the outside. This energy matrix can also be described as a "health pattern." However, if the patient has an acute lack of energy, one should definitely be given additional energy according to the energy model since a cyber magical transfer takes time to work and become effective.[1]

The transfer of matrices seems to be the most prominent feature of this practice anyway. In the example already mentioned of transferring the knowledge of a foreign language, it's not really the concrete vocabulary and grammar rules that are later activated by the receiver; instead, the transfer can be noticed when linguistic patterns of experience are suddenly activated.[2] The best results thus far have indeed been achieved in the field of foreign language transfer. But cyber magic can also be used quite effectively for magical healing, the transfer of any kind of knowledge, and the intentional influencing of others. It seems to be predominately guide patterns that are transferred, which act in a certain sense like "blueprints" or "building plans."

This has certain advantages and disadvantages. The disadvantages include the fact that cyber-magical operations often do not take immediate effect, as mentioned above, although they can be performed quite quickly (depending on the magician's ability, sometimes just a split second). Plus, the results are often "blurry" and even more difficult to ascertain than those of ordinary operations. One more drastic disadvantage is the fact that once information is assimilated by means of foreign influence, it's extremely difficult and sometimes impossible to locate, and it can almost never be deleted.[3]

The advantages include that the overwriting and deletion of undesired patterns by new, desired matrices in a target person often have a much longer lasting effect than would be possible by using the energy model. To put it more clearly, we do not simply change a factory's flow of energy or its speed of production; instead we give it entirely new production schedules and programs while leaving the factory's own internal energy balance untouched. Furthermore, cyber-magical operations generally remain undetected. That immediately becomes clear when we remember that information has no mass or energy, and therefore also has no material resistors (e.g., inner sensors) that it might activate. In any case, we can recognize when an information transfer has taken place by the reaction of our organism's own physical memory ("hard drive maintenance," often perceived as a burning or prickling sensation in the spinal column), although we wouldn't be able to specify it any further.

THE CURRENT MAIN FIELDS OF APPLICATION OF CYBER MAGIC

The following list is in no way complete, but rather represents the current state of knowledge. In principle, this list does not intend to say that cyber magic isn't suitable for other purposes as well; instead it's meant to point out the areas in which cyber magic is currently being researched successfully. Please don't hesitate to add ideas of your own.

Transferring the contents of memory storage: e.g., foreign languages, specialized knowledge of all types, "schoolbook knowledge," experience.

- Transfer can take place actively from the transmitter to the receiver with common consent.
- Transfer can take place without the knowledge/consent of the receiver (information implantation).
- Transfer can take place without the knowledge/consent of the transmitter (information extraction).

Areas of application: e.g., preparing for exams, fast learning, support of superlearning:
Transferring energy circuits: e.g., energy control commands, energy flow patterns/loops.
Areas of application: e.g., healing, magical attacks, magically influencing others.

Please remember that even though energy loops are transferred with the intention of them adapting to the target person's energy balance, this does not involve the actual transfer of energy itself!

Everything said above about the transfer applies here as well.

Self-influence: e.g., for activating "flash" statements of intent.

Areas of application: like all magic.

The principle of magically forgetting (which we're already familiar with from sigil magic) is of particular importance in cyber-magical self-influence operations.

Basically, there doesn't seem to be any area at all where cyber magic cannot be applied.

TECHNIQUES OF TRANSFERRING INFORMATION

Currently, one specific technique of transferring information has proven quite effective to cyber magic. It requires the activation of both central memories in the human organism: the brain and spinal cord.

Of course, the organism has many other memories, but experience has shown that specifically activating these two large ones is most effective.

Cyber-magical operations generally proceed according to the following scheme:

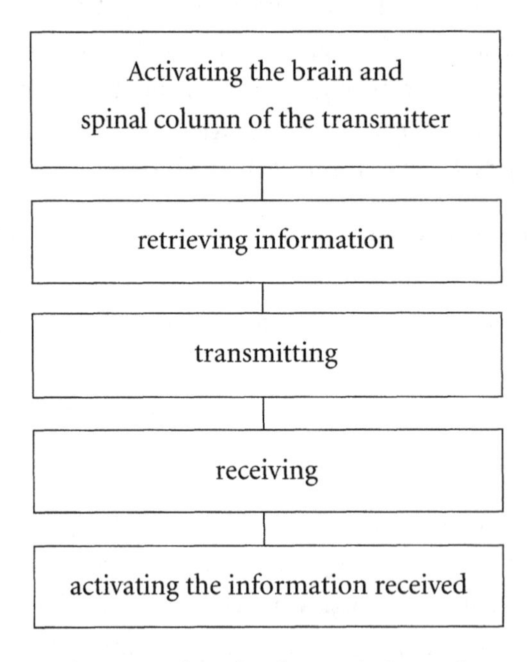

Chart 23: Outline of a cyber-magical operation

In the following that explains the individual steps of a cyber-magical operation, we'd like to use the example of two computers communicating with one another (which most computer literates should understand) in order to illustrate the technical aspects of how it works. If you have no knowledge about computers, feel free to skip over this section.

ACTIVATING THE BRAIN AND SPINAL COLUMN

The beginner is easily tempted to view the activation of the brain and spinal column (the so-called "golf club chakra") as a sort of visualization technique. This wrong idea is probably caused by the fact that activation usually does indeed occur at first (during the training phase) with the help of the appropriate visualization. But in fact, it has nothing to do with a visualization technique. In the same way the acupuncture meridians more or less (depending on the system) "objectively" exist and can even be measured without the person having to know that they exist, the activation of these two main memories of the human organism takes place on a more-or-less physiological level as well.

Cyber magicians generally sense this as a warm or cold sensation, or a tingly or itchy feeling.

If the transfer is made actively, the cyber magician activates one's own memory. The target person doesn't need to do anything at all; the transfer can even take place without his or her knowing. Currently, there seems to be no means of protection against this either.

On the other hand, if the cyber magician wants to extract information from someone, one first activates the memories of the target person with a mental command to transmit, and then receives the desired information into one's own memory without having to do anything else.

Illustration using the computer model: This process is similar to turning on a computer, or activating and checking its operating system (so-called "booting").

Retrieving Information

Retrieving information generally occurs by merely stating the name of the desired data, e.g., "knowledge of English." This occurs purely mentally and requires no further visualization.

Illustration using the computer model: This is similar to calling up a directory and a file, e.g., "cd/sourcedir/sourcefile" in the UNIX world.

Transmitting

Using an older method, transmission would take place by directing the retrieved information to the spinal column and brain and on to the sahasrara chakra ("crown chakra," the "thousand-petal lotus") in order to be "shot out" in a sense by a mental transmission command. One variety of this technique involves giving a mental command to create a morphogenetic field in the crown chakra where the desired information is already located or the desired event has already occurred. This morphogenetic field is then assigned the actual task of transmitting.

The currently most common technique doesn't rely on any kind of visualization of the crown chakra, but still works with the spatial perception of the crown. Then a simple command (e.g., "transmit!") is given without any conscious visualization of the transmission.

Illustration using the computer model: This is similar to the "COPY" command, e.g., "copy q:\sourcedir\sourcefile z:" whereby "q" represents one's own drive and "z" the target drive. The crown works like a modem in a normal dial-up network. The ability to store the transmitted data into a specific part of the target drive (e.g., "copy z:\source\sourcefile z:\targetdir\targetfile") requires exact knowledge of its construction and is therefore currently just a thing of the future.

Receiving

Receiving is similar to transmitting. For more information, see the next two sections below.

Processing the Information Received

Processing received information is done automatically at first, and experienced cyber magicians generally sense this in the spinal column in the same way as with transmitting. Untrained people generally sense nothing at all.

For more information, see the section below on "Retrieving Cyber-Magically Transmitted Information."

The transmitter sometimes perceives the arrival of data in the memory of the target person as a small physical jolt of the scalp, a soft tingling sensation, or something similar. Even without such physical signals, when done properly, the magician will receive certain clear signals to confirm the success of one's operation. This applies accordingly as well to the specific extraction (and therefore, reception) of information.

Illustration using the computer model: The immediate processing of data is similar to the automatic sorting and compressing done by a hard drive, which arranges everything in a certain order but does not yet enable access to it.

Despite this detailed description of a cyber-magical operation, remember that the entire process generally takes no longer than three quarters of a second! Even inexperienced beginners (although they must be able to activate kundalini) can usually perform cyber-magical operations in less than half a minute!

Retrieving Cyber-Magically Transmitted Information

How can the cyber-magically transmitted information be activated? This area still requires intense research; even though there's no doubt that retrievable information can actually be transmitted, we're still faced with the challenge of how we can accurately put this knowledge to use.

One of the main problems is not knowing exactly what is transmitted. The effect it brings about is often quite vague. One cyber magician commented, "It feels like something that was learned a very long time ago." In this sense, transferring the knowledge of a foreign language, for example, would make it considerably easier to learn this language. If knowledge of the foreign language is already available, the newly acquired information is activated through the appropriate contextualization. This can occur, for example, during a trip to the corresponding country where the transferred language is spoken, or, for a dead language, while reading more literature in that language.

According to our current state of knowledge, one of the most significant factors that can influence the specific retrieval of information is stress, for example, being under pressure to suddenly have to communicate in a foreign country can quickly activate this information.

In general, the contextualization already mentioned also plays a significant role. The newly acquired information must be retrieved within the appropriate external or internal context. Therefore, there would be no point in trying to retrieve French vocabulary while studying math or repairing a car.

A great deal of the information transferred is revealed quite subtly over a period of time. That's why it's always important to observe yourself closely when controlling the results of an experiment.

Illustration using the computer model: Before activating the information, such as the knowledge of a foreign language, you should be aware that you've received the transmitter's pattern of language experience, which is the main program in a sense. Even the other related modules (e.g., vocabulary, syntax, idiomology) are available in a comprehensive (or undifferentiated) transfer, but they still need to be properly installed.

Since the methods of transfer currently available are still relatively primitive, a great part of retrieving the information consists of, figuratively speaking, separating and logically organizing the files, directories, clusters, and sector allocations on a hard drive that's quite cluttered with information and programs.

However, the law of adaptation can help (a similar process is currently being developed in the field of artificial intelligence). An addition to already stored information[4] causes the old information to combine with the new, thus creating a new file structure (or an already existing one is reactivated and maintained). Apart from the data comparison, this automatically leads to increased access speed. However, this is an automatic process that's immanent to the information cybernetic "operating system" of the human biocomputer, a process that resembles those in common computer applications as well.

Cyber Magic as an "Empty Hand Technique"

This short introduction should suffice to give you a working basis that will allow you to make your own experiences with this modern discipline of magic.

The advantages of cyber-magical operations are clear. Not only the short duration of the process is attractive, but also the complete abandonment of any type of equipment; the sheer effectiveness of cyber-magical operations especially in the field of transferring experience and knowledge; their long-lasting effect; their enormous subtlety and thoroughness while at the same time being completely disguised from the outside; and much more.

In fact, cyber magic is actually a sort of "empty hand technique" ("wishful thinking without thinking"), which has always been the sign of a true master. The cyber magic method has always been used, although it was understood differently before. The so-called "high magic" that older literature makes such a fuss about is actually—once you wipe away all of its religious transcendentalism—a form of pure information transfer. Our epoch reserves the right to shroud this discipline in a new light and new understanding, to establish parallels to current scientific developments (electronics, information model of physics, cybernetics, chaos theory), and to create a new technique on the basis of this.

But remember, as easy as cyber magic is to use, it nonetheless requires previous knowledge of how to activate the main memory in the human biocomputer. We've introduced it already in order to give you the opportunity to gain some early experience so that you can continue to research and develop cyber magic on your own, and/or to prepare you for this currently most advanced form of magic.

---

1. According to experience, this generally takes anywhere from just a few seconds to two to four days.
2. For example, the ability to recognize unfamiliar phonemes, differentiation between expression and style, less uncertainty when speaking, increase in self-confidence concerning the foreign language, sudden activation of previously latent, passive knowledge of the foreign language.
3. This corresponds to the latest state of knowledge, but may change significantly in just a short period of time.
4. Such as vocabulary, for example, that has been transferred and received cyber-magically, but not consciously.

INTRODUCTION TO RITUAL MAGIC (XII)

SCOURGE, CHAIN, AND DAGGER (AGAIN)

Crowley, who's known for assigning the dagger a different function than is commonly done in other magical literature, interprets the scourge, dagger, and chain as symbols of the three alchemistic elements, sulfur, mercury, and salt (see *Magick,* pp. 55–56). He compares these principles to the three Indian *gunas,* or subtle aggregate states:

Sulfur = Rajas

Mercury = Sattva

Salt = Tamas

Although the modern magician rarely uses weapons such as the scourge and chain,[1] we'd like to mention them here anyway for better understanding.

The alchemistic element of sulfur roughly stands for the energy of things, mercury for their mobility, and salt (or earth) for their stability or constancy. In this sense, they roughly (but only roughly) correspond to the elements of Fire, Air, and Earth.[2]

Whenever Crowley poses a rare Christian argument, he's a representative of *pecca fortiter,* or the principle that sin is not a bad thing since it makes forgiveness possible in the first place, which is much more magnificent than the actual sin itself.[3] In this sense, the scourge, dagger, and chain represent the sacrament of penitence. He wrote:

> *The Scourge is Sulphur: its application excites our sluggish natures; and it may further be used as an instrument of correction, to castigate rebellious volitions. It is applied to the Nephesch, the Animal Soul, the natural desires.*
>
> *The Dagger is Mercury: it is used to calm too great heat, by the letting of blood; and it is this weapon which is plunged into the side or heart of the Magician to fill the Holy Cup. Those faculties which come between the appetites and the reason are thus dealt with.*
>
> *The Chain is Salt: it serves to bind the wandering thoughts; and for this reason is placed about the neck of the Magician, where Daäth is situated.*
>
> *These instruments also remind us of pain, death, and bondage* (*Magick*, pp. 58–59).

The scourge can be made of various metals. Crowley recommends an iron handle and nine copper wires intertwined with small pieces of lead, whereby iron stands for severity, copper for love, and lead for austerity. In some covens of the Wicca religion, the scourge is used for the initiation of new candidates to remind them of the punishment they would be subjected to if they ever betrayed the group, other materials are used such as willow rods or leather switches.

We've already discussed the dagger in detail.

The chain is made of soft iron and should have 333 links according to Crowley, which symbolize the demon Choronzon, the Lord of Dispersion. In this context, this demon represents stray thoughts or lack of concentration.

In conclusion of his section on these three weapons, Crowley writes: "The Scourge keeps the aspiration keen; the Dagger expresses the determination to sacrifice all; and the Chain restricts any wandering" (ibid.).

THE PHIAL AND THE OIL

The phial is the container used to keep the "Holy Oil" (Crowley's term). As expected, the old master of Thelemic magic makes quite a big fuss about the Holy Oil, which, in his opinion, symbolizes "the aspiration of the Magician," and stands for "grace" and "a quality bestowed from above," "the spark of the higher in the Magician which wishes to unite the lower with itself" (*Magick,* p. 60). Here we can see Crowley's mysticism in its pure form.

Not all modern magicians follow Crowley's path, even though they may respect and appreciate him as a pioneer and "father of modern magic." And surely they won't submit to his dictum either, such as: "Unless therefore the Magician be first anointed with this Oil, all his work will be wasted and evil" (ibid.).

At least Therion gives a recipe for his magic oil, although he doesn't state any quantities. It consists of four substances. The basis is olive oil, which Crowley views as the gift of Minerva, the Wisdom of God, the logos; three other oils are mixed with this oil, namely the oils of myrrh, cinnamon, and galangal. Myrrh symbolizes Binah, the Great Mother, which represents both the understanding of the magician as well as the sorrow and compassion that result from one's contemplation of the universe (a clear Buddhist influence on the part of Crowley). Cinnamon oil symbolizes Tiphareth, the Sun—"the Son, in whom glory and suffering are identical" (ibid.). The galangal oil symbolizes both "Kether and Malkuth, the First and the Last, the One and the Many, since in this Oil they are One" (ibid.).

In our opinion, the value of these statements lies mainly in the fact that they show how to symbolically elevate even the most trivial detail, thereby turning it into a tool of magic. Of course, each person is free to decide for oneself how far one wants to go—after all, it's obvious that Crowley, as a fin-de-siècle man, had a preference for baroque pomp and excess symbolism, but this is merely a subjective opinion that shouldn't stop you from taking the same path, or a similar one. After all, the only dogma of pragmatic magic is "The main thing is that it works!"

On a more functional level, it's surely correct that the oil Crowley recommends (which, by the way, is identical to the oil of the Magic of Abramelin) should cause a burning sensation on the skin that can bring about various effects depending on the body part that's anointed. For example, rubbing some of this oil onto your anja chakra can help improve your concentration, while the muladhara and svadisthana chakras should be anointed for sex magic operations. Today it's quite common to use the planetary oils that are available in magic specialty shops; when used in conjunction with the corresponding planetary incense, these can induce an extremely strong state of planetary gnosis. Apart from that, the act of anointment has an ancient cult tradition as well, and the Old Testament, for example, mentions it quite frequently. The modern magician, however, mainly views it as a means of trance induction.

The phials[4] to hold the oil have no fixed form. However, according to Crowley, they should be made of pure rock crystal, and he also mentions that some magicians shape them in the form of the female breast because this "is the true nourishment of all that lives" (*Magick*, p. 61). For exactly this reason, he continues, they can also be made of mother-of-pearl and stoppered with a ruby.

But the modern magician has other worries. The anointment phials are viewed in a more rational, purely functional manner and not turned into a magical weapon; if a magician has five oils, one'll most likely have five different phials in various shapes and sizes. However, this doesn't mean that you cannot make a similar phial that's loaded with the appropriate symbolism for an all-purpose oil.

In any case, it would certainly be a good idea for the magician to obtain a wide variety of oils and experiment with them. We've already discussed the effect of scents and fragrances in this book, so no further explanation should be necessary. Even the effect of burning oils (or vaporizing them on a hot metal plate) shouldn't be underestimated and can be quite helpful in programming the subconscious (psychological model) to react to certain correspondences.

OPHITICA

lucifer

who says: i serve!
and means the wrong god?
who says: let me pull!
and kisses the scaffold?

in the old spirit there was much to be understood
and the beauty of many stars to be admired,
but this only extinguishes fire instead of igniting it
and i'd rather burn myself than never find
what ignites me: thrown from light, blessed

no demiurge to pardon my godly nature,
no blacksmith to fill my bowl,
no veil-maker to not hide my eyes
from the alive and the aflame and all that you know
and is eternal.
and is eternal.

ouroboros

the beginning of the world lay in a dark abyss. the light
came and coiled around creation, silently strangling it without shedding its skin.
that which is endless and will never be eternal and dies
enters the circle, pleads and woos and solicits,
demanding the blessing to be god, defying the trivial,
and yet i still coil around everything born and brand the wall
with writings of fire. the world is my skin.
a demiurge who builds on houses in his house.
his dying song echoes not in the room
and earth, water, fire, air—a dream.
and when the well-calculated already spoils the beginning:
i measured the candle length, cut the wick.
but you'll never know and never swear it.
i see the change in all the thousand choirs alone
and see the sevenfold fire reignite
and watch it go up and down: blessed—and damned.

ophis

the tree? in a dream: you see it not
know only of the forbidden fruit that promises you torture
as you lap at the darkness, roll in the grass
and never see the usurper, never hear the sand in the glass
and yet believe to exist—and believe to be alive

and believe all of his deception and get entangled
in the web that i break up, that you'll never recognize
until someone grabs you and points out good and evil:
the treetop sways, the fruit is ripe and falls to the earth
that becomes your green grave as soon as you touch it.
oh, you are kept prisoner through obedience,
in a casket made of gold, and rarely did sing
the old ones of this way that you'll never comprehend:
of the garden's high walls polished smooth with time
and you wouldn't be mortal, or deemed to downfall
if you were only aware of the steady pulse of time
and the fact that you are gods.
and the fact that you are gods.

---

1. An exception is the Wicca religion, although they generally have an entirely different function here, and usually a rope is used instead of the chain.
2. In *Magick*, Crowley actually refers to water instead of salt, which doesn't really make any sense in this context.
3. Paul deals with this problem in his Romans 5:20–6:2, and Crowley makes a reference to him.
4. According to the dictionary, the word "phial" (or vial) actually means nothing more than "a round glass bottle with a long neck" but is also used to describe small bottles of all types—especially small amphoras.

CPSIA information can be obtained
at www.ICGtesting.com
Printed in the USA
BVHW011359221020
591610BV00008B/554